Praise for Theresa Howes

'Truly gripping . . . I loved it.'
Jill Mansell, *Sunday Times* bestselling author of *Promise Me*

'I absolutely loved this . . . Vivid and heartbreaking.'
Lana Kortchik, *USA Today* bestselling author of *Sisters of War*

'War, passion and tragedy unite in this
atmospheric and moving tale.'
S D Sykes, author of the Oswald de
Lacy Medieval Murders series

'A wonderfully immersive, emotional read.'
Annabelle Thorpe, author of *The Enemy of Love*

THERESA HOWES lives in London, and has a background as an actor. Her work has been longlisted for the Mslexia Novel Award, Bath Novel Award, Caledonia Novel Award, Lucy Cavendish College Prize and the BBC National Short Story Award.

Also by Theresa Howes

A Matter of Persuasion
The French Affair
The Secrets We Keep

An American Scandal

THERESA HOWES

ONE PLACE. MANY STORIES

HQ
An imprint of HarperCollins*Publishers* Ltd
1 London Bridge Street
London SE1 9GF

www.harpercollins.co.uk

HarperCollins*Publishers*
Macken House, 39/40 Mayor Street Upper,
Dublin 1 D01 C9W8
This edition 2026

1
First published in Great Britain by HQ,
an imprint of HarperCollins*Publishers* Ltd 2026

Copyright © Theresa Howes 2026

Theresa Howes asserts the moral right to be identified as the author of this work.
A catalogue record for this book is available from the British Library.

ISBN: 9780008666880

This novel is entirely a work of fiction. The names, characters and incidents portrayed in it are the work of the author's imagination. Any resemblance to actual persons, living or dead, events or localities is entirely coincidental.

All rights reserved. No part of this publication may be reproduced, stored in a retrieval system, or transmitted, in any form or by any means, electronic, mechanical, photocopying, recording or otherwise, without the prior permission of the publishers.

Without limiting the exclusive rights of any author, contributor or the publisher of this publication, any unauthorized use of this publication to train generative artificial intelligence (AI) technologies is expressly prohibited. HarperCollins also exercise their rights under Article 4(3) of the Digital Single Market Directive 2019/790 and expressly reserve this publication from the text and data mining exception.

Printed and bound in the UK using 100% Renewable
Electricity by CPI Group (UK) Ltd

For more information visit: www.harpercollins.co.uk/green

For Bill

'Jack shall have Jill;
Naught shall go ill.'
A Midsummer Night's Dream

'Varnish and gilding hide many stains.'
Mansfield Park

Chapter 1

New York, 1895

Hugh took his sister's hand and gave it an encouraging squeeze. 'This is it, Maddie. Are you ready to go inside?'

Madeline lifted her eyes from the gutter and shivered. The solid yellow brick exterior of the New York Metropolitan Opera House, with its straight lines and square shoulders, appeared more like an industrial building than a house of music and lacked the elegance of the European opera houses they'd visited on their travels during the past two years.

How many times had she stood on this very spot, gazing up at its forbidding façade, longing to see inside, to hear the grand music from the comfort of its plush seats? Now, the dream was about to come true. Her stomach gave an involuntary flip at the thought of mingling with the audience. The elite. New York's finest and most unforgiving society.

She pulled her silk velvet mantle tighter around her shoulders to protect herself against the chill wind, her ribs catching against the bones of her corset as she drew in a breath.

'Perhaps we should come back another night instead.'

A huddle of self-possessed women strapped in the latest Paris fashions nudged past her, eager to escape the cold night as they tottered in high-heeled shoes towards the unnatural glow of electric light and the warmth of the opera house foyer, the men on their arms as proud as peacocks in their tall hats and long-tailed suits. Madeline's eyes snagged on the diamond studs glittering in their cuffs and starched collars as they hurried past, her heart sorry for the hothouse flowers already wilting in their lapels.

She wasn't ready for this. Mixing with society in Paris and Milan had been one thing, but New York was something else altogether. She turned to her brother, twisting her mouth into what she hoped would pass as a smile.

'I've changed my mind about being here. I want to go home.'

They'd been anticipating Madeline's entrance into society all the time they'd been travelling in Europe. Now wasn't the moment to lose courage. Hugh blew out his cheeks, a mixture of frustration and understanding clouding his eyes.

'I've secured us a box, Maddie. Do you know how difficult it was at such short notice, the strings I had to pull?'

At twenty-eight, good looking and of independent means, Hugh was more than a match for the self-made men, who had recently amassed fortunes in banking and industry, who were now barging their way through the crowd as if they owned the place, and he had no problem with being seen among them. As far as he was concerned, he didn't see why old and new money couldn't get along.

Admittedly, he was more at home with the members of New York's knickerbocker society to which he belonged. Descendents of bourgeois colonials who claimed to have come over on *The Mayflower*, who'd made their money in real estate before the Civil War, men whose wives insisted on calling themselves *the social aristocracy* even though they were strictly middle class, and who were so high-minded, they purposely avoided wearing the latest fashions because they believed it vulgar to be seen to be too up to date.

Many of these old families would be here tonight. Having been away for so long, Madeline sensed Hugh's growing unease at meeting them again as he acted as her escort, despite his right to be there. He took her arm and pulled it closer into his body, an unspoken gesture of support that was meant to hold them both up. 'Come on, Maddie. Let's go inside. I don't want you to miss the start.'

He'd arranged to see *Aida* this evening purely for her sake. Music was her passion rather than his. As her older brother and protector, he saw it as his duty to ensure there were things in her life that made her happy.

She owed him more gratitude than this, more genuine thanks. She threw back her head and presented her brightest smile. No one must see her fear, her trepidation, least of all Hugh.

'Of course, you're right.' She gave his arm a gentle tug, encouraging him forward. 'What are you waiting for?'

They drifted through the foyer, caught up in the sway of the crowd, a hundred heady perfumes and pungent colognes mingling with the satisfied sound of friends and allies greeting one another. Madeline held her head high, taking in the gilded interior, the polished mirrors and the chandeliers, revelling in the reassuring give of the thick carpet beneath her shoes.

Heads turned to look at her with each step she took, voices dropping to a whisper each time her name was mentioned. It wasn't her imagination. Hugh increased his pace, leading her up the stairs towards their box. 'You mustn't mind the home crowd, Maddie. They can't help themselves when they see a beautiful young woman. Their jaws drop uncontrollably, and they lose all sense of decorum. You mustn't hold it against them.'

During the two years they'd spent in Europe, Madeline had transformed from a shy twenty-year-old girl into a confident young woman with a keen intelligence and a wit that enabled her to hold her own in any company, or so she thought until tonight.

She tried to laugh off the stir her appearance had created,

which had already made her the talk of the evening. She would be the reason certain society ladies would pay calls on each other tomorrow afternoon. Most young women in her position would see this as a victory, but Madeline was smart enough to wait and see before forming an opinion on how she was being perceived.

They were about to take their seats in the private box when a young man burst in and slapped Hugh on the shoulder. He must have followed them through the foyer and up the stairs without them realising.

'Crosby, I thought it was you. When did you get back from Europe?'

'Just a few days ago.' Hugh turned to shake the young man's hand, but his attention had already shifted to Madeline.

'Aren't you going to introduce me to your lovely companion?'

His eyes were everywhere, devouring every curve of Madeline's face, her tall figure, noble as a Greek statue, shown to the best advantage in an off-the-shoulder emerald-green silk dress, cut to within an inch of its life.

'I'm not so much his lovely companion as a minor irritant,' replied Madeline with a brittle smile. The way he looked at her made her feel cheap.

Hugh cleared his throat, suppressing a laugh. 'This is my sister, Miss Madeline Crosby.' Hugh flashed her a look which she read as *beware*. 'This is Mr Leonard Forster, an old acquaintance from school, also known as Ginger.' To explain the nickname, Hugh patted his top lip with his forefinger, drawing her attention to Ginger's auburn moustache.

Ginger stepped forward, lifting his chin to meet her eye. 'I'm delighted to finally know you, Miss Crosby. I've heard so much about you.'

'Everything you've heard about me was good, I hope, especially if you intend to repeat it.'

He gave a nervous laugh. 'You're as beautiful as you are quick.'

'That may be so, but I doubt either of these attributes will win me any admirers among the society ladies here tonight.'

Hugh gave her another look, this time a warning to temper her wit. Madeline held her tongue. She didn't need her brother to tell her she'd gone too far. If she was to make a good impression, she needed to appear more demure. It was one of the rules of the game. Nobody appreciated a smart woman.

She looked out across the auditorium at the golden horseshoe of boxes that were quickly filling up, raising her eyes to take in the glass chandelier struggling to pass as crystal, and the thin layer of gold paint adorning every hard surface. Running her fingertips along the edge of the gilded box, she wouldn't have to scratch too deeply to reveal the dull metal beneath. Her heart sank at the sight of such outward show, at the shallowness of it compared to the grand opera houses of Europe. New York was still a young city and she had to accept it for what it was, growing pains and all.

All this time, she hadn't realised Ginger was still talking to her, gazing up at her in awe, like a mountain he was determined to conquer.

'You'll do me the honour of wearing my flower, Miss Crosby.' With the swift gesture of a magician pulling a rabbit out of a hat, Ginger tugged the limp gardenia from his lapel and offered it to her.

Madeline blinked at the curling white petals of the exotic flower which were already fading to yellow, her nostrils twitching at the once floral scent, now past its best and adding a sour note to the air. Before she could work out how to politely refuse it, a woman's voice bellowed from a box on the other side of the auditorium.

'Don't you dare acknowledge that woman, Leonard. You'll have me to answer to if you do.'

Suddenly, the clamour of people finding their way to their seats stopped. Hundreds of pairs of eyes turned to stare at Madeline, following an invisible line from where the woman was pointing and shouting. Madeline felt the colour rise in her cheeks. She might as well have been standing centre stage rather than in a discreet box, high up on the side of the auditorium.

Ginger clapped his hand over his mouth and withdrew the offer of the gardenia, allowing it to drop to the floor. 'It's my mother. I didn't know she was here tonight.' He gave Madeline a half-hearted bow and began to back away. 'You must excuse me. She'll be expecting me to join her.'

He'd gone before either of them could summon the wit to ask him to leave. Hugh turned his back on the audience, most of whom were still staring at the box, and buried his face in his hands.

'I'm sorry, Maddie. I never for one minute imagined this would happen.'

'It's not your fault.'

She slipped into the shadows behind the seats, putting herself out of sight of the audience who'd paid to see a different kind of drama to the one unfolding before them, but who were no less pleased by what they saw, judging by the chorus of whispers and sniggers.

'I know you meant well, bringing me here tonight, but I won't subject myself to being the object of such attention.'

Hugh gently took her arm as she edged towards the door. 'Let's not go yet, Maddie. At least stay and listen to the first act. I know how much you've been looking forward to it. Don't let the behaviour of one stupid woman spoil it for you.'

But it wouldn't be the behaviour of just one stupid woman. It would be all her friends too. By the time word of Madeline's appearance had spread, everyone in New York society would be talking about her. Memories were long, especially those attached to unforgiving hearts.

'You're a new face, Maddie, that's all, and a very beautiful one. Your presence is bound to ruffle a few feathers, particularly mothers trying to find rich husbands for their less attractive daughters.'

He was trying to make her feel better and she was grateful for it, grateful for his love, for without it, she'd be nothing. Since the deaths of both their parents, she had no one else to rely on. She forced a smile, conscious that people were still watching her. The evening was spoiled, but she wouldn't give anyone the satisfaction of knowing it.

'You might be right, but let's go anyway.' The words snagged in her throat as she tried to sound matter of fact. 'I won't enjoy the music with Ginger's mother looking dagger-eyed at me all evening.'

They crept out of the box and along the snaking corridors of the opera house. Hugh muttered under his breath, trying to make the best of what was, in reality, a very public social banishment, while Madeline fought to hold back her tears.

'Ginger always was a snivelling little creep, even at school. I can't believe he had the nerve to offer you his rotten gardenia. Did you get a whiff of it? It smelled like yesterday's kippers.'

It might have been an exaggeration, but it was exactly what Madeline needed to hear. After suffering such humiliation, it was all she could do to hold herself up and put one foot in front of the other. Thankful for her brother's support, she gripped his hand as they fled the stuffy atmosphere of the opera house and ran out onto the street into the drizzling rain.

Madeline's thoughts turned to the gardenia as their cab hurtled along Broadway. The image of the wilting flower was a reminder of how something so beautiful could turn ugly in a matter of moments. She glanced at Hugh sitting opposite her, his arms resting on his thighs as he leaned forward, head bowed. It broke her heart to see him looking so downhearted.

'If Ginger treats exotic flowers with such disrespect, imagine how he must treat the women in his life.'

Hugh looked up, his face softening at her comment. 'He always was a stinker.'

'I could see that. I could even smell it. Perhaps I should send his mother a note, thanking her for rescuing me from her awful son.'

In truth, she never would. There was enough satisfaction to be had in simply thinking of it. There was no need to go through with the actual deed. There was enough cheap cruelty in the world without adding more to it. She'd suffered too much of it herself to ever want to inflict it upon others.

She gazed out of the window at the dark New York sky, the clatter of horses' hooves from the passing cabs a background to her thoughts. If she closed her eyes, she could have been on any busy street, in any city, but it wasn't any city, it was New York, the place that was meant to feel like home.

Hugh had done his best for her but tonight had proven that she couldn't rely on anyone to give her a sense of belonging. For all she treasured her brother's love, nothing he could do would ever banish the desolation that dragged at her heart or temper the grief she felt over her mother's death that even after all these years, still cast a long shadow over her existence.

She'd been too young to remember the final days of her mother's life clearly, but she recalled the two small rooms they'd lived in at the back of the hotel on West 25th Street. Known as the Tenderloin district, the area was notorious for its brothels and gin joints, cheap boarding houses where rooms were rented by the hour to those without luggage, and French-style cabarets, which loosely translated as sex shows. It also had the highest crime rate in New York City, which in itself had the highest crime rate in the world. It was no surprise it was known as Satan's Circus.

Despite being a small child at the time, Madeline could still picture the seven brothels in a row, run by seven sisters: the paint-scratched front doors and cheap curtains at the windows. Most of all, she remembered the men who used to visit. Sometimes, there were two or three a night. She would sit in a chair facing the corner while her mother took them into the adjoining room. When the door closed behind them, she would bury her nose in a book, trying not to hear the forced laughter, and the other noises that came through the wall, trying not to breathe in the smell of drink that lay heavy on the men's breath and lingered long after they'd gone.

She remembered her mother growing sick, remembered her sending a letter to a Mr Crosby only hours before she died. Afterwards, she remembered being collected in a fancy carriage in the dead of night and being taken to a school for young ladies, where she stayed for the next five years.

It was only after Mr Crosby's wife, Hugh's mother, passed away that their father welcomed Madeline into his home. For the last years of his life, he treated her as his long-lost daughter, even going as far as to bestow an independent fortune on her. It was guilt that drove him to be so generous and his enduring grief for her mother, who was the true love of his life, if he was to be believed.

He claimed Madeline's mother had disappeared after a misunderstanding, five months before Madeline was born. He'd tried to track her down, but there was no trace of her until he received her deathbed letter. He acted on her cry for help straight away, but by the time he reached her it was too late.

This was the story he related to Madeline and Hugh once they were old enough to understand. It was the only version of events they had, and so whether it was true or not, they had no way of knowing.

After their father's death, it meant everything that Hugh had honoured the terms of his will and continued to accept Madeline as his sister and take over as her protector. It was fortunate they got on so well, because as tonight's visit to the opera had proven, no one else in New York was prepared to acknowledge her.

'I know tonight didn't go so well,' said Hugh, who must have been ruminating on the evening's events, 'but if we persevere, I'm sure that by the end of the season we'll have established your reputation. You're too special not to win people's hearts, Maddie. Look how you were admired in Europe.'

In Europe, they'd had no idea her mother had been her father's mistress and not his wife, or that she'd died in a brothel. However Madeline behaved, it would make no difference to the people of New York. Reputation was nothing but an illusion, a state of grace or disgrace, imposed by others, and it had little to do with anyone's true nature. In this society, one slip was enough to undo a lifetime of impeccable behaviour, and as Madeline was learning, you didn't even have to do anything wrong to be damned.

Hugh's attempt to introduce her into New York society had been a disaster. She'd always known it was likely to end this way, but still a small part of her had hoped things would turn out differently. Despite her brave face and her forced laughter at Hugh's attempts to cheer her, she despaired at the fact that she'd never be welcome in the society where her father's family had thrived for generations. And if she wasn't accepted here, then would she ever belong anywhere?

Chapter 2

Madeline woke early the next morning, disturbed by a shaft of sunlight travelling across the room as Bessie, one of Uncle Morris's maids, drew back the curtain, her sing-song voice cheerful as the dawn chorus.

'Morning, Miss. It's a beautiful day. I'll bring your breakfast up to you on a tray to save you coming downstairs for it.'

Madeline stretched her limbs into the cool reaches of the bed. The feather mattress and the crisp linen sheets were a luxury she would never take for granted. The room, decorated in white and gold, with chintz-brocaded drapes, matching poufs, and a heavily patterned oriental carpet, had once been occupied by her late aunt. Even after all this time, Madeline couldn't bring herself to change anything to suit her own taste.

Her aunt's clothes still hung alongside her own in the wardrobe, her hairbrushes and bottles of scent still cluttered the dressing table. Hugh said she should make more effort to claim the space as hers, that it was the only way to make it feel like home. He was right, but still she couldn't bring herself to do it. Perhaps this was why the house felt like a temporary resting place, as if she was only passing through.

The two of them had moved into their widowed uncle's

brownstone, just off Fifth Avenue and Madison Square Park after the death of their father. At the time, Hugh had been too young to set up a home of his own, having not yet come into his inheritance, and it had made sense to consolidate what was left of the shrinking family. Devastated by the loss of his father, Hugh had been in need of his uncle's support, and Madeline, who was still a young girl, hadn't had any say in where they lived.

She blinked at Bessie, narrowing her eyes against the sun as it flooded the room. 'I'll come downstairs for breakfast. It'll save you the trouble of bringing up a tray.'

'It's no trouble, Miss.'

'Thank you, but I'd prefer to go downstairs.'

The maid dropped a curtsy. 'If you're sure, Miss.'

It might have been Madeline's imagination, but Bessie's tone suggested she thought she'd made the wrong choice.

The ormolu clock was striking nine when Madeline entered the breakfast room. Hugh appeared tight-lipped as he reached across the table and poured her a cup of coffee.

'I instructed the maid to bring breakfast up to you on a tray this morning.'

'I decided to join you instead. It's not fair for Bessie to have to fetch and carry for me unnecessarily when she has so many other things to do.'

'In that case, eat up quickly and we'll take a walk in Central Park while the sun's shining.'

'Don't you want to read the newspaper first?' Hugh rarely shifted until he'd read *The New York Times* from cover to cover. This morning, he seemed uncharacteristically restless.

'Anyone would think you were trying to get me out of the way. What is it?'

He pushed aside his untouched plate of kedgeree and gulped the last dregs of his coffee. 'I have to tell you something. It's best if we discuss it away from the house.'

Madeline reached for a slice of toast and sank her knife into the butter. 'You can't leave me dangling now. You have to tell me what it is.'

Before Hugh could reply, the door flew open and Uncle Morris entered, still wearing his silk dressing gown and bedroom slippers. He wasn't alone. There was a woman hanging on his arm. Although she'd taken the trouble to dress, last night's lipstick and rouge remained smeared across her unwashed face.

Her eyes scanned the breakfast table, the scrambled eggs and the griddle cakes dripping with golden syrup, the black grapes and the freshly baked bread. 'How civilised it is to sit down to a family breakfast.'

Morris offered her a chair, fussing around her as she settled into the seat. 'Let me introduce Miss Treacle to you.'

Hugh raised his eyes to his uncle's face. 'Miss Treacle?'

'It's Letty, dear. Miss Treacle is my professional name. If we're all going to be living under the same roof, you must call me Letty.'

Hugh glanced at his uncle. 'So it's all settled then?'

'As I said last night, there's no point in Letty paying rent on a tiny attic room in Hell's Kitchen when she could be living here with us. It's not as if we haven't got the space.'

Letty gave Morris's hand a squeeze. 'I'm grateful to you.' She looked at Madeline, tears budding in her eyes. 'You can understand why, I'm sure.'

She was less than half their uncle's age; that much was clear. The soft lilt of her Irish accent suggested she hadn't been long in New York. It wasn't hard to guess what she'd been reduced to doing to make ends meet.

Hugh got up from the table, beckoning Madeline to follow him. 'We'll leave you to enjoy your breakfast.'

Madeline grabbed a second slice of toast and followed him out of the room, brushing the crumbs from her day dress as she went. She didn't speak until they reached the drawing room, the door firmly closed behind them.

'Did you know about Letty? What has Uncle Morris said to you?'

'He told me about her last night after we got back from the opera. He claims to be in love with her. He intends to give her a home, here with us, to protect her.'

'Is he planning to marry her?'

Hugh shook his head. 'He intends to keep her as his mistress.'

'Well, that's hardly any protection. Where did he meet her?'

'In one of the brothels in Hell's Kitchen. He's been visiting her for months apparently.'

Madeline sank onto the sofa, trying to see the situation from all angles. 'I'm all for rescuing women in her position, but keeping her as his mistress isn't going to help her in the long run.'

'I suggested he set her up in her own apartment and gave her an allowance, but he insists on having her live here. It's his house. He can do as he pleases.'

'That's all well and good,' said Madeline, 'but what happens when he grows tired of her? What will become of her then?'

'I've been asking myself the same question, but it's not my only worry. The situation will reflect badly on the family, especially on you, Maddie. We can't have you living in the same house as our uncle's mistress. I don't care so much for myself, but it'll be too damaging to your reputation.'

'My reputation is already in tatters, in case you hadn't noticed.'

'If you're going to find a husband—'

'I don't want a husband.'

'Then, if you want a fulfilling life, to make friends and be accepted in society, you can't be seen to be living under the same roof as Letty.'

It was fine for men to do as they pleased, to take as many casual lovers as they wished, but any hint of scandal around a woman tainted her forever. She'd be ostracised by her friends and disowned by her family. 'So our lives are to be dictated by what other people think.'

'I'm afraid so,' said Hugh.

Madeline thought of the unfairness of it all. When it came down to it, Letty was no better or worse than any of the women in so-called 'good society'. It was only circumstances that made it seem so. She probably came from a perfectly respectable family in Ireland, and if pressed, would no doubt like nothing more than to return to them. Whatever the reality, their uncle's decision to have her live with him as his mistress wouldn't lead to the secure, respectable life Madeline imagined Letty was hoping for.

'What do you think we should do?' she asked.

'Now I've come into my inheritance, I can set us up in our own home. We could take a lease on a brownstone nearby, or find something grander in the French style, nearer to Central Park if you prefer.'

Morris's house had never felt like home, but still the idea of moving was unsettling. They'd been travelling for two years, moving restlessly from one European city to another. She was ready to pause and take a breath, to find out who she was when the merry-go-round stopped, and to work out what she wanted from life.

'All right, let's take a walk through the streets and see what takes our fancy.'

He was doing it for her benefit. As a wealthy man, Hugh didn't have to worry what people thought about the way he lived his life, while Madeline was judged at every turn and denied the privilege of living on her own terms.

They were interrupted by a quiet knock on the drawing-room door. 'There's a couple of letters just arrived for you, Miss.'

Bessie slipped into the room and presented Madeline with two cream-coloured envelopes on a silver tray, her name written on the front of each one in different but equally elegant scripts. They must both have been hand-delivered, as they bore no address or post mark. In each case, the paper was thick and expensive, one smelling faintly of violets, the other of roses.

Hugh instantly cheered up. 'It looks like you've made a conquest or two among the ladies, Maddie. I'll bet they're invitations to tea.'

Remembering Ginger's clumsy overtures at the opera, Madeline gritted her teeth. 'One of them is probably the bill for Ginger's gardenia. I couldn't help trampling on it as we fled the box.'

'Then you did a good thing, putting it out of its misery.'

She opened the first envelope, hoping for good news in spite of her misgivings. The single sheet of paper inside contained no more than two lines. The anticipation fell from her face as she read it. She'd been right not to hope for anything positive.

Stay away from our sons and our husbands.
You're not welcome here.

Madeline's hand shook as she handed the letter to Hugh. The challenge of finding a new home no longer seemed worth it. It would make no difference where she lived. The people here, many of whom were once their father's closest friends, were unwilling to accept her.

Hugh gave the letter a quick glance before tearing it in two and tossing it into the fire. Whoever had sent it hadn't even had the courage to put their name to it.

The second letter was from a charity Madeline had approached the day before, offering to support their cause in helping fallen women find respectable work. The terse reply made it only too clear that their high-minded ideals prevented them from accepting money from someone of Madeline's background. The irony was so cruel it made her want to scream.

'I'm sorry, Maddie. This is worse than I expected. I should never have brought you back to New York.'

It was lonely for Hugh too. While he protected her, he was also tarnished. 'I should go to a place where nobody knows me and leave you to get on with your life. You'll never find a decent wife otherwise.'

'I won't abandon you, Maddie, so don't even think of trying to talk me into it.' He was quiet for a moment while he considered their options. 'Would you like to go back to Europe? You loved Paris. Or we could settle in London. At least there we can speak the language.'

She shook her head at all his suggestions. 'We've only just come home.'

'Do you really think of this as home?'

It was impossible to lie to him. She'd travelled so much, lived through such upheaval since her mother's death that nowhere really felt like home. She looked at her brother, anxiously biting his nails.

'Tell me honestly, Hugh. In the whole of your life, where have you been the happiest?'

'That's easy,' said Hugh. 'Beachlands, our summer cottage in Newport.'

Beachlands had been shut up since their father's death. Madeline didn't know it very well, but Hugh had spent all his childhood summers there and had often talked fondly of the place.

'Then let's go there.'

'Are you sure? I can't promise there'll be much to occupy you.'

She thought of the hard stares she'd received from the women at the opera, the way the men had looked at her, assessing her like meat on a butcher's hook. Every set of critical eyes had either wanted to condemn her or to possess her, while the worst of them had wanted both, even as they demonstrated their contempt. There was no future for her in New York, no promise of happiness. There had to be a different kind of life out there somewhere, one where she wasn't looked down upon. She wouldn't find it unless she went in search of it.

'Let's go and find out, shall we?'

Chapter 3

Their uncle didn't appear too concerned when Hugh announced his and Madeline's intention to leave New York so soon after arriving. If anything, he seemed relieved at the prospect of having the house and Letty all to himself.

A tearful Bessie helped Madeline pack the clothes that only the week before they'd so carefully unpacked, the maid gasping with joy at the sight of each beautiful dress as she'd lifted it from the trunk. Beyond her hairbrushes and her trinkets, her favourite rose-scented soap and a dozen beloved books, Madeline had few personal possessions. Her harp, which had been a present from Hugh on her sixteenth birthday, was her most treasured item. Too large and too fragile to travel around Europe with them, it had remained in the corner of their uncle's drawing room for the past two years, untouched apart from the dusting it received from Bessie each morning. Now they were leaving New York, it seemed unlikely that Madeline would have the pleasure of playing it again anytime soon, and she was sad to say farewell to it.

Bessie ran a soft cloth over the leather binding of *Jane Eyre* before placing it carefully in one of the trunks. 'If you find yourself in need of a lady's maid, Miss, you only have to ask. I attended to your dear departed aunt for years before she passed, and she never had reason to complain.'

Bessie, with all her neat and particular ways, couldn't hide how appalled she was at the prospect of having to wait on Letty. Despite not having her own maid, Madeline couldn't bring herself to offer her the position. Uncle Morris would never forgive her if she tempted her away.

As a parting gift, Madeline gave Bessie the equivalent of a month's wages and asked her to be kind to Letty, who probably had more in common with Bessie than Bessie could imagine. Although appearances being what they were, Madeline knew better than to say it.

Everything Madeline owned fitted into four large trunks. It wasn't much to show for the life she'd lived, and it reflected her unsettled nature. Her father had left her a generous inheritance and there was enough money to buy whatever she desired. Yet without a true home she had no wish for material possessions beyond what was necessary. It didn't seem worth having anything when there was nowhere to put it. With the move to Beachlands, she hoped all that was about to change.

On their last evening in New York, while Hugh was out having dinner with friends, Madeline took the opportunity to conduct a little secret business. It was after dark when she left the house. Undeterred by the fine spring rain, she hailed a cab and directed the driver to take her to West 25th Street.

'Stop on the corner, near Buckingham Palace, please.'

Each brothel was famous for its grand name. The cheap painted signs fooled nobody and had become something of a joke among the clientele.

The driver raised his eyebrows. 'Are you sure you want to go there, Miss? You know it's . . .'

Madeline nodded, urging him along. If she was to get there and back before Hugh returned, she had to hurry.

Once they arrived at the destination, the cab driver turned to her again. 'Are you sure this is where you want me to drop you, Miss? It's not safe. Even I wouldn't step out onto these streets.'

If nothing else, Madeline was grateful for the concern of a stranger. She was too focused on her task to worry about what might happen to her if she stumbled across the wrong kind of man.

'I'll only be a minute. Would you mind waiting for me? I'll pay double your usual fare.'

'I wouldn't leave you here alone, Miss, even if you didn't pay me.'

The rain had grown heavier, blurring the bright lights of the cabaret signs as she dashed across the street, heading for the shadows where a young woman stood huddled against the cold, waiting for trade. She looked up with startled eyes as Madeline put out her hand and offered her a bundle of notes.

'Please, take this.'

When the woman refused to accept it, Madeline gently nudged it against her clenched fingers before letting go of it, causing the woman to grab it before it landed on the wet ground.

Horrified by her instinctive reaction, the woman gasped. 'What's all this for?'

'Please, share it among your friends and take some time off. Catch up on some sleep and get your children something good to eat.'

No thanks were necessary, but Madeline accepted them graciously before she ran back across the street, narrowly avoiding a group of drunks in bowler hats and stained breeches as they veered towards her. She jumped into the cab, mud splashing the hem of her silk dress and ruining her shoes.

Despite the look of surprise on the woman's face, Madeline had the reassurance of knowing she'd done something good. The only way she could be certain money reached the women who needed it was by putting it directly into their hands. To this end, she determined there and then that she would instruct a lawyer to ensure a designated amount of cash, drawn from her personal bank account, reached them each month. She didn't need the approval of the women's charity who'd rebuffed her to help the women who worked in these brothels. She would do it on her own terms.

Chapter 4

The next day, Hugh and Madeline boarded the train at Grand Central and left New York without giving it a backward glance. If Madeline was to thrive and make a life for herself, she had to keep looking forward.

Hugh talked animatedly during the train journey, describing everything she was going to love about Newport: the tennis and the horse riding, the year-round entertainment at the Casino, a club which had nothing to do with gambling and everything to do with sport, musical evenings and socialising. Then there were the wide-open spaces, the endless beaches, and the ocean, where she could learn to sail or indulge her romantic nature by simply gazing out to sea like a heroine in any one of the novels she was so fond of reading.

Beachlands was situated on Ocean Drive, overlooking the Atlantic, in an area surrounded by dunes and low hills, which could almost have been wilderness if it wasn't for the grand summer houses that continued to be built along the shoreline.

Despite being so close to the water, Madeline thought

Beachlands was a strange name to give a house, and she wasn't ready to consider it hers, rather than her father's, or Hugh's. Acceptance would come with familiarity, both of which would take time and a little application on her part. Whether it would ever feel like home was another matter altogether.

The house, which Hugh was in the habit of referring to as a cottage, had been built in the colonial style before the Civil War. It had twelve bedrooms spread over three floors and was surrounded by acres of formal garden. Situated in the most exclusive part of Newport, it had been one of the grandest houses in the area. In recent years, it had been dwarfed by a series of mansions commissioned by the newly rich industrialists and bankers, who were keen to spend their summers in the same place as old money New Yorkers. Built in classical French or Italian style, the new residences were like nothing America had ever seen, boasting fifty-foot-high ceilings, Baccarat chandeliers, marble floors, mirrored ballrooms, and hothouses to rival the famous gardens at Kew.

Left to stand empty for much of the year, the houses were owned by the very people Madeline and Hugh had been determined to escape.

'Are you sure you want to settle here?' asked Hugh. When he'd mentioned his fondness for Beachlands, he hadn't thought that coming here would be like jumping out of the frying pan into the fire. 'We don't have to stay if you don't like it. There are other places we could settle. I hear Boston is quite nice.'

'Those people aren't here for much of the time,' reasoned Madeline, realising Hugh's concern. 'And it won't be as claustrophobic as New York. There's no opera, for one thing.'

Despite misgivings over the society they might encounter, they decided to give it a try. They couldn't live like hermits, after all. At least Beachlands was a home they could call their own, and Madeline was prepared to put up with a great deal to ensure Hugh lived in a place that had always made him happy.

Although Beachlands had been at the centre of Hugh's childhood, Madeline had only ever visited once, briefly, on her way back to boarding school. It had always been a retreat for the Crosby men rather than the women of the family. Madeleine hadn't been given an opportunity to get to know it well enough to feel entitled to any part of it, or for that matter, to feel she was being denied it in any way.

She was standing in the grand entrance hall when Finch emerged from the shadows. Madeline hadn't heard her approach, and the housekeeper's small figure, which seemed to materialise from nowhere, appeared sinister rather than welcoming.

'Can I help you?'

She addressed Madeline as if she were a stranger who'd wandered in off the street and likely to run off with the family silver at any minute. Madeline's jaw clenched in response to her scrutiny and the chipped tones of her question.

'Mr Crosby is outside seeing to the luggage. Perhaps you could arrange for some tea. We've had a long journey.'

'You must be Miss Crosby. He said you were coming.'

The housekeeper held her ground, inspecting every crease and soot mark on Madeline's coat, and clearly in no hurry to send for the tea. She looked older than her years. Her hair, knotted tightly on the back of her head, was completely grey, and the angles of the deep lines on her face indicated they were the product of frowning rather than laughter. It's what happens when you spend too much time alone, thought Madeline, when you don't find enough to laugh about. It was a timely warning not to take life too seriously.

Hugh had told Madeline that before their father married, Finch had been one of his mistresses. At the end of one summer, having finally grown tired of her, he'd tried to shut up the house and return to New York without her, but she'd refused to leave. Penniless and with her reputation in tatters, her family had disowned her and she had nowhere else to go. Finch had assumed that after taking her to his bed, their father would marry her. Her mistake had been to overestimate his integrity.

Eventually, a compromise was reached. Their father allowed her to stay at Beachlands as long as she agreed to take on the role of housekeeper. In return, she was paid a fair wage for her labour.

The offer had been made purely to placate her, and nobody had expected her to stay beyond a matter of months, but as far as Finch was concerned, she now had a fine home and respectable employment, which was more than could be said for most discarded mistresses. Her enduring presence was the reason the women of the family had stayed away, or at least, until now.

It had all happened more than three decades ago, before Hugh was born. Now, after so many years of living as the unofficial mistress of Beachlands, Finch appeared to view Madeline's appearance as an intrusion. Madeline imagined she'd spent her life roaming the rooms, reliving the memories of her one love affair, playing out the scenes of that precious time, during which she'd allowed herself to believe that one day it would all be hers, and she wasn't about to relinquish her position now.

It had been written into their father's will that Finch must be allowed to see out her days in the house, if that was what she wished, and her remains could be buried in the grounds. Now, as they stood face to face, Madeline couldn't help feeling she was seeing a living ghost.

Hugh had been paying the cab driver and seeing the trunks were removed from the carriage safely. He entered the house, looking surprised to see Madeline still standing in the hallway, as if she were waiting for permission to embrace her new home. He rubbed his hands together, breaking the ice in the atmosphere.

'Finch, there you are. Please show Miss Crosby up to her room. We've had a long journey. I'm sure she'd like to freshen up.'

His familiarity betrayed he was a regular visitor. The two years in Europe had done nothing to loosen his bond with the place, or his casual relationship with Finch for that matter. Finch, on the other hand, seemed less pleased to see them.

'Miss Crosby has asked for some tea.'

'You can do both, can't you?' asked Hugh, his eyes skimming the floor for dirt and checking the silver gewgaws on the ornamental table had been polished. 'You have our rooms ready, I take it? I gave you plenty of notice that we'd be arriving today.'

'I thought we could put Miss Crosby in one of the rooms overlooking the ocean. If the sound of the waves proves too much of a disturbance, she can always move to a room at the back of the house.' Finch spoke as if Madeline weren't present, as if she didn't exist.

'A room overlooking the ocean sounds just fine,' said Madeline. The thought of waking up to the sound of the ocean sent her heart soaring.

'You must consider Miss Crosby the mistress of the house from now on,' said Hugh. 'Take your orders from her as you would take them from me.'

Finch sighed, not even attempting to hide her resistance to having another woman ruling what she believed to be her domain. She gave Madeline a narrow look. 'Follow me.'

The carpet was as plush as any Madeline had trodden in the best opera houses, the walls along the landing lined with portraits of their father's ancestors, posing as the founding fathers of America in their buttoned-up waistcoats and calico shirts. The faces, so familiar in their resemblance to Hugh and their father, were a reminder to Madeline that this was where she belonged, that she had a right to be here. If she ever had any doubt, all she had to do was look into their eyes and see her own reflected there.

She followed Finch through a door at the end of a long corridor, only to find herself in a dim room, the air stale with the smell of dust and unwashed linen.

'Are you sure this is the right place?'

She stumbled over the words, disorientated for a moment as

Finch threw back the curtains, allowing the bold afternoon light to infiltrate the room.

The unmade bed was the first clue to the source of the stale smell, the discarded night shirt and underwear beside it on the floor, the second and the third. No one from the family had visited the house for at least two years, so unless Finch had been entertaining male visitors, which seemed unlikely but not impossible, the unwashed linens had been lying around for a considerable time.

Madeline pulled off her gloves and opened a window, allowing the sound of the ocean and the scent of the fresh salt air to flood in. Beyond the front lawn and the coastal road, there was nothing but an endless stretch of beach and billowing dunes, the rolling waves and an expanse of sky that seemed to stretch to infinity. The view was as magnificent as anything she'd seen in the Mediterranean.

When she turned around to comment on it, Finch had already slipped away and closed the door quietly behind her. Assuming she'd gone to instruct one of the housemaids to clean the room, Madeline went downstairs to join Hugh for tea.

It took three attempts to find the drawing room. Hugh laughed at her confusion and promised to give her a grand tour as soon as he'd drunk his tea and enjoyed a slice of Finch's fruit cake, which she always made to celebrate his arrival.

'Is everything all right?' he asked, brushing crumbs from his jacket with a satisfied sigh.

'Everything's fine,' said Madeline, making light of the discomfort she felt at Finch's looming presence in the corner of the room. The housekeeper appeared to have no intention of leaving until she'd watched Hugh consume the cake, and Madeline didn't feel it was her place to dismiss her while Hugh was there.

She didn't mention the state of her bedroom, trusting that by the time she returned upstairs to unpack and change out of her travelling clothes, it would have been cleaned and tidied, the bed made up with fresh sheets. She would manage the situation herself. There was no need for Hugh to know about it.

Hugh seemed particularly excited to be there, drinking his tea and praising Finch's cake. Madeline thought it a rather dry affair and lacking in vine fruits, but kept her opinion to herself. For Hugh, so much of the joy of it was tied up with his childhood memories and she didn't want to spoil them. Perhaps the cake had tasted better in those days. She would never know because she hadn't been there to taste it.

The house, when she was finally given a tour, was bewildering in its size and layout. Their uncle's brownstone in New York and the small, select hotels where they'd stayed in Europe were nothing in size compared to Beachlands. Each room was decorated in the same overblown style: the patterns of blues and greens on the papered walls and the rosewood furnishings giving it an atmosphere of gloom, the heavy curtains and rugs creating darkness where there should have been light.

After the full tour, Hugh walked Madeline back to her room, which she now realised was on the first floor, tucked in the far corner of the house. She kept her opinion on the decor to herself as he grinned, assuming she was impressed by what she'd seen.

'How do you like your room, Maddie?'

'I couldn't ask for anything better.' Tired from the journey, Madeline wanted nothing more than to change out of her travelling clothes and wash her hands and face. 'I'll see you downstairs once I've unpacked.'

'Do you mind if I come in and take a look at the view? You can see the old lighthouse if you squint in the right direction.'

Before she could object, he'd opened the door and wandered into her room. Someone had been in and closed the window while she was downstairs drinking tea and the stale smell was as bad as ever. This time she recognised the stench as not only unwashed clothes, but also lingering tobacco.

'What the devil . . .'

Hugh stared at the mess in the room, the discarded male underwear and the dirty sheets on the unmade bed. Someone had placed Madeline's trunks in the corner, but beyond that, and the closing of the window, everything remained just as Madeline had discovered it an hour before.

'What does Finch think she's playing at?'

Hugh charged from the room before she could stop him, bellowing Finch's name, and taking the stairs two at a time as he headed towards the housekeeper's private quarters.

Madeline went after him, trying to cool his temper. 'I'm sure there's a reasonable explanation.'

'There's no excuse for it, Maddie. Finch was given plenty of notice to prepare the house for when we arrived.'

'Perhaps there was a misunderstanding.'

It was at that moment that Finch chose to do her magic trick of appearing out of nowhere. It dawned on Madeline that there were hidden doors everywhere, enabling the servants to move about the house without being seen or heard.

'Did you call me, sir?'

Hugh's mouth gaped as he tried to contain his temper. 'Why wasn't Miss Crosby's room prepared for her?'

Finch gave Madeline a cool look before turning her attention back to Hugh. 'I didn't realise you expected me to wait on her.'

'I've made it quite clear that my sister is the mistress of Beachlands. If you refuse to accept her authority, then you're free to leave this house.'

'You seem to be forgetting that my position here is protected by your father's will.'

'It was also in my father's will that Madeline is to be accepted as a member of this family. If you're unable to do that, then you'll find yourself living in the gardener's cottage on the edge of the grounds.'

The housekeeper's face was like stone. 'I'll see to the room now, sir. If I'd known which one she wanted in advance, I'd have made it ready for her.'

Hugh clenched his fists, trying to contain his temper until Finch left them. 'I'm sorry, Maddie. I don't know what the problem is. I gave her very clear instructions about preparing a room for you. She's never behaved like this before.'

'She's used to being the only woman in the house,' said Madeline.

Knowing she had a battle on her hands, Madeline decided to play the situation down. Experience had taught her that women like Finch were best won over gently.

When Madeline returned to her room an hour later, Sara, one of the young housemaids was unpacking her trunks. The place had been cleaned and aired, and the bed had been made up with fresh linen.

'There's new pillows on the bed, Miss. I didn't think you'd want to sleep on those old ones. The feathers didn't smell right.'

Madeline offered her a violet sweet for her trouble and helped her put away the dresses, smoothing out the creases with the flat of her hand and sprinkling the armoire with fresh lavender to keep the moths at bay. The smile on the young maid's face, her willingness to work with Madeline, was enough to prove that she'd have at least one ally in the household, and for now, that would have to be enough. She would win over her enemies one day at a time.

Chapter 5

The sun had already risen, casting a sprinkling of light across the ocean when Sara appeared in Madeline's room the next morning with a tray of poached eggs, toast and coffee.

'Mr Crosby thought you might like to take your breakfast in bed as you had such a tiring day yesterday, Miss.'

It was typical of Hugh's kind-heartedness that he would think of this. He didn't know she'd been awake since dawn, watching the ocean waves roll in across the beach. The sea air blowing through the open window was as refreshing as any night's sleep. She climbed down from the window seat and helped herself to coffee, thanking Sara for her trouble. Despite Finch's best efforts, Madeline suspected she was going to like it here.

Sara hesitated at the door, indicating she had one more message to deliver. The smile bursting on her lips suggested it was good news. 'Mr Crosby has a surprise for you, Miss. He'll be waiting in the drawing room whenever you're ready.'

Hugh had been so generous already, Madeline couldn't imagine what he'd found to surprise her with. Excitement tingled in her veins as she washed and dressed, pinning up her hair in a way that meant she didn't require the services of a maid.

A quick learner, she'd already memorised the layout of the

house and this time she had no trouble finding the drawing room. She knocked quietly on the door, wondering what was lying in wait for her.

Hugh's voice boomed from inside the room. 'You don't have to knock on your own door, Maddie. Come and see what I've got for you.'

She took a deep breath, prolonging the anticipation. All at once she was a child again, revelling in the excitement of receiving a gift, knowing that this time she was unlikely to be disappointed.

'What do you think?' he asked, unable to hide the eagerness in his voice.

She stepped into the room and began looking for the present, taking in the sofas and the chairs upholstered in red velvet, the fringed brocade curtains at the tall windows, the occasional tables, and the oriental rug.

Hugh watched her search the room. 'Try behind the parlour palm.'

Madeline's eyes drifted to the tall potted plant that dominated the farthest corner of the room. It was only now she realised it had been pulled forward, allowing something to be hidden behind it. She peered between the long stems and fine arching leaves of the plant, examining the telltale shape, which had been covered with a gold bedspread.

She turned to Hugh, biting her lip as she smiled, imploring him to help her drag the object to the centre of the room.

'Have you guessed what it is yet?'

Her eyes filled with tears as she nodded, carefully lifting the cover from the delicate, familiar object. Her beloved harp. She ran her hand along the contours of the wooden frame, allowing her fingers to trail lightly across the strings, filling the air with a delicate sound.

'I had the devil of a job transporting it here from our uncle's house in New York. If it hadn't been for these modern trains, I don't know how I'd have managed it.'

'I hope it didn't cause anyone too much inconvenience.'

Hugh shrugged. 'They were amply rewarded for their trouble.'

He refused to say any more about how it came to be there, and she gave up questioning him, simply glad to have her instrument back so she could start playing again.

Hugh set aside his coffee and gazed out of the window, stretching his long legs in front of him. It wasn't her imagination. He was more relaxed here than she'd ever seen him in New York or in any of the places they'd visited in Europe. It wasn't just his holiday mood. Being here had helped him reconnect with his old carefree self.

'There's a polo match this afternoon,' he said. 'A group of English army officers have challenged some of the local boys to a game. It might be fun to watch.'

Everyone was going mad for polo since it had crossed the Atlantic from England. 'Are you thinking of taking it up?' Hugh needed to put his energy somewhere if he wasn't to grow bored.

He frowned at her question. 'I don't know.'

Madeline could see the uncertainty in his face. If he joined a team, they'd need a commitment from him. Since their father's death, he'd become a drifter, moving from place to place and attaching himself to no one but her. No decision had been made as to whether they would make their home here permanently. If they didn't want to remain outsiders, they had to make a stand, claim somewhere as home, and stick with it. The constant travelling was a privilege, but it was also self-indulgent. They couldn't run away forever.

Since they'd arrived here, everything about Hugh's demeanour told her that this was where he belonged, that Beachlands was his true home. If she was to convince him to settle, she had to prove to him that it felt like her home too.

'Let's go and watch the match. You can show me what's so fascinating about men on horseback hitting a ball with a stick.'

'It's a mallet, not a stick,' he laughed, knowing she knew exactly what it was, and that she probably understood more about the rules of the game than he did.

The polo field was on a stretch of land near Bellevue Avenue, where many of the newly rich industrialists had built their summer residences, outshining the old New Yorkers' summer cottages with their splendour, or as Madeline preferred to think of it, their mock-European vulgarity.

By the time Hugh and Madeline arrived, the edge of the pitch was already busy with spectators. Women in lightweight silk or sprigged muslin day dresses were gathered in elegant huddles, their faces protected from the sun by gossamer veils and large brimmed hats, while the men stood about in well-cut jackets, boasting exotic buttonholes, their straw boaters tipped at halting angles, throwing shade across their eyes.

It wasn't just the new money here, but members of the so-called New York aristocracy too. It was only late spring, but already they were flooding in, escaping, before the oppressive summer city heat arrived. Madeline had known there'd be no avoiding them by coming to Newport. She just hadn't expected to have to face them quite so soon.

'It's the wilting flower brigade all over again.' She winked at Hugh, determined to make a light of their presence. 'Please tell me Ginger isn't here. I couldn't stand to see another precious gardenia suffer rough treatment.'

Hugh grinned. 'You were the one who trod on it so mercilessly.'

'It was already in its death throes, thanks to Ginger's neglect.' She shook her head at a young man who made a point of catching her eye, a pink rose wilting in his lapel. 'No flower should ever be treated so brutally.'

The crowd cheered as the players rode onto the field. The visiting team scored within minutes, outclassing their opponents without difficulty. It was clear early on which way the game was going. The long-limbed Westchester team appeared gangly and uncoordinated in their saddles compared to the English army officers whose shorter, sturdier limbs were more suited to the physique of the ponies.

'Hurlingham rules dictate the size of the ponies,' commented Hugh, with some disappointment after yet another goal had been scored against the Westchester team. 'That's why we're losing.'

'They have to try harder,' replied Madeline, pretending not to notice a group of women who were making a great show of turning their backs on her. 'Resilience is key when it comes to victory.'

By the end of the first chukka, the English team were already a long way ahead. Lacking in experience and technique, the Westchester boys were a sorry sight, dribbling the ball and clinging to their ponies' necks, while the Englishmen swept past them, swinging the mallets with a devil-may-care finesse and sending the ball flying down the field to the opponent's goal.

'The English are here to teach us how it's done,' said Hugh, as the polite clapping dissolved into discontented murmurs.

'It's the sport of kings,' replied Madeline. 'They're here to get their own back on us for the War of Independence.'

A quiet laugh came from behind them. Hugh turned to see who'd been listening to their conversation.

The young man bowed his head as Hugh caught his eye. 'Forgive me. I couldn't help overhearing.'

The man was more soberly dressed than the rest of the crowd, in a well-cut blue linen suit, designed for style rather than show. His eyes were kind rather than judgemental, his face as good looking as any Madeline had ever seen. The fact that he'd laughed at her joke only increased her curiosity about him. Beyond this, there was something unassuming about his manner that she instantly warmed to.

He smiled at Madeline before tearing his eyes back to Hugh. 'Please allow me to introduce myself. My name is Edward Booth.'

Recognition snagged at the back of Madeline's mind. 'Are you the lawyer who represented those poor people in Hell's Kitchen? The ones threatened with eviction by that awful robber baron?'

'Yes, that was me.'

Madeline thrust out her hand for him to shake. 'I applaud you for your work, Mr Booth.'

Edward took her hand. 'It's a pleasure to meet you, Miss . . .'

'Madeline Crosby. This is my brother, Hugh.'

Edward looked thoughtful. 'Forgive me. Your name sounds familiar, but I can't quite place it.'

'I'm the Miss Crosby who donated a considerable sum to fund your campaign for the steelworkers' right to shorter hours.'

Her knowledge of his work seemed to unsettle him. 'You've put me at a disadvantage, Miss Crosby. You appear to know more about me than I know about you.'

'I've followed your career in the newspapers. It's a rare person who is prepared to risk their professional reputation to fight for the rights of those less fortunate than themselves.'

'I don't always win, but I do the best I can.'

He was younger than she'd expected from reading the transcripts of his speeches. He must have been around the same age as Hugh, and yet there was a steadiness and a wisdom in him that went far beyond his years.

His eyes lingered on her face. 'I haven't seen you here before. I would have remembered.'

Madeline brushed off his obvious admiration, refusing to show how much she was affected by it. He was after all only judging her by her appearance. He had nothing else to go by, other than her obvious wealth and her history of spending it charitably. 'We've been travelling in Europe.'

'Are you here for the summer?'

His question sounded eager, just like so many other men who'd tried to get to know her. Still, she was thrilled by his interest. She knew from his work that Edward Booth was a good man.

'We might stay longer. It's hard to say.'

He handed her a calling card. 'I must introduce you to my sisters. They'd be delighted to know you.'

Hugh gave her a questioning glance, waiting for his sister's permission before offering Edward his card in return. Once it had been given, Edward slipped it into his top pocket, placing his palm over the spot where it nestled as if to keep it safe. 'Come to tea tomorrow afternoon.'

'Only if you promise to tell me more about your work,' said Madeline.

'I shall look forward to it.' Suddenly remembering his manners, he glanced at Hugh. 'You must come too, of course.'

Hugh grinned. 'Wherever my sister goes, I also go. You can be sure of that.'

Chapter 6

Madeline looked up at the imposing mansion, fronted by a sweeping lawn edged with marble statues of eighteenth-century milkmaids, their heads inclined towards the circular fountain that stood in the centre, presided over by a bronze cherub. Anyone passing along the road could easily have mistaken it for a miniature version of the palace of Fontainebleau.

'This can't be the house,' said Madeline, as Hugh halted the buggy in front of the tall iron gates. 'You must have taken a wrong turning.'

Hugh checked the address on the card Edward had given them the previous day. 'This is it.'

Despite its ancient look of grandeur, the pale-yellow brick façade shone like new. Everything about the house gleamed, from the rows of windows to the roof tiles, the perfectly upright chimneys and the horseshoe staircase leading to the main entrance. Even the gravel, winding a serpent path around the lawn, appeared to be made of highly polished stones.

A young boy, dressed like a miniature footman in burgundy breeches and a brocade waistcoat appeared as if from nowhere and opened the wrought-iron gates. The gold-painted fleur-de-lis insignia glinted in the afternoon sun as they swung silently open;

the hinges too new, too well oiled to squeal.

After the beautiful houses they'd seen in Europe, well worn and steeped in age, this particular house appeared out of joint, not only with what it pretended to be, but with the landscape in which it sat.

'New money, and lots of it, I'd guess,' murmured Hugh, nodding to the miniature footman as he negotiated the buggy through the gates and up to the house.

This wasn't what Madeline had expected, knowing what she did of Edward's career as a lawyer. She assumed his home would be modest, more in tune with his social conscience. This house would have put the tastes of Madame de Pompadour in the shade.

The front door opened before they'd stepped down from the buggy. The maid, who could have passed as the slightly older sister of the little boy at the gate, bobbed a curtsy and welcomed them to Mountview. Her black dress, with its starched white collar and apron, would have appeared contemporary, if it hadn't been for the oversized mob cap, which had a decidedly ominous French revolutionary feel to it.

The sound of the front door closing behind them echoed around the grand entrance. A house built on this scale would always have a sense of emptiness, however many expensive objects filled the rooms. It was a showpiece masquerading as a home, and Madeline shuddered at the chilly impersonal nature of it.

There was no fear of the inside of the house being overshadowed by its exterior, as the black and white marble floor gave way to elaborately gilded walls, which stretched up to a high ceiling painted with frescoes depicting nymphs and cherubs, their modesty protected by swathes of diaphanous fabric in what appeared to be an imitation of the Baroque style. At the centre of it all was a grand marble staircase, erected on a scale that would put any public building to shame.

The maid led them through a pair of double doors into a large sunlit drawing room where the family were already gathered.

Edward stood up to greet them before the maid could announce them.

'Mr and Miss Crosby. Welcome. You're just in time for tea.'

Four sets of eyes interrogated Madeline's face as Edward introduced them to his sisters, Marianne and Jane, his mother, Mrs Booth, and finally Mrs Norton, the widowed sister of Mrs Booth and aunt to the siblings.

'What do you think of our home?' asked Mrs Booth, who was lying on a chaise longue which had been angled in front of the French doors to catch the ocean breeze. There was a drowsiness to her manner as she forced out her words, as if the afternoon heat was too much for her delicate constitution to bear.

Madeline cast her eyes over the gilded panelling that covered all four walls, the confection of rose-chintz sofas and armchairs, the clashing rugs in violent oranges and blues.

'It's . . .' She bit her tongue. The words *mock Baroque* sprung to mind, but it would be an indelicate thing to say.

Hugh jumped in to save her as Madeline faltered. 'Yes, it's very . . .'

'Isn't it,' interrupted Edward, relieving them of their obligation to comment further.

Madeline met his eye, silently thanking him for rescuing them from the awkward exchange. It wasn't in her nature to be so familiar with a stranger, but everything about his manner made her feel it was safe to let her guard down.

A different maid to the one who'd answered the door led the procession as the tea tray and a variety of cake stands, displaying sandwiches and sweet treats of the sort only usually found in the best European hotels, were brought in. Madeline took advantage of the distraction to study Edward's sisters. They appeared conventional in their pale-coloured silk dresses with puff sleeves, nipped-in waists and bell-shaped skirts, so like every other young woman in society, that Madeline would never have connected them to their campaigning brother.

Marianne proved she was the eldest by taking precedence in helping herself to the sandwiches, while appearing to pay little attention to anyone in the room. Tall and well built, with elegantly fashioned hair that must have taken half the morning for her maid to construct, she was a more imposing version of her sister, Jane, who was fairer and slighter, and showed a little more reticence when it came to attacking the sandwiches.

'Help yourselves to tea and cakes,' said Mrs Booth, tugging the fluffy ears of the white long-haired Chihuahua who lay sprawled across her stomach. 'We don't stand on ceremony in this house.'

The dog raised its right lip at the disturbance and released a trembling growl, its brown eyes bulging like marbles in its apple-shaped head. 'Don't mind Mimi,' added Mrs Booth. 'She hardly ever bites.'

Madeline, who had eaten very little lunch, for reasons she couldn't now remember, forewent the sandwiches in favour of a strawberry tart. Caught in the rapture of the butter pastry and the melting softness of the crème pâtissière, she failed to notice a small figure slip into the room. Suddenly, Mrs Norton, who until that moment had remained as silent and rigid as the hard-backed chair upon which she sat, snapped her fingers and demanded the young woman bring a selection of sandwiches from the table.

She appeared to be about twenty, a year or two younger than Jane, the youngest sister, and wore a simple cotton dress, unadorned with lace or any kind of decoration. Her hair was pinned back in a simple knot and betrayed no evidence of a maid's hand. The way she jumped to Mrs Norton's bidding suggested she was a paid companion to one of the women of the family. Her lack of style and panache certainly ruled her out as being a lady's maid.

'This is Miss Flora Pierce,' said Edward, when no one else bothered to introduce her. 'She lives with us.'

Madeline smiled at her through a mouthful of strawberry tart, still no wiser as to who she was. Judging by the uncomfortable look on Flora's face, she wasn't pleased to be the object of attention.

'Never mind her,' said Mrs Norton, snatching a cucumber sandwich from the plate before Flora could set it down in front of her. 'Tell us about your family.' She gave Hugh a pointed look. 'Are you from New York? What kind of business are you in? Would we know your father?'

'My father died a few years ago,' said Hugh.

'I'm sorry for it,' replied Mrs Norton, investigating the thickness of the cucumber between the slices of bread. 'And your mother? Where is she now?'

Hugh visibly flinched at the question. 'She died too.'

'I see. Do you run the family business?'

Hugh helped himself to a sugar lump and dropped it into his tea, squirming under the interrogation. 'There's no family business in the sense that you mean.'

'You're old money?' asked Mrs Norton, the tone of her voice rising with the question.

Madeline sensed Hugh's discomfort as he cleared his throat. The family fortune had been built over generations through clever long-term investments and property speculation. Inherited wealth was a fact of their lives and something neither he, nor his father, nor his grandfather had needed to work to achieve. It wasn't so much that Hugh took it for granted, but that he'd been brought up never to talk about it.

Marianne thrust a spoon at him, encouraging him to stir his tea before the lump settled in the bottom of the cup.

'We don't usually have the honour of mixing with your sort,' continued Mrs Norton. 'We've certainly never had one of you in the house before. We find old money likes to keep itself to itself and prefers not to mix with new money.' She gave him a hungry look. 'I hope you'll prove the exception, Mr Crosby.'

Madeline sipped her tea, resisting the temptation to make a joke about endangered species laying low in their natural habitat and only mixing with their own kind for the sake of their protection.

She wasn't sure her wit would be appreciated by those who had yet to know and understand her. Heaven forbid they should take her flippant comments seriously.

'You mustn't be too shocked when I tell you our money comes from trade,' said Mrs Booth, pushing the corner of a sandwich into Mimi's mouth to silence the growling. 'My husband, that's Mr Booth, and his father before him, earned the money for everything you see around you through good, honest work, and we're not afraid to admit it.'

'He should be proud of his achievements,' said Hugh. 'It's men such as your husband that have made the country what it is today.'

Madeline thought it was a little rash of Hugh to give such endorsements without knowing exactly how the money had been accrued. Many of today's self-made men weren't known as robber barons for nothing.

'He spends most of his time in New York, seeing to things,' continued Mrs Booth. 'Our eldest son, Theo, works alongside him.' She paused, giving way to an elaborate yawn. 'Edward has no interest in the business and prefers to go his own way.'

'If we're discussing our next generation of men, we have to include our dear Rawdon,' piped up Mrs Norton who'd been following the conversation with growing intensity. 'He's the greatest banker of them all.'

Madeline pretended to wipe the crumbs from her lips with a napkin to hide her smile. Mrs Norton's pronouncement had been so ridiculous she didn't dare catch her brother's eye.

'You'll have read about Rawdon in the business pages of the newspapers,' continued Mrs Norton.

'I'm afraid not,' replied Hugh, his tone overflowing with good manners. 'We've been abroad for some time.'

'Then you won't have heard the news,' said Mrs Booth, pushing Mimi from her lap as the dog started to cough up the crusts she'd been fed.

Madeline tried to look interested in the conversation, while keeping one eye on the dish of profiteroles that had just been set down by yet another maid in a French revolutionary mob cap.

'Our dear Marianne is to marry him.' Mrs Norton jumped in before Mrs Booth could make the announcement. 'They became engaged after knowing each other for only a month.' She looked at Marianne, triumph written large on her face. 'Isn't that so?'

Marianne nodded, her eyes set adrift on the profiteroles. 'Yes.'

'And aren't you the luckiest girl alive?' asked Mrs Norton in a tone that suggested it wasn't so much a question as a statement of fact.

Finally succumbing to the temptation, Marianne grabbed a profiterole and pushed the whole thing into her mouth, nodding in answer to her aunt's question.

Following the precedent set by Marianne, Madeline leaned forward and helped herself to a profiterole. 'Congratulations on your engagement,' she muttered, before sinking her teeth into the confection.

'You should see the house she'll be living in,' continued Mrs Norton, rescuing Marianne from having to reply with a mouth full of profiterole. 'Of course, there wouldn't have been an engagement if I hadn't encouraged it. It doesn't do to be shy when it comes to these matters. If she hadn't been quick, some other gold digger would have grabbed him.'

A snigger escaped Hugh's lips, which he quickly disguised as a cough. Madeline didn't look at him for fear of giving him away.

'We're not saying Marianne is a gold digger,' said Edward after an awkward silence. 'She'll be taking a very handsome dowry into the marriage.'

'I was simply referring to the less wealthy women out there,' added Mrs Norton, completely unabashed. 'Precious few young women are as deserving of a man like Rawdon as my dear niece.'

There it was again, the talk of money, as if love were a financial transaction rather than a dictate of the heart.

'Is Rawdon handsome?' asked Madeline, dragging the subject

onto more civilised ground. After all, she hardly knew these people and had been brought up to understand the importance of first impressions.

'He's a fine man, indeed,' blurted Mrs Norton after Marianne failed to answer.

Made curious by Marianne's silence, Madeline looked at her and raised her eyebrows as if to repeat the question.

Having been cornered in the most subtle of ways, Marianne reached for another profiterole and shrugged. 'He's a man of the highest standing, and as my aunt says, he has the most marvellous house.'

Mrs Norton sipped her tea with a satisfied air, her eyes firmly fixed on Hugh. 'Now Marianne is all but settled, I shall turn my matchmaking energies to finding a suitable husband for Jane. She's just as great a beauty as her sister, don't you agree, Mr Crosby?'

It didn't seem to have dawned on Hugh that Mrs Norton was addressing him directly until he heard his name mentioned. He froze in his seat, his eyes widening like a rabbit facing a shotgun.

'I . . .'

'Of course, we don't expect to find anyone quite as wealthy as Rawdon for Jane,' added Mrs Booth, who must have sensed Hugh's panic, 'but I'd like to think the perfect match is out there somewhere.'

Hugh needed rescuing from the ambitions of Mrs Norton, who clearly wouldn't rest until she'd secured advantageous marriages for both Marianne and Jane. Madeline was also beginning to regret eating so much sugar without lining her stomach with a sandwich first. A breath of ocean air was what she and Hugh needed, and a brisk walk along the shore.

Madeline swallowed the last of her tea and looked at her brother, indicating she was ready to leave. Before they could politely escape, the door burst open and a man of middling years and a large girth blustered in. Madeline assumed it was Mr Booth senior until Mrs Norton gasped.

'Speak of the devil and he's sure to appear. Here he is, our own Rawdon.'

Appearances can be deceptive, particularly at first sight, but in this case, Madeline didn't think so. Not only was Rawdon old enough to be Marianne's father, but the way he entered the room, launching himself at the tea table like a toddler who hadn't been fed since breakfast, suggested he lacked much in the way of charm or manners.

All eyes rested on him as his clumsy fingers turned over the remaining sandwiches on the plates. It didn't escape Madeline's notice that Marianne moved to the other side of the room, squeezing onto the edge of the chaise longue next to her mother's feet, where she began ruffling the fur around Mimi's neck and kissing the poor creature's nose as if no one else in the room existed.

Mrs Norton gave her niece a critical stare before turning her attention back to Rawdon. 'We've been telling our guests about the summer cottage you've had built on Bellevue Avenue.'

'Fifty rooms, not including the ballroom,' boasted Rawdon through a mouthful of smoked salmon. 'Five hundred tonnes of marble has been shipped in for the floors, and I couldn't tell you how many chandeliers there are, but there's a lot. More than any other house on Rhode Island, I've been assured of that.'

'Has it been built in the French style?' asked Madeline, trying to build a picture of it that she could relate to the lumbering man in front of her.

He stopped chewing for a minute while he thought about it. Seemingly unable to come up with an answer, he turned to Marianne. 'What would you say it is?'

'It's in the English tradition,' said Marianne, her face still buried in the dog's fur, despite the low rumble of its growl.

Images of moated castles with battlements appeared in Madeline's head, Tudor mansions displaying heraldic flags, and brooding gothic piles surrounded by woodland, but none of them seemed an appropriate fit for the man she saw in front of her. 'I love the style of old English houses and their formal gardens. We visited some beautiful ones during our stay in England.'

'They'll have been nothing compared to our dear Rawdon's house,' said Mrs Norton, exhibiting a pride that wasn't hers to claim. 'You should see it for yourself. You won't believe your eyes.'

'You must all come tomorrow,' said Rawdon, his offer sounding more like an order than an invitation. 'We'll make an afternoon of it. I'll give you a tour of the house then we can have tea and play games on the lawn.'

Games. Madeline tried not to cringe as she finally asserted her intention to leave. Edward gave her a sympathetic smile as he stood up to show her out, and she hoped she hadn't betrayed her ungenerous thoughts.

'There's a formal garden in the grounds you might like,' said Edward as he led her out of the house and handed her into the buggy, Hugh following faithfully at her heels. 'You must allow me to show it to you. Even though it's newly planted, the rose garden is worth seeing.'

Edward had picked up on her comment about her love of gardens. Madeline hadn't realised he'd been paying so much attention to her words.

'I'd like that.'

She was flattered that he'd shown her such consideration and saw it as a reflection of his character. He was so different from the rest of his family, devoting his professional life to fighting for the rights of those less fortunate than himself. He could have whiled away his days as a man of leisure, or joined the family business, taking the credit for its success without assuming any of the responsibility for it.

It was rare to meet a man of such good nature, and her spirits lifted at the thought of seeing him again. Putting up with his garish aunt and his annoying mother and sisters would be a small price to pay for being in his company and getting to know him a little better.

Chapter 7

From the outside, Rawdon's house looked like an Italian Renaissance palace. The limestone front, with its rows of Doric columns, and the marble statues on the roof acting as ineffectual lookouts across the rolling lawn, reminded Madeline of the classical buildings they'd seen in Rome.

'I thought Rawdon said the house was designed in the English style,' said Madeline as Hugh drove up to it in the buggy.

'It was Marianne who said that,' reminded Hugh. 'Something tells me she was having a joke at his expense. Their engagement doesn't strike me as a meeting of hearts and minds.'

'Love conquers all,' said Madeline. 'And if that fails, there's always his vast wealth to fall back on.'

The Booths' carriage was already parked in front of the house. Mrs Norton was standing in the porch, midpoint between the mock-classical stone columns, shaking the creases from Marianne's silk dress that had suffered from being squashed during the carriage ride.

'We might as well have walked for all the fuss it's caused,' said Jane, her spite aimed at her sister. 'It's not exactly far.'

'It's important that we're seen to arrive in style,' snapped Mrs Norton, who had now turned her attention to Marianne's hair and was pulling at the flowers that had been woven into her curls. Not for the first time, Madeline wondered what the fascination was with wearing fresh flowers and allowing them to slowly die on your person.

Thanks to all the fuss, it was a moment before her and Hugh's presence was acknowledged. Edward stepped forward to greet them.

'You must forgive our little family drama,' he said. 'Our aunt insisted on taking the carriage, while Jane prefers to walk. You can never please everyone.'

All sense of awkwardness fell away as Edward took Madeline's arm. Gratified by his attention, the day suddenly felt so much brighter for seeing him.

The scowl dropped from Jane's face as soon as she spotted Hugh. 'I'm sure you wouldn't have denied me a walk, if it had been up to you, Mr Crosby.'

'Only dogs cry for walks,' said Marianne, giving her sister a stiff look as her aunt continued to fiddle with her hair.

The mention of dogs brought Mrs Booth to Madeline's mind. 'Is your mother not joining us today?'

'The visit would have been far too tiring for her,' said Mrs Norton, 'which is why I've made it my duty to take her place.' She nodded to Flora, who was standing behind the family group, laden down with the three mantles and various sets of gloves which must have belonged to the women of the party. 'Come along, girl. Don't lag behind. And if you want to show how grateful you are to be here, look cheerful.'

'Yes, do come along,' said Marianne, aping her aunt's manner. 'We haven't got all day.'

Madeline's heart went out to the young companion, struggling under the weight of so many accessories and trying to put on a brave face. She offered Flora an encouraging smile, but the girl was determined not to catch her eye, and the effort was wasted.

Finally, the front door was opened and Rawdon appeared. 'Come in, come in. Why didn't you ring the bell?'

'You should have a boy stationed at the entrance to keep watch, Rawdon,' said Marianne. 'Your guests shouldn't be expected to have to ring the bell, nor should they be kept waiting.'

Jane sniggered behind her sister's back. 'You're going to have your work cut out, bringing him up to scratch.'

Rawdon looked shamefaced. 'No doubt things will improve once you're the mistress here, Miss Booth.'

There was a formality and a coolness to the exchange that sent a shudder through Madeline. She held her tongue, reminding herself to reserve her judgement. Not every story was a love story.

Edward, who was still at Madeline's side, spoke softly. 'The house is spectacular, isn't it? Although it looks Italian on the outside, everything inside is in the French style.'

'Not English then?' asked Madeline in the most innocent way she could muster.

'No,' said Edward. 'That was my sister's little joke.'

There was a fine line between humour and cruelty. Sometimes it was hard to know which side of the line people were on.

They followed Rawdon as he charged through an entrance hall of cathedral-like proportions. The harshness of the floor-to-ceiling marble was softened only by the flash of red velvet drapes and gilded panelling – the assault on the eyes proved it was possible to have too much of a good thing. Madeline couldn't help thinking it was the perfect setting for a tragic opera. It didn't take much to imagine the body of a slain king lying face down in front of the granite fireplace.

Rawdon didn't stop for breath until they reached the nearest drawing room, where the atmosphere was altogether calmer, thanks to the pale-blue walls and tumbling lace curtains. Here, the stark marble tiles gave way to parquet flooring and oriental rugs, while the Napoleon-III-style easy chairs, upholstered in oyster damask, were clustered around the rosewood occasional tables in a manner of forced informality.

'I've decided to name the house Southsea,' he bellowed to no one in particular.

'Are we south of the sea then?' asked Jane, hooking her arm through Hugh's, as if she suspected he was about to make a run for it at any minute. Now she had a hold of him, Madeline feared he wouldn't get away without a struggle.

Rawdon seemed confused by Jane's question. He frowned at his future sister-in-law. 'Does it matter which way the house is facing?'

Mrs Norton gave her niece a warning look to silence her before she could come back with a cruel remark.

'We'll have tea and then I'll show you around,' said Rawdon, moving on from Jane's question, either out of confusion or good manners. He was so set on impressing them it was hard to know which it was.

Madeline's eyes were everywhere, examining the stencilled ceilings, the antique French furniture, some plundered, some copied, with gilded wood polished to a high shine, but it was all too much to take in. It was as if a magic spell had been cast, transporting her to the French court. If it hadn't been so vulgar, so humourless, she'd have considered the decor a parody. Did Rawdon have nothing more worthwhile to spend his money on or did he lack the imagination to do some good with it?

'I can see how impressed you are with the house, Miss Crosby,' said Rawdon, misreading her expression of wonder. 'Despite its classical look, it'll surprise you to know it was built with a modern steel frame.'

The fact that cold steel lay at the heart of the house did nothing to surprise her. Uncertain how to respond, she offered him a noncommittal smile.

After tea, the talk turned to taking a tour of the house. At the prospect of wandering around the rooms, Marianne became more animated than Madeline had ever seen her.

'Would you like me to show you the billiard room?' Marianne asked Hugh. 'It has a mosaic-tiled floor, like you see in the ancient Roman houses.'

Hugh gave her an uncertain look. 'Um . . .'

'If we're to tour the whole place, we should start with the gardens while the weather's fine,' said Madeline, knowing Hugh must be longing to be outside.

Edward offered Madeline his arm again. 'The last time we met, I promised to show you the rose garden.'

It touched her that he'd remembered. She wasn't used to such personal attentions from anyone other than Hugh. Here was a man who admired her for herself. She only hoped his opinion of her wouldn't change if he learned about her past.

Rawdon looked downcast at the suggestion that they should go outside. 'The men have just finished covering the fireplace in the music room with platinum leaf. It shines brighter than gold. Wouldn't you like to take a look at it first?'

It was churlish to try to change the plan now minds had been made up. Jane threw open the French doors and escaped onto the terrace that overlooked the ocean, shouting to Flora to fetch her parasol from the carriage. The instruction was quickly followed by Mrs Norton demanding her gloves, not the pair Flora was already carrying, but the other ones, she said, and her veil, which she'd also left in the carriage.

'It must be a great test of patience, being a paid companion to Mrs Norton,' said Madeline as Edward led her away from the terrace.

'Flora isn't a paid companion. She's our cousin.'

It was unusual for Madeline to misjudge a situation so completely. Flora behaved with such a downtrodden air and was generally spoken to so roughly that anyone not knowing her relationship to the Booths would have come to the same conclusion.

'Then it's very good of her to be at everyone's beck and call.'

'Flora likes to be useful to the family.'

It was obvious from the way she was treated that the Booths

didn't consider her an equal. Madeline only had to look at the clothes Flora wore to see the difference. 'Has she been living with you for long?'

'Since she was a child. Her mother, Frances, is my mother's youngest sister. She eloped with one of Father's clerks when she was barely seventeen and moved to a small town in Wisconsin. She had this romantic notion that the two of them would make their fortune panning for gold, but it didn't work out that way. It was nothing but a dream. The gold rush had long passed.

'It was years before she was heard from again. By then, she had a brood of young children and a husband whose drinking habits didn't leave enough hours in the day for anything else. He was too unreliable to hold down a job, and she was keeping the family above water by whatever means she could, largely by dressmaking and taking in laundry. It was our aunt, Mrs Norton, who suggested we invite Flora for an extended visit. No one anticipated that she'd stay with us for so long, but she's made herself indispensable to everyone.'

'Mrs Norton lives with you as well?'

Edward frowned, as if he'd never before considered it. 'She came to stay after her husband's death and has never really left.'

Madeline's curiosity returned to Flora. 'She must miss her mother and father, her brothers and sisters.'

'She has the kindest nature. Over the years, I've come to look upon her as a sister.'

This was all well and good, but she wondered how Flora felt about the situation. Mrs Norton treated her no better than a drudge. 'Is Flora in or out?'

'In or out of what?'

'Society. Does she go to parties with your sisters?'

'She stays at home to keep Mother company. Today is an exception. She was keen to see the rose garden here at Southsea, which is why I insisted she join us. She doesn't go out into society the way you mean.'

'Does she wish to find a husband?'

'She's never said so. Mother will need her more than ever once Marianne marries. Jane will marry too one day. It wouldn't do for Mother to be left without a young companion.'

And so Flora was meant to be the stay-at-home surrogate daughter. Had they considered what would happen to her when she was no longer needed? With no fortune and no husband, what would become of her? Would any of the Booth siblings be considerate enough to give her a home?

They passed through a tall iron gate into a walled garden. Madeline was instantly greeted by the sun-warmed scent of the roses. Whichever direction she looked, flowers bloomed on mature shrubs, displaying every shade from red to pink to the softest white, from orange and yellow to the palest cream. She settled on a nearby bench to enjoy the spectacle, her senses reeling from the combined fragrance of the flowers and the confection of colour.

'I've never seen so many types of rose in one place.'

'Rawdon arranged it for Marianne as soon as he finished building the house. Roses are her favourite flower.'

It was hard to believe the rose bushes had only been planted the previous winter. You didn't need time and patience to build a garden after all as long as you had unlimited money and labour to throw at it.

'It's a grand romantic gesture, don't you think?' asked Edward.

His comment put Madeline's cynical thoughts to shame. She nodded, bowing to his better nature. 'Yes, it is.'

A man like Edward could make the world a better place just by encouraging her to see it through his eyes.

'What else do you enjoy, apart from gardens?' he asked.

'Music is my greatest love. Hugh gave me a harp for my sixteenth birthday. It was the one thing I'd always longed for. I missed it so much while we were travelling in Europe. Now I have it here with me in Newport, I intend to practise every day.'

'I'd love to hear you play.'

'Then you must visit us at Beachlands. Come any time you please. I like nothing more than an appreciative audience, so you must promise to flatter me, even if you find my ability lacking.'

They'd only been seated a few minutes when Jane appeared, her face flushed from too much activity.

'Are you all right?' asked Madeline. She looked as if something terrible had happened.

'It's too hot, and the ocean breeze keeps blowing.' She stamped the ground, as if such an effort would put a stop to the waves tumbling. 'Have you seen Mr Crosby and Marianne? By the time Flora returned with my parasol they'd disappeared. The three of us were supposed to be exploring the animal topiary garden together, but I can't find them anywhere.'

The last time Madeline had seen Hugh, he'd been trying to disentangle himself from Jane's grip. Something must have occurred in the intervening minutes, resulting in Jane being given the slip, leaving Marianne to claim Hugh for herself. It seemed a curious way for an engaged woman to behave towards a man she hardly knew.

After they'd assured her that they hadn't seen them, Jane stormed off, throwing her soiled handkerchief to the ground, as if it hadn't strained someone's eyes to embroider the intricate pattern in the poor light of a sweatshop.

Two words rang in Madeline's head. *Animal topiary.* She turned to Edward, who seemed unconcerned by his sister's behaviour, as if this kind of tantrum was something that happened all the time.

'Animal topiary?'

He suppressed a smile. 'Allow me to show you.'

A short walk brought them to an adjoining area of the garden, where a series of large animals carved out of box hedging had been carefully arranged. 'It's a folly of Rawdon's mother,' explained Edward. 'She grew them on her estate and had them transplanted here as a present when the engagement was announced.'

Madeline stared up at the enormous green elephant, the tiny leaves of the box trimmed neatly to shape its trunk, its tusks and its ears. Beside it stood a giraffe, which was at least twelve feet tall. Next to that, there was a bear and a lion, each one carved out of leaves and branches to be larger than the real thing.

'Did Rawdon's mother cultivate these?'

'Her gardeners grew and shaped them over decades. This is only a small selection. Her own garden is like a green zoo.'

Edward kept the tone of his voice neutral as he explained the heritage of the topiary so as not to give away whether he admired them or considered them ridiculous. She found herself drawn to his diplomacy. He never fell into the trap of saying the wrong thing just to make someone smile, the way she did. He didn't need to try hard to be liked.

'Rawdon would have only been a child when these animals were first cultivated,' commented Madeline. 'They must have grown as he did.' Offering them as a gift for his garden suddenly seemed a loving thing to do and not foolish at all.

A burst of laughter erupted from the other side of the wall. Peering through one of the arches, Madeline spotted Marianne and Hugh, wandering an irregular path across the lawn that overlooked the ocean. After the enclosed space of the topiary garden, it seemed a vast expanse, the view carrying as far as the eye could see across the ever-shifting water.

Madeline waved to catch their attention as she and Edward approached them. 'Jane was looking for you both. She seemed upset to have missed you.'

'We promised to wait for her,' said Hugh with some dismay, 'but Marianne was impatient to show me . . . everything.'

Marianne's eyes shifted to the horizon. 'I still can't believe all this will soon be mine.'

There was something unreal about the house and the garden, just as there was something forced about the relationship between the engaged couple that Madeline couldn't quite comprehend.

She understood the concept of marrying for money, of money marrying money, but there seemed more to it than that.

'It'll be quite an undertaking after you're married, being mistress of this estate,' said Madeline, not sure whether she meant the comment to indicate awe, or a reason not to marry.

'I suppose it will.' Marianne tapped Hugh on the shoulder with her parasol. 'How about you, Mr Crosby? Are you planning to take a wife any time soon? There must be any number of young ladies vying for your attention.'

Hugh waved his hand as if to dismiss the subject. 'I have no interest in marriage. I'm perfectly content to share my life with my sister.'

Marianne's eyes grew wide at his answer. 'That's because you haven't met the right woman.'

'My brother has met many charming women, but I've yet to see him fall in love with any of them,' said Madeline, coming to his defence.

Marianne linked her arm through Hugh's and pulled him closer. 'We'll have to see what we can do about that.'

'I've never been in love and never intend to be,' said Hugh, with more vehemence than the situation required.

'You should leave the poor man alone,' said Edward, trying to make light of the situation. Marianne was, after all, attached to someone else and couldn't have any interest in pursuing Hugh. Nor was she yet in a position to act as a matchmaker, which was a role that usually fell to married women.

Undaunted by Edward's rebuke, Marianne turned the same question on Madeline. 'How about you, Miss Crosby? Do you intend to marry?'

'I . . .'

She met Edward's eye as he searched her face, showing more interest in her answer than someone of such short acquaintance had a right to.

The conversation was interrupted by the sound of Rawdon's

voice carrying across the lawn as he shouted Marianne's name from the shrubbery.

Marianne clutched Madeline's arm and gave it a tug. 'Quick, let's go before he sees us.'

It seemed cruel to run away from their host when he was so determined to show off his home. 'You go,' said Madeline. 'I'd like to stay here and enjoy the view for a while.'

Marianne and Hugh had only just disappeared out of sight when Rawdon appeared, red-faced and out of humour. 'Have you seen Marianne? She was meant to meet me in the rose garden. We were supposed to be having a tryst.'

Madeline couldn't lie, least of all to a frustrated lover. She pointed vaguely in the direction of the house. 'They went that way.'

Rawdon's scowl deepened. 'What do you mean, *they*? Was she with her sister and Flora?'

'She was with my brother,' said Madeline.

Rawdon tugged at the waistband of his trousers where they'd begun to sag. Having been designed for standing and sitting rather than for moving around in, they'd started to impede him. 'That brother of yours is far too charming for his own good.'

Madeline agreed. 'You wouldn't believe the trouble it causes.'

She and Edward watched as Rawdon trundled off in the direction of the house. It was hard for Madeline to equate the grandness of the property with the smallness of the man who owned it. Even though he wasn't small in stature, he appeared to be so in every other way.

'How did Rawdon make his money?' she asked, cringing at her own question. It wasn't done to bring money into the conversation, but curiosity had got the better of her.

'It was his father who made the fortune,' said Edward. 'Rawdon simply inherited it. He spends enough time at the bank to make people believe he plays an active part in its continued success, although I'm not convinced he does very much. His father was wise enough to employ an excellent team of people to run it after his death.'

'Rawdon must consider himself fortunate.'

'His only responsibility is to produce an heir to inherit the family fortune. He's had every advantage in life, although you have to wonder if it's done him any good.'

'You only have to look around you to find the answer to that.'

Edward shrugged. His enduring silence was more telling than anything he could have said to fill it.

'So, tell me,' said Madeline, determined to change the subject. 'What made you decide to go into the law?'

'I was never interested in joining the family business. My older brother, Theo, will inherit it. He's in New York, working alongside our father.'

'And so, as in all the best English novels, you found yourself with the dilemma faced by the younger son. You either had to take up the church or the law, and you chose the law.'

Edward laughed. 'It wasn't quite like that.'

'So, you don't see yourself as a romantic hero?'

He looked at the ground, appearing too awkward now to meet her eye. 'If only I were tall enough and good looking enough, I'd throw myself at the feet of the heroine without a second thought.'

'Heroes come in all shapes and sizes. You shouldn't underestimate yourself.'

It wasn't in Madeline's nature to be so forward. Realising what she'd said, she took a deep breath, telling herself to slow down, to hold her tongue.

Edward must also have sensed they were at risk of becoming too familiar and retreated to safer ground. 'Growing up in New York, I witnessed enough social injustice to realise that someone had to stand up to it. I can't change the world for everyone, but if I can improve the living and working conditions for some by fighting for their rights, then I can make a difference to a few, and it's better than nothing.'

'If more rich men acted like you, the world would be a better place.'

'Not everyone feels that way. My father is disappointed I haven't joined him and Theo in the hotel business.'

'You're in the hotel business. I had no idea. When your mother mentioned you were in trade, I assumed you were involved in buying and selling goods of some kind.'

'Not goods, but services. We own a string of hotels across the county. You'll be familiar with the Trident name. We have half a dozen establishments in New York alone.'

There was a pause while Madeline took in the information. Surely, she'd heard him incorrectly. 'Your family own the Trident hotel chain?'

'My grandfather built it from nothing to what it is today.'

'I see.'

The air had suddenly grown hot. Madeline could feel it clawing at the back of her throat. The insistent sound of the waves crashing on the rocks, the cry of the sea birds circling above her head, all became too much. She pulled herself free of Edward's arm and marched ahead.

'You must excuse me, Mr Booth. I think I've had too much sun.'

Madeline continued towards the house as fast as she could without breaking into a run. She couldn't stay here a minute longer, not in the company of these people. She wanted to go home, or at least to Beachlands, which was the closest place she had to a home. She needed to find Hugh. The last time she'd seen him he was heading towards the house with Marianne. He must be nearby somewhere.

When Madeline returned to the terrace, Flora was sitting alone on the bench, red-faced from too much sun. For all the care she'd taken of everyone else's parasols, she'd neglected to carry one for herself.

'Have you seen my brother?' Madeline asked, trying to keep the urgency out of her voice.

'I've seen no one for this past hour. Edward was supposed to meet me here. He promised to show me the rose garden, but he must have forgotten.'

A pang of guilt shot through Madeline like a hot wire. She'd monopolised Edward's company when he was supposed to be with Flora. It had been the girl's express wish to see the gardens. So far, she'd seen nothing but the terrace. Anger gnawed at Madeline for the way Flora had been neglected.

'Let me show you the rose garden.'

Flora shook her head. 'Please don't go to any trouble. It really doesn't matter.'

Edward must have been following not far behind because a moment later he appeared on the terrace. Madeline barely glanced at him as he approached. 'There you are, Mr Booth. You promised to show Flora the rose garden.'

Flora shrank further into her seat as Edward threw himself down beside her. 'Forgive me, Flora. I've already walked around the garden with Miss Crosby and it's grown unbearably hot. You must allow me to show you another time.'

Madeline was confounded by his response. She held out her hand to Flora. 'Come with me. I insist you see the roses while the blooms are at their best.'

'There's no need to trouble yourself, Miss Crosby. I'm quite content sitting on this bench.'

Everyone was hot and bothered and the atmosphere had become strained. If Flora didn't want to visit the rose garden, Madeline wasn't going to force her. She glanced across the terrace, just as Hugh and Marianne approached from the shrubbery. Something must have amused them because their heads were leaning into one another and they were laughing like children.

Madeline tried to keep the agitation out of her voice as she greeted him. 'Hugh, at last. There you are.'

Before Hugh could respond to Madeline's greeting, Jane appeared from the drawing room where she'd been sitting with

Mrs Norton. She stormed across the terrace towards her sister. 'How dare you go off to explore the garden without me?'

Marianne gave her a cold stare. 'I was showing Mr Crosby the view of the ocean.'

Not for the first time that afternoon, Jane stamped her foot. 'You shouldn't have gone off with him alone when you know I wanted to join you.'

'He's a guest. I was showing him around.'

'Rawdon's been looking for you. He's in a foul mood. You were supposed to meet him in the rose garden.'

At the mention of Rawdon's name, Marianne became suddenly deflated. She dropped Hugh's arm and sighed. 'Where is he now?'

'He's in the billiard room, practising his shots.'

Marianne marched into the house, quickly followed by Jane, who continued to berate Marianne at full volume for neglecting Rawdon and monopolising Hugh's attention.

Madeline went up to her brother as soon as they were out of sight, murmuring quietly so no one else would overhear.

'I want to go home.'

'Not yet, Maddie. It would be bad manners to leave before we've had a tour of the house, and then there's supposed to be games.'

'Please, Hugh.' Madeline had seen enough games. She didn't want to be witness to any more. 'I'll tell them I've got a headache. I can't stand to be in the company of these people a minute longer.'

She knew it sounded melodramatic but she didn't care. She needed to impress on Hugh how strongly she felt about leaving.

Given the strain of the afternoon, no one seemed too displeased when Hugh announced their sudden departure. Madeline was awarded a suitable amount of sympathy for her headache, although nobody seemed too troubled by it, which was exactly as it should be, given the fact that it was a white lie.

Brother and sister remained silent during the return journey to Beachlands. Madeline needed to process everything she'd learned during the course of the afternoon before she could discuss it with Hugh. Even then, she would find it difficult to confess the real reason she'd wanted to leave so urgently, when it was such a sensitive matter.

She was still reeling from the fact that the Booths were behind the Trident hotel empire when it was in one of their associated brothels that her mother had lived her final days. For all Edward's high-mindedness and his good work, it was a shock to learn he was connected to such a company.

How foolish she'd been, allowing herself to be attracted to him before taking the trouble to find out the kind of man he truly was. It was a harsh lesson in trust, and Madeline would feel the bruises of her disappointment keenly for some time to come. She must learn to harden her heart, to steel herself against the man who had benefited so spectacularly from the exploitation not only of her mother but of so many other vulnerable women, both past and present.

Chapter 8

Hugh called for tea as soon as they arrived back at Beachlands, insisting it was just the thing to ease Madeline's uncharacteristic attack of ill temper. Soothed by the cool shade of the drawing room, Madeline was still distracted by the revelations of the afternoon. She'd been a fool to think she could run away from the past. That it wouldn't continue to snap at her heels wherever she went. How could she have allowed herself to be taken in by Edward's charm? All men were the same and rich men even more so.

'Did you hear what I said, Maddie?' Hugh touched her gently on the arm. 'Edward asked if we'd like to join the Booths for lunch on Saturday. I said I'd check with you first.'

Sara had baked macarons from the recipe Madeline had given her. One bite through the crisp shell into the soft centre and she was transported back to Paris. Even now, she longed for the freedom and the dignity she'd felt in the French capital, where no one knew of her past.

'I'd rather not see any more of the Booths. They seem a complicated family.'

Hugh helped himself to a macaron before Madeline ate them all. She was already on her third and gave no indication of stopping until she'd finished the plate. 'I thought you liked Edward. You approve of his work.'

'That was before I got to know him.' She picked up the newspaper and pretended to read, indicating the subject was closed.

'What made you change your mind?' Hugh leaned forward in his seat, obliging her to look at him. 'Did something happen between the two of you? Is there something I should know about?'

'No, it's nothing like that.' She offered him another macaron, but it wasn't enough to distract him from his questions.

'Is it because the Booths made their money in trade? I didn't think that kind of thing would bother you.'

Her brother had touched a nerve. 'There's trade and there's trade.'

Hugh scratched his head. 'I'm sorry, Maddie, but I don't understand. He seems decent enough. You were very taken with him when you first met him. I don't know what you've suddenly got against him.'

If Hugh was going to accept why she didn't want to see the Booths again, she'd have to explain her reasons. She hated having to mention it and had sworn never to go into such matters again. They'd agreed a long time ago that they couldn't move forward with their lives if they kept dwelling on the past, but given Hugh's insistence, she had no choice but to bring it up.

'The Booths own the Trident hotel chain. It's how they made their fortune. It's the profit from the business that enabled them to build that huge house.'

'Are you sure?'

'Edward told me himself this afternoon at Southsea. Why do you think I was suddenly so keen to leave? The news of it made me sick.'

'I'm sorry, Maddie. I had no idea.'

'Not dwelling on what happened to my mother is the only way to throw off its stranglehold. I'd convinced myself I could do it until this afternoon, but socialising with Edward and his family, knowing their lifestyle is built from the profits of the Trident business has brought the past straight into the present.'

Hugh was silent for a moment while he considered his sister's plight. 'Tell me, Maddie. Is there anything you'd like me to do?'

'You must send a note saying we won't be joining them for lunch on Saturday. Don't give an excuse. That way, they'll know we simply can't be bothered with them. They'll soon lose interest in us.'

'Edward is never going to lose interest in you. You only have to see the way he looks at you to know that.'

These weren't the words Madeline needed to hear. Not now she'd vowed to put all thoughts of him out of her mind.

Hugh slurped his tea while he considered the situation further. 'None of what you've told me tallies with Edward's social conscience. He doesn't charge a cent for the legal work he does fighting for the rights of those less fortunate than himself.'

'Maybe he has a guilty conscience or maybe he's a hypocrite. I don't intend to get to know him or his family well enough to find out.'

'You're sure he said it was the Trident hotels they owned?' Hugh didn't like to think badly of anyone and it was obvious he was still struggling to take it all in.

'I would hardly have mistaken it. He went on to say they had six hotels in New York alone. I didn't tell him my mother had lived and died in one of them, that I'm only here with you now because our father rescued me, before I too could be set to work in one of the brothels they run from their outwardly respectable establishments.'

Madeline's words came out more sharply than she'd intended. After all, it wasn't as if her brother really needed reminding of what had happened.

Hugh hung his head. 'Don't say it, Maddie. Please don't say it.'

'Perhaps if I told Edward where I really came from, he might be a little less interested in me.'

'You come from here, Maddie. You're a Crosby. Father gave you his name. You belong here with me. You must never forget that.'

'Imagine how the Booths would treat me if they knew the truth. You only have to consider how they behave towards Flora to know they'd look down on me, and she's only guilty of being a poor relation.' Madeline snatched the last macaron from the plate and bit into it. 'We came here to escape the memories of my past and my mother's tragic life. Now I find myself confronted by it in the cruellest way possible.'

'I'm sorry, Maddie.'

'How can the Booth women be so high and mighty when their lifestyle is funded by the sex trade? It's bad enough that everyone in old New York society insults me without giving the people who exploited my mother's misfortune the opportunity to shun me as well.'

'They need to take a hard look at themselves before they judge anyone else,' said Hugh. 'You can't tell me Marianne hasn't been pressured into marrying Rawdon for his money. I've no doubt the family will put the same pressure on Jane when the time comes to marry her off. They have no right to judge the circumstances of your early life, Maddie. Your mother was left with no choice but to do what she did. You can't say the same when it comes to the Booths marrying off their daughters, or should that be *selling* them off?'

'How could they encourage Marianne to marry without love?' asked Madeline. Even now, she found it impossible to understand the situation and accept it for what it was. 'Love is what makes the difference to every human interaction. In spite of what happened to my mother, I still believe that.'

Hugh blew out his cheeks. 'Marianne admitted to me that the only thing she loves about Rawdon is his estate.'

This came as no surprise to Madeline. 'Then Marianne knows what she's doing. It's not her fault. She's been conditioned to it. Nothing as sentimental as love will get in the way of her becoming mistress of Southsea.'

'We shouldn't put all the blame at the door of the Booths for what happened to your mother,' said Hugh. 'Father should have looked after her when she told him she was having his child. He'd taken her as his mistress and should have been prepared for the consequences. It was his fault she ended up in one of the Trident brothels. It was desperation and having nowhere else to turn that led her there.

'People can sometimes attempt to repair the damage they did in the past even though it's impossible to undo it,' he continued. 'Whatever his mistakes, I believe it's what our father tried to do.'

'He failed to rescue my mother, but at least he rescued me,' said Madeline. 'I have to give him credit for that.'

'Neither Edward nor his sisters are to blame for what happened to your mother,' said Hugh. 'Just as you and I are not to blame for the way our father treated her. The Trident hotels and the associated brothels were established during the Civil War. The damage goes back beyond our generation.'

'Are you saying I should embrace the Booths as friends even as they continue to live off the profits of their family's brothels?'

'What would you really like to see happen, Maddie?'

'I'd like women to be able to earn a living and feed their children without having to sell their bodies and souls to do so.'

Madeline thought back to her last night in New York when she'd slipped out of her uncle's house and given money to the women who worked in the brothels. However much she gave, her actions could only ever make a temporary difference.

'Until the brothels are shut down nothing will ever change.'

'You won't improve things from the outside, Maddie. We'll only be able to influence the Booths to close the brothels and compensate the women they've exploited if they consider us their friends.'

Madeline shuddered at the thought of it. 'I don't know, Hugh. Mixing with them is a lot to ask.'

'You're intelligent and witty. If anyone can influence their thinking, you can. This could be your opportunity to make a difference to so many women's lives.'

She considered what her mother would have thought of the plan, remembering the words she said to her as she lay dying. *Do everything you can to build a good life for yourself. Be kind to the strangers you meet. Don't be quick to judge them. You never know what's brought them to where they are.*

If she was to be true to her mother's teaching, Madeline had to apply her philosophy to everyone and not allow bitterness or prejudice to influence her actions. Otherwise, she was no better than Ginger's mother, looking dagger-eyed at her at the opera.

Madeline's thoughts turned to Hugh. His love and respect lit up his face every time he looked at her. He'd stood by her so steadfastly she couldn't bear to let him down.

She nodded, forcing herself to appear more confident than she felt. 'Let me think about it.'

Chapter 9

Hugh was pouring himself coffee when Madeline came down for breakfast the following morning. Trying to look her best after a sleepless night, she'd put on a pale-blue silk dress and made an extra effort to pin up her hair. He passed her the drink he'd intended for himself and selected a second cup.

'Are you feeling better?'

Madeline nodded as she sipped the coffee and helped herself to a griddled pancake, drizzling it with maple syrup. Seeing her eat always put his mind at rest, and she didn't want him to fret over her. She would get over the disappointment of Edward in her own time.

It was only after she'd forced down a second pancake that she noticed he was dressed for going out.

'Do you have plans for the day?'

'Rawdon mentioned a local horse breeder was auctioning off some livestock. I thought I'd go and see if there was anything worth buying. I know how much you missed riding regularly when we were in Europe, and it's ridiculous to keep hiring a horse for the buggy every time we want to go out.'

If Hugh was ready to acquire horses, he must have made up his mind to stay. It was Madeline's instinct to raise an objection, to suggest they move on and settle somewhere else, where nobody knew them, but what was the point? This place was as good as anywhere, in spite of its shortcomings. Hugh had been connected to it since childhood. His roots were here. That, in itself, was a good enough reason to stay. And the ocean was a balm, its vastness and its endless motion rendering every petty humiliation insignificant. It wasn't possible to change the past. She told herself this every time she received a sidelong glance from a stranger, a disparaging look from Finch. All Madeline could do was look to the future and strive to make the best of it.

'I'll come with you,' she said. 'I'd like to see the stock for myself.'

'I'd like nothing more, but we don't know what sort of a place it is. These events tend to attract all sorts of rogues.'

It frustrated her to be constrained like this, and it annoyed her even more that Hugh was right. It was unfair that women were locked out of so many interesting places in the name of propriety. She was just as good a judge of horseflesh as he was.

'I don't want anything less than sixteen hands and nothing more than three years old.'

Hugh nodded at her instructions. 'If I purchase anything, I'll do so on approval. If you don't like the horses I choose, we won't keep them.'

'If you're preparing to open up the stables here, you must also speak to Mr Coombe. Sara mentioned his son is looking for a job. He's not keen to work alongside his father in the garden, but perhaps he'd like the position of groom.'

Hugh swallowed the last of his coffee. 'I'll have a word with him on my way out. It was considerate of you to think of it. I knew you'd take to being mistress of this house.'

Madeline walked him to the front door, wishing she was going with him, that she had a task that involved more than just passing the time. Idleness was the worst thing for the soul and the day spread out before her like an endless chasm.

'If you want to go out, Maddie, you could always ask Finch to accompany you.'

It was another one of those rules made by men, dictating that young women of a certain social standing shouldn't leave the house without a chaperone. The rule didn't apply if you were of the class that had to work for a living. Then, you could go anywhere, be seen anywhere. It confounded Madeline as to why some women should need protecting more than others, as if those who served no purpose other than to ornament men's lives and produce male heirs should be better valued than those who nursed the sick or worked in the factories.

She nodded, so Hugh would think what he'd suggested was a good idea. 'I might do that.'

The thought of spending time in Finch's company gave Madeline the shivers. In the short time they'd been here, her open contempt for Madeline had morphed into a quieter form of determined neglect. It manifested itself in the smallest and most petty inattentions, such as failing to make sure her shoes were polished after she'd requested it, or serving only marmalade at breakfast when she'd specifically asked for honey; small irritations that weren't worth remarking on, but designed to slowly wear down her spirits over time.

Occasionally, Finch's hostility towards Madeline would cross into something more sinister. Only yesterday, she'd discovered a dead mouse rotting beneath her dressing table. The shocking sight of the poor creature suggested it had been deceased for some time, yet it hadn't been there that morning. Given its position, there was no way that either she or Sara wouldn't have seen it.

None of these things were worth mentioning to Hugh, and Madeline wouldn't give Finch the satisfaction of raising them, and revealing they bothered her. If Madeline didn't respond, Finch would eventually tire of her malice or her imagination would run out of ways to torment her.

The clock in the drawing room had just struck eleven when

the bell at the door rang. The sound echoed around the quiet house, where the staff, it seemed, had learned to move around in silence. The sweep of dusters and brushes were so deft as to be inaudible. Madeline could have been in a house of ghosts for all the life she felt there.

A moment later, Finch appeared beside the desk where Madeline was studying a piece of sheet music. Despite repeated requests, Finch still refused to knock before entering a room, confirming Madeline's suspicions that she was determined to undermine her.

'There's a Mr Booth to see you. Shall I show him in?'

The arch of Finch's eyebrows expressed her disapproval. Edward's arrival had caught Madeline off guard. She'd forgotten she'd given him an open invitation to come and listen to her play the harp. Despite her promise to Hugh that she'd consider befriending the Booths so they would have an opportunity to address the issue of the brothels, she wasn't prepared to see Edward, not now.

'Tell him I'm not at home.'

Finch threw a look over her shoulder, as if she expected him to walk in at any minute. 'Someone must have given him the idea you'd be here. He said he was expected.'

'Then he's mistaken. Ask him to leave his card on his way out.'

The housekeeper turned to leave, knocking Madeline's sheet music from the desk as she went. 'It seems you're just like your mother, after all.'

Madeline refused to rise to Finch's jibe. She crossed to the window, placing herself at an angle behind the curtain so she wouldn't be seen if Edward happened to glance in her direction as he left the house.

After pausing on the doorstep to straighten his hat, Edward turned, casting his eyes about him as if he sensed someone watching him, before he made his way back along the gravel path towards the gate. A couple of heartbeats and he was gone.

He couldn't possibly have seen her. An expert in concealment, Madeline had hidden herself too well.

Her spirits sagged for the rest of the morning. Picking up the sheet music from where Finch had determinedly knocked it to the floor, she tried to play her harp. It was no use, her fingers were clumsy and uncoordinated, her mind elsewhere when she tried to concentrate on the notes.

Her first impression of Edward had been misleading. Men were all the same. She only had to look at Finch and her mother to see how badly her own father had treated women. She paced the room, her arms folded against her agitation. She'd been right to turn Edward away. She would tear up his calling card, which was waiting for her on the hallway table, and that would be the end of it.

She was sitting on the terrace with a novel when Hugh returned. She greeted him with a smile, casting aside the book she'd been holding for the past hour without reading a single page.

'Any luck with the horses?'

'Not this time. Your requirements were very specific. They were all too tall or too small, too old or too young.'

'Am I being difficult?'

'You're not difficult, Maddie. I understand your heart as well as my own. It has to be the perfect match or nothing at all.'

Hugh was uncompromising, a perfectionist in all matters. It was the thing she loved most about him. It was also the reason she doubted he'd ever find a wife.

He sat beside her on the bench, inclining his head towards her as if he were about to make a confession.

'I hear Edward Booth called on you this morning.'

Madeline had removed Edward's calling card from the hallway table and put it out of sight, so how did Hugh know he'd visited? She tried to sound measured in her response.

'Who told you?'

'Finch happened to mention it when I came in. She said you refused to see him.'

Of course Finch would have mentioned it. She watched Madeline's every move and saw it as her duty to report back to Hugh.

'I'd forgotten he said he'd call.'

'I'm sorry, Maddie. Was it very awkward?'

'Not at all.'

'Would you like me to have a word with him? Tell him his attentions are unwelcome.'

'There's no need.'

Madeline was used to fending off unwanted approaches from men. It went with the territory of her past. Knowing what her mother had been reduced to, many assumed she was fair game. She only had to remember Ginger's behaviour at the opera to know society's view of her hadn't changed, and it never would.

It was different when it came to Edward. His conduct hadn't been influenced by her past. This time, the tables were turned. On no account would she allow his charm and kindness to affect her, and the sooner he realised this, the sooner her peace of mind would return.

Chapter 10

Madeline hadn't wanted to attend another polo match when Hugh suggested it. There would be too many members of the old New York society there for her taste, but Hugh loved the group camaraderie of rooting for a particular team. Something a natural outsider like Madeline could appreciate but never fully relate to. She couldn't bring herself to deny him the pleasure of it and agreed to go anyway.

If Edward happened to be there, she would do her best to avoid him. It had been weeks since Madeline had refused to see him. She was still considering Hugh's suggestion about befriending the Booths in order to approach the issue of the Trident hotels being run as brothels but was struggling to come to a decision on it. It seemed unfair to give Edward false hope regarding her affections when her only intention would be to influence his business affairs.

The sun was high, and a crowd had already gathered around the pitch when they arrived. The first of the summer fashions were on display, and wide-brimmed hats and silk dresses with cinched waists were the dominant features. The excitement in the atmosphere was typical of the early season, and as friends greeted one another the air was afire with gossip. Madeline observed it all with detachment, fascinated by the social rituals. Even after all this time of being out in society, she still found it forced and ridiculous.

'Crosby, how good it is to see you.'

It was Edward, making his way towards them. He must have spotted them in the crowd and seemed determined to say hello. In spite of herself, Madeline's heart lifted at the sight of him.

'We haven't seen you for so long. I thought you must have gone back to New York.' Edward's tone betrayed none of the disappointment he must have felt at being rejected without reason.

Madeline couldn't work out if he was insensitive to the snub or conditioned by his good manners not to show it. Judging by the way he avoided her eye, she gathered it was the latter.

Hugh swerved the subject, describing his failed attempts to find suitable horses, smoothing over the awkwardness of Madeline's coolness as she kept her eyes on the pitch, even though the match wasn't due to start for another few minutes.

Everything would be much simpler if Edward would just go away and leave them to get on with their lives. That way, she could pretend he didn't exist. Even after such a short acquaintance, he had the capacity to mean so much more to her, but his connection to the Trident hotel chain made such a thing impossible.

'My sisters and my brother, Theo, are here. Theo is taking a brief holiday from the family business in New York. Won't you say hello?'

Edward's words were directed at Hugh rather than Madeline. Her rebuff must have stung him deeply, even if he was trying not to show it.

'Another time, perhaps,' said Hugh.

'The game is due to start any minute,' added Madeline, determined to avoid joining the Booths' party. 'We don't want to miss it.'

'My sisters are just over there,' said Edward, his tone almost desperate.

There was no way out of the invitation without making a scene. Before she could invent another excuse, Edward had taken her to an area where the crowd was thinner and people gathered in clusters to chat and picnic, rather than watch the polo match. Hugh had given Madeline an apologetic look as he'd hurried to keep up with Edward's pace.

The Booths had arranged themselves in a series of wicker chairs around a large picnic table. Marianne squealed as soon as she set eyes on Hugh and demanded he sit next to her.

'Where have you been? We haven't seen you for so long.'

'Most of my time has been spent trying to find a pair of horses for myself and Maddie,' said Hugh, remaining his usual genial self, even in the face of Marianne's shocking forwardness.

Not one to be left out of the conversation, Jane began questioning him about the exact qualities he looked for in a horse. Rawdon hung around at the edge of the group, near to where Madeline stood. If he had any thoughts on the subject of horses, he chose not to share them. Madeline noticed how his eyes remained fixed on Marianne in a way that went beyond adoration. Whatever she'd done to attract him, he seemed completely under her spell.

'I promised to introduce you to my brother, but he seems to have wandered off,' said Edward, interrupting Madeline's observations.

She smiled, not knowing what she was supposed to say in return. 'The match will be starting soon. Hugh won't want to miss it.'

'I'm sorry not to have seen more of you during these last weeks, Miss Crosby. If I've done something wrong or offended you in any way then . . .'

The hurt in Edward's eyes was genuine. She couldn't allow herself to succumb to it. 'You left a calling card. It was rude of me not to respond. It's just that . . .'

'You don't have to explain. You're from a distinguished family. I understand the reluctance of many in your circle to mix with people like us, the so-called *new money*.'

His tone was matter of fact, as if he accepted the situation for what it was and didn't blame her for it. But it wasn't that at all. If he knew the real reason for her reluctance to associate with him, he'd be appalled.

Looking for a way to escape the conversation, she smiled at Flora who instantly appeared beside her, mutely offering a glass of lemonade. Red-cheeked from the sun, she'd put down her parasol to hand around the refreshments. By catching her eye, Flora must have assumed Madeline was asking for a drink.

Madeline sipped the lemonade, mortified by Flora's display of subservience, not only to herself but to the whole Booth family. She wanted to make conversation with her, but it was hard to know where to start with someone who always seemed reluctant to engage with anyone beyond her cousins. 'Do you enjoy watching polo?' she asked.

'It's the first time I've seen it,' said Flora, lowering her eyes as if she expected a scolding. 'Marianne is mad for it and insists on coming to watch every match. I usually stay at home and keep my aunt company when the young people go out, but today she decided to come along too.' She glanced over Madeline's shoulder to where Mrs Booth had fallen asleep in a chair, Mimi snoring quietly on her lap, a silver dog bowl filled with stewed liver and rice on the ground beside them.

The way Flora referred to *the young people*, when she was the youngest of them all, made Madeline wonder how she saw herself, what hopes she had for her future life.

'Do you see much of your parents, or your brothers and sisters?'

'I owe the Booths a great deal. I'm very happy to be here.'

It wasn't an answer to the question Madeline had asked. Madeline covered her confusion with a smile. 'The lemonade is delicious.'

The awkwardness was broken by the appearance of two young men. Edward clapped the tallest one on the back. 'Miss Crosby, allow me to introduce my brother, Theo, and his very good friend, Mr Joseph Young.'

Madeline would never have taken Theo for Edward's brother. There was nothing in his features or his manner that resembled him. She could only imagine Theo took after his father rather than his mother.

'I'm delighted to meet you, Miss Crosby. My brother hasn't stopped talking about you. I see now why he believes you're far beyond his reach.'

Edward squirmed at his brother's comment. He was a flirt, but Madeline could tell there was no harm in him. Theo was too interested in catching Mr Young's eye for validation each time he spoke for her to feel any kind of threat or serious intention from him.

'Your brother needs to find a new subject to occupy him,' said Madeline. 'He must be very dull company if all he can do is talk about a woman he barely knows.'

Theo threw back his head and roared, making much more of her reply than it warranted. 'He said you were a great wit.'

'He bored you with that too? He really does need to find himself some new interests.'

It hadn't been her intention to humiliate Edward or turn his admiration for her into a joke. Her wit was her defence against the world. It was sharp enough and cruel enough to stop anyone getting too close. It didn't mean she was proud of it, but in this case, she believed it to be necessary. Heaven forbid she should find herself falling in love with Edward, or he with her.

With Marianne still monopolising Hugh's conversation, Jane turned her attention to Mr Young, who was helping himself to the fresh sandwiches as quickly as Flora could lay them out. Madeline observed their body language, their familiarity as they shared a joke, and she wondered where he fit into the family, what expectations Jane had of him. His shoes, which always said so much about a person's station in life, were decidedly down at heel, suggesting he wasn't as wealthy as the Booths, but then few people were.

Her gaze drifted away from the group towards the polo field, even though she wasn't the slightest bit interested in the match. She sensed Edward's eyes on her and wondered what he was thinking, hoping he wouldn't try to catch her attention again. It was then she heard the words, sharp enough to pierce her soul.

'Just look at her standing there in that fancy frock as if butter wouldn't melt in her mouth.'

The comments came from just behind where Madeline was standing. The familiar voice was high pitched to express the woman's indignation and to ensure the message reached Madeline, who felt the colour rise in her cheeks. Turning around, she found herself face to face with Ginger's mother, her dragon-eyed stare drilling into her. Insulting Madeline in full public view at the opera wasn't enough. She was determined to humiliate her here in Rhode Island too.

Hugh was at her side in an instant. He took her hand and led her towards the picnic table. 'You look hot, Maddie. Let me get you another glass of lemonade.'

He had the presence of mind not to dignify the insult to his sister by acknowledging it. Removing her from the line of fire demonstrated it had meant nothing, that Ginger's mother, for all her venom, couldn't harm them. Hugh's actions were enough to send the dreadful woman on her way, summoning her cohorts to follow. She wouldn't countenance the humiliation of being ignored, even by someone she disregarded.

Madeline's hand was shaking as Hugh refilled her glass. She stared at the pale liquid, reluctant to meet anyone's eye.

Hugh gave her arm a squeeze. 'Don't worry. Nobody here heard what was said. They're all too wrapped up in themselves to notice anything going on around them and even if they did, no one would think the comment was aimed at you.'

She only had to risk a glance around her to realise he was right. Marianne was fluttering her eyelashes at Rawdon to pacify his jealousy after she'd spent so long talking to Hugh. Jane was feeding the discarded crusts from the sandwiches to Mimi, and Edward and Theo were laughing at Mr Young's rambling tale about a four-legged duck, while Mrs Booth's sleep remained undisturbed. As usual, no one was taking any notice of Flora, who was quietly warning Jane against feeding Mimi too much bread.

The distant cheers coming from the area near the pitch indicated the polo match had begun. Madeline gave Hugh's arm a discreet tug to get his attention. 'Shall we go and watch the game?' It was after all what they'd come for.

Marianne heard her suggestion and piped up. 'Yes, let's go and watch the match, Mr Crosby. I do so love it and we're missing all the excitement.'

Hugh's answer was interrupted by Mimi, who at that moment began making terrible heaving noises. Flora gently lifted the animal from Mrs Booth's lap. The sudden movement must have been enough to dislodge whatever was troubling the poor creature and before Flora could place Mimi on the ground, the contents of the dog's stomach came up, soaking the front of Flora's dress.

Having been woken by the disturbance, Mrs Booth let out a howl worthy of the dog itself. Flora gasped, placing the creature carefully on its own four legs so it could recover undisturbed. Everyone else look on horrified, apart from Hugh, who dashed forward to offer Flora his handkerchief, insisting she use it to wipe away the partly digested crusts and stewed liver the dog had thrown up all over her dress.

Now she was fully awake, Mrs Booth demanded to know what Flora had done to upset Mimi so much, while Marianne and Jane silently observed the drama.

When he realised the handkerchief wasn't big enough for the job, Hugh reached for the clean table napkins and passed them to Flora. Mortified by Hugh's attention, Flora begged him not to trouble himself.

'I can't stand by and see you in such a wretched state, Miss Pierce.'

Meanwhile, the dog who now appeared to be feeling much better, climbed back onto her mistress's lap, seemingly unrepentant for the trouble she'd caused.

'What were you thinking, feeding Mimi so much crust?' Mrs Booth shrieked at Flora, tugging the dog's ear to soothe her as she tensed at the pitch of her mistress's voice. 'You know she has a delicate stomach.'

'I . . .' It was all Flora could manage to say as she sniffed back her tears.

Indignation boiled in Madeline's veins. She threw a look at Jane, who refused to catch her eye. 'It wasn't Flora's fault, it was—'

Flora held up her hand to silence her. 'Please don't say any more about it, Miss Crosby. If you'll excuse me, I'll take Mimi to stretch her legs. She'll feel better after a walk.' As Flora spoke, she lifted the dog from Mrs Booth's lap, using the creature's little body to hide the stains on her dress.

The meaty smell was abominable. Madeline offered Flora a little eau de cologne to mask the worst of it, but she shook her head, silently refusing it without looking up, pausing only to thank Hugh for coming to her rescue.

Once Flora had gone, the conversation picked up again. The soiled napkins were discarded along with the rest of the food, which after Mimi's display, no one had the stomach for. Madeline silently raged at the injustice on Flora's behalf. Everyone must have known she wasn't responsible for the dog's sickness, but no one had spoken up for her; while her failure to stand up for herself was no doubt part of the reason she commanded so little respect within the Booth family.

Appalled by the unfairness of it all, Madeline was desperate to set matters straight, to force Jane to confess that she'd been the one guilty of feeding crusts to the dog. But Flora had asked her to remain silent, so anything she said would be a betrayal. Flora must have her reasons for staying quiet, and whatever they were, Madeline knew to respect them.

Having witnessed the injustice, Madeline now understood why Flora always appeared beaten down, why she rarely had the confidence to look anyone in the eye.

She placed a hand on Hugh's arm and whispered, 'Let's go, before anyone invents a reason to detain us.'

Hugh nodded, appearing as keen to get away from the party as she was. He waited until the Booths were out of hearing before he picked up the conversation.

'It was bad form on Jane's part not to own up to being the one who'd fed the crusts to the dog, don't you think, Maddie?'

'If Flora had spoken up for herself, Jane wouldn't have got away with it,' said Madeline, still indignant on Flora's behalf.

'There's probably more to it than we know.'

It was typical of Hugh to be so generous-hearted, to give everyone the benefit of the doubt. It was one of the many traits Madeline adored about him. And as Madeline led him back towards the polo match, ignoring the grim stares she received from Ginger's mother and her equally unpleasant friends, she thanked him for sacrificing his handkerchief to a good cause.

Chapter 11

Madeline was practising the harp the following morning when the Booths' carriage pulled up in front of Beachlands. Hugh put aside his newspaper and gave her a confounded look.

'I didn't invite them, Maddie, I promise.'

However good an idea it seemed to befriend the Booths, so she could try to influence them to close the brothels, Madeline went cold every time she thought about it. Edward's display of fondness at the polo match had left her more conflicted than ever.

'You mustn't mind our intrusion,' said Marianne, bursting into the drawing room without waiting to be announced. 'We've had a wonderful idea and couldn't wait to share it with you. You'll be as excited as we are when you know what it is.'

A flustered Finch came charging in after Marianne. 'I'm sorry, Mr Crosby. I asked her to wait while I announced the party, but she insisted on barging ahead of me.'

Before Hugh could assure her it was fine, Jane entered the room, quickly followed by Theo, Mr Young and finally Edward, who offered his apologies for disturbing them. The smile fell from his face when he saw Madeline step away from the harp.

'Perhaps one day you'll allow me to hear you play. I do so look forward to it.'

He hadn't forgotten her offer to play for him or that she'd turned him away the day he came to listen to her, but he was too polite to mention it directly. She made a vague gesture that could have meant anything before asking Finch, who was loitering in the corner of the room assessing the ladies' outfits, to bring tea. When she failed to respond, Hugh repeated the instruction.

'Finch, Maddie asked you to bring some tea. Please see to it.'

As usual, Madeline's request was ignored until Hugh repeated it. Marianne, who had already made herself at home on the sofa, didn't fail to miss the snub. 'I wouldn't put up with such disrespect from a servant. You should dismiss her on the spot.'

The arrangement was far too complicated to go into, and as far as Madeline was concerned, it was no one else's business. 'She's very loyal to my brother.'

'You're the mistress here, not your brother,' said Marianne, clearly piqued by Madeline's defence of an insubordinate member of the household staff. 'No housemaid will be allowed to behave like that when I'm mistress of Southsea.'

There was a loud bang as Finch slammed the door behind her. Madeline hoped Sara would be instructed to make the tea, knowing it would be heavily laced with spite if Finch made it, and even more undrinkable than usual.

'What is it you want to tell us?' asked Hugh, trying to move on from the awkwardness.

'It was Mr Young's idea,' said Jane, encouraging Hugh to sit next to her. 'He must tell you about it himself.'

Before Mr Young had the chance to speak, Marianne jumped in. 'We've been so bored lately that we've decided to put on a play and we want you both to be in it.'

Whatever Madeline had been expecting, it wasn't this. 'A play? What kind of play?'

'One of those Shakespeare ones,' said Jane. 'Mr Young will explain, if Marianne will let him get a word in.'

It turned out that Mr Young was an actor by trade, which

explained the down-at-heel quality of his shoes. Currently finding himself between engagements, he was staying at the Booths' summer cottage indefinitely, at Theo's invitation.

'I thought we could stage *A Midsummer Night's Dream*,' said Mr Young. 'Not the whole play, but a few selected scenes, purely for our own amusement.'

Madeline was mesmerised by Mr Young every time he spoke, not because of his charisma as an actor but because of the exaggerated drawl of his speech. She and Hugh had seen many plays, both in America and Europe, but she'd never heard anything like it. She could only describe it as lying somewhere between foppery and parody. Giving him the benefit of the doubt, she wondered if his manner was the style expected for Shakespeare's comedies these days.

'What scenes were you thinking of?' asked Hugh, who appeared keener on the idea than Madeline had expected.

Marianne almost leapt out of her seat. 'The lovers' scenes.' She batted her eyes at Hugh. 'You'll play a star-crossed lover with me, won't you, Mr Crosby?'

Mr Young held up his hands as if he were playing to the gods. 'If I'm to direct the actors, you must let me decide on the casting.'

Marianne's face turned to thunder. 'If you want to stage your production in our garden, Mr Young, and remain a guest in our home, you need to consider my wishes.'

'I'm not sure it's a good idea for the ladies to act in a play,' said Edward, who had been looking increasingly uncomfortable with the direction of the conversation. 'It might not be seen as respectable.'

'Why not?' asked Mr Young. 'I've acted with ladies in every play I've ever appeared in.'

'They were professional actresses. There's a difference in social standing between the women who take to the stage and my sisters and Miss Crosby,' said Edward. 'They have their reputations to consider.'

Madeline tried not to flinch at the implication. Women who appeared on the stage were viewed as no better than prostitutes. In some cases, desperation forced the women into both trades. She also found Edward's remark highly hypocritical, given the source of the Booth family fortune.

'I don't think it's appropriate to put on a play,' continued Edward, 'and I won't be taking part in it.'

'Pooh to reputation,' said Jane. 'Marianne can play the lover with Rawdon. There's no harm there as they're soon to be married.'

'Rawdon should play Bottom, the fellow with the ass's head,' said Marianne, letting out a great laugh. 'It'll suit him better than playing a lover.'

Jane flashed a smile at Hugh. 'I'm prepared to risk my reputation with Mr Crosby if he'll be Lysander to my Hermia.'

'Who do you expect me to play?' asked Marianne, suddenly indignant.

'Titania, of course,' said Jane, her tone matter of fact. 'She's the one who falls in love with an ass.' She turned to Madeline. 'You could play Helena, and Edward could be your Demetrius. It'll be so much fun, with everyone falling in and out of love with each other.'

'I see no harm in it,' said Hugh. 'We're all friends and it'll be a strictly private affair. What do you say, Maddie?'

All eyes in the room were on her, as if the fate of the play lay in her hands. She hated the idea of it, hated the association with fallen women and the exposure that acting the love scenes would bring. She would prefer to remain an observer while the rest of them made fools of themselves, and yet Hugh was right. This might be the kind of situation she could exploit for her own ends. If she were to have any chance of gaining influence with the Booths, she needed to insert herself into the family. She could only persuade them to reform their business practices and shut down the brothels if she first gained their trust.

Sometimes it felt as if her whole life were a performance. If she had to put on yet another act to achieve her goal, then that was what she'd do. Taking her courage in both hands, Madeline sat up straight and offered an arch smile, casting her eyes around the drawing room.

'So, tell me, what gentleman am I to make love to?'

Chapter 12

The first rehearsal was to take place the following afternoon at Mountview, the Booths' grand summer residence. When Madeline and Hugh arrived, they were shown into the garden where Theo and Mr Young, Marianne, Jane and Rawdon were seated in a circle of chairs on the lawn.

Already Madeline was beginning to regret her impulsive decision about agreeing to appear in the play. She was more than capable of acting a part, but faced with spending so much time with the Booths, she didn't know how she would stand it.

Mr Young stood up to greet them with a manner of someone who had put himself in charge. 'At last, our love interests have arrived. Now we can finally get started.'

The emphasis was on the word *finally*. Madeline gave Hugh an uncertain look. She'd hoped this would be no more than a little gentle fun. Surely, they weren't taking it too seriously.

'I've saved you a chair next to me, Mr Crosby,' said Jane, furiously patting the seat. 'If we're to fall in love we need to sit close to one another.'

Hugh gave her a gracious bow as if he were already acting the role of a courtier, while Madeline slipped into the only other available chair, which happened to be next to Rawdon, who was scowling at the pages on his lap.

'Confounded play,' he muttered. 'I'll be damned if I can make anything of it.'

Mr Young was about to begin when Flora came running across the lawn towards them. 'So, you've finally made up your mind to play Puck,' said Marianne, squinting into the sun as she looked up at her.

'N . . . no.' Flora's cheeks reddened as all sets of eyes interrogated her. 'I've come to return this to Mr Crosby.' She turned to Hugh, presenting the handkerchief he'd given her to wipe Mimi's vomit from her dress at the polo match, which she'd washed and pressed into a neat square.

Hugh blew out his cheeks. 'I never expected to see this again. I wouldn't have blamed you for throwing it away, considering the mess it was in.'

'Not at all, sir,' said Flora. 'It's a beautiful piece of linen. It would have been a crime to throw it away.'

He considered the handkerchief, rubbing its smoothness between his fingers and thumb. 'It's never been laundered so well. I'm grateful to you.'

'It's just a handkerchief,' said Marianne, rolling her eyes. 'Anyone would think it was something that mattered.'

It was the kindness that mattered. Even if no one else could see it, Hugh had noticed and appreciated it. As an attractive, wealthy man, most people wanted only what they could get from him. It was rare to see his thoughtfulness returned, and Madeline could see it had touched him.

'Can we get started now,' bellowed Mr Young. 'Important decisions have been made about the play and I need to tell you about them.'

There was nothing new to impart beyond the announcement that Mr Young had cast himself as Peter Quince and that Theo would take on the parts of the mechanicals, apart from Bottom the weaver, who was to be played by Rawdon.

'Theo and I will rehearse our scenes in private,' he continued. 'The rest of you don't need to be there.'

Madeline didn't claim to know the play that well, but she was confused as to how Theo could perform the roles of Flute, Snug, Starveling and Snout when they all appeared on the stage at the same time. 'Forgive me for asking, but how is it going to work? Will you have different hats for each part?'

Mr Young dropped his eyes to the script and scratched his head with an air of a man who didn't know what he was doing. 'We'll work it out as we go along.'

'Perhaps we should consider doing a different play,' suggested Madeline. 'One that's better suited to fewer players. Something less ambitious.'

'Hear, hear,' added Rawdon. 'You can't expect us to learn these lines. Most of it doesn't even make sense.'

'We can't give it up now,' said Marianne, her eyes drilling into Rawdon's troubled face. 'One of the gardeners has been ordered to make you an ass's head.'

Rawdon was only allowing Marianne to appear in the play on the condition that she acted opposite him as Titania. On no account was he prepared to watch her pretend to fall in love with anyone other than his Bottom.

Whichever way they considered the casting, they were still short of actors to play Demetrius, Puck and Oberon.

'Perhaps you could convince Edward to play Demetrius, Miss Crosby,' said Jane. 'If anyone can influence him, you can.'

'I don't know,' said Madeline. 'I don't think—'

'You must give it a try,' insisted Jane. 'The success of the play depends on it.'

No one had noticed Flora was still there until she suddenly spoke out. 'He won't do it. You can't expect him to do it when he doesn't approve of it.'

It was the loudest Madeline had ever heard Flora speak, and she hadn't realised she had it in her to be so assertive.

'Flora will be making the costumes for us,' said Theo. He narrowed his eyes and nodded at her. 'Isn't that right?'

Meek as a kitten, Flora nodded back at him. 'If you insist.'

It struck Madeline that this was the first Flora had heard of it, that the order was her punishment for refusing to play Puck. 'We could always wear our own clothes.'

Mr Young shuddered at Madeline's suggestion, as if something revolting had bitten him. 'That won't do. The play is set in Athens. We shall all wear white robes and the girls shall have flower garlands in their hair.'

The memory of Ginger's limp gardenia flashed through Madeline's mind. She cast a worried glance at Hugh. It was getting more ridiculous by the minute, although her brother didn't seem to mind a bit. For the first time in as long as she could remember, he appeared to be enjoying himself.

Mr Young clapped his hands. 'Let's start with the scene where Titania wakes up and finds herself in love with Bottom.'

Rawdon looked confounded. 'Bottom? That's me, is it?' He stared at his copy of the play and starting furiously flicking through the pages. Madeline's heart went out to him.

'Wouldn't it be a good idea if someone explained the plot first,' she suggested, 'so everyone understands what the scenes are about and how the characters relate to one another?'

Theo and Mr Young exchanged glances. What she was suggesting would involve work and hard thinking.

'We haven't got time for that now,' said Mr Young, dismissing her suggestion with a flick of his wrist. 'If you don't know the play, you should read it in your own time. We're only doing a few selected scenes from . . .' he gave another vague gesture, once again dismissing the detail '. . . somewhere in the middle, so we shall concentrate on those.'

Mr Young clearly wasn't prepared to explain the plot, which made Madeline wonder if he actually knew what it was all about. 'Who is to play Puck?' she asked, raising the question again. 'The character is crucial for the lovers' story.'

When he failed to answer, she tried again. 'Who is to put the love juice in the lovers' eyes?'

The awkward silence was broken by a maid running across the lawn towards them and announcing it was time for tea. The sense of relief among those gathered was palpable.

'Too much of this will make us dull creatures indeed,' said Marianne, linking her arm through Hugh's and smiling at him, much to Jane's obvious irritation.

They trailed inside the house where afternoon tea had been laid out in the drawing room. Madeline's spirit lifted at the sight of the cakes that once again wouldn't have looked out of place in a Parisian patisserie. Edward was already drinking tea with Flora and Mrs Booth when they arrived.

'Just the man we were looking for,' said Jane, grinning at her brother. 'Miss Crosby has a question for you.'

Suddenly, all eyes were on Madeline. She adopted her liveliest manner, putting on an act before the rehearsals had even begun. If she was to persuade Edward to convince his father to close the brothels, she had to get close to him, no matter the risk to both their hearts.

'The play is in ruins unless you agree to play Demetrius, Mr Booth. There's no drama unless I have a lover to play opposite me.'

His face paled at her directness. 'Perhaps a little less drama wouldn't be a bad thing.'

Madeline had gone too far and come across as brazen. This was no way to win Edward's confidence, but there was no going back now.

She followed him out onto the terrace, where he seemed determined to set himself apart from the rest of the party. 'You shouldn't worry about the play, Mr Booth. It's just a little fun among friends. There's no harm in it.'

'Perhaps not for you, Miss Crosby, but even setting aside the damage your playacting might do to your reputation if word of it spread, I'm not sure my heart would stand having you pretend to be in love with me. Not all of us are as accomplished at artifice as you appear to be.'

His declaration left her lost for words. However much she was determined to harden her heart against him, she felt his sentiments deeply.

She returned to the drawing room and helped herself to a cream slice. Edward had no right to accuse her of artifice when he behaved like a hypocrite, publicly fighting for the rights of those less fortunate than himself, when his family fortune was founded on the exploitation of women.

'Do sit down, Miss Crosby,' said Mrs Booth. 'You're staring into space like one of those ancient Greek statues, and that's before you've put on one of the costumes.'

It was the most Madeline had heard Mrs Booth say in one afternoon. The excitement over the play had enlivened her to the extent that she was sitting upright on the chaise longue. Even Mimi was more animated, her marble eyes bulging in expectation as she stood at her mistress's feet to catch the crumbs from her sandwich before they reached the floor.

'I've been considering my darling little Mimi,' continued Mrs Booth between mouthfuls. 'She should have a carry-on part. There must be a place for her in the drama.' She tilted her head at Mr Young. 'Perhaps she could appear in one of the scenes with you and Theo. You must be getting on very well with them by now, the number of hours the two of you spend locked in Theo's bedroom rehearsing your parts.'

All eyes were fixed on Mr Young as he stared at the dog. 'Does she have any special talents?'

'Only vomiting and scratching,' offered Theo. 'I don't think we should risk her upstaging us.'

'Flora must carry her on,' insisted Mrs Norton, who had slipped into the room during the course of the discussion.

'That's an excellent idea,' said Jane. 'It's not as if she's got anything else to do, apart from making the costumes.'

Flora began to back out of the room, her fingers trembling as she struggled to open the door. 'You must forgive me. I couldn't possibly set foot on your stage. I wouldn't feel right about it.' She'd gone from the room before anyone could insist otherwise.

'I don't know what's wrong with her lately,' said Mrs Norton, scowling at the door as Flora closed it behind her. 'She's here to do as she's told. She has no right to feel anything about anything unless we say so.'

Edward gave his aunt an indignant look. 'I'll go and see if she's all right.'

Jane and Marianne had their heads together and were mumbling furiously in a way that looked suspiciously like plotting, while Rawdon had retreated to a chair in the corner beside the parlour palm, his face set in a murderous scowl.

It had been a long, fraught afternoon and it was beginning to feel eternal. The laziness of the general mood suggested no more work was to be done on the play scenes that day. Madeline gestured to Hugh, who'd been quietly sipping his tea and, like the perfect guest, keeping his opinions to himself. 'Time to go,' she whispered.

They were almost home before Hugh brought the conversation round to the real reason they'd spent the afternoon with the Booths. 'Did you make any progress with your campaign to get the brothels closed?'

'Not in the least.' Edward had been the obvious member of the family to target, but she'd failed to make a good impression on him. It was going to be a slow game if she was to achieve anything.

'Flora's a curious one,' said Hugh, after a long silence. 'Returning my handkerchief like that was the sweetest thing anyone has ever done for me.'

'It was only a handkerchief, Hugh. Don't get carried away.'

'Most people would have thrown it on the fire. It seems unfair, the way the family put upon her.'

Madeline knew exactly what he meant. Behind Flora's quiet demeanour Madeline suspected there lay an intelligent mind and a good heart. 'Don't pay her too much attention, Hugh. She doesn't deserve to fall victim to your charm.'

'I wouldn't dream of it.' He paused, offering her a wounded look. 'Anyway, I don't know what you mean.'

Madeline gave him a warning nudge. He was too good and too kind, too innocent in many respects when it came to love. She feared it was only a matter of time before his unassuming manner landed him in trouble with at least one of the Booth women.

Chapter 13

Marianne and Jane were in the drawing room with Rawdon when Madeline and Hugh arrived at Mountview the following afternoon to begin rehearsals. The conversation came to an abrupt stop the moment the Crosbys were shown in. There was no sign of Theo or Mr Young, and Madeline had the feeling they'd walked in on an argument. Despite being obviously pleased to see Hugh, Madeline couldn't help thinking Marianne looked annoyed.

'I hope we're not interrupting anything.'

'We'll start as soon as everyone else arrives,' said Marianne, refusing to rise to Madeline's comment.

Madeline responded with a warm smile, hoping Marianne wouldn't see through it. Despite her determination to gain influence with the Booths, she was finding it increasingly difficult to be in their company.

'There you are, Mr Crosby,' said Jane, crossing the room to greet Hugh and leading him to the sofa. 'I've been looking up the flowers that are mentioned in the play in this botanical book I found in Father's library. Let me show you *love-in-idleness*, which is the name of the flower Puck uses to make the lovers fall in love with one another. Did you know it's a purple pansy?'

Gracious as ever, Hugh did Jane's bidding, nodding as she

pointed to the illustrations and slowly turning the pages of the book whenever she instructed, even though he didn't have the slightest interest in plants. All the while, Marianne, who professed to be learning her lines, didn't take her eyes off them.

Distracted by the family drama that appeared to be bubbling under the surface, Madeline failed to notice that Rawdon was trying to catch her attention.

'Miss Crosby.' He dropped his voice to a whisper as soon as she looked at him. 'Would you explain the story of the play to me? I have so many lines to learn and I'm confounded if I can understand any of them.'

'The play is about unrequited love, power and control.'

'That's all well and good, but what does it mean?'

'Your part is quite simple,' said Madeline. 'A spell is cast over Titania, queen of the fairies, played by Marianne, to make her fall in love with you.'

'It needs a spell to make Marianne love me? Am I not lovable enough without it?'

'Bottom is a simple weaver. A queen would never usually bestow her love on someone so lowly.'

He cast a look at Marianne, whose eyes in turn were fixed on Hugh. 'So, she won't fall in love with me simply for the man I am.'

'Remember, a spell has also been put on you, turning you into an ass.'

Rawdon turned the crumpled script over in his hand. 'It's all nonsense. I don't know why we're wasting our time with it.'

'Because it is great art,' bawled Mr Young, bursting through the door just in time to hear Rawdon's comment.

There was a thunder of feet as Theo came in after him. 'Good news,' he shouted. 'Edward has agreed to play Demetrius.'

Mr Young gave a loud cheer as Edward followed his brother into the room. Madeline tried to catch his eye, but he looked the other way.

Jane clapped her hands. 'Now all we have to do is find a Puck to drop the potion in our eyes and we're all set to fall in love with one another.'

We also need to find an Oberon, and more mechanicals, thought Madeline, but no one seemed to want to consider the knotty problem of casting. Whichever way Madeline considered it, she couldn't see how they could make even a few selected scenes work with the actors they had. Details, she realised, weren't high on Mr Young's list when it came to putting on the play.

After reading through the scene where Demetrius rejects Helena, they took a break for tea. Edward had said nothing all afternoon beyond the lines prescribed by the script, and he didn't appear to have any stomach for the refreshments. When he wandered onto the terrace, away from the noise of the tea table, Madeline took the opportunity to speak to him alone.

'What made you change your mind about appearing in the play?'

'Mr Young said if I wouldn't do it, he'd ask one of his friends in New York to take the part. I couldn't risk a stranger coming into our private party. I won't have the reputation of you or my sisters compromised.'

'It's very gallant of you, riding to the rescue to protect our virtue. We should get you a white horse.' She tried to make light of the situation. It wasn't usually this difficult to bring a smile to his face.

'Acting out these scenes involves too much intimacy.'

'None of it is real. Reminding ourselves it's pretend is the way we protect our hearts.' Even as she said it, she wished it could be true.

'Marianne is about to make an advantageous marriage to Rawdon. I'm sure you understand the delicacy of the situation. We wouldn't want anything to happen at this late stage to put it in jeopardy.'

Edward didn't have to spell it out for Madeline to understand that he wasn't talking about hearts being broken if the wedding was called off. The marriage would result in a closer business alliance between Rawdon's bank and the Trident hotel chain. It was a sharp reminder, as if she needed it, that women in this society were no more than commodities to be bought and sold for the benefit of men.

'Running a business such as yours must force you to make a lot of moral choices.'

He frowned at her comment. 'Some lawyers find that to be the case if they defend those who are obviously guilty. I'm more selective about the clients I represent.'

'I wasn't talking about your law practice. I was talking about the Trident hotels and the associated businesses.'

'There are no associated businesses, only the hotels, although we are looking to expand.'

This was why they needed Rawdon's money, to grow their already blossoming empire, to put even more women to work in their brothels. Madeline felt her blood begin to burn in her veins. Did he not understand that those women's reputations were just as important as those of his sisters? That they deserved the same respect and consideration, the same protection he insisted on for those closest to him?

'You don't think there's room for reform in your family business?'

'There's always room for improvement, I don't doubt it, just as there is with any business. I leave all that to my father and Theo. My brother is the one who'll one day take over the running of it. I want no part of it. I intend to remain working in the law.'

'Why's that?' She didn't care if the directness of her question offended him. She needed to understand his position, why he prided himself on being a man of honour when he was riddled with double standards.

'The law is my vocation. I thought you knew that. My father is a difficult man to get along with. Theo manages him better than I do.'

'Considering the work you do as a lawyer, don't you think you should step in to address the lack of morality and improve the ethics of the company and its culture? They say charity begins at home. Don't you think the same of morality?'

'I don't know what you mean.'

His nervous throat clearing convinced Madeline he was lying. He must understand what she was getting at. He couldn't expect her to speak of it directly.

'What you're saying, Mr Booth, is that you're happy to live in the luxury the family business provides, but you're not prepared to address the exploitation of others that underpins your wealth and privilege.'

He looked at her as if she were mad, as if she were reciting lines from a different play to the one he'd agreed to take part in.

'I'm sorry, Miss Crosby. I don't understand what you're saying. I have my father's assurance that all employees in the hotels are treated well and paid a fair wage.'

'It's not the maids or the doormen I'm referring to.'

'Then what is it?'

Rather than appearing angry, he seemed upset by her questions. It was a clever act, but he was an expert lawyer and she wasn't fooled by him.

'You must know what I'm referring to.'

'If I've done something to offend you, Miss Crosby, you must tell me what it is.'

He was a convincing liar. She could see why he was so effective in fighting his clients' battles in court.

'I won't accept your ignorance on the matter when it's the foundation of your family business.'

'I—'

Whatever Edward was about to say was lost, as Mr Young chose that moment to call everyone back to the rehearsal. Refusing the offer of Edward's arm, Madeline returned to the drawing room, where Rawdon, who was still struggling to understand the relationship between the crossed lovers, was sitting with his head in his hands as Flora talked him through the diagram she'd sketched.

'It's quite simple,' she explained. 'Helena, played by Miss Crosby, is in love with Demetrius, played by Edward, but Demetrius is in love with Hermia, who is played by Jane. Hermia is in love with Lysander, played by Mr Crosby, but she is being forced to marry Demetrius.'

Rawdon looked more confused than ever. 'Can you explain it again?'

'Hermia and Lysander run away together. Demetrius and Helena follow. Thanks to the love potions administered by Puck, it all works out in the end and the star-crossed lovers marry who they are meant to be with, and everyone lives happily ever after.'

'Bravo, Flora,' said Madeline. 'We can only hope all our lives turn out as happily as it does for those star-crossed lovers.'

Flora handed the diagram to Rawdon. 'All we need now is a Puck to make everything right.'

Ignoring Flora's comment, Mr Young looked around the room to make sure everyone was present. 'Where's Miss Booth and Mr Crosby?' he asked, throwing his script in the air like a circus clown who no one finds funny. 'They wouldn't get away with this behaviour in the professional theatre.'

'I'll go and look for them,' said Madeline, who'd noticed them slip out into the garden while she was talking to Edward on the terrace.

She made her way across the lawn, but there was no sign of them until the sound of Marianne's laughter revealed they were on the other side of the yew hedge that marked the boundary of the formal garden.

'Hugh, are you there? We're waiting to start the rehearsal.' Madeline heard a snigger from the other side of the hedge. If they were trying to hide, they were making a poor show of it. 'Can you hear me?'

Of course they could hear her. They were simply pretending not to. She slipped round the hedge and found the two of them sitting side by side on a bench.

'Didn't you hear me calling? We're waiting to start.'

Marianne's face was red from too much sun and laughter. She pointed to her script, which lay abandoned at her feet. 'Can't you see we're rehearsing?'

'Mr Young wants us all up at the house,' said Madeline, who was too hot and too out of sorts to be playing games.

'I was helping Miss Booth with her lines and lost track of the time,' said Hugh, who at least had the decency to look shamefaced.

Marianne threw back her head and laughed. 'Yes, that's exactly what we were doing.'

'Shouldn't you be rehearsing your scenes with Rawdon?' asked Madeline. 'He's the one you're playing opposite.'

'Yes, but it's so much more fun rehearsing with Mr Crosby.'

'Maddie's right,' said Hugh, getting up from the bench. 'We should get back to the house. Everyone must be wondering where we are.'

By the time they returned to the drawing room Mr Young and Theo had grown tired of waiting and gone to rehearse in Theo's room. Rawdon had suddenly remembered some business he had to take care of at Southsea and had also disappeared. This left only Edward and Jane, who stamped her foot at Marianne and demanded to know why she insisted on ruining everything, while Flora quietly moved around in the background, clearing away the tea things.

Madeline and Hugh left before they were dragged into the argument. 'You know I blame you for this,' said Madeline, as Hugh handed her into the buggy.

'I don't know what you mean.'

'You're the reason the sisters are bickering. If you insist on paying attention to one of them, please make it the one who isn't about to get married.'

'I'm only being friendly. There's no harm in it. There can be no misunderstanding. The fact that Marianne is about to marry means it's far safer for me to enjoy her company than her sister's.'

'You realise they're both a little in love with you, don't you?'

Hugh laughed off the suggestion. 'Not everyone considers me as fondly as you do, Maddie. Anyway, I've made it clear I'm not interested in taking a wife.'

Madeline knew this wouldn't deter Marianne or Jane if either of them had set their hearts on him. If anything, his declaration never to marry would make them more determined to catch him. 'Promise me you'll be more careful.'

'I'll do my best, but Marianne follows me like a lost lamb bleating for its mother. She's everywhere I turn, demanding my attention. It would be rude to snub her when I'm a guest in her family home.'

Madeline gave his arm a squeeze, just hard enough for it to register as a reprimand. 'Think of poor Rawdon before you flirt with his future wife.'

Hugh nodded, his tone suddenly serious. 'Ah yes, poor Rawdon. No one's likely to forget him in a hurry.' He gave her a worried look. 'You don't think Marianne will be fool enough to actually marry him, do you?'

Now wasn't the time to encourage Hugh to think about what Marianne might or might not do, and so Madeline kept her thoughts to herself. Marianne was set on her course, and Hugh, for all his well-meaning nature, couldn't be allowed to disrupt it.

Chapter 14

Madeline was word perfect when they arrived at Mountview for the rehearsal the following day. She and Hugh had spent the previous evening and most of the morning going over their lines until they not only knew their own parts, but everyone else's too.

Madeline had enjoyed the challenge of setting her mind to the discipline. The concentration had lifted her spirits in a way she hadn't felt since her schooldays. She was grateful to her father for sending her to a school that had given her a rigorous education, when it was often only sons who were treated to it. Now, she wondered what it would be like to have a real purpose in life, to use her intelligence and education in a practical way, to have a profession or a business, to go out in the world and make a difference.

She wondered if other women felt this way. Whether they too mourned the squandering of their potential, having been brought up to be nothing more than ornaments; married off to seal business transactions; provide heirs for their husbands or used simply for the pleasure of men.

'Are you all right, Maddie?'

Hugh gave her a curious look. She was glad he couldn't read her thoughts. Not all men were bad. Some were just as much a victim of their society as women. For all his good fortune, Hugh was a pauper when it came to love. He'd grown up witnessing their father take a string of mistresses to compensate for his unhappy marriage. Instead of bringing joy, it had simply spread the misery to his wife, himself and every woman he took up with, including Madeline's mother and Finch. It was the reason Hugh had vowed never to marry. He couldn't allow himself to love any woman other than his sister. The consequences were too tragic if he got it wrong.

The fact that young women like the Booth sisters vied for his attention only proved to Hugh that he was right to protect his heart against their advances. A lifetime was too long to give to one woman, especially if that woman had ulterior motives for marrying or turned out not to be who you expected her to be. First impressions, along with many that followed afterwards, could be misleading.

The day was overcast and so the rehearsals were to take place inside. Theo had ordered the furniture be cleared from the drawing room and decided that the French doors and the view of the garden would serve as the backdrop for the stage.

None of the family was there when Madeline and Hugh were shown in. Hugh looked around the empty space, which appeared cavernous without the antique gilded tables and chairs and Mrs Booth's chaise longue.

'Do you think they've cancelled the rehearsal and not told us?' he asked.

There was every chance of it. Madeline suggested they wait on the terrace until they could be sure. She felt like an intruder, standing in the empty room when the family weren't in attendance.

They'd only been outside a few minutes when Flora appeared in the drawing room with Mrs Norton. Hugh moved to join them inside until Madeline held him back. Flora's face was swollen and tear-stained. It didn't take much to see they were in the middle of a difficult conversation. To save Flora's embarrassment, Hugh and Madeline hid behind a statue of a milkmaid.

Hugh had left the French doors open and Mrs Norton's voice, hissing with venom, carried out to the terrace. 'I've never known such an ungrateful creature in the whole of my life.'

Flora sobbed. 'You must forgive me. You can't expect me to do it when I don't believe it's proper.'

'And who are you to have an opinion on anything? Your cousins are asking you to play Puck. There's nothing special about that. The character is no better than a servant so you should have a lot in common. It's not as if any of the young men want to make love to you.'

'Edward said if I'm not comfortable with it, I shouldn't do it.'

'You don't see him spoiling his sisters' fun. He knows how important it is to find a suitable husband for Jane. Men like Mr Crosby don't appear every day. He's old money. Imagine what it could do for the family if we were able to move in the elite social circles in New York. Imagine the benefit to the hotel business.'

Madeline gasped. 'They're out to trap you.'

'Then they're going to be disappointed,' replied Hugh, his face sagging with misery.

The heavy slam of the door indicated Mrs Norton's departure from the drawing room. Madeline risked a glance around the edge of the statue. Flora was standing with her back to them, still sobbing.

'Should we go in and speak to her, do you think?'

'Let's give her a minute to compose herself,' said Hugh. 'She wouldn't want us to see her upset.'

They were still watching from behind the milkmaid when Rawdon crashed into the room. Flora jumped at the sight of him, as if he'd pointed a shotgun at her.

'Have you seen your mistress?'

'Mistress?' Flora hiccoughed as she said it, the sobs catching in her throat.

'Marianne, Miss Booth, whatever it is you call her. The hussy who's supposed to be marrying me.'

Madeline gaped at Hugh. This was a side of Rawdon they hadn't seen before. He wasn't only a lumbering fool. He was also a bully.

'The last time I saw her she was with Jane.'

'And where was that?'

Flora continued to sob. 'They were in Mrs Booth's dressing room, selecting trinkets to wear for the play.'

'Blasted play. I curse the day they ever came up with the idea.'

Like Mrs Norton before him, he stormed out of the room before Flora could think of anything else to say, or perhaps she knew it was better to simply say nothing.

Madeline flinched at the sound of his exit. 'What is it with the door slamming? Do people not realise some of us have delicate constitutions and are sensitive to unnecessary noise?'

'I'm going to comfort Flora,' said Hugh. 'It's not fair for her to be treated so roughly.'

Madeline suggested they give her another minute to compose herself so they didn't embarrass her. By the time they'd debated it, Flora had already fled.

Now they were alone, they relinquished their hiding place behind the statue and wandered back into the empty drawing room.

'I feel like I'm in a French farce with all this coming and going,' said Madeline, trying to make light of the family rows they'd witnessed. 'We even have the doors leading onto the terrace to complete the setting.'

'Poor you,' said Hugh with mock gravity, 'having to suffer all that slamming.'

They were considering giving up on the afternoon and going home when Theo and Mr Young came strolling across the lawn holding hands and looking dishevelled. Like any self-respecting actors, they too entered the scene through the French doors, dropping hands when they realised they'd been spotted.

'Where is everyone?' asked Mr Young, as if he wasn't as guilty of being as late as the rest of them.

'I'll go and round them up,' said Theo as he left the room, slamming the door behind him.

'French farce,' mouthed Hugh, purely to make Madeline laugh.

Within a few minutes, everyone had gathered. Marianne stood sullenly beside Rawdon as if all the sunshine had been knocked out of her, while Jane sidled up to Hugh and asked his view on the weather, as if it were the only thing she could think of to talk about. Edward had his back to everyone, his head buried in the script as he tried to learn his lines. It was a minute before Madeline realised Flora had crept back into the room, her face betraying the signs of recently shed tears.

Mr Young clapped his hands to get everyone's attention. 'I apologise for the late start to the rehearsal. Theo and I were running through our scenes and lost track of time.'

Madeline still wondered how they could rehearse their scenes without the requisite actors and wanted to know why Rawdon hadn't been included when Bottom also appeared in them, but she'd given up asking. Rehearsing the Mechanicals' scenes was clearly an excuse for them to spend time alone together without questions being raised. She also still wondered what they were going to do about an Oberon, but as they didn't have a Puck, perhaps it didn't matter anyway.

All this while, Mr Young was still talking. 'I'm pleased to announce that Flora has agreed to take on the role of Puck.'

Not agreed, thought Madeline, *but forced*. She glanced at Hugh, who appeared surprised at the news, while Flora stood in the corner, red-faced and refusing to catch anyone's eye.

'Bravo, Flora,' said Hugh. 'You understand the play better than anyone and probably already know the lines, going by how much time you've spent helping everyone else learn theirs.'

'She certainly knows Rawdon's,' said Marianne, not without sarcasm.

'Perhaps we should get on then,' suggested Edward without much enthusiasm.

Mr Young decided they should jump straight into the scene where Lysander and Demetrius witness the argument between Helena and Hermia. He gave the actors their positions, ordering Madeline, who was pretending to be Helena, to crouch on all fours, while Hugh and Edward stood over her, as if to protect her from Hermia's anger, which was ably demonstrated by Jane waving her fingers in front of Madeline's face and proclaiming:

'How low am I? – I am not yet so low

But that my nails can reach unto thine eyes'

Everyone was so involved in the scene that nobody heard the door open or took any notice of the thunder of heavy feet crossing the room until a loud voice roared, 'What the hell is this?'

There was a pause before Theo had the presence of mind to respond to his father's question.

'I thought you were in New York, sir.'

This wasn't what Tobias Booth wanted to hear. 'What's going on?' He glared at Mr Young, Hugh and Madeline. 'Who are these people?'

'We're rehearsing a play,' said Theo. 'This is my very good friend, Mr Joseph Young.'

Mr Young gave a bow as if he were taking a curtain call. 'I'm delighted to meet you, sir. I'm the one in charge of the performance you see before you.'

'And this is Mr and Miss Crosby,' added Theo, eager to continue with the introductions. 'They—'

'Where's the furniture?' demanded Tobias Booth, ignoring Madeline and Hugh as his eyes narrowed on the empty drawing room. 'And where's the carpet?'

'All safely stored, sir,' replied Theo, who'd begun wringing his hands in the face of his father's rage.

'I don't want it *safely stored*. I want it all back in place, right now. And don't ask the servants to do it. It looks to me as if you've wasted enough of their time on this foolhardy exploit.'

'But this is our rehearsal space,' said Mr Young, suddenly indignant. 'The weather's too changeable for us to rehearse outside as I originally planned.'

Tobias Booth slapped his silver-topped cane against his leg, the anger sparking from every part of him. 'There'll be no more rehearsals and there'll be no play. I won't have this scandalous behaviour in my house.' He turned to Edward. 'I thought you'd have more sense than to allow your sisters to behave in this manner. Anyone would think they were common whores.'

Mr Booth was about to turn his verbal assault on Flora when Edward stepped in. 'Please don't blame Flora. This is none of her doing. She's only here because she's been forced into it.'

Edward's words seemed to take some of the bluster out of his father. 'Get out of my sight, all of you. And put this room back to how it should be.' He smiled at Rawdon, turning on what must have passed for his charm. 'You must forgive this chaos, sir. I hope it hasn't damaged your opinion of Marianne.'

Rawdon glanced at his fiancée as she hurried out of the room. 'I instructed my lawyer to send over the agreement regarding the transfer of funds for her dowry. I hope you found everything in order and the amount you pledged to pay still stands.'

'Of course, of course,' said Mr Booth, nodding furiously at his future son-in-law. 'We look forward to our families joining together as one. The sooner, the better, I say.'

Hugh and Madeline decided to make a dash for it, or as Madeline called it, a French exit, before they were forced to suffer Tobias Booth's attention. Even when he tried to be charming, he was full of bluster.

They'd reached the front door when Madeline realised she'd left her gloves on the terrace. She looked back over her shoulder at the long hallway, the imposing maze of rooms. If she retraced her steps to the drawing room she'd have to risk crossing paths with Tobias Booth, and she refused to give him the opportunity to speak to her in the same disrespectful way he'd spoken to Mr Young. Everyone in the house, whether they were guests, family or strangers, appeared to be treated with the same level of contempt. Knowing what she did of his business practices, she'd find it impossible to be civil to him. His display of hypocrisy, demonstrated by his concern for the moral welfare of his daughters when he was responsible for the running of numerous brothels, made her blood boil.

'They're only gloves,' said Hugh. 'Can't you leave them?'

The gloves were a delicate shade of cream, made from the finest kid leather and a perfect match for every summer outfit. She couldn't leave them behind. She'd bought them in Paris, which meant they wouldn't be easy to replace. 'You go ahead. I'll slip round to the back of the house through the garden and collect them. It'll only take a minute.'

'Are you sure you want to do this, Maddie? If you're seen, we might be expected to stay for tea.'

'Wait for me in the buggy. I'll be there and back before you know it.'

Madeline crept around the exterior of the house at double speed, her shoes slipping on the polished gravel as it gave under her feet. All the while, she kept her head down, relying on the fallacy that if she didn't look up, nobody in the house would see her if they happened to glance out of the windows.

The gloves were beside the statue of the milkmaid, exactly where she'd left them. As she dashed across the terrace to grab them, she overheard the booming tones of Tobias Booth lecturing Theo.

'Why are you wasting your time here with your mother and sisters when you're supposed to be in New York? It's time you started taking responsibility for the business. I need to know I'll be leaving it in safe hands when I'm gone.'

'It's only a few weeks,' said Theo, the lilt of his voice making light of the transgression. 'There's no point having this house if we don't enjoy it from time to time.'

'You don't just take off without my permission. There's work to do, decisions to be made. Hundreds of people rely on the hotel business for their livelihoods, not to mention your own flesh and blood. This house doesn't pay for itself. You can't simply walk away from your obligations whenever you feel like it.'

'Mr Young is between professional engagements. I'd promised to bring him down here and I thought—'

'I don't care what you thought. Your duty lies with your family, not with Mr Young.'

Madeline hoped they wouldn't notice her as she crept across the terrace gripping her favourite gloves. All the while, Tobias Booth continued to berate his eldest son.

'Mr Young is a bad influence. I forbid you to see him again. You need to find yourself a wife. You need an heir, Theo. The Trident hotel business needs an heir. Why is it I never see you courting any women?'

Madeline had overheard too much. She made her way back to the front of the house feeling like an intruder. She hadn't meant to listen in on the private conversation and was reeling from the disclosure. It wasn't only the women in the family who were being bartered to benefit the family business, Theo was expected to marry and produce an heir too. From the little she knew of him, he didn't seem inclined to settle down and his temperament appeared ill-fitted to running a business, or maybe he just wasn't ready to step up to it.

'Is everything all right?' asked Hugh, as he handed her into the buggy. 'You were gone a while.'

She waved her gloves in the air, as if recovering them had been a victory. There wasn't time to tell him what she'd overheard or why it had taken her so long to retrieve them.

'Let's go.'

They were almost home before Hugh spoke again. 'I think we can assume that's the end of the playacting.'

'I can't say I'm sorry,' said Madeline. 'Whatever Mr Young

might have thought, we were hardly equipped to perform scenes from *A Midsummer Night's Dream*.'

'It's Flora I'm most relieved for,' said Hugh. 'She was mortified at the thought of having to act on the stage. She told me she's never been to the theatre or seen a play. She had no idea what she was supposed to do.'

Rehearsing the play had been Madeline's opportunity to get to know Edward properly. She had to gain his favour if she was to convince him to rid the Trident hotel chain of their brothels, but now she considered it, she realised it had been a bad idea from the start. She'd misjudged his character. He didn't have the sense of justice and morality that her first impressions of him had suggested, and her plan to use her influence with him to get the brothels shut down seemed hopeless. And from what she now knew of Theo and Tobias Booth, there was no chance of convincing either of them to close the brothels. She sighed, frustrated by her fruitless efforts. She'd put herself through the indignity of the last few days for nothing.

Chapter 15

Two days later, Madeline and Hugh received an invitation to Marianne and Rawdon's wedding. Madeline examined the card, written in Mrs Norton's formal hand. The gold-leaf silhouettes of the bride and groom facing each other from opposing corners glinted in the sun as she held it up to the light.

She frowned at the date, which was only a few weeks away. 'It's quite soon, but I suppose we're obliged to go now we've been invited.' She handed the invitation to Hugh, hoping he'd come up with an excuse to get them out of it.

'It might be fun. You never know, Maddie. You might even enjoy yourself. It seems to me you need cheering up.'

Lately, Madeline had been suffering from an overwhelming sense of deflation and it was all to do with the play. She'd enjoyed the intellectual challenge of learning a part and the discipline of having somewhere to be at a given time. Despite their differences, there'd been a sense of camaraderie growing between the Crosbys and the Booths as they worked towards the common purpose of putting on a performance, even if it was only a few half-baked scenes that had been cobbled together and without enough actors to fill the roles. For all their crossed purposes, and in spite of her better judgement, she even found herself missing Edward.

Now, because of Tobias Booth's intervention, all that was gone and Madeline's days stretched before her like a wilderness. There was only so much time she could spend playing the harp, and with no one to listen to her, there seemed little point in it beyond her own indulgence.

Later that morning, Hugh went to visit another livestock auction in the hope of finding them a pair of suitable horses. Madeline wandered from room to room with no obvious purpose. The house was too big for just the two of them and overwhelmingly gloomy, but it was part of their family heritage, particularly Hugh's. She didn't feel it was her place to suggest making changes to the old-fashioned decor or the drab furniture when Hugh loved everything just as it was.

Despite feeling like an outsider, Madeline was determined to make the best of settling here. She reminded herself every day of her privilege and her lucky escape from the life that had been awaiting her in the brothel. Hugh had gone to great lengths to make her feel at home, and yet she could never be comfortable here, never let her guard down while she was forced to suffer the disapproval of Finch and her small acts of hostility.

Something had to be done about it. Her tricks had become increasingly petty, but still Madeline had resisted bringing them to Hugh's attention. She refused to sound like a whining child or risk boring him with her complaints. Instead, she continued to give the impression of turning a blind eye to them, refusing to admit that the dead flies in her pot of face cream or the splinters of glass in her bath were wearing her down. Nevertheless, the battle couldn't be allowed to continue.

It was already the afternoon when Madeline made the decision to go down to the kitchen to ask one of the maids to make coffee, rather than summoning Finch to pass on the instruction. As mistress of the house, Madeline was entitled to go anywhere she pleased, but it didn't stop her feeling like an intruder as she crept down the back stairs to the kitchen.

The door creaked as she pushed it aside. Finch was sitting in a comfortable chair beside the stove reading the newspaper. She must have heard Madeline's approaching footfall, because her shoulders twitched as she made her way into the room.

'Do you want something?' Finch raised her eyes from the newspaper, glaring at Madeline as if she were a trespasser 'I didn't hear the bell.'

There was an assertiveness to Finch's tone that made Madeline question who was actually in charge.

'I didn't ring the bell,' said Madeline. The kitchen was empty but for the two of them. 'Where are the maids?'

Finch folded the newspaper and put it aside with a sigh. 'I gave them a few hours off. With the master out of the house, I didn't think they'd be needed.'

It wasn't Finch's job to instruct the maids on anything beyond their day-to-day tasks, not now Madeline was mistress of the house.

'You should have checked with me first.'

'Why?' Finch's back was rigid, despite the give of the chair, the generous padding of the cushions. 'What do you want them for?'

'That's for me to decide,' said Madeline, her voice rising with indignation, despite her effort to control it.

Hugh had made it clear to Finch who was in charge. Still, Madeline was reluctant to instruct her to make the coffee. She didn't want Finch waiting on her and she didn't trust her not to add something unpleasant to the pot.

'I came to ask you to join me for coffee.'

This was the last thing Finch must have expected. She narrowed her eyes, a hunted animal caught in a sudden shaft of sunlight. 'Why would you want to do that? We're nothing to one another.'

'You're the housekeeper here and I'm the mistress. If the house is to run smoothly, it's important we work together.'

Finch cleared her throat. 'I've managed well enough all these years without your interference. I don't see why I should put up with it now.'

'Because it's my house and it's up to me to decide how it's run. For instance, the maids have their allocated half days and holidays. If they need time off on any other occasion, I need to be consulted. Is that clear?'

'I have just as much right to be here as you do,' said Finch, her voice succumbing to a hiss. 'You should remember that.'

Madeline stood her ground. 'You have a right to live and work here, but it is not your house.'

'You won't get rid of me. Hugh will never let you.'

'I have no intention of getting rid of you. I'm simply making it clear what the boundaries are.' Madeline filled the kettle and put it on the stove to boil. 'Where do you keep the coffee? Or would you prefer tea?'

The gesture rendered Finch speechless. Pushing herself out of the chair, she reached up to the high shelf and retrieved the coffee tin, her voice softer as she handed it to Madeline.

'You must show me how you like it, so it's more to your taste in future.'

'You can instruct Sara on the method. I don't expect you to make it for me. That's what the maids are for.' Madeline wasn't prepared to betray the fact that she knew Finch had been doctoring her drinks to make them unpalatable. There was no victory to be won here, only better relations and the restoration of dignity on both sides.

Finch gave a small acknowledgement of Madeline's gesture and handed her the coffee pot. 'It's a big change having you here. I can't deny it.'

'I respect the fact that this is your home, just as much as it's mine,' said Madeline.

'There was a time when I thought it really would be mine, that I'd be the mistress here. That was before Mr Crosby senior decided to marry someone else.'

'None of us are to blame for what my father did. Nor can I be held responsible for the choices my mother made. She paid dearly for them.'

Finch took a deep breath, as if to prepare herself for what she was about to reveal. 'I had a child too,' she said, the words barely audible. 'A little girl. A half-sister to you and Hugh.'

The news that Madeline had a half-sister was too much to take in. Why hadn't she been told this before? 'Where is she now?'

'I had no choice but to give her up. Your father didn't acknowledge her the way he acknowledged you, giving you his name and a share of his wealth. He was a younger man then. I don't think he understood the responsibility of a child, what it meant to cast her aside and me along with her. By the time he realised his error, it was too late. It's the reason he allowed me to become the custodian of this place. It was his way of trying to make up for what I'd lost.

'You must forgive me for resenting you, Miss Crosby, but every time I see you, I think only of my own daughter, how but for the whim of your father, she'd be the mistress here, wearing your fine gowns and travelling the world with Hugh whenever her fancy takes.'

'Does Hugh know he had another half-sister? He's never mentioned her.'

Finch shook her head. 'Perhaps if I'd died, as your mother did, my little girl might be here in your place.'

'You mustn't think like that.'

'It's hard not to.'

'Where's your daughter now?'

'She died of cholera. The orphanage was good enough to let me know. They said it would help me let go of her. They knew how difficult it had been for me to hand her over. They were wrong, of course. Some things are impossible to let go of.'

'I'm sorry. I—'

Finch raised her hand, indicating the subject was closed and never to be spoken of again.

The coffee was cold by the time they came to drink it, but Madeline hadn't really wanted it anyway. It wasn't the reason she'd ventured into the kitchen.

As she got up to leave, Finch handed her the newspaper. 'There's a piece in here about that lawyer friend of yours, Edward Booth. It seems he isn't such a bad sort, after all. You should think twice about turning him away next time he visits.'

Back in the drawing room, Madeline was still reeling from everything Finch had told her. No wonder she was so resentful of her presence. No wonder Hugh's mother never visited the house when she was alive. Madeline wondered if Hugh had ever learned about his other half-sister from their father. She would never mention it, never risk dragging up the past. If he knew about her, he'd chosen to keep it to himself, and if he didn't know, then Madeline wouldn't be the one to break it to him. Hugh carried enough guilt for their father's behaviour. His determination to repair the damage of the past was the reason he looked after Madeline so well, the reason he protected Finch. There was no point in layering more guilt on his shoulders.

Still holding the newspaper, Madeline's thoughts returned to Edward. The article reported on another of his campaigns, this time to help a group of female factory workers win the right to keep their jobs after they married. It was a victory on a small scale, relating to only one employer, but it gave hope that more would follow suit, that the law would one day protect the basic rights of all working women.

Despite the prospect of a better future, nothing that had happened in the past could be undone. This went for her mother's life and for Finch's, and for all the other women who'd been exploited, as well as those who continued to suffer.

Reading about Edward's latest campaign convinced Madeline she was right to try to influence him to close the Trident's brothels. He might think he could fool her by denying their existence, but he was mistaken. She would win this battle. He had to be a better man than he'd shown himself to be when they spoke of the hotel business. She had to believe he was the man he presented to the world, not the man protecting his family secrets, the man that despite everything, her heart was drawn to, and she wouldn't rest until she'd achieved her purpose.

Chapter 16

Hugh returned later that day with two fine black stallions and an old grey mare he'd won at the livestock auction. 'I couldn't leave the mare behind, Maddie,' he explained. 'No one else was bidding for her and she's so sweet.'

The mare, with its ageing limbs and barrelled stomach was too docile for Madeline or Hugh to ride but would make an excellent stable companion for the more excitable horses. 'I was worried what would happen to her if I didn't buy her.'

It was typical of Hugh, rescuing the waifs and strays. He was too kind-hearted for his own good.

They took the stallions out the following day, riding into the scrubland in the hills above the beach. Madeline was glad to get out into the fresh air, to be her wild, untrammelled self again. This was how freedom felt, driving forward against the wind in an open space, the energy of the horse beneath her powering her on.

'Will he do?' asked Hugh, when they finally stopped to catch their breath.

Madeline ran her hand along the smooth neck of the horse, feeling the blood pump through his veins, the thick skein of muscle beneath his fine coat. 'He's perfect.'

They were making the long descent down to the beach when

they saw Edward coming towards them on horseback. Madeline narrowed her eyes against the sun, the tension returning to her body as he waved to catch their attention.

He pulled up his horse in front of them and raised his hat, his formality fully restored now they were no longer acting as star-crossed lovers.

'I'm glad to see you both.'

His eyes shifted nervously from Hugh's face to Madeline's and back again, trying to disguise his awkwardness behind a display of good manners.

'I must apologise for the way your recent visit to our house ended. We weren't expecting my father to return so suddenly or to take against the play the way he did, although his reaction was completely understandable. He's a man of the highest moral standards.'

Madeline tried not to react to the absurdity of Edward's comment regarding his father's morals. He was either trying to cover up for him or he didn't know his father at all.

'His intervention must have come as a relief to you,' said Madeline, once she'd regained her composure. 'After all, he managed to put a stop to the play where you'd failed.'

'He saved us all from further embarrassment,' said Edward. 'I'm grateful to him for that.'

Madeline flashed him a smile. The devil in her was determined to play on his discomfort. 'Please don't apologise, Mr Booth. Some of us are more shameless than you give us credit for.'

'Forgive me, Miss Crosby. I don't think . . . I didn't mean . . .'

Hugh gave a roaring laugh. 'Maddie is teasing you, Mr Booth. You don't want to take anything she says too seriously. She'll tie you in knots with her sharp wit.'

She almost felt sorry for the look of confusion on Edward's face. The man she saw before her, awkward and self-conscious, was a far cry from the person he must present himself as in court, fighting for the rights of those less fortunate than himself. He was essentially a good man and there would be a lot to admire about him if it wasn't for the brothels.

Her horse was growing restless. She patted his flank to calm him. 'It was wrong of us to leave without saying goodbye the other day. You must forgive us.'

'I don't blame you for fleeing from my father's temper. Once he gets into a rage, there's no stopping him.'

Tobias Booth's behaviour explained why Edward refused to work alongside him in the family business, and why Theo had abandoned his post in the New York office.

'I wanted to call on you,' said Edward, 'but I didn't know if you'd receive me.'

He couldn't have forgotten the time she'd invited him to listen to her play the harp, only to have Finch turn him away at the door. Her behaviour seemed cruel and inconsistent when she considered it from his point of view.

'I've been trying to work out why we're suddenly so at odds with each other,' he continued, all the while staring at the ground. 'I don't know what I've done to upset you, Miss Crosby, but whatever it is, I'm deeply sorry for it.'

Madeline gripped the horse's reins, suddenly heady with emotion and fearing she might fall. Whatever confusion Edward was feeling, she didn't doubt his remorse.

'The issue I mentioned before, about the morality of your family business. Did you raise it with your brother or your father?'

'Our employees are all treated fairly. I—'

'But did you ask? Did you look into it?'

Edward was beginning to flounder, the frustration leeching out of him. 'The hotel business is nothing to do with me, Miss Crosby. I know nothing of its affairs or of the day-to-day running of it. I made the decision a number of years ago never to be a part of it. It's not my place to interfere in it now. My father would never allow it. Nor would he countenance the questions you insist I should ask him.'

It was the same conversation they'd had before. There was no point going over it again if he wasn't prepared to listen. She gave a gentle tug on the reins, encouraging her horse to begin its slow descent down the hill.

'Then there's nothing left to say.'

'Madeline, please . . .' Edward called after her, his voice dying on the wind.

Hugh threw Edward a sympathetic look over his shoulder as he turned to follow his sister. 'If you want to win Maddie's heart, you'll to have to try harder than that.'

Brother and sister rode on in silence, the horses negotiating their way through the dunes and onto a long stretch of beach where the ocean breeze and the sound of the crashing waves went some way to restoring Madeline's sense of peace.

Hugh rode alongside her. Every now and again, he cast a curious glance in her direction. 'You know he's in love with you.'

It was a statement rather than a question. Madeline shrugged it off. 'You've been reading too many novels. You know how love stories go to your head.'

'This isn't fiction, Maddie. It's real. You only have to see how he looks at you. He's completely under your spell.'

'I'm not a witch and I've done nothing to encourage him.'

'You didn't have to encourage him, Maddie. He needed no help to fall for you. You should take it as a compliment.'

'He wouldn't feel that way if he knew where I came from or who my mother was.'

'Is that the reason you're pushing him away?'

'You can't have forgotten his family business is based on a chain of brothels or that my mother died in one of them. If it hadn't been for Father's intervention, I'd probably be working in one right now.'

Hugh nodded, not disagreeing with her. 'So, are you in love with him or not?'

Madeline batted away the question, encouraging her horse to

gallop across the beach. What a ridiculous thing for Hugh to ask, given the nature of everything that connected their families. It was impossible that she could allow herself to love Edward or have any kind of feelings for him. Despite his legal work, his family's wealth was founded on the exploitation of women. She understood Hugh's argument about leaving things in the past where they belonged, but the brothels were still in operation today, and while Edward continued to deny their existence there could be no place for him in her heart.

Chapter 17

Madeline was considering which of her new dresses she should wear for Marianne and Rawdon's wedding the following day, when a grand coach drove up to the house. Desperate for distraction, she wandered over to the drawing-room window to find out who the visitors might be.

'Three guesses,' she said, throwing a look at Hugh, who was catching up with *The New York Times*.

'Only three? Surely, we're more popular than that.'

'I'm not counting all the women who've set their hearts on you,' said Madeline. 'That would be—'

Before Madeline could finish, Finch appeared at the door, her best manners tipping over into solemnity. Since Madeline's visit to the kitchen, relations had thawed a little between them and the iciness was now only several inches thick.

'There's a Miss Booth and a Miss Pierce to see you both.'

'Thank you, Finch,' said Madeline. 'Please show them in. And ask Sara to bring some tea, would you?'

Marianne barged into the room before Madeline had finishing speaking to Finch. Flora trailed half a dozen steps behind, apologising for the intrusion under her breath.

'You'll forgive our sudden appearance,' said Marianne,

arranging herself on the sofa without waiting to be invited, 'but I had to see you.'

'You're very welcome,' said Madeline, throwing a look at Hugh, while trying to work out if he had anything to do with the unexpected visit. She smiled at Flora who was still hovering by the door gripping Marianne's parasol. 'Won't you sit down?'

'I'm so sorry,' said Flora, clearly flustered at finding herself in the gloomy drawing room. Madeline gathered from her nervousness that she didn't get out much.

Hugh gave Flora a gentle look. 'There's nothing to be sorry for. I doubt you've done anything wrong.'

'Oh, but we shouldn't have intruded in this way.'

Flora's hat sat at a crooked angle as if she'd dressed to go out in a hurry and without the benefit of a mirror, while Marianne, sitting with a straight back and ankles crossed, was perfect from button to bow.

'You must excuse Flora,' said Marianne. 'I only brought her because I needed a chaperone, and I couldn't ask Jane to come.'

The comment suggested the sisters weren't on the best of terms. If Marianne had needed a chaperone, it would have been more prudent to bring Mrs Norton rather than Flora, who appeared so uncomfortable in social situations. Madeline knew better than to stir up trouble by giving an opinion on it. It seemed a good idea to change the subject.

'We're looking forward to attending your wedding tomorrow.'

'That's what I've come to talk to you about,' said Marianne, her gaze fixed on Hugh. 'Can I speak to you alone?'

Panic lit Hugh's eyes as if someone had set fire to him. 'Maddie and I have no secrets. You can say whatever you need to in front of her.'

Madeline nodded, desperate to know what all this was about, while trying not to make her curiosity too obvious.

Without warning, Flora shot out of her chair. 'I'll wait outside.'

'Whatever for?' asked Madeline, looking up at her as if she'd gone mad.

'So you can speak in private.' Flora bowed her head, presenting herself once more as no better than the hired help.

Madeline felt her heart give at the unfairness of it, the cruelty of the way Flora was treated by the Booths. Anyone who bothered to look would see she was kind, intelligent and sensitive. 'You're our guest, Flora, and I'd like you to stay here with us.'

Marianne was about to say something when Sara interrupted with the tea tray. Madeline offered the maid a smile, silently thanking her before urging her gently out of the room. If she didn't find out what Marianne had come to impart to Hugh soon, she was going to burst.

There was a further moment of silence while Flora, who had finally returned to her seat, insisted on pouring the tea. Madeline took a sip to satisfy herself that Sara had made it rather than Finch. The truce between them was delicate, and there was no saying when another fit of outrage would come upon the housekeeper again, rendering the tea undrinkable.

'So, Miss Booth, what was it you were about to tell us?' asked Hugh. 'Did you say it was something to do with the wedding?'

'I might as well come straight to the point,' said Marianne. 'I want to know whether you think I should go ahead with it.'

Hugh let out a nervous laugh. 'I'm not the one you should be asking that question of. Only you can answer it.'

'She shouldn't marry Rawdon if she doesn't love him,' said Flora, jumping into the conversation. 'It isn't right and it isn't fair on him.'

'Few people marry for love,' replied Madeline, with more feeling than she'd intended. 'Although the world would be a better place if everyone did.'

'And if I don't love Rawdon?' asked Marianne, spilling tea in her saucer in her eagerness to ask the question.

'It's a bit late to start thinking about that now,' said Madeline.

'The wedding is less than twenty-four hours away.'

Marianne nodded, her shoulders stiff, as if she were holding up against defeat. 'All the agreements have been drawn up. The money has changed hands.'

Goods and chattels, thought Madeline. *Objects to be bought and sold.* That was all women were, no matter how prettily you dressed them up.

'It's not too late,' insisted Flora. 'You have until the second before you walk down the aisle to change your mind.'

'Why would you change your mind?' asked Hugh. 'I thought you wanted to be mistress of Southsea?'

'There are other houses I could be mistress of.' Marianne raised her hand, gesturing to the room as she spoke. 'There's this one, for instance.'

Hugh shifted uncomfortably in his seat. 'Maddie's the mistress of this house and she always will be.'

'Not if you choose to marry,' said Marianne.

'But I never will.'

'Not even for love?'

'I'm not in love.'

Marianne put aside her teacup and crossed the room to sit beside him. 'You could learn to love someone if they loved you dearly enough.' She pushed her face into his, brushing his cheek with the tip of her nose. 'How could you not love me?'

Flora gasped at the impropriety as Hugh disentangled himself from Marianne's proximity and crossed the room, putting himself out of her reach.

'You must forgive me, Miss Booth. As far as I'm concerned, we're social acquaintances and could never be anything more to one another. I have too much respect for Rawdon to act in any way that would come between him and his bride-to-be.'

'The attention you've shown me every time we've met suggested something very different,' said Marianne, her voice brittle around the edges.

'We were having fun, enjoying each other's company. I treated you no differently to the way I treat Maddie.' Hugh glanced at his sister, begging her with his eyes to help him.

Even though she was furious with him for the way he'd behaved, Madeline nodded. 'He's right. He's a terrible tease, but there's no harm in him.'

'I never meant to mislead you, Miss Booth. The fact that you're engaged to Rawdon was the reason I felt I could enjoy your company freely. As far as I'm concerned, you're as good as being a married woman. I thought you would see my attention for what it was.'

'And what was it, sir?'

Hugh gritted his teeth. 'A bit of fun.'

There was a beat of silence while Marianne took in Hugh's words. 'So, you have no other intentions towards me?'

'I never made it a secret that I have no intention of marrying.'

Flora, who'd been quiet for the last few minutes, suddenly spoke out. 'Shame on you for breaking Marianne's heart, Mr Crosby. You must have seen how taken she was with you.'

'She's about to marry another man. Why would I even consider it?'

Marianne rose from the chair with as much grace as she could muster. 'Come, Flora. It's time to go home. There are people there who love us and they'll be wondering where we are.'

Marianne turned as she reached the door. There was one last arrow to shoot. 'At least have the decency not to marry Jane. I couldn't stand to see the two of you together.'

Hugh looked her straight in the eye. 'I have no intention of marrying anyone and that includes your sister.'

'You might find she has something different to say about that, Mr Crosby. Don't say I didn't warn you.'

After Marianne had climbed into the carriage, Madeline rushed to the front door and called Flora back, handing her the parasol that had been left in the drawing room during their hurry to leave.

'I know Hugh can be a bit high-spirited sometimes, but he would never deliberately have done anything to spoil Marianne's chances of marrying Rawdon. Whatever you might think, he's not that kind of a man.'

Flora turned the parasol nervously in her hands. 'Someone has to rescue Marianne from Rawdon,' she whispered. 'If your brother won't do it, I don't know who will.'

It seemed rather a dramatic statement for Flora to have made, and Madeline had no answer for it. She could only hope Flora was wrong, that Marianne was simply suffering pre-wedding nerves, and that there'd be no more talk of rescue.

Hugh was still in the drawing room, staring at his untouched cup of tea when Madeline returned, the sound of the retreating carriage wheels disappearing along the driveway. He raised his eyes, innocent as a puppy expecting to be slapped.

'Did I really give her the wrong impression?'

'I fear you did.'

He threw up his hands in frustration. 'I have no intention of marrying. Everybody knows that.'

'You might say as much, Hugh, but it's not the impression you give.'

'I don't understand.'

'You're rich and good looking, clever and kind. No woman's heart stands a chance of surviving when you seek out her company and make her laugh, when you pay her a hundred small attentions that most men wouldn't even think about.' Madeline sighed, trying to work out a clearer way of explaining it. 'All those small kindnesses add up to so much more than you simply announcing you'll never marry. When most men say it, what they really mean is they have every intention of marrying, but they haven't found the right woman yet.'

'That's not the case with me, Maddie, and you know it. I won't marry in case I turn out to be a terrible husband like our father and Uncle Morris.'

Madeline pursed her lips. 'Promise you'll be more cautious in future. If you tell a woman you have no intention of marrying, don't assume she believes you.'

'I thought I was on safe ground with Marianne.'

'There's no such thing as safe ground where women are concerned. You're lucky Rawdon hasn't come after you with his shotgun. Or Tobias Booth. There's a man capable of revenge if I ever saw one.'

'Am I not to have any fun?'

'Most women are forced to lead sheltered lives. There's no armour around their hearts. They have no defence against your charm or that handsome face of yours.'

Hugh was quiet for a long time before he spoke again. 'You don't think she was trying to use me to get out of marrying Rawdon, do you?'

'Possibly, but if you hadn't made yourself so agreeable the idea might never have crossed her mind.'

Madeline thought back to Flora's farewell comment before she climbed into the carriage. She hoped for Marianne's sake that her fears were overblown and that Rawdon, for all his bluster, would turn out to be a better husband than she anticipated.

Chapter 18

Marianne and Rawdon's wedding was to take place at the white clapboard church with the needle spire where George Washington was once said to have worshipped. Knowing there was no risk of outshining the bride, Madeline had chosen to wear the lemon silk dress she'd bought in Paris during the spring, which she topped with a wide-brimmed hat.

A number of guests had already gathered outside when they arrived, and the lawn was a riot of puffed taffeta and lace, wilting flowers and oversized parasols.

The crowd separated as Marianne climbed down from the wedding coach. Her silk dress, the colour of green poison bottles, was a surprise but not a completely strange choice in a society where almost any colour was deemed suitable for a bride, as long as it looked expensive. And it was true that no expense appeared to have been spared on Marianne's ensemble, from the cream satin shoes to the matching veil and every lace frill and seed pearl in between.

Everyone watched as Jane thrust a bouquet of orange blossom into Marianne's hand. Her dress, which was a rather uninteresting lilac, appeared to have been chosen so as not to put her sister in the shade and would have been better suited to the third phase of mourning than a wedding.

'Do you think Marianne will go through with it?' asked Madeline, slanting her parasol across her face so no one would read her lips as she whispered to her brother.

Although she was speculating, there was a serious point to her question. It was a mystery as to how Marianne could throw her life away on Rawdon, dismissing love as inconsequential after everything she'd declared to Hugh the day before. But of course, love wasn't the point of this particular union. It was Madeline who was being naive. She only had to count everything Marianne and her family were about to gain just by muttering a simple *I do* to understand the reason behind it. Love was nothing in comparison to Rawdon's vast wealth.

Considering it was such a grand affair, the bride seemed rather lonely, with only Jane in attendance. Although it was meant to be the happiest day of her life, an air of reluctance hung over Marianne like a storm cloud, as if she were heading to the gallows rather than the wedding altar. When she failed to make her way towards the church, Madeline wondered if she'd paused to take in the scene, or whether her feet were frozen to the spot.

Noticing the bride's hesitation, Mrs Norton dashed to Marianne's side. Despite the aunt's victory in arranging what was deemed the match of the season, her frown went deep. Her cheeks, which were mottled by any number of emotions, were only slightly paler than the unadorned plum satin dress she'd chosen to wear.

'Come along, Marianne. There's no time to waste.' Mrs Norton's voice carried farther than she probably realised as she encouraged the reluctant bride to put one foot in front of the other. 'You don't want to give Rawdon the idea that you're having second thoughts by being late to your own wedding.'

When her words failed to have the desired effect, she grabbed Marianne's wrist and resorted to marching her towards the church under the watchful eye of Tobias Booth, who stood apart from the crowd, his arms folded across his chest as he watched the proceedings.

There was no sign of Flora, who Madeline would have expected to see in attendance. Hugh must have been having the same thought, because he began muttering about how Flora would have made a most appealing bridesmaid as they dashed into the church just ahead of the bride.

Madeline could hardly bear to watch as the couple took their vows, as Marianne's heart was slain on the sacrificial altar of matrimony. She was marrying Rawdon, even though she didn't love him. Everybody knew it, even if nobody dared to say it.

For the wedding breakfast, Rawdon had arranged for the ballroom at Southsea to be decorated with swathes of hothouse flowers, interspersed with antique urns filled with blue hydrangeas and goldenrod. Perched on a gilded throne at the farthest end of the room from the orchestra, Marianne was finally queen of all she surveyed. It wasn't the miserable-looking man sitting next to her she'd married, but everything he stood for.

'So, she really did it,' said Madeline, raising her champagne glass to Hugh. 'I hope she finds a way to live happily ever after.' She studied the newlyweds, sitting side by side in all their majesty, an array of sterling-silver asparagus tongs, grape scissors and nut picks that had been presented as wedding gifts laid out on a table beside them. 'We've been so preoccupied with whether Marianne loves Rawdon, we've never stopped to ask ourselves whether Rawdon loves Marianne.'

Hugh helped himself to a lobster canapé from a passing footman, his eyes lazily tracking the dancing couples now the orchestra had struck up. 'You concern yourself far too much with whether other people are in love, Maddie. You should pay more attention to matters of your own heart.'

As far as Madeline was concerned, love was for other people. Given her origins, it was unimaginable that a man of honour and good sense would ever want to marry her, and so she was content to spend her life with Hugh.

The sharp sound of a yap announced the arrival of Mrs Booth

at Hugh's shoulder. She was cradling Mimi in her arms like a newborn baby, the tiny flower garland circling the dog's ears having done nothing to improve the creature's temper.

'You must forgive Mimi's rough little greeting,' said Mrs Booth. 'She's not used to so many people. Thank you for coming. How are you enjoying the day?' Her eyes glazed over, as if she'd already asked the question a dozen times and had little care for the answer.

Hugh thanked her graciously for the hospitality, risking his fingers near the dog's jaw as he attempted to pet her.

'I wouldn't do that, if I were you,' said Mrs Booth, stepping away from him more swiftly than Madeline had ever seen her move. 'She's not accustomed to men.'

Hugh clasped his offending fingers to his chest. 'Forgive me, I—'

But already Mrs Booth had drifted to the next group of guests, the restless dog wriggling for freedom in her arms as once again she thanked people for coming and asked if they were enjoying the day.

'Mr Crosby, there you are. I've been looking for you everywhere.'

It was Jane, trying to catch Hugh's attention by waving her arms in the air, her words running into one another as she moved unsteadily across the ballroom towards them, the effects of the champagne she'd drunk having gone to her head.

'Dance with me, sir.'

Hugh gave Madeline the panicked look, that always made her suspect someone had set fire to him, before he responded to Jane's demand.

'You should get some fresh air first, Miss Booth.' He took her arm, attempting to keep her steady. 'It's rather warm for dancing, don't you think?'

'Be careful, Hugh,' whispered Madeline. 'If it comes to it, tell her you're betrothed to an Austrian princess you met in Paris. Let her down gently. Don't break her heart.'

Hugh gave his sister a narrow glance as he led Jane into the garden where a little fresh air might restore her. If that failed, at least the champagne would be out of easy reach.

Madeline was watching the dancing couples make their pretty pairs across the ballroom floor when Edward approached her.

'Would you like to dance, Miss Crosby?'

'Are you any good, Mr Booth?'

Her question was bold enough to make him smile. 'Not really, but if you wish to dance, I'd be glad to.'

She cast her eyes around the room. 'There must be many fine dancers among all these good-looking men.'

'That's what worries me. I fear one of them might whisk you away before I've had a chance to talk to you.'

'Lucky for you, I'm not in the mood for dancing.' She offered him her arm. 'Shall we get some air?'

Many of the guests were already outside, enjoying the early summer sunshine as they strolled through the gardens. Refreshment tables had been set up at regular intervals across the lawn enabling the guests to help themselves to drinks and gorge on wedding cake to the soothing tones of an outdoor string quartet.

The sight of the musicians must have reminded Edward of Madeline's harp. 'You promised to play for me, Miss Crosby. I'm determined to hold you to it.'

'Perhaps I'm just not very good and don't want you to find out.'

'I hope you play very badly. It'll make me feel so much better.'

'Why's that?' She feared he was about the get the better of her with his wit and she could hardly stand it.

'If you play badly, perhaps I won't be quite so in awe of you.'

His comment wasn't what she'd been expecting and she was lost for words. She stared at the ground, at her beautiful silk shoes that had come all the way from Paris. How exquisite they were and how undeserving she was of them.

'There's nothing awe-inspiring about me, Mr Booth. I'm lowlier than you could ever imagine, and I'm not very good at playing the harp.'

'The only way to resolve this is for you to let me hear you play.'

She smiled, refusing to commit to anything more than the here and now. 'Tell me about your latest crusade to win women the right to return to work after they're married.'

'Who told you about that?'

'I saw it in the newspaper. It was Finch, our housekeeper, who brought it to my attention.'

'It's a small step, but hopefully the first of many towards improving the rights of women working in the factories.'

Hugh had spotted Edward talking to Madeline and came to join them, lowering his voice so only Edward would hear. 'I suggested that Miss Booth find a quiet room to lie down in until she's feeling better, but she refused to listen. Perhaps you might have a word with her?'

Edward sighed. 'It's the champagne, isn't it? I warned her it would go to her head. She's not used to it. Do you know where she is?'

The three of them retraced Hugh's steps to the topiary garden where Jane was sitting on the green elephant's trunk, swinging her legs and shouting, 'Here comes the bride' to anyone who happened to pass by.

'I'd better rescue her before she makes any more of a fool of herself,' said Edward. 'It's been hard for Jane, seeing Marianne married. It's the only thing my sisters have been brought up to expect in life. If you ask me, she's feeling left out.'

'I'm sure she'll be the next to marry if she sets her mind to it,' said Madeline, as Edward helped his sister climb down from the topiary. 'She's young, rich and pretty. Those are all the qualities she needs to make a good match, especially in this society. At this gathering alone, there must be more millionaires to the square inch than anywhere else, outside of the opening night of the season at the New York Metropolitan Opera House.'

'You're right,' said Edward. 'I've no doubt we'll all find good matches sooner or later.'

'Apart from me,' laughed Hugh.

'And me,' said Madeline. 'I have no intention of marrying, either.'

She stole a look at Edward, who rather than reacting to her comment, started to walk an unsteady Jane back to the house.

Hugh linked his arm through his sister's and gave it a tug. 'I've had enough of the Booths' company for one day. Shall we go and eat some cake?'

They found themselves a table on the lawn, which was perfectly placed to watch the comings and goings of all the guests. Edward had managed to convince Jane to go for a lie down, but it hadn't lasted long. Hugh and Madeline were on their second slice of cake when they spotted her at a nearby table with Theo and Mr Young.

'I thought Mr Young had been sent back to New York with a flea in his ear,' whispered Madeline.

Hugh shrugged, trying to appear as if he wasn't watching them. 'Perhaps he's been allowed back. It is a special occasion, after all.'

Almost as if their speculation had summoned him, Theo wandered over to their table. 'Thank you for coming. I hope you haven't felt too neglected by the family today. There are so many guests to greet that I fear we might have missed some of you.'

'Not at all,' said Madeline. 'We've been very well looked after, and the entertainment has been second to none.' She glanced at Jane as she said it, wondering how much longer Mr Young would put up with her whispering drunken nonsense in his ear.

Madeline had to admit that Mr Young was good looking in an *actor-ish* sort of way. She couldn't help suspecting his outfit had been lifted from the costume store of a travelling theatre troupe, as it owed more to a French revolutionary freedom fighter than to a suit purchased on Fifth Avenue for a society wedding. If he couldn't afford good clothes for the wedding of his closest friend's sister, how would he ever afford to keep a wife like Jane? And if he did make a play for Jane, what would Theo make of it?

It wasn't long before Mr Young grew tired of Jane's company

and unceremoniously abandoned her. He and Theo disappeared into the house, their heads leaning into one another as they laughed and whispered over a private joke. Madeline envied their intimacy, the sense of completeness that seemed to embody them whenever they were unconscious of being watched.

Jane approached the Crosbys' table and dropped into the chair beside Madeline. The effects of the champagne still hadn't worn off.

'Why does nobody like me?' she asked, leaning a little too closely into Madeline's face. 'You can be honest with me, Miss Crosby. Why is it?'

'You just haven't met the right man yet,' said Hugh.

Jane nodded, as if to accept the gentle message he was sending to her. 'Mr Young is so handsome, don't you think?'

'He is,' said Madeline.

'But he isn't rich,' said Jane.

'No, he isn't.'

'I don't think people should marry for money. Do you, Miss Crosby?'

Before Madeline could answer, Marianne appeared at their table, the voluminous skirts of her dress spilling over the small chair as she squeezed herself into it.

'Thank you for coming to my wedding. Hasn't it been a beautiful day?'

Her face carried a fixed look that didn't seem to be the result of alcohol or happiness, but something else altogether. Shock, perhaps.

Madeline gave her hand a gentle squeeze. Her skin was surprisingly cool to the touch. 'Are you all right? It's been a big day.'

Marianne nodded. 'I'm absolutely fine.' She turned to Madeline without seeming to focus on her. 'I did it, didn't I? I married him.'

'You did.' There was a beat of silence while Madeline tried to think of something else to say. 'And now you're the mistress of this magnificent house and all its grounds.'

Marianne nodded again, this time, frantically. 'Yes, that's absolutely right. I am the undisputed mistress here. And it's the biggest and the grandest home on the whole of Rhode Island.' She took a breath, puffing out her chest. 'I'm now one of the richest women in America. It's all mine and nobody can take it away from me.'

Jane leaned forward, cupping her sister's face in her hands as if to emphasise her message. 'From today, neither Father nor our aunt can tell you what to do. You're finally free, Marianne.'

Apart from the dictates of Rawdon, thought Madeline, but now wasn't the time to say it.

'Do you have plans for a honeymoon?' asked Madeline, moving the conversation onto safer ground.

'I want to go to Europe, but Rawdon insists on returning to New York. He says he's wasted enough time away from the banking business as it is.'

It didn't bode well for the future if Rawdon wasn't prepared to make time for a honeymoon. 'Europe will always be there whenever you have the time to visit,' said Madeline, trying to sound consoling.

Marianne grabbed her sister's hand and clutched it. Whatever differences had been between them before the wedding, they seemed to have been mended. 'I'm taking Jane to live with me in New York. I'm making it my mission to find her a husband.'

Jane gave Hugh a resigned look. 'I see now I have no hope of finding a suitor in Rhode Island.'

'How about Flora?' asked Hugh. 'Are you taking her too?'

If anyone would benefit from a husband, it was Flora. It had to be the right kind of man, of course. She was too sensitive a soul to pass off to just anyone.

'Flora has to stay here with Mother,' said Jane. 'With me and Marianne gone, she'll need a companion more than ever.'

What she needs is someone to fetch and carry for her, thought Madeline, *a lady's maid or a paid companion.* That was the truth of it. 'If she's to stay here, I'll make an effort to see more of her.

She'll be lonely without the two of you for company.'

'There's no need,' said Marianne, who seemed rather put out by the idea. 'She's perfectly happy on her own.'

'Where is Flora?' asked Madeline. Now she came to think of it, she hadn't seen her all day.

'She's upstairs, helping my maid unpack my clothes,' said Marianne. 'You wouldn't believe what a huge job it's been transporting my summer wardrobe from Mountview to Southsea. There were carriage loads and carriage loads of trunks. Someone had to oversee it.'

'It had to be done today?' asked Hugh, not bothering to hide his indignation.

'It couldn't wait,' said Marianne, rising from the chair and dragging Jane with her. 'You must excuse us. We have so many other guests to greet.'

Madeline was about to suggest they leave when Edward stepped forward and asked her once more to dance. The orchestra had struck up a slow song and the evening was drawing in, bringing with it the cool ocean breeze. The chandeliers were being lit in the ballroom and everyone was beginning to move inside.

'I might not be a very good dancer, Miss Crosby, but I won't take no for an answer.'

'For pity's sake, Maddie,' said Hugh, 'put the poor man out of his misery and allow him one dance at least.'

She considered Edward's request, knowing it would be a mistake to get too close to him, but in spite of everything, she couldn't find it in her heart to resist his offer again. In many ways, she didn't want to.

'One dance and no more,' she murmured, taking his hand and allowing herself to be led by him, feeling the warmth of his breath on her neck as they moved in time to the music.

Secure in his arms, she knew this was how life should be, with no past or future to worry about, only the present moment to fill her heart. When she closed her eyes, she could almost imagine herself free of cares, imagine there was nothing to stop them continuing like this forever, but as the music stopped and the dancing couples stood away from one another, the magic faded. The lightness of being that came with the music and dancing could only ever be fleeting and not relied upon to last. The enchantment that had lifted her heart was nothing but an illusion and couldn't be trusted.

Now the music had ended, Madeline said goodbye to Edward and returned to her brother. They'd had their one dance and it was over. That was all there was, and all there could ever be between them.

Chapter 19

Madeline was as good as her word, and a few days later, she sent a note to Flora, inviting her to tea. There was no motive behind the invitation other than to do good. She didn't particularly crave Flora's company, although company of any sort was preferable to the long days spent at Beachlands with no one to talk to but Hugh. Beyond practising the harp and horse riding, she found little to occupy her time. Her mind remained restless, set free to roam dark places. She needed a cause, a battle to fight and she needed a friend, and there was no reason why Flora couldn't be that friend.

'I don't think she'll come,' said Hugh, when Madeline mentioned the invitation. 'She thought I paid too much attention to Marianne before her wedding and gave her false hope that I'd rescue her from Rawdon.'

'That'll teach you to behave like a rake.'

Suitably chastened, Hugh buried his face in his newspaper. The remorse he displayed in the everyday gesture made Madeline's heart go out to him. Sometimes he was too charming for his own good.

Despite Hugh's assertion, Flora accepted the invitation and appeared the following afternoon clutching a large bunch of yellow roses, picked only an hour before from the Booths' garden.

'I guessed you like yellow because of the dress you wore to Marianne's wedding,' she said, holding the flowers at arm's length as if she were embarrassed to offer something so simple, so pure.

Madeline pictured Flora in the rose garden in the heat of the afternoon sun, selecting the best blooms, her fingers scratched by thorns. It was a thoughtful gift and one that would have taken some trouble to acquire. She reached for the flowers, breathing in their honeyed scent. 'They're perfect, Flora. Thank you.'

'It was kind of you to think of it,' said Hugh, who had insisted on joining them for tea, even though Madeline had considered it a bad idea.

With all the talk of the flowers, Madeline had failed to acknowledge the presence of the young man standing at Flora's side. Flora touched his arm, gently drawing her attention to him.

'This is my brother, Will. I hope you don't mind me bringing him. He's visiting from New York. We haven't seen each other for so long, I don't like to miss spending a moment with him.'

Hugh held out his hand, his smile broad and welcoming. 'I'm delighted to meet you, sir.'

Will had the same dark eyes as his sister, the same intelligent look. His smart suit, which wouldn't have looked out of place in any New York office, gave him an air of self-assurance that stayed just on the right side of confidence. Over the course of their tea, Madeline learned that for the past year, he'd been working as a junior clerk in one of his uncle's hotels.

'And how do you like it?' she asked, trying not to show any ulterior motive in her question.

'I've learned a great deal. It was very good of Uncle Tobias to pay for my education, and to give me an opportunity to work in his business.'

The comment showed Will in a favourable light, but it didn't answer the question. Madeline couldn't resist pressing him a little further. If anyone had insider knowledge about the immoral practices of the Trident hotel chain, it was Will.

'Do you plan to make your career in the hotel business, working alongside your uncle?'

There was a hint of uncertainty in Will's manner as he searched for an answer. He was definitely hiding something. Madeline had an instinct for these things and could sense discomfort as readily as she could smell a rotting gardenia. She packed the thought away for another time. It was unfair to press him for sensitive information when she'd only just met him, and he was clearly too smart to say anything disparaging about his benefactor to a stranger.

He turned to Hugh, proving his adeptness at changing the subject. 'I'd like to thank you, sir, for the kindness you've shown my sister.'

'I've done nothing in particular,' said Hugh, taken aback by the comment.

'It might not have seemed a lot to you, sir, but Flora told me you lent her your handkerchief when she was in need of it one day. We also appreciate you inviting her to take tea this afternoon. It means a great deal.'

Such gratitude for these small acts made Madeline's heart give. How cruelly was Flora treated by the Booths that the offer of a handkerchief or an invitation to tea should mean so much to her?

'It was Maddie's idea to have you over to tea,' said Hugh, his eyes softening as he turned them on Flora. 'Although, I'm very glad she thought of it.'

Despite Will's polite words, Madeline still sensed an enduring coolness on Flora's part towards Hugh. She'd made no secret of the fact that she thought him careless when it came to breaking women's hearts. Even today, her disdain was written in her expression, in the way she turned from him every time he tried to catch her eye.

It wasn't a bad thing. Hugh needed to learn that not every woman would be taken in by his charm. He might not have meant any harm where Marianne was concerned, but he was too full of high spirits for his own good. It pleased Madeline that Flora, who was so unlike the privileged women in his usual social circle, was too wise to be flattered by him.

If he wasn't to make the same mistakes as their father, Hugh needed to learn that he would always be judged by how people perceived his actions, no matter what the intentions behind them. It seemed Flora might be the one to teach him that lesson where others had failed.

Despite their paths crossing, they lived in different worlds. Madeline only had to look at Flora to see the dissimilarity in their circumstances. The dress she wore was made of rough cotton, made rougher from having been laundered so many times, no doubt by Flora herself. Her shoes, although highly polished, were well worn, and her gloves, for all they were spotless, showed signs of stitching where they'd been repeatedly repaired over time.

Most good families wouldn't even allow a lady's maid to be dressed so poorly, let alone a first cousin. Madeline was tempted to offer some of her clothes from last season, most of which had hardly been worn, but feared the suggestion might embarrass her. Still, Flora was a heart-rending sight, made worse by her determination to regularly express her gratitude for her circumstances. Whichever way Madeline turned the conversation, Flora was always quick to emphasise how lucky she was to have been taken in by the Booths.

As they moved on to their second plate of cakes, Madeline learned that the rest of Flora and Will's family were still living in a small town in Wisconsin. It was only the two eldest siblings that Tobias Booth had seen fit to rescue from their poor upbringing. The younger children remained with their mother, Mrs Booth's sister, and their drunken father. Their father's failings weren't described in so many words, but it didn't take much for Madeline to piece together the facts from Will's general comments and Flora's evasions. Both brother and sister were highly conscious of being charity cases and were too grateful to say anything against their benefactors.

After tea, Madeline suggested the four of them take a walk along the cliffs to blow away the cobwebs of the afternoon. The more time she spent outdoors, the more she seemed to crave the ocean air. It gave her a sense of freedom she could never feel in the gloomy confines of the house. In the great outside, there was no society to judge, no artificial standards to live up to and no hard stares from Finch. For a few precious minutes, Madeline could be herself, whoever that self might be.

This wasn't the only reason she suggested a walk. If she was to have any chance of finding out what Will really thought about the Trident hotel business, she had to get him into a more relaxed environment. He would never let his guard down otherwise.

She took his arm as they strode up the cliff path, obliging Flora to walk a few steps behind with Hugh. Will's eyes were everywhere, taking in the big sky and the crashing waves below.

'This is spectacular. I never knew there could be such wildness, such freedom. Who knew the ocean was so big. It's as if it goes on forever.'

'Perhaps you should have been a sailor,' said Madeline. 'It's not too late to join the Navy.'

'It's a tempting idea, but I intend to find a new position in New York. I don't want to be too far from Flora.'

'You're looking for a new position?'

'I don't mean to sound ungrateful when Uncle Tobias has done so much for us, but I want to earn my living in a way I can be proud of.'

He stopped what he was saying, as if he realised he'd strayed into territory he knew better than to breach.

'The hotel business isn't to your liking?' asked Madeline, encouraging him to continue.

'It's not what I expected. I hope to find something that suits me better.'

He didn't have to say any more. She suspected he knew about the brothels and it would have been unfair of Madeline to press him further on the subject. His evasiveness had told her all she needed to know.

The silence was broken by a sudden burst of laughter from Flora. Madeline turned to where she and Hugh were following behind. Flora's eyes were shining, her face unrecognisable with joy. She blushed when she realised all eyes were on her.

'Are you going to share the joke, Hugh,' asked Madeline, 'or is it too silly to make any sense to the rest of us?'

Hugh gave Flora a conspiratorial look. 'Shall we share it, Miss Pierce, or shall we leave my sister and your brother in their misery?'

'I think we should keep it to ourselves,' said Flora.

'Let me guess,' said Madeline. 'The joke was so ridiculous that you only laughed to be polite, and now you're too embarrassed to admit your overreaction in case we think you're as silly as Hugh.'

Flora laughed all the more at Madeline's explanation. 'That's exactly it.'

'Go ahead and make me look a fool,' said Hugh, joining in the joke at his own expense. 'I'd rather have you laughing at me than with me.' He frowned, full of mock seriousness. 'Isn't that how the saying goes?'

His comment made Flora laugh even harder. It delighted Madeline to see how much more confident she appeared in Will's company, how easily she laughed and was prepared to share in a joke. She even seemed prepared to humour Hugh, seeing his silliness for what it was. One glimpse of the real Flora and Madeline liked her so much more than her cousins. This was the friend she was in need of. Flora's easy-going kindness was the company she craved.

They were ruddy cheeked and windswept after their cliff-top walk, but it didn't matter. Their dishevelment was all part of the fun of the afternoon. Madeline felt more relaxed than she had in any company since her father had brought her out into society.

Back at the house, Sara served hot chocolate and shortbread to fortify them. It only took a minute for Hugh to spill the chocolate on his cuff. Flora handed him a napkin, alerting him to the offending spot before Madeline could tease him over it.

Hugh took the napkin gratefully. 'Thank you for not scolding me for my messiness the way my sister would.'

'I wouldn't dream of it,' said Flora, her face suddenly solemn. 'If anything, I should be asking for your forgiveness.'

'Admit it, it was you who splashed my cuff with the offending chocolate when I wasn't looking,' said Hugh, trying to make light of Flora's sudden seriousness, which suddenly changed the tone of what had so far been an agreeable afternoon.

'I won't plead guilty to that,' said Flora. 'But I am guilty of misjudging you.'

There was a beat of silence while Flora took a deep breath, summoning the courage to continue. 'It wasn't your fault Marianne had second thoughts about her wedding. Before she left for New York, she admitted she'd tried to use you to get out of marrying Rawdon. It was wrong of her to do such a thing. She behaved badly towards both you and Rawdon, and I should never have taken her side.'

There was an awkward silence while the enormity of Flora's confession sank in. Hugh was too gracious to admit that he'd suspected as much, even though Madeline knew he'd believed it to be the case. There was nothing to be gained by saying it. Flora was looking uncomfortable enough as it was.

'I don't think we should put all the blame on Marianne,' said Madeline. 'After all, if Hugh hadn't been so charming, it wouldn't have put the idea into her head.'

Hugh bowed to his sister's comment. 'From now on, I promise to bore everyone I meet. I shall restrict my conversation to dogs and horses.'

Flora almost jumped out of her seat. 'Oh no, I didn't mean—'

'He's teasing you,' said Madeline, relieved to see Flora's face change as she began to see the comment for what it was. Finally, she was beginning to understand Hugh, which meant they could all enjoy each other's company without the risk of Flora falling prey to his charm. With a new friendship in the making, the long summer ahead didn't seem such a lonely prospect after all.

Chapter 20

Perhaps it was because his two daughters were no longer there to torment him that Tobias Booth began to pay more attention to Flora. Or it might have been the questions that had been raised about her status during the course of Marianne's wedding festivities that set him thinking. Madeleine couldn't have been the only one to ask, *is she out or not out*, now her cousins were no longer there to put her in the shade. It might even have been Will's gentle hints that prompted it, but whatever it was, Madeline was delighted to receive an invitation to Flora's coming-out ball, which was to be held at Mountview.

'It'll be a small affair,' insisted Flora, trying to find ways to play it down. It was the third time in a week that Flora and Will had dropped in to Beachlands for tea. 'It's as much an honour for Will as it is for me. A celebration while he's here on an extended holiday with us.'

Even the celebration was tinged with sadness as Flora failed to hide how much she would miss her brother when he returned to his job in New York. His presence had encouraged her to be herself. Once he was gone, Mrs Booth, with all her lazy, selfish ways, would demand more of her time and Flora would once again lose any sense of self.

'I have just the thing for you to wear,' said Madeline.

Refusing to hear any excuses, she took Flora upstairs to her dressing room, where earlier that day, Finch had helped her select something suitable from Madeline's wardrobe.

She showed Flora the amber silk dress, which had been laid out on the bed in preparation for her arrival. 'The colour is just right for you, don't you think?'

The quality of the silk shone through the simple design, the puff sleeves and discreet lace cuffs the only ornament. Flora was bound to reject anything too fussy, and as far as Madeline was concerned, its quiet elegance was perfectly suited to Flora's understated dignity. There was no show about it, just as there was no show about Flora.

'I bought it in Paris last year but have never worn it. I never felt the colour was right for me.' Madeline hesitated, not wanting to offend or patronise, desperately wanting Flora to be pleased with the dress, to feel able to accept it in the spirit it was meant. The gift had originally been Hugh's idea, but Madeline didn't want to risk embarrassing or compromising Flora by mentioning it. The thing that mattered most was that she had something beautiful to wear on the occasion of her coming-out ball.

'Will you accept it as a coming-out gift?'

Flora stared at the dress, her eyes running over every inch of the amber silk, the clench of her fists hinting at how desperate she was to own it. 'It's very kind of you, Miss Crosby, but I couldn't possibly accept it. It's far too good for me.'

There it was, the sense of inferiority that Madeline recognised so well. How many times had she had the same thought whenever she'd considered a beautiful dress or trinket for herself? How many times had she felt the same shame at not being good enough? It had to stop. And one way of making it stop was by being kind to others, to help them recognise their own worth.

'I think it's exactly right for you, Flora. Sara will make any alterations that are necessary, although I suspect little will be needed. It could have been made for you.' She watched as the tears clouded Flora's eyes, not tears of gratitude, but something more complex and less discernible.

'Please say you'll accept it. If you don't estimate yourself highly enough to wear a lovely dress, you can't expect others to hold you in esteem. Respect starts with the self.'

Again, how many times had Madeline told herself this? How many times had she tried to convince herself she was more than just the daughter of a prostitute, more than just an illegitimate child? How hard it was to believe you were worth something when society insisted otherwise.

She picked up the dress and held it against Flora's body, encouraging her to touch it, to be seduced by the liquid feel of the silk. 'There are shoes to match and a cashmere shawl for when the evening gets chilly.'

Slowly, Flora's hand reached for the silk, her fingers trailing the delicate folds and pin tucks of the dress. 'It is very fine indeed.'

'Then please don't let it go to waste.'

Flora made a gesture that could have been a nod or a shake of the head, as if part of her soul was accepting the gift, while the other part refused it. 'How can I ever thank you?'

'By taking pleasure in wearing it,' said Madeline. 'By being happy in it and accepting that you're beautiful.'

The smile that slowly spread across Flora's face was all Madeline needed to reassure herself the gesture had been the right one, that her generosity had been taken in the spirit it was meant. It was time for Flora to shine and Madeline would be the one to help her do it.

Chapter 21

On the day of the ball, Edward sent Madeline a posy of pink roses from the garden. He must have heard how touched she'd been by the bouquet Flora had picked for her and wanted to similarly please her. Madeline stared at the flowers, wondering if he meant her to wear them to the ball, the memory of Ginger thrusting his limp gardenia at her in the opera house flashing through her mind.

If she didn't pin at least one rose in her hair or to her dress, Edward would be offended, and if she did, he would see it as encouragement. Neither of which was an outcome she intended. In the end, her aversion to wearing slowly wilting flowers won the day, and the posy remained intact at home, just as it had been delivered.

Not wanting to outshine Flora, Madeline wore a simple dress of oyster-grey chiffon. She had nothing to prove and every reason not to draw attention to herself. This was Flora's evening, and Madeline's enjoyment would come from observing her happiness.

Edward greeted her and Hugh as soon as they arrived. 'Miss Crosby, I'm here to claim the first dance, and the one after that, if you'll indulge me.'

She'd been prepared for his advance and had already decided

on her answer. 'You must forgive me, Mr Booth, but I won't be dancing this evening. You must oblige the other ladies with your requests.'

His face fell, his eyes searching for a sign of the roses he'd sent her. 'I'd hoped you'd do me the honour of wearing my flowers.'

'It was kind of you to send them, but I have an aversion to displaying wilting flowers on my person. It's cruel to make them suffer. You wouldn't leave a fish out of water to flounder. I feel the same about flowers and refuse to inflict a slow, painful death on them just to indulge my vanity. You'll be glad to know they're sitting very comfortably in water at home where they can drink to their hearts' content.'

She didn't confess how delighted she'd been with the flowers, or that she'd placed them in a crystal vase on her bedside table, so they'd be the last thing she saw at night and the first thing her eyes fell upon in the morning. Her better judgement had told her to give them to Sara to enjoy, but when it came to it, Madeline hadn't had the heart to part with them.

Edward's jaw gaped as if he didn't know what to make of her reasoning, whether she was teasing him by comparing the cut flowers to dying fish, or truly mad enough to care for the well-being of a simple rose. 'I didn't realise you were so tender-hearted.'

'Only when it comes to flowers. I can be quite brutal when it comes to anything else, apart from dogs, cats and horses. I'm very fond of those.'

She hoped her cruel wit would make him turn away from her, but if anything, it only drew him closer. He was determined to understand her; that was the problem. Instead of alienating him, her strangeness was only serving to fascinate him.

He held out his hand. 'You won't refuse me one dance, at least.'

Of course she wanted to dance with him. She wanted it more than anything, but it was wrong to give in to a man with such divided principles, and there was no saying where it would end. Whenever she was tempted by him, she thought of her mother, dying in a back room of one of the Trident hotels, her future having been taken away from her long before her life ended. While Edward denied the exploitation of women in his family business, Madeline couldn't respect him, and she certainly couldn't dance with him.

He gave her a desperate look. 'We were getting along so well. Now, I'm losing you and I don't know what I've done.'

Hugh, who had watched the whole exchange, suddenly piped up. 'For pity's sake, Maddie, don't make the poor man beg. One dance won't kill you.'

She gave Hugh a disparaging look, but before she could protest, Edward was leading her onto the dance floor. She felt herself tense as her heart pulled instinctively towards him. She couldn't let it happen. Under no circumstances could she allow herself to fall in love with him. 'I warn you, Mr Booth. This is the very last time I'll dance with you.'

He looked at her as if it was another one of her cruel jokes. 'You don't mean it.' He led her around the floor, his hand hardly cupping hers, as if to hold it too tightly would break it. 'I had hopes . . . I thought perhaps we might spend more time in one another's company, to get to know each other better, to find out if we might have a future together.'

It was a bold statement, and she knew what courage it must have taken to say it. It had been a mistake to have let things go so far. She pulled away from him and moved to the edge of the dance floor, slipping out of the ballroom quietly so as not to draw attention to herself. It was too hot, and in the midst of so many people, the air was too oppressive to think clearly.

She hadn't realised Edward had followed her until she heard his voice, gentle to the point of pleading.

'Miss Crosby, I—'

'Don't say anything else. I wouldn't want to disappoint you.' Unable to look at him, she had refused to turn around, instead she'd spoken the words over her shoulder.

'Tell me what I've done to offend you so I can put it right.'

His voice was almost desperate as he traced her steps into the garden. The moon was already high and there was a cool wind blowing off the ocean. Seeing Madeline shiver in her thin chiffon dress, he took off his coat and put it around her shoulders.

The gesture felt kind and yet too intimate. The comfort of his residual body heat, the smell of his pomade was too intense. This wasn't how it should be. She couldn't allow him to get this close.

'You can't expect me to allow you to court me when you're guilty of such double standards.' She blurted out the words without giving herself time to consider them. She hadn't planned to raise the issue in such a careless manner, but he'd pushed her too far and now it was done.

'I've only ever tried to do the very best in my legal work. I might not always have got it right, but . . . tell me, Miss Crosby, tell me what I've done that offends you so badly.'

'It's nothing to do with your legal work. I know about the business behind the Trident hotel chain. I know what you're covering up. It's been going on for decades.'

He looked at her as if she hadn't spoken sense. 'I don't know what you mean.'

'There's no point trying to hide it. Your legal work won't make up for the exploitation that goes on behind the closed doors of your family's business.'

'I've been assured that my father's employees are treated well and given a fair day's pay for a fair day's work. There's no exploitation of workers in the hotels. I've already made this clear to you.'

'I'm not talking about the hotels. I'm talking about the brothels. The dedicated back rooms that are a fixture in every one of the Trident establishments, where women are rented out by the hour as if they were just another service, along with breakfast and shoe cleaning and the provision of the morning newspaper. These women are workers in your family hotels just the same as the doormen and the chambermaids.'

Edward lowered himself onto a nearby bench as the reality of what Madeline was saying sank in. 'You're mistaken. Whoever told you this is lying. They're trying to damage our business. Father has made a number of enemies over the years. Someone is spreading these rumours to ruin him. You mustn't believe them.'

With his face hidden in his hands, and only the moonlight to judge him by, it was impossible to tell if he really believed what he was saying.

'How can you be so sure?'

'Because it's unthinkable. My father would never allow such a thing.'

'Do you know that for a fact?'

'It's unimaginable.'

'Just because you can't imagine it, Mr Booth, it doesn't mean it doesn't exist. Is it true you have no hand in the running of the business?'

'I swear to you. You're familiar with my legal work. You know the values I stand for.'

'You can't *not* know such things go on,' said Madeline, fighting to keep her voice steady. 'It strikes me you've chosen not to know.'

He shook his head, confused by what he was hearing. 'I can't believe it.'

'I think it's more that you *won't* believe it. Look at the luxury you live in, the advantages your wealth has given you. Have you ever, just for one minute, stopped to question where it comes from, what the cost of it might be to others?'

He stood up from the bench and began pacing back and forth, his face paler than the moon. He cast his eyes up to the sky, as if he were searching for answers among the stars. 'I won't question how you claim to know such things about my family's business, but if they are true, you put me to shame.' He lowered his eyes to the ground, his mind lost in deep thought, the silence remaining a cavern between them, until without so much as a goodnight, he made his way back to the house.

He'd left without taking his coat, but she wouldn't go after him. She slipped it from her shoulders and placed it on the bench where he'd sat. If he didn't come back to retrieve it, one of the maids would find it in the morning and think nothing of it, putting its abandonment down to high spirits or drunken carelessness. They would never guess it was due to disillusionment and heartbreak.

She took a few minutes to compose herself before returning to the house, where she lingered at the edge of the ballroom, watching the couples dance, listening to the laughter as it carried across the floor.

It pleased her to see Flora looking so well, outshining everyone in the amber silk dress. Hugh had engaged her for half a dozen dances, and all eyes were on her as she moved around the room in his arms.

Madeline only realised Will was standing beside her when he spoke. 'Thank you for taking Flora under your wing. I've never seen her looking so happy.'

'She's enjoying having you to visit. She'll miss you when you've gone.'

His face clouded over at the mention of his departure. 'I don't mind admitting how much I dread returning to my job in New York. I'm grateful for the experience I've gained working for my uncle, but I count the days until I can find new employment.'

His words were said with such feeling that Madeline didn't need to question the motivation behind them. He knew about the brothels and he was no longer prepared to be tarnished by his association with them.

Madeline saw no more of Edward that evening, but still she couldn't stop thinking of their exchange. It was hard to understand how a man of such outward integrity could lie about the nature of his family's business. It didn't seem possible that he didn't know. If a man like him could lie with such conviction, then no man could be trusted.

She didn't have the opportunity to speak to Hugh until they were in the carriage on their way home.

'What a pleasant evening,' he said, his eyes alive from too much champagne. 'Not too many guests and not too few.'

Madeline agreed. She wasn't ready to discuss what had passed between her and Edward. She needed time to think about it, to work out what she really felt. At the moment all she could feel was the dull ache of disappointment. All she wanted was to sleep and to wake up refreshed, with a clearer head and a clearer view on Edward.

'I have to say,' continued Hugh, filling Madeline's silence, 'Flora was the most charming company this evening. Now she's out of the shade of her cousins, she's truly come into her own. She really is the sweetest creature.'

'Don't be swayed by the fact that she laughed at your jokes, or indulged you with too many dances,' said Madeline. 'She was the hostess. It was her job to make you feel welcome.'

'She certainly did that. You've been a good influence on her, Maddie. It won't be long before an eligible young man steps in and sweeps her off her feet.'

There was something in her brother's tone that set alarm bells ringing in Madeline's head. 'You've caused enough trouble in that family, Hugh, whether you meant to or not. Please don't pay Flora too much attention, even if you only mean to be friendly. She doesn't deserve to have her heart broken.'

'Consider this, Maddie. Women aren't the only ones with hearts. A gentleman can feel things too, you know.'

'Not you, Hugh. You've hardened yourself against love. You've told me this a hundred times.'

Hugh clenched his fist against his mouth, preventing whatever reply he was tempted to make from escaping.

'Did you hear what I said?' she asked.

'Of course. I wouldn't dream of breaking Flora's heart. She's the gentlest creature, yet so solid and reliable. She'd be the easiest woman in the world to love.'

'Don't forget, after the example set by our father and uncle, you swore never to marry.'

Hugh nodded. Most of the Crosby men were brutes where women were concerned and he feared turning into one of them. Remaining a bachelor was the only way to avoid the kind of unhappiness their father had inflicted on his mother.

'And don't even think of making her your mistress,' added Madeline. 'She doesn't deserve it.'

'I wouldn't dream of such a thing, even if she'd have me.' Hugh was quiet for a minute. 'It doesn't mean we can't be friends. We all need friends from time to time.'

Madeline knew exactly what he meant. Flora was turning into a true and trusted friend, taking the edge off her loneliness and insecurity. Her kindness was proving a balm for the impossible situation Madeline found herself in with Edward, for the love he offered that despite her heart's calling, she found impossible to accept.

Chapter 22

Despite the need for sleep, Madeline lay awake for most of the night, listening to the waves crashing against the shore, relentless as her beating heart, her mind confused by the way Edward had reacted to the mention of the brothels. Surely, it couldn't be true that he didn't know of their existence.

She joined Hugh for breakfast, blaming her swollen eyes and pale skin on having drunk too much champagne the night before, although barely a drop had touched her lips. Hugh served her a plate of scrambled eggs dripping in butter, just the way she liked them, with a little bacon on the side.

'This will fortify you.' Considering he'd drunk so much the night before, Hugh was as fresh-faced as ever. He glugged the last dregs of his coffee and pushed an envelope across the table. 'This arrived just before you came down for breakfast.'

She frowned, not recognising the handwriting. It slanted elegantly across the paper, the sender having used the finest of nibs such as an artist would choose. The only letters she was used to receiving were from society ladies, reminding her to know her place. She waited until Hugh was distracted, pouring them both coffee, before opening it.

My dearest Madeline,

Forgive me the impertinence of calling you dearest, but it's what you are to me. However cruelly you try to dismiss me, I love you and I always will.

Edward

She put aside the letter and picked up her fork, but the eggs, which were usually so delicious, were like rubber in her mouth, the bacon, hard and bitter. His words were beyond the impertinence he spoke of, and yet she read the truth in them, the anguish. How could someone so tender-hearted be associated with such criminal exploitation? And how much longer would he continue to deny it?

Hugh looked up, his eyes full of curiosity. 'Is there anything interesting in your letter?'

Madeline shook her head, burying the note in the pocket of her dress. 'Nothing. Nothing at all.'

She knew Hugh didn't believe her, but she wasn't ready to talk about it. However sympathetic he was, he could never truly understand where she'd come from, how it had felt to watch her mother die in a brothel, how it affected her view of the world, her view of herself.

'I hope you'll be well enough to come out with us this afternoon.'

Hugh had arranged to go horse riding with Will and Flora. This was the first Madeline had heard of it. It had been agreed the night before while Madeline was in the garden with Edward, *taking the air*, as Hugh called it, with a teasing grin.

'I offered Flora the use of Brodie. She claims not to be a very confident rider and the ageing mare will suit her perfectly.'

'And how about Will? What will he ride?'

'Theo has offered him the use of his horse. It should be fun. You'll come, won't you?'

'Of course. Someone has to make sure you don't pay too much

attention to Flora. She doesn't deserve to have your charm inflicted on her.'

'You mustn't worry, Maddie. Flora's far too sensible to be taken in by all that.'

'There's nothing more attractive to a woman than an unattainable man,' said Madeline, feeling the truth of the words as she said them. It was no good. She had to stop thinking of Edward.

'Most women will do anything to get my attention when they discover my net worth,' said Hugh, crunching a piece of toast, 'but she's the opposite. There's no vanity about her, only sweet temper and goodness. I can't get over how she shone at the ball, and it was all thanks to you, Maddie. Having you as a friend has given her so much confidence.'

Madeline brushed off his comment. She wanted to believe it was the time Flora was spending with Will that was making her happy, and that it was nothing to do with the attention Hugh was lavishing on her. For all Madeline's warnings and his good intentions, he seemed to have no idea what he was doing.

Flora and Will arrived promptly at the stables where Brodie had already been saddled, ready for Flora. She let out a nervous sound as Hugh helped her mount.

'You're sure she won't make any sudden movements?' she asked, gripping the reins as if they were about to be ripped from her hands at any minute.

'Only if you ask her to,' answered Hugh, grinning up at her. 'Otherwise, she's as meek as a lamb.'

'I'll ride alongside you,' said Madeline, throwing a warning glance at her brother. She knew how hard it was to appear comfortable in the saddle if you hadn't been brought up with it. She'd only started riding herself at the age of fifteen, after her father presented her with a horse. Although she made a good pretence of it, she'd never be as natural as those who'd ridden from a much younger age. Just as so many other things in life, Madeline made a show of being more confident than she was and hoped, through a demonstration of bluff, never to be found out.

'Have you been on a horse before?' she asked Flora, as the two of them fell back, allowing Hugh and Will to go ahead at a faster pace.

'Only now and then, whenever Marianne or Jane granted me the use of their horses. My aunt's need of my company leaves me little freedom for leisure or exercise. I'm grateful to her for letting me spend this time with Will.'

'I hope we'll still see each other regularly after he returns to New York,' said Madeline.

Flora's face fell at the mention of Will's departure. 'I doubt it very much. My aunt needs me more than ever now Marianne and Jane are no longer here.' She shifted her weight in the saddle, checking it was secure on Brodie's back. 'Edward sends his good wishes.'

What exactly was Madeline expected to say to that? She'd already made her feelings clear. It was unfair of him to use Flora as a messenger.

'You always speak so highly of him.'

'Edward's a good man. He was the only one of the Booths to make me feel welcome when I arrived in the family as a displaced ten-year-old, the only one ever to listen to me or give me the time of day.'

'Do you know anything about the Booth family business?'

'It's never talked of.'

Flora had no idea about the brothels or that her life was funded by the exploitation of fallen women. 'Your loyalty to the Booths does you credit.' Madeline nudged her horse, gently encouraging it to break into a trot. 'Come on; let's catch up with our brothers.'

The four of them were high up on the cliff path when they heard a cry in the distance. Hugh stood up in his stirrups to get a better view of the surroundings, trying to identify the source of the noise, whether it was animal or human.

'I think it came from over there,' said Will, pointing to a narrow turning that led to a steep path.

Madeline and Flora followed at a slower pace as the men set off in the direction of the sound. 'Do you think it could be a trapped animal?' asked Flora, clinging to Brodie's reins.

It sounded more like the cry of a child, but Madeline didn't want to alarm her, and there was no saying her assumption was correct. Her early life experiences had taught her to always jump to the worst conclusion. The response was instinctive, even though it was irrational.

By the time they'd caught up with the men, Hugh and Will had dismounted and were standing in a clearing near the edge of a cliff. Will was comforting a young woman who was in some distress, while Hugh stood with his hands on his hips, staring up into an enormous beech tree, its branches blowing fiercely in the wind.

The young woman, dressed soberly in a grey serge dress, sobbed into her handkerchief. 'I told him not to go climbing the tree. What will my mistress say when she finds out, and however will he get down alive?'

'Can you hear me?' Hugh cupped his hands around his mouth and hollered up to the boy who was crouching like an enormous owl on a branch twenty feet above them.

'His name's Julian,' sobbed the governess. 'We were meant to be collecting wildflowers to make a nosegay for his mother. He wasn't supposed to climb the tree.'

At the mention of his name, Julian let out a great wail, the words in between his cries indicating he was stuck and couldn't get down, as if they hadn't already known.

There was only one thing for it. Assessing the tree, Hugh took off his hat and coat and handed them to Flora before beginning his ascent.

'There must be another way to get him down,' cried Madeline. 'You'll break your neck if you fall.'

'We can't just leave him there,' said Hugh, beckoning to Will to give him a leg up.

Will did as he was asked and within a minute Hugh was climbing the tree, pulling himself up from branch to branch.

Flora clung to his hat and coat as if embracing his clothing would keep him safe. 'I can hardly bear to look.'

'Take your time, Hugh,' shouted Madeline. 'And don't look down.' She placed her arm around Julian's governess to calm her. The last thing Hugh needed was the distraction of a sobbing woman.

He was almost there. Exposed on the high cliffs, the branches swayed in the wind. Madeline was dizzy just looking up at them.

Once he was within arm's reach of Julian, Hugh instructed him to take his hand, but the boy was rigid with fear and refused to move. There was nothing for it but for Hugh to climb higher. Madeline winced at the thought of it. The branches above his head were thinner and there was no saying they'd take his weight.

He paused for a minute, working out his path through the canopy of leaves before gradually venturing a few more feet. Once he'd steadied himself, he slowly turned around until he had his back to the boy. Madeline held her breath. Surely, he wasn't foolish enough to do what she thought he was going to do.

Flora rushed over and grabbed Madeline's hand and the three women stood silently in a huddle. Will waited at the base of the tree. Should Hugh's mission fail, he was preparing himself to break the fall of anyone who came tumbling down.

Madeline watched as Hugh took a deep breath and braced himself against the trunk.

'Julian, climb onto my back. Move slowly and try not to jump.'

When Julian didn't move, his governess made encouraging noises. 'Do as the gentleman says, Julian. It's the only way down.'

Eventually, Julian placed first one hand and then the other on Hugh's shoulders, before relinquishing the lower branch with his feet, allowing his body to slide towards Hugh, until he was able to wrap his legs around his waist.

'Hold on tight, young man.'

Madeline heard the strain in Hugh's voice as he struggled under the boy's weight. She watched as he negotiated his way down, inch by inch, branch by branch, with Julian clinging to his back.

The moment he was within reach, Will lifted the boy from Hugh's shoulders and placed him on the ground before helping Hugh clamber down the remaining few feet.

Julian ran to his governess and threw his arms around her waist. 'I'm sorry, I'm sorry.'

Once he was safely on the ground, Flora made a beeline for Hugh, who was shaking Will's hand and thanking him for his help. 'I can't believe you did that,' she blurted, thrusting his hat and coat at him. 'You were so brave, putting yourself in danger to save the child.'

Hugh shrugged off her admiration. 'Anyone would have done the same.' He clapped Will on the shoulder. 'I couldn't have done it without the assistance of your brother.'

The governess had begun crying all over again, this time with relief. 'I don't know how to thank you. I don't know what I'd have done if you hadn't come along.'

Hugh ruffled the boy's hair. 'I suspect he'd have found his own way down eventually. After all, he had the ability to get himself up there.'

The sun was already going down and the afternoon was growing cooler as evening began to set in. The four of them rode back to Beachlands, exhausted from the adventure. Madeline had the horrors every time she pictured Hugh climbing the tree. She'd spotted the grazes on his wrists that he'd taken pains to hide from them, and the small cut on his ear, which he wouldn't notice until he got home.

Still, he was determined to make light of his bravery as he rode alongside Flora, gently guiding the old grey mare and laughing off her comments every time she told him what a hero he was.

'Your bravery surprised me, Mr Crosby. I would never have believed it of you.'

'Don't praise him too much,' said Madeline, trying to make light of the risk he'd taken. 'At this rate, we'll never get his head through the stable door.'

But the warning was lost somewhere on the breeze as the two of them trotted ahead, Hugh lapping up every second of Flora's praise and fawning over her like a puppy who'd been starved of attention.

Alarm bells rang in Madeline's head at the sight of them, but surely there was nothing to worry about. After what had happened with Marianne, Hugh had learned his lesson and was wise enough not to tangle with Flora's heart. And if Hugh couldn't be trusted to be sensible, then Flora must know him well enough by now not to be caught up in his charm.

Chapter 23

Madeline was practising the harp in the drawing room when Finch silently made her presence felt. The housekeeper's expression was as unreadable as Madeline had ever known it.

'There's a Mr Booth to see you.'

Finch rolled her eyes as Edward shouldered his way past her and blustered into the room.

'Please don't turn me away, Miss Crosby. I beg you to let me speak. Five minutes of your time is all I ask.'

Startled by his intrusion, Madeline stepped away from the harp. 'This is most irregular, Mr Booth. What gives you the right to come barging into my home like this?'

'I'm asking for a fair hearing, that's all.'

Finch rubbed her hands together, stirring herself up for a battle and giving every indication she was prepared to manhandle Edward out of the house, if that was required. 'Shall I fetch Mr Crosby? He's in his study answering his letters.'

'No, it's all right,' said Madeline, regaining her composure. 'Thank you, Finch. You can leave us now.'

'Only if you're sure.' Finch threw Edward a warning look. 'I'll be standing outside the door if you need me.'

Once they were alone, Madeline gestured to Edward to take

a seat. 'You've got five minutes, so don't waste it.'

'What I said in my note. I—'

'Is that all you've come to say, because I don't need to be told again.'

'No, it's not about that.' He faltered, staring at his hands as they lay in his lap. 'The issue you raised about my father's business . . .'

'You mean the brothels. Let's state it for what it is.'

He cleared his throat, betraying his nerves. 'Yes . . . that.'

His indirectness was beginning to annoy her. 'You might as well say the word. It won't bite you.'

'Yes, of course. The brothels.' He paused before continuing, as if the very mention of the word had shaken him. 'I didn't want to believe it when you told me about them, but you were so vehement, I confronted my father about their existence. He denied it at first, but after some pressing, he finally admitted that everything you claimed is true. I don't know how you found out about them, but you were better informed than me. It seems it's been going on since the Civil War, long before my father played any part in the business.'

'So, your father simply carried on with them when he took over. He never questioned the ethics of it, let alone the legality.'

'The law turns a blind eye to the practice. The brothels provide a much-needed service for many men and a source of employment for women.'

'You consider it a crime without victims?'

Edward squirmed in his seat. 'It's not for me to judge, but in some cases, yes, I believe it is.'

'But not in all cases?'

'I couldn't say.'

'And you think it's acceptable? You're content that your family's wealth has been built on this exploitation?'

'You should consider, Miss Crosby, that if men have an outlet for their desires among women who are willing to oblige them, then respectable women aren't troubled by their unwanted advances.'

'You think that the women forced into this trade are less respectable than me or your sisters? That they don't deserve the same decency and protection? Have you never considered that it is only circumstances that have put these women in this position, that many of them are reduced to such work because they've been let down by the men in their lives and cast out into a society that offers them no protection?'

He looked at her blankly, as if such ideas were new to him.

'Have you any idea how easy it is for a woman in this society to fall?' she asked. 'The women working in your brothels are no different to me or your sisters. You might want to think upon that.'

'The brothels are not the whole source of our wealth, Miss Crosby. There are also the hotels.'

Madeline let out a gasp. She turned her back on him and stared out of the window, trying to control her rage.

'I'm sorry. That was the wrong thing to say.'

'Not if it's how you feel.'

'This has come as a great shock, Miss Crosby. I'm still trying to come to terms with it. I can't understand why my father has allowed it to continue, or how Theo hasn't questioned it.'

'Have you asked your brother about it?'

'Theo is so under the influence of my father, so terrified of him, that he's frightened to express an opinion on anything. That confident, fun-loving young man you've seen is simply an act. The real Theo isn't who you think he is. You wouldn't recognise the real man behind the façade if you met him.'

'Then perhaps it's time for you to start working together to stand up to your father. The two of you are the future of the company. The family legacy is in your hands.'

Edward nodded. 'I've already expressed my displeasure at the situation and asked for it to be brought to an end, but as I have no role in the company, I have no power to compel him. As I said, Theo is too scared to stand up to him.'

'But you're both happy to live off the revenue it generates.'

'I take no money from the family business. I can't stress that strongly enough.'

'You've benefited from the wealth it provides for your family all your life, the home you grew up in, the education you've been given, the position it offers you in society.'

'I've never been complicit in this, Miss Crosby, and I'm as appalled by it as you are. Every advantage I've been given I now use to help improve the lives of those less fortunate than myself.'

His hand shook as he rubbed it across his face. 'I understand your disgust of my family and how they made their wealth. Scratch below the surface of any rich man and you'll find secrets they would rather remain hidden. In many cases, you'll even discover an element of shame. Why else would so many give as much as they do to charity, offering up their art collections to the public, or building opera houses and schools, hospitals and orphanages, if not to make amends for their misdemeanours and exploitation. I appreciate your rage, Miss Crosby, but I don't understand why you're taking this particular issue so personally.'

What difference would it make now if she told him the truth? Anything that could possibly have been between them was ruined. There was such bitterness in his tone, such recrimination, that the love he'd professed to feel for her must have been destroyed.

He must hate her now for having exposed the dirty family secret he'd known nothing about. She'd given him a burden he never knew existed, and now he had to live with it. She might as well tell him the rest of it and answer the questions still rumbling in his mind.

'You ask how I knew about the brothels and their connection to the Trident hotels. You wonder why I'm so enraged by it, why I take the exploitation of these women so personally.'

'You're a woman of social conscience.'

'It goes deeper than that. I was born in one of your family's brothels, Mr Booth. I was forced to watch my mother die in a back room of one of the Trident hotels when I was seven years old.'

Edward gaped at her words as they slowly sank in. 'I don't understand. How—'

'My mother was Mr Crosby's mistress, not his wife. After my mother's death, he arranged for me to be cared for and educated. His wife died when I was twelve years old. It was only then that he officially acknowledged me as his daughter and brought me to live with him and my half-brother, Hugh.'

'I had no idea.'

'It's the reason we left New York. The closed, upper-class society to which the Crosby family belongs refuses to acknowledge me. It's all credit to Hugh that he stands by me and treats me as if I were his true sister, rather than the illegitimate waif of his father's mistress.'

'That's no way to describe yourself, Miss Crosby.'

'To many that's who I am. It's something I've come to terms with. I don't crave the acceptance or the respect of those who look down on me because of the circumstances of my birth. Instead, I use the wealth I inherited from my father to help improve the lives of the women who, like my mother before them, are reduced to selling themselves to feed their children.'

'I now understand why you're so angry with my family.'

'It was Hugh's idea that I cultivate your friendship with the intention of gaining some influence over you. He thought if you came to regard me, you'd act on my wish to see the brothels closed. I wasn't convinced it would work. Now I see it was naive to even consider it.'

'I see.' Edward's shoulders sagged as he stared at the floor. 'Given the circumstances, I was a fool to hope you could ever love me.'

She took a deep breath, steeling herself against his admiration. It would be so easy to give into it and yet it was impossible to even consider it. She pointed to the clock on the mantelshelf, its hands poised to strike the half hour.

'Your five minutes are up, Mr Booth. It's time for you to leave.'

She stared out of the window as he rose from his seat and picked up his gloves. If he had anything else to say in his defence, he chose to keep it to himself, and after one final lingering moment, he bid her good day.

His carriage had only just disappeared through the gate when Finch slipped into the room and joined her contemplation at the window. 'I couldn't help overhearing your conversation.'

'It had to be said.'

'Your mother would have been proud of you.' She took Madeline's hand and gave it a squeeze. 'I'll be downstairs in the kitchen. If you need anything from me, you only have to ask.'

Madeline considered Edward's reaction to learning about the brothels. His state of shock was understandable. She'd forced him to re-evaluate everything his family stood for, and it had rendered him speechless. He'd also proven himself too scared to stand up to his father and too weak to force him to close the brothels. She'd expected more of him than cowardice. At the end of the day, he'd chosen to put family loyalty before doing what was right. She admired his faithfulness but despised where he'd chosen to place it.

Later that evening, she sat with Hugh and told him about the conversation she'd had with Edward, how she was left with no option but to take matters into her own hands.

'If he won't see to it that the brothels are closed, then I will.'

Her brother blew out his cheeks. 'It's all credit to you, Maddie, but are you sure you want to do this?'

Her determination was driven by rage, and her rage made her fearless. 'I've made up my mind. There's no going back on it.'

'There's a good chance your past will be exposed even more publicly than it already has. It'll be used to discredit your character. I'm not only thinking of you, Maddie, but also of your mother's memory.'

It wasn't only her mother's memory that would suffer, but their father's too. Hugh already felt the burden of the way their father had behaved towards women in the past and had been marked by it. If it came to wider public attention, then he would have to carry that burden too.

Still, it was a fact of life that a man's reputation didn't suffer the way a woman's did. Men were seen as rogues, and admired for their sexual conquests, whereas women were simply ruined. They were cast out by even their closest friends and family, as Madeline's mother had learned to her cost, as Finch and so many other women had also learned.

'I'm not saying you shouldn't do it,' said Hugh. 'I'll stand by you, whatever you decide, but give it some thought. Consider all the consequences before you take any action. There's no saying what Tobias Booth might do if you damage the reputation of his business.'

Hugh reminded her that he was leaving for New York the following morning. He had some matters to attend to but would only be gone a few days.

'You won't do anything rash while I'm away, will you.'

Madeline didn't answer. Her mission was set, and she was determined to see it through. All she had to do was work out the best means of achieving it without causing more damage than was necessary.

Chapter 24

Madeline heard nothing from Edward during the following days. Her handling of their last meeting had been so brutal that she had no expectation of hearing from him ever again. It had been unfair to inflict her anger on him when he wasn't personally responsible for the brothels. He happened to be the wrong person in the wrong place and had been made to suffer the unleashing of Madeline's pent-up rage and grief.

She couldn't expect him to view things the same way she did when they had such different life experiences. He was probably still in shock and needed time to digest the revelations. Despite all the excuses she made for him, his response had disappointed her.

Hugh returned three days later, full of good spirits and refreshed from his time in New York. Madeline couldn't feel envious of the fact that he'd been to the opera without her after their last disastrous visit. Her presence beside him would only have drawn the wrong kind of attention and spoiled his enjoyment of the evening.

Living so close to the ocean, the city now seemed a million miles away. The rhythm of the waves and the turning of the tide supplied a different kind of background music to her life and was a world apart from the bustling streets of New York. It was only now, as she forced herself to consider the change, that she discovered she didn't miss the city at all. Beachlands, she realised, was beginning to feel like home.

'How is Uncle Morris and Letty?' asked Madeline. 'I hope he's treating her well.'

'Letty's no longer there,' said Hugh. 'Uncle Morris paid for her passage to Ireland, so she could visit her family. After she'd left, Bessie let slip that she'd received a marriage proposal from her childhood sweetheart, which she'd accepted. There's no chance of her returning to New York. Uncle Morris is pining for her like a lost puppy.'

So, the tide had turned and Uncle Morris finally knew how it felt to be exploited. She didn't wish heartbreak on anyone, but it was time he learned his lesson. If Letty was back with her family, where she was loved and respected, and had made a good marriage, then as far as Madeline was concerned, all had ended well for her.

The following afternoon, Flora and Will joined them for a ride across the cliff tops. Flora had confessed to growing quite fond of Brodie and was determined to become a more confident horsewoman. The fresh air and exercise were doing her good. She'd gained weight and there was a bloom to her cheeks that hadn't been there before. Will's visit had brought happiness with it and although she was still withdrawn in comparison to her cousins, there was a growing self-possession about her that Madeline found enchanting. Flora's coming-out ball had not only brought her out into society, but it had also brought her out of herself. If Madeline hadn't known better, she'd have suspected her of being in love.

After the way things had been left with Edward, Madeline was surprised Flora wanted to go out riding with her. She assumed that if sides were to be taken in an argument, then the ever-loyal Flora would side with her cousin. It quickly became apparent from her easy manner that she knew nothing of the disagreement between her and Edward, which suggested she also knew nothing about the brothels. Madeline wouldn't cause upset by raising the issue. The exploitation was, after all, none of Flora's doing. If Edward wanted her to know about it, then he would tell her himself.

It had been Hugh's idea to take a picnic. He'd gone to the trouble of organising it himself, directing Sara on the selection of cold meats and cheeses they required, the fruits that were to follow, and the fine wine that would complement everything. He'd even chosen a sheltered spot, an hour's gentle ride from Beachlands, where they could lay out the picnic blanket beneath an overarching tree, its canopy protecting them from the ocean breeze and the direct heat of the sun.

Flora looked at the feast with wonder as Hugh made a performance of laying it out. 'You've thought of everything, Mr Crosby. This is far too much.'

'It's the everyday wine glasses, I'm afraid,' said Hugh, holding one up to the sun to check for smears. 'I didn't want to risk carrying the best crystal.'

Everything had been neatly arranged into two large picnic hampers, which had been strapped like panniers to his horse. Despite the precariousness of the journey, everything, even the soft-boiled quails' eggs, had survived the ride intact.

'Anyone would think we had something to celebrate,' said Madeline, surveying Hugh's largesse with suspicion. It was unusual for him to pay so much attention to domestic details. As much as he loved good food, he always left the planning and execution of it to Finch.

Hugh poured a glass of wine and thrust it into Madeline's hand. 'It's funny you should say that, Maddie.' He glanced at Flora and Will, making sure their glasses were full, and cleared his throat.

Madeline sipped her wine which was slightly warm and all the more delicious for it. 'You're not going to make a speech, are you?'

'I am if you'll let me get a word in.' Hugh looked away from his sister's grinning face and turned to Will, who was already tucking into the French cheese.

'While I was in New York, I had dinner with John Edgerton, an old school friend, who's now something big in the Utility bank. I mentioned you were looking for a new position, and that you were a smart, hardworking young man.' Hugh dug in his pocket. 'This is his card. There's a position for you at his bank should you wish to take it. The salary is guaranteed to be fifty per cent higher than what you're earning now. If you prove yourself, it'll steadily increase year by year.'

Will wiped the crumbs from his hands and took the card, staring at it in disbelief. 'But Mr Edgerton hasn't even met me. How could he offer me a job?'

'My recommendation was enough. I know you won't let me down.'

'I'm lost for words . . .'

'You mentioned the hotel business wasn't to your liking,' said Hugh. 'This is an opportunity for you to try something different and it'll be more rewarding financially. The problem with working in a family business is that you can often be taken advantage of. Here, you'll be recognised for your true worth.'

'You've been so kind, Mr Crosby,' said Flora, fighting back tears. 'I don't know how to thank you.'

'You can thank me by calling me Hugh and by agreeing to be my wife.'

The words came out so flippantly they sounded like a joke. Madeline laughed, trying to disguise her annoyance. His flirting had gone too far this time. 'Don't say such things to Flora. It's not funny.'

Oblivious to his sister's warning, Hugh gave Flora an intent look. 'I'm deadly serious. I want you to be my wife.'

The three of them froze as the meaning of Hugh's words sank in. Flora's jaw worked up and down three or four times before any sound came out.

'I'm . . . I'm sorry, Mr Crosby, I don't understand what you're saying.'

'Marry me, Flora.'

Madeline slammed her glass down on an uneven piece of ground, where it inevitably tipped over. 'This has gone beyond a joke, Hugh.'

'It's not a joke, Maddie. I'm asking Flora to marry me. I'm sorry if I made a hash of it, but there it is.' He clambered to his feet and brushed the dirt from his trousers. 'Perhaps I didn't make myself clear enough. I love you, Miss Flora Pierce, and I would like you to be my wife.' He sniffed, running his fingers through his hair. 'There, I've said it again. This time I hope you'll take me seriously.'

Flora stared at the ground. 'This is all very sudden.'

'It might appear that way, Miss Pierce . . . Flora, but I can assure you, it isn't. I've given it a great deal of thought.'

'But you've given no indication of it to any of us,' said Madeline, 'least of all to Flora, judging by the look of horror on her face. Did you not think to approach the subject in a more subtle way, or at least try courting her first? You've knocked Flora out of her senses.'

Flora got to her feet and backed away from the group. 'Please don't talk about me as if I'm not here.'

Hugh shouted after her, spilling his wine as he waved his arms. 'Will you marry me or not?'

'No, I won't marry you, Mr Crosby, and I beg you to stop asking me. It's all too . . .'

Her words tailed off as she broke into a run, the ribbons of her bonnet trailing in the wind as she gathered speed.

'Flora, where are you going?' Madeline tried to follow, but Flora gestured at her to stay away.

'Please, leave me alone, Miss Crosby. I need a moment to myself.'

All this while, Will had remained silent, watching the drama unfold in front of him. 'You've paid my sister a great honour, sir. You must forgive her surprise.'

'Do you think I should go after her?' asked Hugh, the

determination already gone from his eyes. Now he simply looked bewildered. He usually got his own way, especially where women were concerned, and he wasn't used to being disappointed.

'I'd leave her alone for now,' said Madeline. 'She's had a shock.'

Already, Flora had mounted Brodie and was heading along the cliff-top path at a greater pace than any of them had ever seen her ride.

Will climbed to his feet, his eyes fixed on his sister as she galloped into the distance. 'I'd better follow her, just to make sure she gets home safely. I'll see Brodie is returned to your stables.' He shook Hugh's hand. 'Thank you for the job opportunity, sir. I'm very grateful. I'll make an appointment to see your friend, Mr Edgerton, as soon as I return to New York.'

'It's a genuine offer,' said Hugh, his eyes following Flora's progress in the distance. 'There are no strings attached. The last thing I wanted to do was upset your sister. Please look after her.'

'You can be sure of it. And whatever happens, sir, you've shown us both far more favour than we deserve, and I'll be forever in your debt.'

Madeline waited until Will had ridden off before addressing her brother. 'Whatever were you thinking, proposing to Flora like that? Have you gone out of your mind?'

He turned to her, his eyes as wide as a puppy's. 'I love her, Maddie. It's as simple as that.'

'But to propose marriage out of the blue in front of me and her brother. Did you really expect her to say yes, just like that?'

'It's been on my mind so much lately, it just came out. We've been getting on so well, I didn't think it would come as such a shock to her.'

'Have you given her any hint of your feelings before today, any expectation of a marriage proposal?'

Hugh's eyes roved the landscape while he thought about it. 'Many women have assumed far more after receiving less attention from me.'

'But do you think it was enough for her to understand your intention?'

'I didn't expect her to turn me down flat.'

'Your reputation with women goes before you, Hugh. She'll have hardened her heart to your advances. You've made it quite clear that you have no intention of marrying. What did you expect?'

Hugh buried his head in his hands. 'I've gone about it all wrong, Maddie. How could I have been such a fool?'

She let him wallow in his misery for a minute before placing a consoling hand on his shoulder. 'Why didn't you tell me how you were feeling? We could have discussed it.'

'It was while I was in New York that it struck me. I missed her like you wouldn't believe; her kindness, her simplicity. I couldn't get her out of my mind. The night I went to the opera, I sat alone in the box. All the beautiful society women were there, batting their eyelashes and waving their feather fans at me, but all I could think about was Flora, how much she would have enjoyed it, how proud I would have felt having her sitting beside me.'

'But you hardly know her.'

'She's like no other woman I've ever met, apart from you, Maddie. She wants nothing from me. Her artlessness makes me want to give her everything. She's never been to the theatre. Did you know that? She's never travelled. Imagine the beautiful clothes I could give her, the fine life she could have at my side. She'd never be at anyone's beck and call ever again. Everyone in society would look up to her. The Booths treat her like a maid. She deserves so much better.'

'You're making her sound like one of your charitable causes.'

'It's not charity, Maddie. It's love.'

'You've always said you'd never marry, that the men in our family only make their wives unhappy and you refuse to do the same.'

'I can be different, Maddie. I know I can. I'm confident Flora would bring out the best in me, just as you do.' He turned to the picnic and poured himself another glass of wine. 'You wouldn't mind if I married Flora, would you? You've nothing against her.'

'If anyone could make you a good wife, then she could.'

He nodded at her comment. 'I can see all three of us living happily together at Beachlands.'

He seemed to be ignoring the fact that Flora had turned him down. 'Don't get your hopes up, Hugh. She hasn't said yes, and there's no guarantee she'll change her mind.'

'She'll come round when she's had time to think about it. I'll talk to her again tomorrow.'

'You need to give her longer than a day to get over your clumsy proposal.' Madeline picked up her glass from where it had tipped over on the ground, the soil displaying a dark patch where the wine had spilled. 'Tread carefully and promise me you won't break her heart.'

'She's the first woman, apart from you, to ever show an interest in me, Maddie. When I say, *me*, I mean me as a man, not my wealth or my fine house. When she looks at me with those serious eyes, I feel seen for the first time. I feel like someone of value.'

'Is this all because she returned your handkerchief?'

'Don't mock it, Maddie. Love is built on small acts of kindness. A freshly laundered handkerchief, a questioning look that asks me if I'm all right from someone who cares about the answer. It's all I'm asking for.'

With all the expectation of happiness gone from the day, they packed up the remains of the picnic and made their way home in silence. Madeline was too preoccupied by the things Hugh had confessed to make conversation. It was the first time he'd revealed this side of himself and for all their closeness she was seeing him in a new light. She'd never before realised his sensitivity, how being marked as an eligible man by every woman he'd ever met had affected his confidence. When his wealth was such an object of desire, how could he be sure any woman would ever love him for himself? She'd be gentler with him in the future and less quick to tease. Whether it was too late to save his heart from being broken by Flora was another matter altogether.

Chapter 25

Madeline gave Flora a week to settle her thoughts before paying her a visit. She didn't tell Hugh where she was going, and he hadn't asked her to speak on his behalf. Flora's name hadn't been mentioned between them since their conversation immediately following his proposal.

Since the picnic, Hugh had withdrawn into himself, taking long walks along the beach, or sitting alone in his study. In the evenings, he would listen to Madeline playing the harp, lost in his own thoughts, or stare unseeing at the pages of a novel. During this time, it dawned on Madeline what a solitary figure he was, exiled from his usual circle in New York. She only now realised how much society he'd give up for her by relocating to Beachlands.

It was noticeable that he chose to spend less time with his friends who were visiting Newport for the season. She didn't question him over it, even though she felt responsible. It could simply be that he was outgrowing his youthful habits. The sudden change in his attitude towards marriage certainly suggested as much. The death of their father had been a blow to him, in spite of the fact that he'd deplored his moral weaknesses. Uncle Morris's decision to move his mistress into their New York home, obliging Hugh and Madeline to leave, had been another disappointment. Their uncle was the only man Hugh had to look up to, and he too had let him down. For Madeline's sake, Hugh had taken on the full responsibility of acting as head of the family, and she only now realised what a lonely place it was for him.

Flora was sitting with Mrs Booth and Mrs Norton in the drawing room when Madeline was shown in. She'd gambled on Edward being too busy with his law practice to be at home in the afternoon and was relieved to find he wasn't there. After their last conversation, it would have been too awkward to drink tea with him as if nothing of significance had passed between them. Still, she'd taken the risk of having to face him. Her desire to see Flora, to make sure she hadn't been too upset by Hugh's clumsy proposal, was stronger than any reluctance she felt about being in Edward's company.

Madeline assumed a confident attitude as she greeted the three women, breezing into the room as if she hadn't a care in the world. 'Please forgive my unexpected visit, but I happened to be passing and thought it would be rude not to say hello.'

Mrs Booth yawned, positioning herself in a more upright position on the chaise longue, careful not to disturb Mimi, who was tucking into a bowl of fricasseed bones near her feet. 'It's good of you to come. We're very dull these days without Marianne and Jane to liven up the place.' She dangled a languid hand in the direction of her sister, sitting upright in a hard-backed chair. 'We long for youthful company. Isn't that right, my dear?'

'There's nothing wrong with a little peace and quiet,' said Mrs Norton, who barely acknowledged Madeline before turning her attention to Flora. 'Put down that sewing and fetch us some tea. Be quick about it.'

Madeline tried to catch Flora's eye, but she wasn't having any of it as she focused on neatly folding away the satin dress she'd been mending on Mrs Booth's behalf. A cloud appeared to have fallen across her spirit, casting her into the shade now Will had returned to New York. Even though it had only been a few days, much of the bloom had already left her cheeks. With no one for company but her aunts, and with much fetching and carrying to do, the new Flora had crawled back into her shell and the old downtrodden Flora had re-emerged.

When she returned with the tea, Madeline made a point of asking her directly how she was. Flora shrugged, hardly looking up from beneath her eyelids, while admitting she was fine and thanking her for her concern. She didn't ask about Hugh, just as Madeline didn't ask after Edward.

The house was unnaturally quiet without the younger members of the family, and Madeline struggled to sustain the conversation as they drank their tea and picked over the accompanying strawberry tarts. Mrs Booth, who was never one for conversation, concentrated on feeding slithers of pastry to Mimi, who had finished the fricasseed bones and was begging for a treat, while Mrs Norton watched Flora's every move in her quest to find fault. For all she had a sweet tooth, Madeline struggled to enjoy the pastries in such inhospitable company.

Once Flora had cleared away the plates, Madeline suggested the two of them take a walk in the garden. Her heart sank at the look Flora gave her aunts, silently begging permission to be excused.

Mrs Norton looked down her nose at the suggestion. 'Flora ran an errand to the haberdasher for me this morning. That's enough excitement for one day.'

'You must think of the sun, Flora,' added Mrs Booth. 'No young lady likes to be seen glowing. I wouldn't risk Mimi out in this heat.'

There'd been no mention of taking the dog for a walk. Madeline would never have suggested it at this time of day, given its fur coat. She remarked on this to Mrs Booth as she repeated her request.

'There's a cool breeze blowing off the ocean, and Flora and I have parasols to shade us.' She glanced at Flora, encouraging her to speak up for herself.

Taking the cue, Flora inclined her head towards Mrs Norton.

'I'll pick some of the peach tea roses you're so fond of while I'm in the garden.'

The suggestion of the roses was enough to influence Mrs Norton's mind. 'Very well, but don't speak to any of the gardeners. You don't know what it might lead to.'

If it hadn't been for the hint of bribery, Madeline suspected their request for fresh air would have been refused.

Flora's mood seemed to lift as they escaped the confines of the drawing room for the freedom of the garden. As they sat on a bench among the roses, enjoying the scent of the blooms, she was quick to begin the conversation.

'I received a letter from Will this morning. He's been to see Mr Edgerton and agreed a date to begin working at the bank. Uncle Tobias isn't at all pleased that he's leaving the family business but won't stand in his way.'

'That's good news,' said Madeline. 'I'm glad Hugh was able to help.'

She cringed as she said her brother's name. She wasn't here to make excuses for him, but now she'd mentioned him, there was no keeping him out of the conversation.

'We're very grateful to Mr Crosby for his help in advancing Will's career,' said Flora. 'He'll be much happier in his new job.'

'I'm glad to hear it,' said Madeline. 'Please say you weren't offended by the offer Hugh made you. He didn't approach it in the most thoughtful or sensitive way, and he's deeply sorry for upsetting you.'

'It came as a surprise. That must have been obvious from my reaction. I hope I didn't insult him after he's been so kind to Will.'

'You have nothing to apologise for.'

There was a beat of silence before Flora found any more words. 'I shouldn't have responded the way I did. How is he?'

'I've never seen him so sad. It's like he's lost.'

'I'm sorry to hear that.'

'I haven't come to plead for him, Flora. Please don't think

that. I couldn't wish for a better wife for my brother than you. As much as I'd love to have you as my sister, I'm not here to try to influence your decision.'

Flora looked surprised at Madeline's comment. 'I'm flattered you feel that way, but it's impossible. Mr Crosby is full of fine words, and even if he meant them when he said them, how could I be sure he'd still mean them tomorrow, or next year, or the year after that? Fine words are fleeting, but marriage is for life and life is long.'

'When it comes to love, you have to trust your instincts,' said Madeline. 'Only you know how you feel.'

'This isn't about how I feel. No woman could fail to have their head turned by Mr Crosby's attentions. It's how he feels that matters most. I saw how he flirted with Marianne. He can't expect me to take him seriously now he's suddenly shown an interest in me. Next week or next month, someone else might take his fancy. I can't risk my heart to someone so inconstant.

'It's not like the play we rehearsed with Mr Young,' continued Flora. 'There's no Puck among us to put us right if we fall in or out of love with the wrong person, to guarantee we'll all live happily ever after, no matter what mistakes we make along the way. I have no alternatives, no other suitors. My life is limited. I'm not Marianne or Jane, with a dowry large enough to tempt any man. There are no other options for me. If my heart is broken, it will stay that way forever. If I fall, there's no safety net to catch me.'

'You consider Hugh to be frivolous, and based on his behaviour towards Marianne, you have every reason to think so,' said Madeline, 'but there is another side to him, one that few people are allowed to see. You must take my word for it when I tell you he is generous and honourable, loyal and steadfast.'

'You must forgive me for saying it, Miss Crosby, but I've seen little of that side of him.'

'Life isn't as black and white as we'd like to believe,' said Madeline. 'Good and bad don't come in separate packages, clearly labelled and tied with a neat bow. All families, even the Booths, have their shame and their hidden secrets, even if it's not always apparent to everyone, least of all those closest to them.'

'Are you saying there are things in my family I don't know about? Bad things?'

Madeline had said more than she'd intended. She couldn't lie to Flora, but it wasn't her place to tell her about the brothels.

'I believe few of us would stand up to moral scrutiny if we were truly tested.'

'You think I've judged your brother too harshly?' asked Flora.

'I know him better than you. I see him differently because of the love and care he shows me. There are things you can't know about, things it would be wrong of me to share with you.' Madeline paused, realising that once again she was stepping on perilous ground.

'You have to decide on your feelings without interference, basing your judgement on your experience, your current life and your hopes for the future. Whether you change your mind about marrying Hugh or not, it's a decision you'll have to stand by for the rest of your life, and so it has to be your decision.

'Women in our society have little control over their lives,' continued Madeline. 'Choosing a husband is one of the few powers we have. There'll always be people trying to influence us for their own ends, but it's important to choose wisely and to be true to your heart.'

She hadn't meant to make Flora cry, but she'd veered unwittingly close to it. There was a lot more Madeline could say, but the most important things needed to remain unspoken. She wasn't ready to admit the truth about her own past, not here, where she still garnered some respect, where people judged her on her own terms, and she wouldn't betray the true nature of the Booths' business to Flora, who relied on the family for her home and security.

Madeline rose from the bench. 'Whatever happens, I hope we can still be friends.'

Flora nodded, lost in her own thoughts as Madeline took her leave, slipping quietly through the garden gate without returning to the house. If she didn't make too much noise, Mrs Booth and Mrs Norton might forget she'd ever visited, but for the half-eaten strawberry tart she'd regrettably left behind.

Chapter 26

Hugh was waiting on the front doorstep when Madeline returned home. 'You've been to see Flora. You have, haven't you, Maddie?'

She nodded. Seeing the sadness in his eyes, she couldn't lie to him. 'Let's go inside.'

'What did she say? Has she changed her mind about marrying me?'

'You need to give her more time, Hugh. You can't force your love on to her.'

'I should send her a letter. Would that help? Or flowers. I'll send her roses, dozens of them.'

'I don't think that would be a good idea.'

He followed her into the house, waiting at her side like a faithful dog while she unpinned her hat in the mirror. 'She'll see them as shallow gestures. That's what you think, isn't it?'

She turned to him and sighed. His desperation was too painful to watch. 'I'm afraid so.'

'Tell me, Maddie. What should I do to prove my love to her?'

If only she had the answer, she'd give it to him in a heartbeat. He might be a grown man, experienced in all areas of life, but when it came to romantic love, he'd never had a role model worth following. There hadn't been a decent man in their family to show him how to do it. Now his heart was on the line, he was like a little boy lost.

'I don't know, Hugh, but I think Flora needs time to get used to the idea of you.'

'Are you saying I might have a chance with her?'

'Reading between the lines of what she said, I think you might. But you mustn't rush her.'

He nodded, the misery lifting from his eyes. 'I'll listen to what you say, Maddie. I won't give up on her. I'm not beaten yet.'

They lived quietly for the next few weeks. Madeline didn't raise the subject of Flora again, and Hugh didn't mention her. He would speak about her when he was ready, or not at all. Madeline wouldn't be the one to force it. She'd never seen him struck by a woman like this. The protestations he'd made about never marrying proved he'd never been in love before. His determination had been easy to express when he didn't know what it would cost him and had no sense of what he'd be sacrificing. The words would never have slipped so easily off his tongue otherwise. His feelings for Flora were the first real test of his resolve.

Madeline wouldn't go as far as to say that Hugh was moping. It was more that he was shadowed by a cloud of regret, which he betrayed now and then when he thought she wasn't looking. He would remove the handkerchief Flora had laundered and pressed from his pocket and turn it over in his fingers with reverence, as if it were the relic of his lost love. Whether he was regretting his feelings, or simply the clumsy way he'd expressed them, Madeline didn't know and she respected his privacy too much to ask.

There was no word from Edward during these long weeks. Madeline made no effort to contact him, and his continued silence suggested her revelation had driven him away. It wasn't only the old New York society who rejected women of her background. The people with new money didn't want to know her either. She'd disgusted him with her honesty, by revealing the truth of who she was and where she came from. At least this made the breach easier. By keeping his distance, Edward had shown his true character. It was easier to profess love for a mysterious heiress than for the illegitimate daughter of a rich man and his mistress, the daughter of a woman who died in one of his father's brothels.

At least the situation was cut and dried. Despite her undeniable feelings for him, there was no room for hope or for the resolution of a misunderstanding. The situation was what it was, and Madeline took his absence at face value. He was appalled by her past and no longer wanted anything to do with her, which meant he could only love her for the person he imagined her to be, not for the person she was.

Refusing to waste her energy on regret, Madeline decided to spend her time planning the most effective way to expose the brothels. Tobias Booth was a powerful man. If she was to protect herself against his wrath, she had to remain anonymous. As long as he didn't know she was behind the exposé of his criminal business, he wouldn't be able to exact revenge on her. She had to work strategically if her plan was to succeed and prove herself twice as cunning as the man himself.

To support her campaign, she instructed her lawyer to gather testimonies from a number of the women currently working in the brothels, along with their permission to bring them to public attention. She'd already won their trust, thanks to her regular and direct financial assistance. She hadn't realised it at the time, but by helping them, she'd already laid the foundations for the downfall of the Trident brothels. Now, with everything in place, there was nothing left to do but sit back and wait for the fallout.

Chapter 27

Madeline and Hugh were having breakfast on the terrace, enjoying the early morning sun when Hugh suggested they go to a polo match.

'We've been too quiet for our own good lately, Maddie. We need a distraction to bring us out of ourselves.'

The day was promising to be a hot one, and so she put on a white muslin dress with a forgiving outline that didn't require her to be laced too tightly into a corset. She'd been much taken with the Rational Dress Society during their stay in London and longed for the fashion to catch on in America. If women's lives were to be less constrained, if they were to be allowed to breathe freely enough for their voices to be heard, they needed to rid themselves of corsets, high-heeled shoes and weighted skirts.

The polo match was already underway by the time they arrived. They milled through the crowd, looking for a spot that would give them a decent view of the playing field, but it was hopeless. It was the height of the season and the visiting team from New York had attracted a larger number of onlookers than usual. They should have planned the day better and arrived earlier.

The combination of the heat and the failure to get a good view of the match put Hugh out of sorts. Madeline suggested they retreat to the hospitality tent, hoping a cool beer would restore his spirits and make up for missing the best part of the match.

'Mr Crosby, it really is you. And Miss Crosby. What a delightful surprise.'

Madeline would have recognised Mr Young's voice anywhere. She forced herself to smile as he made his way through the crowded tent towards them, waving his arms above his head as if he were calling the sparrows hither. It was soon apparent that he wasn't alone. Theo and Jane were with him.

'We thought you were all in New York,' said Madeline, forcing herself to appear more pleased to see them than she actually was.

It was only after she'd spoken that she realised there was a fourth member to their party. Edward was trailing behind them, his head down as he moved through the crowd, trying not to collide with the sea of elbows, hats and unruly parasols.

'We were,' exclaimed Mr Young. 'But it got a bit hot.' He waved his black leather fan rapidly in front of his face. 'You know how the city boils at this time of year. We all needed to escape, didn't we?'

It might have been her imagination, but Madeline was sure Jane rolled her eyes and turned her back on Mr Young as he spoke. This was a big change in her behaviour towards him. The last time Madeline had seen them together Jane had hung on his every word. She must have finally realised he would never have any romantic intentions towards her. However much she preyed upon him, he only had eyes for Theo. Madeline felt sorry for her naivety, for her failure to see what was plainly in front of her face.

Jane didn't save all her contempt for Mr Young. She also had plenty to spare for Hugh, glaring at him as he tried to make polite conversation by asking her if she was enjoying the weather.

'Why would you want to know that, Mr Crosby?' she snapped.

The corners of Hugh's mouth twitched with irritation. 'I was making conversation. Forgive me if you found my question too intrusive.'

Jane's face reddened. She'd made herself look foolish and Hugh's measured response had ensured she felt it.

'How's your sister? Is she still in New York?' asked Madeline, trying to smooth over the awkwardness. Bringing Marianne into the conversation wasn't the best way to improve matters, given what had happened in the past, but as the subject of the weather had already been covered, she was at a loss as to what else to say.

Jane began her reply with a sullen look. 'Marianne is at Southsea. The city heat doesn't suit her.'

'Is she not with you today?' asked Madeline, glancing over her shoulder as if to search her out. 'I know how much she enjoys watching polo.'

'Her time is no longer her own,' said Jane. 'Not now she has Rawdon to please.'

It seemed strange that Rawdon would deny his new wife the pleasure of attending a polo match with her family, but the scornful look on Jane's face warned Madeline against commenting on it. When Hugh tried another subject, she turned her back on both of them, just as she'd turned it on Mr Young.

Her behaviour was a determined snub. Madeline would have been affronted on Hugh's behalf if she hadn't been conscious of Jane's childishness. It was obvious she still resented Hugh. She had hoped after Marianne married Rawdon that his attentions would turn to her, despite his repeated assertions that he would never marry. If she had tried to attract Mr Young to make Hugh jealous, she had wasted her time. Now, Jane's ill-manners proved how sheltered her life had been, how little she understood the complex nature of human relations. She couldn't be blamed for it, but seeing how much she was spoiled, Madeline couldn't find it in her heart to feel sympathy for her.

All this time, Edward had been standing at the edge of the group. Madeline made a point of looking away from him as he stared at his feet. He appeared as uncomfortable with the meeting as she did, while Mr Young, seemingly insensible to the uneasiness around him, continued to talk over everyone's heads about the weather.

Just when Madeline thought the situation couldn't get any more awkward, there was a new addition to the group. Flora. It hadn't crossed Madeline's mind that she might be there until she saw her advancing towards them, weaving her way through the crowd, whispering a continuous stream of apologies as she tried to avoid the crush of bodies in the overheated marquee.

The colour drained from Hugh's face as soon as he spotted her. Madeline gave his arm an encouraging squeeze. 'Do you want to leave? We can slip away quietly. No one will notice.'

Hugh shook his head, taking a sip of his beer for courage. He'd had the advantage of spotting Flora before she noticed him. Now she was only a few feet away, her face flushed red as Hugh caught her eye and smiled.

'Flora.'

Her name was out of his mouth before he could stop it. She hadn't given him permission to use her first name, but it stumbled from his lips anyway. Madeline gripped his arm, silently warning him not to say anything more. No one else in the group knew of his proposal and she was sure Flora would want to keep it that way.

'I'm so glad to see you,' said Madeline, throwing her arms out to Flora and embracing her. 'I've missed you these past weeks. You must promise to come and visit me at Beachlands.'

She placed the emphasis on *me*, making the point that the invitation was nothing to do with Hugh, that it was Madeline who wanted to see her. Flora would never take up the invitation otherwise, after Hugh's clumsy proposal.

Flora moved from foot to foot as she searched for an answer, dropping the parasol she'd been clutching to her chest. Before she could reach to pick it up, Hugh rescued it from the ground. She lowered her eyes, mumbling her thanks as she accepted it from his hand.

'About time too,' said Jane, snatching the parasol. 'You've been an age fetching it from the carriage. My face could have burned to blisters under the direct heat of the sun by now. Whatever have you been up to?'

'Forgive me. It took a while to work my way through the crowds,' said Flora.

'There was no real risk to your face, Miss Booth,' said Hugh, barely hiding his fury. 'You've been in the shade of the tent all this time. If anyone has suffered from exposure to the sun, it's Flora.'

There he went again, calling her Flora instead of Miss Pierce. Madeline caught his eye, willing him to stay calm. Flora wouldn't appreciate him coming to her defence, and judging by Jane's petulance, the poor girl would only be made to suffer for it later.

It was all credit to Flora's resilience that she'd turned down Hugh's offer of marriage in favour of remaining in servitude to the Booths. Or perhaps it was simply that living under such oppression had made her cautious; her familiarity with unhappiness had made her unwilling to put herself in a situation where she could end up faring even worse. After all, Flora didn't know the loving side of Hugh, and she'd been too beaten down by others to have the courage to open herself up to the experience of it. It took courage to allow yourself to be loved, and bravery to risk loving in return. As soon as she'd had the thought, Madeline realised it didn't only apply to Flora, but also to herself.

Seeing Flora hot and bothered, Hugh insisted on fetching her a glass of water, leaving Madeline to the mercy of the Booth family.

While Theo and Mr Young fell into conversation, and Jane made a point of ignoring everyone, Edward finally gathered the courage to speak to her.

'How are you, Miss Crosby?'

'I'm well. Thank you for asking, Mr Booth.'

He cleared his throat. 'It seems we're destined for our paths to keep crossing.'

'I'm sure if we set our minds to it, we can avoid it in the

future. If I'd known you were going to be here today, I wouldn't have come.'

'Whereas I would move heaven and earth just for a chance of seeing you.'

She forced herself to harden her heart against his depth of feeling, so sweetly expressed. 'Then your effort would be wasted.'

A wounded look passed over his face. She took no pleasure in seeing his pain, but what could he expect after his failure to take any action towards shutting down the brothels.

Hugh returned with the water, and as Flora took sips from the glass, the six of them stood looking away from each other in silence. A cheer from the crowd watching the polo match finally gave Madeline the excuse she needed to escape.

'We're missing all the excitement. Let's go and find out what's happening.' She hooked her arm through Hugh's and began to lead him away.

'You're not leaving already are you, Mr Crosby?' asked Flora with what sounded like dismay.

Hugh seemed to grow in height as she spoke to him. It was the first time she'd indicated a desire for his company and he wasn't prepared to let it pass. He offered her his free arm. 'We're going to take a look at the match. Won't you join us?'

Flora glanced at her cousins, as if to ask their permission. When Edward shrugged, suggesting he didn't mind, Jane spoke up.

'You can't go wandering off, Flora. You're needed here.'

Flora lowered her eyes in submission. 'Thank you for the invitation, Mr Crosby. Perhaps we'll see each other another time.'

'Of course we will,' said Hugh, a little too emphatically. 'You can count on it.'

Madeline felt Hugh's hope deflate as they made their way out of the tent. She gave him an encouraging smile. 'Take heart, Hugh. All is not lost.'

He blew out his cheeks. 'She'd have accepted my invitation to join us if Jane hadn't stopped her. I'm sure of it.'

Madeline suspected he was right. If she'd included the others in her original suggestion, things might have gone differently, but it couldn't be helped. She hadn't wanted to risk socialising with the Booths in case she inadvertently betrayed herself. If nothing else, she'd have felt like a hypocrite, making small talk and pretending nothing was wrong after she'd set the wheels in motion to expose the brothels. If they found out what she'd been up to, she'd be the last person on earth they'd want to associate with.

Chapter 28

Madeline was deadheading the roses when Hugh came charging into the garden. The flowers weren't suited to the heat or the sea air, and the blooms were over almost before they'd begun.

'Have you seen this, Maddie?' Hugh held a newspaper in front of her, showing her the headlines.

Trident hotels shamed in brothels scandal. Overnight the company faces financial collapse.

Madeline took the newspaper to a bench in the shade where she could consider it more carefully. Hugh sat beside her, relating the contents before she'd had time to read them, as if he couldn't quite believe it.

'The article says someone informed them of the clandestine business, revealing it had been going on for decades. They gave the locations of the brothels and the specific hotels that provided rooms for the illegal trade. They also supplied testimonies from women who were prepared to talk about their experiences of working there.' He paused, running his hand across his face. 'There are pages and pages of information, giving the women's life stories, explaining how they ended up working in the world's oldest profession. Each one is a tragedy.'

The campaign had finally come to fruition. After all the planning and negotiating, one of the many newspaper editors Madeline approached had been prepared to listen to what she had to say and taken it seriously. They'd even contacted the women whose testimonies she'd provided, women who had agreed to make a further public statement to support her campaign. The dozens of letters she'd written during the past weeks hadn't been a wasted effort. The truth was finally out. If the Booths weren't prepared to put their own house in order, they had to risk the business failing now the true nature of it was out in the open.

Hugh lifted the newspaper from her knees as she stared at it without taking in any of the words.

'Guests are already checking out, while others are cancelling their reservations,' he continued. 'The hotels have always been a popular choice among women travellers. Now, they're abandoning them in droves all over the country.'

Madeline rubbed the newspaper print from her hands as if to remove the contamination of the brothels from her skin. 'I don't suppose all those women's groups campaigning for female suffrage will want to hold their meetings in their public rooms anymore, nor will they book the hotels for their conventions.'

'That's before you consider the rest of the general public who'll stay away,' said Hugh. 'The ordinary men and women who won't want to be associated with such a business, the families with children and those with religious beliefs.'

His voice tailed off as he concentrated on folding the newspaper and put it aside. 'It was you, Maddie, wasn't it? It was you who broke the story to the newspapers. You said you were going to expose the brothels, and you've done it.'

'I gave Edward the opportunity to put things right with the business, and do right by the women affected. His failure to address the situation left me no choice but to take matters into my own hands. The exploitation of the women couldn't be allowed to go on any longer.'

'Why wouldn't he do anything about it?'

'He made the excuse that he takes no active role in the business and has no influence on how it's run. I also suspect he's scared of his father. Or perhaps he sees nothing wrong in it. You should have seen his face when I told him my mother died in one of his family's brothels, that I was born in one of them. He couldn't put distance between us quickly enough.'

'There's probably more to it than that, Maddie. Anyone can see how taken he is with you.'

She wasn't prepared to consider the idea that Edward might still be in love with her, that he'd stayed away because of how she'd treated him rather than for any other reason. 'You don't blame me for doing what I've done, do you?'

'I'm in awe of your courage, Maddie, even if it has ruined any chance either of us ever had of marrying the people we love.'

She hadn't told him she loved Edward. She hadn't even admitted it to herself, so how could he make such a bold statement?

'I'm sorry if I spoiled things between you and Flora.'

'Flora's too good for me, anyway.' Hugh turned to her, his face full of concern. 'This trouble you've caused isn't going to go away quietly, Maddie. The newspapers have respected your anonymity, but I can't see a man like Tobias Booth going down without a fight. If he finds out you're behind his downfall, he'll take you down with him.'

'Then we'll wait and see what happens.' She'd lived her life under a cloud of disgrace. Any more suffering would make no difference to her now.

'You know what the newspapers are like,' said Hugh. 'They have their own political agendas and vested interests. If Tobias Booth has any of the editors in his back pocket, they'll come for you in a very public way.'

'I have no reputation to protect. It's already ruined. And even if it wasn't, it's a small price to pay for doing the right thing.'

'Be careful, Maddie. That's all I'm saying.'

She'd anticipated there'd be repercussions and had rented a boarding house on the outskirts of a small town, many miles from New York, to shelter the women who'd been brave enough to speak out against the brothels, so at least they were safe and taken care of while they found other ways to support themselves and their children. Madeline would never abandon the women who'd helped her and could only sleep at night by knowing she'd put a proportion of her wealth towards protecting them.

If Tobias Booth decided to take revenge against her, then she would face it down. She had her mother's strength and resilience. She hadn't started out in life with wealth or privilege, and if she lost it, she could live without it. She was educated and resourceful, and could make her own way in life if she had to. She was doing this for her mother, and for Finch, and the countless other women exploited by a society that failed to offer them a safety net during times of need.

It wasn't only these women who'd been on her mind lately, but another woman too. One who was in every way more privileged. Madeline hoped her suspicions were wrong, but the only way to find out was to go and see her. She'd already put it off, knowing it would mean stepping into the lion's den, but she knew she had to do it eventually. There had to be a reason why Marianne had failed to attend the polo match with the rest of her siblings when she was so mad for the game, and Madeline wouldn't rest until she found out what it was.

Chapter 29

When she arrived at Southsea, Madeline was made to wait in the grand entrance hall while the maid sought permission to admit her. The maid's hesitancy led her to suspect the Booths knew she was the one who'd exposed the brothels to the newspapers. It was more than five minutes before the maid returned and instructed Madeline to follow her into the drawing room. Given the delay, she hadn't expected to be invited in and now wondered if she was walking into a trap.

Marianne was sitting in a chair by the window, looking out into the garden, her stillness suggesting she'd been there for some time. She jumped out of her seat when Madeline was shown in, as if she wasn't expecting to see anyone and had been caught doing something she shouldn't.

It took Marianne no more than a second to regain her compose. 'Miss Crosby. What a surprise. I didn't know you were here.'

Madeline waited until they were alone before she replied. 'Your maid left me standing in the hallway for at least five minutes. I assumed she'd used that time to ask if you were willing to see me.'

'She'd have been checking with Rawdon to see if she had permission to allow you in.' Marianne seemed nervous as she spoke, running her hands down the silk folds of her dress to smooth out the creases where there weren't any.

'Surely there's no need for that. The maids know me here. I've visited plenty of times before.'

Edward would have known she was the one who'd exposed the brothels in the newspapers and must have made sure everyone in the family was aware of it. Was this why Marianne was so reticent? Although, given the circumstances, Madeline was surprised Rawdon had allowed her to set foot in the house at all.

'Things are different now,' said Marianne, glancing nervously at the door as if she expected someone to burst in at any moment. 'It's not like when you were here before.'

'But you're the mistress here.'

Marianne shrugged off Madeline's assertion. 'Rawdon's in charge.'

This was a different Marianne to the one Madeline had known before the wedding. It had only been a matter of weeks, but already the bloom had gone from her face. Her movements were more hesitant and she lacked any sense of triumph or supremacy. It was hardly how Madeline expected a new bride to look or behave, but then this new bride had married against her inclination.

'I saw your sister and your brothers at the polo match,' said Madeline, trying to bring the conversation around to something more congenial. 'I was surprised not to see you with them when they mentioned you were here rather than in New York. I know how much you like to watch the sport.'

'I—'

Marianne stopped mid-sentence when the maid brought in the tea and only continued once they were alone again. 'Rawdon doesn't like me going out these days.'

The words were spoken so quietly that Madeline struggled to understand them at first. She put the teacup to her lips, the liquid scalding her tongue as she tasted it. She was beginning to see the situation in a different light. The maid hadn't sought

Rawdon's permission for her to enter the house because she'd exposed the brothels, but because he was controlling who his wife was allowed to see.

'Are you not well? Is that why you stay in?'

There was a pause while Marianne considered her answer. 'I'm still getting used to the demands of married life. You can't imagine how much there is to do now I'm the mistress of a grand house like this.'

And yet she'd been sitting staring out of the window when Madeline arrived. Her vacant attitude suggested she'd been in the same position for hours. Her answer had clearly been constructed out of fear or pride. Rawdon was preventing her from going out, keeping her locked up in her own home, deciding who she could see, who she could talk to. However beautiful the surroundings, they were still a prison if you weren't allowed to come and go at will.

Madeline put aside her tea, which was too hot and too bitter. 'Shall we take a walk in the garden? You look like you could do with some fresh air.' If she could get Marianne out of the house, she might be prepared to speak more freely and without the risk of being overheard. That was the thing about a house like this, with its secret passageways and hidden doors, you never knew who was listening.

Marianne looked out of the window, her mouth twisting with indecision. 'I suppose it couldn't do any harm.'

'I'd love to take another look at the topiary garden,' said Madeline, grabbing her parasol to spur Marianne into action. 'I've never seen anything like it before.'

However many times she saw it, she still couldn't get over the great green elephant with its arcing trunk carved out of box. Although if pressed for an opinion, she'd have to admit that her heart belonged to the lion with its catlike muzzle and enormous sprouting mane.

The strategy had been a good one. Marianne appeared to relax as the two of them strolled around the garden, where there were no maids lurking to overhear their conversation or to report back on them.

Their temperaments were so different, that the two of them would never be friends, but it still troubled Madeline to see Marianne in such a state, and she was determined to get to the bottom of it.

'Are you enjoying married life?'

'It's different to how I imagined it. Rawdon is different.'

'He's your husband now, no longer your suitor.'

'My lord and master, as they say in the novels.'

Marianne eased herself down on a stone bench as if the effort might break her. Madeline wondered if she was in pain, but it didn't seem the right moment to ask. Instead, she relied on her observation to work out what could possibly be wrong.

'Rawdon's taking good care of you, though?'

'There's a side to him I didn't know existed. I thought he was simply stupid, but he's cruel too.'

'The stupid ones usually are. They don't have the intelligence or the sensitivity to behave any differently. I'm sorry for you.'

Marianne leaned forward, burying her head in her hands. 'It's as if he's punishing me for every joke I made at his expense while he was courting me, for every humiliation he suffered when I openly paid too much attention to your brother.'

'If Rawdon was bothered by your behaviour, he should have spoken to you about it before the wedding, not punish you for it afterwards.'

'He knew I preferred Hugh to him, that I only married him because your brother wouldn't have me. Now he's determined to make me pay for it for the rest of my life. He thinks I only came to Newport because Hugh is here, that it had nothing to do with wanting to be with my family. He won't accept that there was nothing between us and never will be. For all his high spirits, your brother is too honourable to do anything that would damage a woman's reputation. Still, he's the reason Rawdon won't let me out of the house and why he insists the maids check with him before allowing me to see any visitors.'

'Then I'm surprised I was admitted.'

'He probably wanted to know if you'd come with a message from Hugh. He'll have set one of the maids to spy on us. He'll be furious when he learns we've slipped out into the garden.'

'I didn't mean to get you into trouble. I wouldn't have come if I'd known it would make things more difficult for you.'

'I don't suppose you have a message from him for me, do you?'

Madeline shook her head. 'I'm sorry. His heart belongs to someone else.'

'Of course. And anyway, I'm married. Even if he loved me, there'd be no hope for us. I used him badly. I hope one day he'll forgive me.'

'My brother isn't the sort of man to bear a grudge. It's already forgotten.'

The revelation that Rawdon had set the maids to spy on Marianne made Madeline uneasy. 'Shall we walk a little further?'

If they kept moving, surely the spy would have to reveal themselves. Here, where they were seated, it was too easy for someone to hide behind a hedge and listen to their conversation.

They'd walked as far as the rose garden before Marianne dared to speak again. 'Everything seems to have gone wrong lately. Did you see the report in the newspapers about Father's hotels?'

'You must tell me about it.' Finally, Madeline had an opportunity to find out the family's reaction to the exposé.

'They reported that the Trident hotels are a cover for a number of brothels that operate alongside the legitimate business.'

'Wherever did they get such a story?'

Marianne threw up her hands. 'Nobody knows, but it's sent the family into chaos.'

'I'm so sorry.'

Madeline was genuinely sorry. Not only for the women who'd been exploited by the business, but for the members of the Booth family who had no idea such practices had been going on. Who now had to face public judgement and the consequences of having unwittingly benefited from decades of criminal activity.

'How has your father taken it?' Madeline needed to know how tough an adversary Tobias Booth was going to be if he found out she was the person behind the exposé.

'The scandal gave him a terrible turn. He's gone to a sanatorium in Switzerland to recover. His boat sailed yesterday.'

This was the last thing Madeline had expected. Tobias Booth's guilt was undeniable and he'd fled the country to avoid the consequences. Like most bullies, he'd proven himself a coward when challenged. It didn't mean, however, that the Booths wouldn't retaliate if they discovered she was behind the newspaper reports. Madeline just had to work out who her enemy would be.

'I suppose Theo has taken over the running of the business. Perhaps he'll be able to sort everything out.'

'Theo's gone to Rome with Mr Young. When the news broke about the brothels, he was terrified their relationship would also be exposed. Our society doesn't look kindly on their type of romantic love. They hope Italy will be more forgiving. If not, at least it'll be easier for them to hide.'

Theo was another coward, another spoiled child. 'Who has taken responsibility for the business?'

'Edward's gone to New York to try to put things right and to rescue what he can of Trident's reputation.'

So, Edward had finally been spurred into action. If the business was to be saved, she supposed he'd been left with no choice. 'It must have come as a shock to you all.'

'Rawdon's furious that this has happened now, just as he and Father were planning the expansion of the hotel chain. He's worried the reputation of his bank will be damaged by association.'

They were only concerned for the reputations of their

businesses. There was no concern for the women they'd exploited. 'Did Rawdon know about the brothels?'

Marianne shrugged. 'We don't talk about the business. It's always left to the men.'

'Perhaps it's time you showed some interest in it.'

'Why would I want to do that?' snapped Marianne. 'And anyway, Rawdon won't even let me leave the house to buy a new hat. He'd never allow me to get involved with the business.'

They fell silent as the maid who'd served the tea suddenly appeared beside them.

'Mr Rawdon is asking for you, ma'am.'

Marianne bowed to her, as if it was the maid who was in charge, before dismissing Madeline with a nod. 'It's best if you leave now.'

'Shall I come and see you again?' Madeline couldn't help feeling she was abandoning Marianne to some terrible fate, or at the very least, to an interrogation.

She replied with a slight shake of her head before disappearing from the rose garden, the maid who'd been sent to summon her remaining in close attendance. Madeline was left to see herself out through the side gate, under the scrutiny of what might have been numerous hidden sets of eyes and ears.

Shocked by the realisation of Marianne's situation, Madeline made her way home, fearful not only for Marianne's happiness, but for her safety. Whether Marianne would find the courage to stand up for herself against Rawdon's bullying was yet to be seen, but given the conditioning of her upbringing, Madeline held out little hope for it.

Chapter 30

Madeline told Hugh about her visit to see Marianne over dinner that evening. After she'd finished speaking, he was quiet for a long time, picking at the apple pie Finch had made especially for him.

'You shouldn't have gone to see her, Maddie. You could have got yourself into all sorts of trouble.'

'Marianne was the only person I saw from the family. She doesn't know it was me behind the exposé of the brothels. She was more concerned with her unhappy marriage than with the crisis in the business.'

'She might not know it was you, but Edward's no fool. He'll have worked out who was behind it straight away.'

Of course Edward knew it was her, and what he'd do about it was anyone's guess. At the moment he was probably too busy trying to stabilise the business to think about revenge.

Weeks of quiet uncertainty followed. Madeline was constantly on her guard, expecting the situation to blow up at any minute, for accusations to be made against her in the most punishing and public manner. But there was nothing.

They were finishing their coffee in the drawing room one evening when Finch appeared, her tired expression reflecting the fact that she'd had a long day.

'I'm sorry to interrupt, but this letter has just been delivered for you, Mr Crosby. As it's so late, I thought it might be urgent.'

Hugh took the envelope, his brow furrowing with concern as he thanked her, before advising her gently to go to bed.

Madeline watched him pore over the letter, wondering who it was from. Whatever it was, he was giving it serious attention.

'Is it anything to worry about?' she asked, after he finally returned the two densely written pages to the envelope.

'It's nothing you need to concern yourself with.'

This didn't answer the question, nor did it mean it wasn't worth worrying about, but she knew her brother well enough to understand he didn't want to discuss it.

They sat in silence for another half hour. Hugh stared at the novel that lay open on his lap without once turning a page. Madeline knew something was wrong but didn't want to appear too intrusive.

'Are you all right?' she asked.

Still distracted, he nodded. 'I have to go away for a while. Will you manage here on your own with Finch?'

'Of course, unless you'd like me to come with you.'

'It's good of you to offer, but I'll be better off alone. I'll be back as soon as I can.' He forced a smile. 'I don't want to miss too much of the polo season.'

She resisted asking where he was going and whether the sudden journey had been prompted by the contents of the letter. If he'd wanted her to know, he would have volunteered the information, just as he would have told her who'd sent it, and why it had been delivered at such an ungodly hour. All she could do was trust him and try not to worry.

Hugh had already left when Madeline went down to breakfast the following morning. The house was so quiet it felt as if the rest of the world was carrying on its business without her, as if real life had left her behind.

Somewhere out there, Hugh was attending to a situation that

had required his immediate attention and discretion, while in New York, Edward was fighting to save his family business from the scandal she'd exposed. In one way, she was at the centre of the storm; while in another, she was completely removed from it. Everything in her life seemed to be happening at a distance. Now she'd exposed the brothels, all she could do was sit back and wait to see how the situation played out.

When she came in from the garden later that afternoon, there was a letter waiting for her on the desk. It was too soon to hear from Hugh, and she'd have recognised the informal loops and the slant of his handwriting. This script was far neater, the letters precise and much smaller, as if the cost of the paper and the ink were of a premium, the economy indicating it had come from Flora. She poured herself a glass of Finch's freshly made lemonade and sat down to read it.

Dear Miss Crosby,

Please forgive my writing to you so unexpectedly. I like to think that if things had worked out differently, we might have been friends or even sisters-in-law. You certainly indicated that you'd have liked it to be so, and it is in this spirit that I have taken the liberty of writing to you.

I'm not currently residing at Mountview but have returned to my family at the address you see at the top of this letter. My uncle insisted on the visit after he learned I'd turned down your brother's marriage proposal, which he discovered after reading one of my letters to Will. I had no idea that he read my private correspondence and can now only regret my indiscretion. To say Uncle Tobias was angry that I'd refused such an offer is to understate it. I've seen his anger many times before, but I've never seen him in quite such a rage.

He insisted that returning to my family would instil some good sense into me, that when I'd experienced how it is to be poor and to live in a place of no consequence, I would not only be willing to marry Mr Crosby but would be desperate to do so. It seemed a rather extreme reaction if you ask me, but my opinion is never sought on any matter, not even when it comes to my own happiness.

Although it's very nice to spend time with my mother and father and younger siblings, who I haven't seen for many years, the small house is overcrowded, and given my family's particular circumstances, I'm sure they'd prefer not to have another mouth to feed. Nevertheless, I'm doing my best to make myself useful and am encouraging my sister, Susan, with her reading.

A lot has changed in the Booth family lately. Since banishing me to Wisconsin, Uncle Tobias has travelled to Switzerland to take a rest cure in a sanatorium, and Theo has gone to Europe with his friend, Mr Young, to see the sights. Edward has put aside his legal work and returned to New York to run the Trident hotel chain. This has come as the biggest surprise, as he has never before shown the slightest inclination to involve himself in the family business, but as Uncle Tobias and Theo are taking extended holidays, I don't suppose he had a choice in the matter.

Finally, I come to the real reason for writing to you. I received a letter from Edward yesterday in which he proposed marriage.

It has come as a great surprise and yet, when I think of it, Edward and I have always been friends as well as cousins. He's the only one of the Booths ever to have treated me as an equal, and the only one to make me feel welcome at Mountview. As I have no dowry and no expectation of another suitor, I have accepted his offer.

I trust your brother will welcome this news. I don't imagine the feelings he expressed for me were long lasting, even if he felt they were genuine at the time he professed them. I have no doubt that he now regrets the whole sorry business and considers my refusal to have been a lucky escape.

Miss Flora Pierce

The pages of the letter shook in Madeline's hand as she turned them over and reread them. The news that Edward and Flora were to marry was too much to take in. He didn't love her. She was certain of it. He had a constant heart, a heart that was true and steadfast. He loved Madeline too ardently to have suddenly turned his affections to Flora.

It was only now she was faced with the prospect of losing Edward that Madeline was finally able to admit she loved him, and not only loved him, but loved him deeply. He was the only man she'd ever met who came close to the sensitivity and kindness of Hugh, the only other man who understood her for who she was and who wanted her for herself. The fact that he'd protected her anonymity by not revealing she'd exposed the brothels, nor held her to account for her actions only impressed on her further what an honourable man she'd lost.

What had she been thinking, playing with Edward's heart? Driving him away over the brothels when they were nothing to do with him. She'd punished him for his father's behaviour and now she'd lost him.

And what about Flora? She made no mention of love in her letter. She regarded Edward highly, there was no doubt about it, but only as a wounded animal would regard its carer. She was marrying him out of a sense of gratitude for all the kindness he'd shown her over the years. These were the wrong feelings on which to base a marriage.

It wasn't against the law in New York State to marry a cousin, but it was frowned upon. Such marriages only usually occurred to avoid diluting the family fortune, or to prevent it falling into the wrong hands. Flora wasn't marrying Edward for these reasons, but out of fear of what the future might hold for her if she refused him. She'd already been treated brutally by her uncle for turning down Hugh's proposal. If she suffered any regret over that decision, then this was a way of atoning for it.

If only they could have spent more time together, Flora would have grown to love Hugh the way he deserved to be loved, not because he assumed the right to it, but because he would have earned it. Hugh had failed to give Flora time to understand his feelings before he rushed in with a marriage proposal. After what had happened with Marianne, Flora hadn't been prepared to entrust her heart to him.

Madeline folded the letter and slipped it back into its envelope, regretting the news it contained. Her attempt to close down the brothels had had further reaching consequences than she'd considered. Everyone had been left mismatched and broken hearted, and it was all her fault. How could she have created such a situation, and however could she put it right?

Chapter 31

After a sleepless night, Madeline decided there was only one thing for it. As soon as she'd had breakfast, she packed a carpetbag and prepared to set off to see Flora. The only way to sort this mess out was by discussing it face to face.

'It's a long way for a woman to travel alone,' said Finch, handing her a parcel of food for the journey. 'Are you sure you don't want me to come with you?'

'Thank you, but I'll feel happier knowing you're here, taking care of the house.' Madeline was more touched by the offer than she could express. She tucked the food into her bag, grateful for the kindness that had gone into preparing it. 'If Hugh returns before I do, can you tell him where I've gone?'

Her brother would be furious when he learned she'd travelled alone, but she wouldn't delay her journey until his return. She had to speak to Flora as soon as possible. A marriage between her and Edward would be all wrong, and she had to do what she could to prevent it.

Thanks to the railroad, the journey to Wisconsin was fast and efficient. The steady thump and roll of the train, the stench of the burning coal and the smuts that settled on every part of her, were a small price to pay for the speed of the journey. Still, it was late by the time she climbed into a cab at Wausau Station and directed the driver to take her to the best hotel in town.

As fortune would have it, the best hotel happened to be a boarding house run by the driver's aunt, Lucy. Madeline was too exhausted to comment on the coincidence of the family connection. By the time they pulled up outside a three-storey clapboard house with a discreet sign and lace curtains, Madeline was ready to risk anywhere that provided a decent room, warm water to wash in and a hot meal to fortify her before she slept.

Aunt Lucy, as she insisted on being called, promised all these things and didn't disappoint on any of them, and twelve hours later, Madeline was well-breakfasted and refreshed, ready to begin her mission.

After the grime and bustle of New York's streets and the ocean-swept wildness of Rhode Island, Wassau, with its quiet roads and low-rise buildings, felt eerie. It was a place where people looked over their shoulders at strangers, where no new face was ever missed. In contrast to the cosmopolitan culture of the capital cities of Europe, where no one had marked her as an outsider, Madeline felt like a curiosity rather than a casual visitor.

The town largely relied on the logging industry for its affluence, and in recent years, the depletion of the surrounding pine forests had led to a downturn in the local economy. Madeline could feel the atmosphere of impending decline on the streets, a decline that could only be bad news for ordinary working families such as Flora's, with no inherited wealth to fall back on, no trade or profession and plenty of mouths to feed.

Given the financially precarious situation of her family, Madeline understood why Flora had agreed to marry Edward. Just like Marianne, Flora was prepared to sacrifice herself on the marriage altar for the benefit of her family. Now, Madeline was here to find out if there could be a happy ending without resorting to such extreme measures.

Thanks to Aunt Lucy's directions, Madeline had no trouble

finding Flora's family home, which was situated at the edge of the town, in plain sight of the Wisconsin River and the remaining lumber mills that relied on its fast-flowing water for power.

The Pierce's house was a simple wooden structure, completely in accordance with its rundown location and a world removed from the mock grandeur of Mountview, with its rows of milkmaid statues and manicured lawns. No wonder Flora always seemed so out of place, so grateful for the crumbs of hospitality she was offered by the Booths. As someone who suffered the same poor-relation mentality, Madeline understood why Flora felt duty bound to oblige her benefactors in any way she could.

Madeline knocked on the front door, cursing the dirt from the road that clung to her plain muslin dress and refused to be brushed away. She'd been determined to make a good first impression on Flora's family, but she was already feeling grubby and out of sorts, and anxious about the situation that was about to greet her. It was ill-mannered to appear unannounced and uninvited. She'd considered sending a note in advance but hadn't wanted to give Flora the opportunity of refusing to see her. The family had every right to turn her away. She was, after all, a stranger intent upon talking Flora out of an advantageous marriage.

A pair of heavy feet clattered towards the door before it was flung open, and Madeline was greeted by a flustered maid.

'The master isn't here. What is it you want?'

'I'm looking for Miss Flora Pierce,' said Madeline, refusing to respond in kind to the maid's scowl, however much she felt like it.

The maid rolled her eyes and shouted over her shoulder. 'Flora, there's a strange woman to see you.'

Flora arrived at the maid's side, her eyes widening with panic when she saw Madeline. 'Is everything all right? Has something happened?'

Madeline was quick to dispel any alarm. 'Not at all. I received your letter and wanted to talk to you about it in person.'

'There was no need to go to so much trouble.'

Flora looked even more flustered than the maid at the realisation that Madeline had travelled all this way to see her. She lowered her eyes, inviting her in while the maid stared unashamedly at Madeline, checking every detail from her bonnet strings to her shoes, and every scrap of muslin and lace in between.

'You must excuse how you find us,' muttered Flora. 'We weren't expecting a visitor.' Flora nodded to the maid, whose expression had shifted from curiosity to insolence, and asked her to bring them tea before leading Madeline through to the parlour.

The house was humble and cluttered, but no worse than others Madeline had visited with her mother, when she was still alive and well enough to see friends. The lingering smell of yesterday's cooking and the layers of dust didn't bother her. This was how most people lived. People who struggled daily to feed their children, keep them clothed and ensure they had a roof over their heads. It was a life that, at one time, she herself had fully expected to inhabit.

It soon became obvious that there would be no tea, in spite of Flora's request. The sound of crashing plates and the cursing that travelled through the thin wall from the kitchen indicated a want of cream and lemons, a lack of clean cups and saucers.

All the while, Flora apologised for the cacophony of children's voices carrying from the room above them, the thump of their feet as they ran back and forth, playing their jumping game of dodge the crocodile.

Madeline was working out how to approach the purpose of her visit when Mrs Pierce burst into the room, pulling off her bonnet and casting aside her gloves with a sigh. She stopped in her tracks when she saw Madeline sitting in the one decent armchair, positioned near the window to catch the best of the light.

'Forgive me, I didn't know we were expecting a guest.'

Madeline rose to her feet and introduced herself before Flora had the presence of mind to speak. 'Please excuse my intrusion. Flora is a dear friend and I wanted to see her.'

'You're very welcome.' Mrs Pierce pushed her hands against the creases of her skirt as she spoke. 'You'll have to take us as you find us, I'm afraid.'

Madeline was instantly struck by Mrs Pierce's physical likeness to her sister, Mrs Booth. They had the same delicate features and fine brown hair, the same faraway look in their eyes, as if they longed to be anywhere but where they currently found themselves. It was hard to believe that the two sisters, so similar in every way, could have ended up living such different lives.

It was all down to the men they'd married, the choices they'd made when they were still too young to know their own minds, let alone their hearts. If Mrs Pierce had married a penniless clerk for love, it didn't appear to have brought her any more happiness than Mrs Booth, who'd married a bully and a corrupt businessman for his money. The two of them were depressing examples of a woman's fate when the only self-determination she had in life was the ability to select a husband at an immature age.

Once the introductions had been made, Mrs Pierce excused herself from the room and dashed to the kitchen, where she could be heard ordering the maid to search for the teapot, which appeared to be another everyday object that had unaccountably disappeared.

'I noticed a pretty little tea room on my way here,' said Madeline, rescuing Flora from her embarrassment. 'Shall we go and see what they have to offer in the way of cake?'

'At least there, we'll be able to talk without disturbance,' said Flora, rushing out of the room to fetch her bonnet.

As they made their way to the tea room, Madeline noted the change in Flora. Her reserved manner was as evident now she was back in the heart of her family as when she was living with the Booths. She'd lost weight, and the colour she'd gained in her cheeks from walking along the beach with Will and the afternoons spent horse riding had faded. She didn't look like a young woman who'd recently received an advantageous marriage proposal, a woman on the precipice of wedded bliss.

'You must be glad to spend time with your family after so many years living away from them?' Madeline made it sound like a question rather than a statement, inviting Flora to open up about her situation.

'I've been gone so long, they hardly know me. The house is too full, and Mother's too busy keeping body and soul together to entertain another guest, which is how they see me. The last thing they need is another mouth to feed. Father lost his job at the local brewery three days ago. We won't see him again until he's spent every last cent of his wages on drink and sobered up enough to remember his way back to us.'

'Still, it must be nice to be home again,' said Madeline, struggling for something positive to say.

'I've always called it home, and in my head that's what it's always been, but I don't belong here anymore. That's been made clear to me. If I'm honest, I didn't need to be told. I felt it as soon as I arrived.'

Madeline imagined how it would feel to be sent back to her old life. Flora's mother hadn't sunk to the same ruin as her own mother, but she'd been equally guilty of making a bad choice when it came to giving herself to a man. She forced a smile, pushing away the cold shiver of dread that washed over her at the thought of what might have been if her father hadn't rescued her from the brothel, and if Hugh hadn't stood by her and continued to protect her.

'You must accompany me back to Newport,' said Madeline. 'I'm sure Mrs Booth would be delighted to have you return. She must be missing you terribly, and Mimi must be missing her walks.'

'Edward will send for me when he's ready. I couldn't presume to return until then.'

The mention of Edward's name was the cue Madeline needed to bring him into the conversation. 'I was surprised to hear of your forthcoming marriage.' She couldn't bring herself to offer congratulations when she saw so much wrong in the union, not only for herself and Hugh, but for Flora and Edward too.

'Yes, I . . .'

By now they were seated at a table in the tiny tea room, the smell of warm scones baking in the kitchen offering an unexpected comfort. The conversation stalled as the waitress approached. Madeline ordered sandwiches, tea and a plate of cakes.

'So now you find yourself in the fortunate position of having marriage proposals from two fine men.'

'No, not at all, I mean . . .' Flora looked helplessly around the tea room, as if she was searching for someone to come to her rescue. 'I refused your brother's proposal. I have no obligation to him and he has none to me.'

'I didn't realise you harboured hopes of Edward. You never mentioned it before. It explains why you turned down Hugh's offer.'

Flora stared at the tablecloth. 'Edward has always been very kind to me.'

'You said the same about Hugh.'

'Your brother has shown me great respect, but I hardly know him. Not like I know Edward.'

'Forgive me if I'm speaking out of turn, Flora, but surely Edward is more like a brother to you than a suitor. The two of you are closely related by blood. Your mothers are sisters.'

'There's no law against us marrying.'

'Not in New York State, but in other states—'

'We don't need to concern ourselves with those,' said Flora, more assertive than Madeline had ever known her. 'Edward is a good man. He's safe and reliable. He'll give me a good home.'

'What does your brother think of the engagement?'

'I haven't told him yet.' Flora swallowed, her eyes fixed on the plate of sandwiches that had been placed in front of them. 'I'm sure he'll be relieved to know I'll be well settled.'

She continued to stare at the sandwiches, talking as much to herself as to Madeline. 'You've seen the way my family lives. If I marry Edward, I'll be able to help them. Mother will be able to employ a decent maid. Susan has ambitions to go to college. It'll only be possible if I can pay for it.'

They were finally getting to the crux of the matter. 'Is that the reason you've agreed to marry Edward?'

Flora shrugged, her expression suggesting she didn't know her own mind. 'I'm doing what I think is best for everyone.'

'And how about what's best for you, Flora? Have you considered that?'

'I know you're here to plead for your brother, Miss Crosby, but that's all over and done with.'

'Not as far as he's concerned, it isn't.'

'How can I be sure of his character when—'

'Do you love my brother, Flora?'

Flora's silence told Madeline she wasn't prepared to admit the truth. Nor could she bring herself to lie. There was only one thing Madeline could do to convince her of Hugh's integrity. She took a deep breath, bracing herself for Flora's reaction as she told her about her own origins, how she wouldn't be where she was today if it wasn't for Hugh protecting her, and standing by her in the face of so much public animosity.

Madeline sipped her tea, letting the news sink in before she continued. 'There's no kinder person than Hugh. For all his outward appearances, he's a man of honour.'

Flora stared at the untouched scone Madeline had put on the plate in front of her. 'I don't dispute what you say, Miss Crosby. I've seen his kindness. I'll never forget how he risked his life to rescue the little boy who was stuck up the tree. I see what an excellent brother he is to you.'

'He would be just as good a husband to you.'

'It's too late. I've already refused him.'

'Your refusal has only made him long for you more. I've never seen him so bereft. He's lost without you.'

Flora shuffled in her seat. 'I've accepted Edward now. My fate is sealed. There's no going back on it.'

The fact that Flora was engaged to Edward only served to bring home what a fool Madeline had been to reject him. Regardless of his family's association with the brothels, he was the only man to ever inspire love in her, the only man who ever came close to Hugh in terms of understanding her. How could she have allowed the experience of her early childhood to cloud her judgement? Whatever his family might be guilty of, Edward was a decent man.

It wasn't only her desire for Edward that drove Madeline to stop a marriage between him and Flora. It was for Flora's sake too, and Edward's and Hugh's. No good would come from Flora and Edward marrying. Even if it was for the right reasons, they were wrong for one another. But how could Madeline set things right without causing further harm or breaking more hearts?

'I'm sorry about your mother,' said Flora, reaching for Madeline's hand. 'Mine could easily have suffered the same fate if she hadn't been living in this town. At least here, there are enough sympathetic neighbours to pay her to do their laundry and their mending, enabling her to get by when Father's too drunk to think of anyone but himself.'

'You and I are not so different,' said Madeline, comforted by Flora's touch and the honesty of her words.

'When Uncle Tobias gave me my coming-out ball, he kept referring to me as Cinderella. It was a cruel joke. The rich and powerful will never understand what it's like to be anything other than what they are.'

'Since the exposé, he must understand only too well how it feels to be vulnerable,' said Madeline. 'Why else would he have left the country?'

Flora looked up, her eyes suddenly alert. 'What exposé? What do you mean?'

'Didn't you see it in the newspapers?'

'I haven't seen a newspaper in all the time I've been here.'

It hadn't crossed Madeline's mind that Flora wouldn't have known the reason for Tobias Booth fleeing the country. It had been ill-considered to introduce the subject into the conversation so clumsily.

'You must forget I said anything. It'll no doubt blow over soon enough.'

But Flora wasn't so easily put off. 'What are you talking about, Miss Crosby?'

Now she'd mentioned it, Madeline was forced to reveal the truth, even at the cost of shattering any illusions Flora might have about the fine family that had taken her in as a child, the family she'd spent the best part of her life being grateful to for allowing her to serve them.

Flora sank back in the chair as she absorbed the news. 'Now I understand why Edward wanted nothing to do with the hotel business.'

'He claims not to have known of it. I feel wretched for not believing him.'

'It also explains why Will was so eager to find a new job. He wouldn't tell me why he was uncomfortable working for our uncle after he'd been so generous towards us. Now it all makes sense.'

'He probably thought you'd insist on leaving the Booths' protection if you knew, and he wouldn't have wanted you to feel obliged to give up such a decent home.'

Flora nodded. 'It's all thanks to your brother that Will now has a position where his principles are no longer compromised.'

Once again, the conversation had gravitated to Hugh. Madeline could see the longing in Flora's eyes every time he was mentioned.

The tea had gone cold and the food remained untouched. However tempting it looked, neither could face it. There were too many revelations to digest for them to stomach anything else.

They took a slow walk back to the house. Despite the direction they travelled, neither of them wanted to arrive. Flora paused to look at the river, its fast-flowing surface bubbling over the rocks.

'I finally understand why Edward asked me to marry him. He thinks no other woman will want him now the family is known to be associated with the brothels. That's the reason, isn't it? Someone has to produce an heir. Theo will never do it.'

Madeline couldn't dispute the logic of Flora's conclusion. 'Edward cares for you. You said so yourself.'

'Like a brother though, not like a lover.' She paused, risking an uncertain look at Madeline before she continued. 'He's in love with someone else.'

'Did he tell you that?' Was it true? Had Edward confided his love for her to Flora?

'He didn't have to tell me. I know him well enough to see his heart is broken.'

'In that case, perhaps you should consider calling off the engagement.'

Flora shook her head. 'He wouldn't have asked me to be his wife if he had any hope of marrying the other woman. I'll honour my pledge. I owe it to him and to the family. The Booths have been very good to me and Will. I gave Edward my word and I'll stand by it.'

There was no scorn in Flora's manner, only cool acceptance. Edward and Flora were prepared to marry for the benefit of their families. Romantic love had failed them both, and this was where it had brought them.

They sat on the bank in silence, watching the lumbermen loading the great log rafts with freshly cut timber ready for the journey down the river to St Louis, listening to their shouts and whistles as the orders went back and forth between them.

It was a long time before Flora spoke. 'I had no idea the Booths ran a chain of brothels. I've always been so quick to judge the morality of others while not seeing what was directly in front of me.'

'You mustn't blame yourself,' said Madeline. 'It's been a well-kept secret for decades.'

'It puts a different colour on everything though. Life isn't as black and white as I've always believed.'

'Scratch beneath the surface of any gilding and you'll find grey metal. It's how the world is.'

Flora took a moment to consider Madeline's comment. 'I must seem naive to you, Miss Crosby.'

Madeline gave Flora's hand a reassuring squeeze. 'You've lived a sheltered life. From where I'm sitting, there's a lot to be said for it. No good ever came of exposure to the world's ills.'

'Your early life experience must have given you more wisdom than many of us could ever hope for.'

Madeline let out a helpless laugh. 'Not enough to stop me making mistakes.'

As they walked back to the house, Madeline considered what a wonderful wife Flora would have made Hugh if only things had worked out differently. The situation for all four of them was a waste of everyone's hearts, a waste of the love and the happiness that was once there for the taking. There seemed no going back on the pledges that would inevitably be honoured, no unravelling the mess they'd made of everything.

Chapter 32

The Pierce's maid met Flora and Madeline at the door. Thanks to the three boys running around her legs, she looked more flustered than ever.

'There's a gentleman here to see you. He's waiting in the parlour.' She pushed her unruly hair off her face and shooed the boys upstairs. 'If it's not one thing, it's something else.'

Before Flora could ask who the visitor was, the maid began stomping her way back to the kitchen. 'Don't ask for any tea because I've got enough to do, and there ain't none.'

Either the maid hadn't bothered to ask the caller's name or she hadn't had the presence of mind to mention it. Flora glanced at Madeline. 'Who do you think it is?'

Madeline hoped it was Hugh. If he'd returned to Beachlands soon after her departure, Finch would have told him where to find her. He'd have had time to make the journey there by now. She took Flora's arm and led her into the parlour. 'There's only one way to find out.'

Mrs Pierce was sitting silently in the best chair, her hands neatly folded in her lap in a way that suggested she'd been in the same position for a long time. She looked up as Madeline and Flora entered, casting her eyes to the corner where the visitor stood motionless, his eyes fixed on the empty grate. Not Hugh, as Madeline had hoped, but Edward. Her heart clenched at the sight of him, until she remembered he was here to see Flora.

Edward faltered as soon as he saw her. 'Miss Crosby. I didn't know you were here.'

'I came to see Flora.'

He cleared his throat. It was the thing he always did when he was nervous. 'It's kind of you to do her the honour of visiting.' His eyes were all over Madeline's face, roaming every contour as if he were trying to read her thoughts.

It felt like an age since Madeline had last seen him. Was it really only a matter of months since she'd received his letter, professing his undying love? Now here they were, together in the same room, standing beside the woman who was about to become his wife. One look at his ravaged face told her they'd both made a mistake, that they'd been too cruel to one another. What a mess they'd created.

'Flora's a dear friend of mine. Why wouldn't I want to see her?' Madeline's words came out more sharply than she'd intended. The air was charged with too much emotion; that was the problem.

'It's a pleasure to see you both,' said Edward, falling back on his good manners.

'Is there a particular reason for your visit?' asked Flora, who appeared less pleased to see Edward than Madeline would have expected. Surely a fiancé needed no excuse to visit his intended wife and her family, especially as they'd been apart for so many weeks.

'I've come to take you home,' said Edward. 'A lot has happened in your absence and Mother needs you.'

She needs a lady's maid and a dog walker, thought Madeline, but she knew better than to say it.

'I'll see to your packing straight away,' said Mrs Pierce, darting out of the room, her mood suddenly brightening at the news that Flora was about to leave them.

If Flora noticed her mother's keenness to be rid of her, she didn't comment on it. 'What is it?' she asked. 'What's happened?'

There was a long pause, as if Edward was unsure how to answer. Madeline began to wonder if there was a reason at all beyond Mrs Booth's demand to have Flora waiting on her, hand and foot. He certainly wasn't prepared to mention the exposé of the brothels and the chaos it had caused the family.

'Marianne has left Rawdon and run off with Mr Crosby.' Edward stared at the floor as he broke the news. 'They've taken Jane with them. They left Newport without word or warning four days ago. One of the maids has confessed to acting as a go-between while they planned their escape.'

Could it be true? Madeline sank into the chair recently vacated by Mrs Pierce and tried to make sense of it all. She remembered Hugh receiving a letter the night before he left Beachlands. He'd refused to tell her who it was from or what it contained, but whatever it was, it had prompted him to act quickly and decisively. It wasn't like him to be so secretive. Surely, he couldn't have been foolish enough to fall for Marianne? What had he been thinking?

She looked into Edward's eyes. 'Are you absolutely sure your sisters are with my brother?'

Edward nodded, the bitterness written all over his face. 'I wish I could tell you it wasn't so.'

'Poor Rawdon,' said Flora. 'How is he bearing up?'

'He's furious and demanding a divorce. Marianne is ruined thanks to Crosby.'

'Hugh must have lost his mind or else there's a good reason for it,' said Madeline.

'I appreciate that he's your brother, Miss Crosby, but surely even you can see the damage he's done.'

Edward's words were sharp and exactly what Madeline deserved. But whatever Edward might think, it was out of character for Hugh to act so recklessly. Her brother's broken heart must have affected his judgement, just as Edward's had affected his when he proposed to Flora. Madeline could find no other excuse for it.

Edward picked up his hat and gloves, indicating his intention to leave, before turning to Flora. 'I'll arrange for a carriage to take us to the station while you help your mother finish your packing.' He glanced at Madeline, reluctant now to meet her eye. 'Will you travel with us, Miss Crosby? I'm sure Flora would be glad of your company.'

'It's kind of you to offer, but I'll make my own way, thank you.'

The thought of a long journey in Edward's company was unbearable. Any regrets he might have had about the way she'd rejected him must now be dispelled. Thanks to Hugh's behaviour, the moral high ground she'd claimed against the Booths was lost. She forced a smile and added, 'The two of you are cousins. You don't need a chaperone.'

If either Edward or Flora felt the sting of her words, they didn't show it. It seemed to Madeline that their forthcoming marriage was the last thing on their minds.

Flora waited until Edward had left the room before she spoke. 'If I'd agreed to marry your brother, none of this would have happened. The family is in ruins and it's my fault.' Her hand trembled as she secured the lid on her sewing box, preparing it for the journey back to Mountview. 'Marianne and Jane are lost forever and so is Mr Crosby.'

It was impossible to tell if Flora was upset over the loss of Hugh as a suitor or the damage that had been done to the reputation of her cousins.

'You mustn't blame yourself for the actions of others,' said Madeline. 'Marianne was determined to have Hugh from the first moment she set eyes on him. You told me yourself she admitted using him to try to get out of marrying Rawdon. If you ask me, this hasn't come out of nowhere, however sudden it might appear.'

Still, it couldn't have all been down to Marianne. Whatever

had happened, Hugh was complicit. As much as Madeline was furious with him, she would listen to what he had to say for himself before she condemned him.

Chapter 33

A week later, there was still no word from Hugh. Madeline filled her days at Beachlands with nothingness, taking long walks across the sand and staring at the ocean. The landscape, which had once offered comfort and release, now only served to highlight her restlessness. Practising the harp gave little solace when there was no one to hear her play. No Hugh to gently tease her, and no Edward to remind her she was worth loving, in spite of who she was.

Finch became a companion of sorts as the two women rattled around the empty house, their paths crossing while they went about their daily domestic business, sharing the occasional cup of tea, a passing chat in the garden. The housekeeper had known Hugh all his life and was as confounded by his actions as Madeline. It was too unsettling to consider that the character of their disreputable father could be revealing itself in him after all.

The monotony of the empty days was finally interrupted by the arrival of an unexpected visitor. Finch knocked quietly on the drawing-room door.

'Edward Booth is here to see you. Shall I show him in or would you like me to send him away?'

He was the last person Madeline had expected to call. She put aside the novel she'd been attempting to read and sat up a little straighter. 'Did he say what he wanted?'

Finch shook her head, turning down the corners of her mouth as if to say it was anyone's guess.

If she was to discover the purpose of his visit, she'd have to admit him. 'Please show him.'

The housekeeper nodded at the instruction, indicating Madeline had made the right decision. 'I'll bring you some tea.'

Edward hovered just inside the door after Finch showed him in. He must have hung his hat on the hallway stand and the lack of it left his hands with nothing to do. The freshness still hadn't returned to his face and there were dark shadows in the hollows beneath his eyes. The last few weeks hadn't been kind to him.

'Miss Crosby, thank you for seeing me. I . . .'

She stood up to greet him. For all his ravaged state, he was the same Edward with the same beating heart, the same look in his eyes that said he mustn't love her.

'Won't you sit down?'

He nodded, taking her invitation as an instruction. 'I won't take up much of your time. I know how busy you are.'

She didn't bother to correct him. 'How's Flora? Is she well?'

'Mother's glad to have her back at Mountview where she belongs.'

This wasn't what she'd asked. He stared at his feet, indicating he had no more to add regarding Flora and nothing to say about their forthcoming wedding.

'It's a shame you didn't think to bring her with you.'

'She's looking after Mimi this morning. She ate something that disagreed with her.'

So, she's cleaning up the dog's vomit, thought Madeline. *And scrubbing the carpet to remove the stains of whatever regurgitated treat had been forced on her without any consideration for the sensitivity of her stomach.* 'Please give her my very best and tell her she's welcome to come to lunch tomorrow if her duties allow.'

'Of course she'll be free to join you. You make it sound as if she's the hired help.'

There was an awkward silence while Finch brought in the tea. Madeline thanked her for her trouble. The housekeeper responded with a small smile. 'I'll be just outside the door if you need me.'

Madeline stared at the teapot, willing the contents to brew. There could be only one reason for Edward's visit. 'Have you heard from your sisters or from my brother? Are they safe and well?'

'I've heard nothing. Have you?'

Madeline shook her head. 'No doubt they'll return sooner or later. I've given it a good deal of thought. If the situation is handled carefully, it might all blow over. Very few people know about their disappearance. If we can keep it that way, we should be able to limit the damage to your sisters' reputations. Given the distance of time and a little cooling of tempers, things might not seem so bad. All might not be lost.'

'If you think Rawdon will take Madeline back as his wife, then you're mistaken. I don't know how you could even consider such a thing. You don't understand how serious the situation is.'

'Trust me, Mr Booth, I've seen far worse things than indulged young women behaving badly to get their own way.'

'So, you see nothing wrong in their conduct?'

'I'm not condoning their selfish and immoral behaviour, nor am I excusing the part my brother has played in whatever fiasco they've chosen to indulge themselves in. I'm simply suggesting there may be a pragmatic way of making the best of the situation in the long run, of papering over the cracks of their moral decline. Life is long. We have to find a way of salvaging what we can of the reputations of your sisters for the sake of their futures. I'm also pointing out the need for you to gain some perspective on the situation.'

'I'm sorry, Miss Crosby, but as I see it, it is unforgivable.'

'From what I witnessed on my recent visit to Southsea, I suspect Rawdon wasn't completely blameless when it came to Marianne's decision to leave him. The man is a bully.'

'Nevertheless—'

'You're happy to fight for the rights of less privileged women, most of whom you'll never meet, but when it comes to the welfare of your sister, you're allowing yourself to be blinded by Rawdon's wealth and social standing.'

'Marianne has a very comfortable life, or at least she did until she abandoned it.'

'You're her brother. You must have seen the change in her, seen how unhappy Rawdon's controlling behaviour was making her.'

Edward cleared his throat. She knew her point had been taken, even if he disagreed with it. If she was to find out the purpose of his visit, she had to put the conversation on a more amenable footing. She poured the tea and offered him a slice of cake.

'No, thank you. This isn't a social call, Miss Crosby.'

His irate tone rattled her. 'Then why are you here, Mr Booth? You need to give me a clue, because all you've done so far is stare at the carpet and appear shocked at my suggestion for salvaging your sisters' reputations.'

'I wanted to let you know in person that in the absence of my father and Theo, I've stepped in to run the family business.'

Madeline knew this already. 'So, now you're in charge of the Trident hotel chain and all its brothels.'

'I've closed the brothels and arranged more appropriate accommodation for the women.'

'I'm glad to hear it. And how are the women to support themselves now?'

To his credit, Edward didn't flinch at her question. 'Most have taken respectable jobs within the hotels, which I was able to offer them. We're helping the remaining few find work in other places. None of the women will be left without money or a decent place to live, I assure you.'

He finally raised his eyes to her face. 'You see, I've followed your example in helping these women to better lives.'

This time it was Madeline's turn to look away. He knew she'd already rescued some of the women from the brothels, the ones who'd been prepared to speak out about their situation and put their names to the exposé, just as he knew she was behind the stories in the newspapers, even if he didn't openly accuse her of it.

'The hotels have lost eighty per cent of their business since the public learned about the brothels,' he continued. 'I don't blame decent people for taking their custom elsewhere. It's going to be a long, hard climb to rebuild the reputation of the business and regain public trust, but I owe it to the next generation of my family to do it.

'I can't undo what was done in the past, Miss Crosby, but I can strive to fix the problems of the present and ensure the hotels are run with higher standards in the future. No one will be exploited on my watch, I give you my word.'

Madeline didn't doubt his sincerity. 'You've every reason to hate me for exposing your family business the way I did. It wasn't my intention to destroy the company. The last thing I want is for your employees to be out of work. I only want to see justice done for the women exploited by the brothels.'

He bowed his head. 'I should have paid more attention when you first raised it with me. I didn't want to believe it and certainly wasn't prepared to face it. My father is a difficult man, but that's no excuse for not standing up to him.'

'And now he and Theo have fled the country, leaving you to sort out the mess.'

The comment didn't warrant a reply, and they sat in silence until Edward found the presence of mind to speak.

'I can't stop thinking about the fact that your mother died at the hands of my family just as readily as if they'd taken a gun and shot her.'

'My father had a hand in it too,' said Madeline. 'If he'd behaved differently when he learned she was carrying me, she might still be alive today.' She touched Edward lightly on the arm. 'Your family weren't the only ones responsible for my mother's death.'

He rubbed his eyes, struggling to compose himself. 'Until women are treated as equals in our society their situation will never improve.'

She thought of the way he judged his sisters, how he viewed their behaviour as shameful without considering what might have driven them to it. 'Attitudes have to change radically. Women need to be seen as individuals in their own right, not simply as goods and chattels.'

Edward nodded. 'Once again, your wisdom puts me to shame.'

'You're still set on marrying Flora?'

He stared at the floor for a long time before he answered. 'Flora has everything to gain from the arrangement, and the reputation of the Trident hotel chain will benefit from having a respectable married man at its helm.'

'Has putting business before love made you happy?'

'It has yet to be seen. All I know is that my experience of love has brought me nothing but despair.'

It was the first honest conversation they'd ever had and Madeline was feeling a little drunk from it. She suggested they take a walk along the beach to clear their heads. She didn't care if they were seen without a chaperone. She needed to blow the cobwebs from her mind and put aside the past, to remind herself she was lucky to be where she was now, that it was only the present and the future that mattered. Memories were nothing but ghosts. It would take effort to lay them to rest, but she wanted to be happy.

As they walked along the shore, an explosion of energy from the bowling waves suddenly encouraged her to burst out. 'I'm sorry.'

Edward stopped in his tracks and turned to face her. 'What for? For not loving me?'

'I never said I didn't love you.'

He lowered his eyes, his hair blowing this way and that as he removed his hat and held it against his chest.

'There are many things I could say in response, Miss Crosby, but none of them would be appropriate. Even if I never came to regret them, the words couldn't be taken back and we would both have to live with the knowledge of them forever.'

There were boundaries that could never be crossed. Not now he'd pledged himself to Flora. 'So, you choose to stow them in your heart?'

'As deeply and as safely as I can bury them.'

'Then let me be the one to speak, for then it's been said. Even if it's never referred to again, we'll know it to be the truth. In time we might both take some comfort from it, even if it pains us now.'

She paused, waiting for him to stop her saying what was on her mind. When he didn't, she took it as permission to continue.

'If you were to ask me to marry you now, right this very moment, I would say yes.'

She stifled the sob in her throat, trying to sound like the detached, confident person she always pretended to be, pushing down the sense of inferiority that tortured her soul.

'If I were not bound to Flora I would have already asked you to be my wife.' He looked at her, his eyes intent on her soul. 'I wouldn't be such a fool as to let you get away so easily again.'

Madeline threw out a false laugh, falling back on her bravado. 'Even though I was born in a brothel, have almost ruined your family business, and my brother has run off with your sisters?'

'Yes, in spite of all these things, a hundred times, yes.'

He paused for a moment, as if he were gathering the courage to risk betraying more of himself. 'I was too quick in asking Flora to be my wife. I was trying to prove to myself that I was ready to live a life without you, that I could find happiness elsewhere. It was a mistake to ever think it was possible.' He paused, allowing the sea breeze to snatch his breath. 'I won't dishonour her by going back on my pledge.'

The words were like a knife, twisting in Madeline's heart. 'Flora will make you a good wife.'

'And in return, I'll give her a secure home.'

Despite their connection, and the lock that bound their hearts, such words could never be spoken again. The moment of intimacy had already passed, and there could be no hope of revisiting it, not now Edward had promised to marry Flora.

Madeline returned to Beachlands alone, fighting her despair by reminding herself to be grateful for her privileged life. Not only was she wealthy but she was loved by a good man. Even if that love could never be lived to the full, she would take solace from the fact that Edward loved her for herself and for no other reason.

Chapter 34

Edward was as good as his word in passing on Madeline's lunch invitation to Flora for the following day. Meeting as friends, there was no awkwardness between the two women. Flora hadn't realised it was Madeline who had broken Edward's heart, and given her circumstances, Madeline couldn't blame her for agreeing to marry him. Nothing that had occurred was Flora's fault.

The two of them were picking over a rather uninteresting salad when without warning Hugh returned. Madeline put down her fork and ran to greet him at the front door. After the rumours she'd heard about him and the Booth sisters, she didn't know whether to be surprised to find him alone. Now wasn't the time to ask questions. He was tired and travel weary, and needed to be made comfortable before she began her interrogation.

'Come and have lunch. You must be starving after your journey.' She threw her arms around him and whispered by way of a warning, 'Flora's here.'

Finch relieved him of his coat, hat and gloves, directing his exhausted body with discretion and efficiency. 'Shall I run you a bath, or would you like to eat first?'

Hugh rubbed his hands together as if to brush off the journey. 'I'll join the ladies for lunch, if that's all right.'

Flora had put aside her cutlery and was waiting patiently at the table for Madeline to return and resume their meal. She looked up from her plate as Hugh entered the dining room, swallowing hard as if a lump of food had caught at the back of her throat.

'Mr Crosby, I'm glad to see you've arrived home safely.'

Even though Madeline had warned him of her presence, Hugh seemed unprepared for the reality of it. He hesitated, standing at the edge of the room as if it wasn't his to inhabit.

'Flora.' It seemed it was all he could say.

Whatever Flora was feeling, she didn't show it. She broke away from his gaze. 'I should leave. The two of you must have a lot to catch up on.'

'Please don't go,' said Hugh, still rooted to the spot. 'Stay and finish your meal. I'd never forgive myself if you ran away on my account.'

The idea of running away was an unfortunate one to bring into the conversation given the circumstances, and Hugh blanched as soon as he'd said it.

The ensuing silence was broken by Finch, who appeared with plates of cold meat, potatoes and bread. Hugh took his place at the head of the table and helped himself to the food, heaping effusive thanks on the housekeeper as she slipped quietly from the room.

All the while, Flora was making a great effort to pick over the wilted leaves on her plate, focusing a little too carefully on her fork as she avoided catching Hugh's eye. Madeline guessed it must have taken all the effort she could muster to remain seated at a table with the man who'd played so roughly with her heart and ruined Marianne, and probably Jane too.

Madeline was desperate to hear what he had to say for himself but forced herself to wait until he'd finished eating and fortified himself with coffee before she asked where he'd been for the last few weeks.

'I've been on a mission of mercy, if you'll believe it.' He glanced nervously at Flora, as if he were pleading with her to smile at him.

It wasn't the answer Madeline had been expecting. 'You need to say more than that if you intend to get yourself out of trouble.'

Hugh slumped in his chair. Whatever he'd been up to had taken its toll. 'The letter I received the night before I left Beachlands was a cry for help from Jane, written on her sister's behalf.

'To all intents, Rawdon was keeping Marianne a prisoner at Southsea and refusing to let her see anyone. He'd even set the household staff to spy on her.' He caught Madeline's eye. 'Marianne said you witnessed this the day you visited her.'

Madeline nodded, urging him to continue.

'The sisters managed to communicate with each other through one of the trusted housemaids who was willing to pass letters between them. Together they hatched a plan to get Marianne away from Southsea and away from Rawdon's clutches. Knowing two women travelling alone would draw too much attention, Jane asked for my protection.'

'And you considered yourself the most appropriate person to do this?' asked Madeline.

'I know how it might appear,' said Hugh, glancing at Flora, 'but nothing untoward happened. Following Jane's request, I hired a carriage and waited outside the grounds of Southsea until Marianne was able to slip out of the house without being seen. We then collected Jane, and the three of us left Newport. We travelled to New York where we took up lodgings in an unassuming boarding house, using false names.'

'The three of you stayed together?' asked Flora, her eyebrows rising at the suggestion.

'It was all perfectly proper, I assure you. Jane was there to act as a chaperone as well as a travelling companion to her sister. It took time to arrange their passage on a steamship. They were reluctant to leave the boarding house in case they were spotted by one of Rawdon's acquaintances. They assumed he'd have people searching for Marianne, and the last thing she wanted was to be found. The man had already treated her so brutally, she was terrified of what he'd do if he got hold of her. As their protector, I acted on the sisters' behalf, booking their passage to Europe and making all the last-minute arrangements to ensure their journey was comfortable. As you can imagine, Marianne had left Southsea with only the clothes she stood in.'

'So where are the sisters now?' asked Madeline. 'Are they safe?' After what she'd witnessed during her visit to Southsea, she had no doubt that what Hugh was telling them was true.

'They're on their way to Italy. The boat sailed this morning. Jane has been in touch with Theo, who is currently in Rome with Mr Young, and arranged for him to meet them when they disembark from the ship.'

'And what will they do then?' asked Flora.

'Theo has rented rooms near the Spanish Steps. The sisters will take refuge there while they decide what to do next.' Hugh looked at Flora. 'You mustn't worry. From what I've learned, Marianne will be safer on the high seas than she ever was in Rawdon's house.'

Whatever emotions had been building up in Flora suddenly burst out. She pulled a handkerchief from her pocket and buried her face in it. 'Forgive me. It's all so much to take in. I thought something terrible must have happened, and all along . . .'

The rest of her words were lost as she struggled to stifle her tears. Madeline rose from her chair and embraced her, while Hugh stayed resolutely in his seat staring at his crumpled napkin.

'It wasn't my intention to cause you so much distress, Miss Pierce. I couldn't refuse to assist your cousin's escape when I learned she was in so much danger from the man who'd taken a vow to protect and honour her. I would do the same for any woman.'

Flora nodded. 'I should never have doubted you.'

Madeline looked at her brother, wishing he'd confided in her from the beginning. 'And neither should I.'

The tension in the room was unbearable. Marianne suggested they step out into the garden for some air. The sun was shining and the late roses were still in bloom. They'd be fools not to enjoy them.

She followed at a discreet distance as Hugh took Flora's arm and led her to the arbour where a rambling rose had created a shady retreat. Madeline couldn't help but hear the exchange over the breeze as Hugh spoke.

'I've missed our conversations, Miss Pierce. I've regretted the time we've spent apart.'

'So much has happened these past weeks. I'm still not able to take it all in.'

'My clumsy proposal of marriage is the thing I regret most of all.'

'There's no need to regret your proposal, Mr Crosby. You're not held to it in any way.'

'You misunderstand me. I can hardly think straight when you're so close to me. It's not the proposal I regret, Miss Pierce, but the way I presented it to you. It was badly done, but my feelings are genuine. Will you ever forgive me?'

'Consider it forgotten, sir.'

'I'm not asking you to forget the proposal, Flora, only the manner in which it was expressed. Will you do me the honour of allowing me to prove my constancy to you so that one day you might consider becoming my wife? Please don't say anything now. I'll wait for as long as it takes for you to decide. I live only for your happiness.'

Madeline's heart turned to stone as she listened to her brother's words. He didn't know Flora had agreed to marry Edward, that she was no longer free to accept his proposal.

Having been asked not to speak, Flora remained silent. Madeline suspected it wasn't Hugh's instruction that kept her quiet, but her inability, or perhaps reluctance, to break the news of her engagement.

'Please don't look so sad, Flora,' said Hugh. 'I can't stand it.'

'If you hadn't disappeared without word or trace, Mr Crosby, your sister would have told you of my engagement.'

'Engagement? It's not possible. Who have you pledged to marry? Tell me it's a joke.'

'If I'd have believed your sentiments were genuine and lasting, I would never have accepted him.'

'You're talking in riddles, Flora. My mind isn't as sharp as yours. Please tell me you're not engaged. God knows, I deserve to be punished for the way I've treated you, for not informing you of the reason for my absence sooner, but there's a limit to how much I can endure.'

'While you were away, Edward proposed to me and I accepted.'

'Edward Booth?' There was a long pause while Flora's words sank in. 'But he's your cousin.'

'Now you understand why I can't marry you.'

'How could you accept him when you know how much I love you?'

'Why would I think you were serious after the way I saw you behave with Marianne, after the flippant way you proposed, as if the idea had just popped into your head? After that, there was the long silence, during which I learned you'd disappeared without a trace. Did you expect me to wait until you decided to make your way back to me?'

'I—'

'Please don't say anything else, Mr Crosby. My heart won't stand it.'

Madeline took a further step back into the laurel bush, where she couldn't be seen, resisting the urge to run forward and embrace them both. There had to be a way to fix the situation. If only she could work out how to do it. If only she had a magic potion that would make everything right, just as it had done in *A Midsummer Night's Dream*. But in real life, 'the juice of love-in-idleness' had no such power.

Hugh tried once again to understand the situation. 'You do love me though, don't you, Flora? I know I'm a fool and have lost you forever, but please tell me you love me.'

Hugh's display of emotion prompted Flora to flee the arbour and sent her running towards the house. Madeline gave her a minute to compose herself before going after her.

She assumed a distracted air, as if unaware of what had passed. 'There you are, Flora. Are you leaving already?'

Flora nodded, picking up her parasol and her gloves, which she'd left on the hallway table when she arrived. 'You must excuse me. Mrs Booth will be wondering where I've got to and Mimi will be crying for her afternoon walk.'

'Of course. Let me arrange for a carriage to take you back.'

But Flora wouldn't hear of it. She opened the front door and was already dashing along the path. 'Please don't trouble yourself. The exercise will do me good.'

Once Flora had gone, Madeline wandered back through the house and into the garden, where Hugh remained, staring at the rose he'd picked for Flora, only for her to discard it in her hurry to leave. Even though she probably hadn't meant to drop it at his feet, the gesture had an aura of brutal rejection.

Hugh sat on the bench, his elbows resting on his thighs. He must have heard his sister approach and spoke without looking up. 'How could I have made such a mess of things?'

'Love makes fools of us all. Isn't that what the poet says?' She reached for his shoulder and gave it a squeeze. 'Are you sure you love her?'

Hugh nodded, too overcome with emotion to express it. 'I blundered in like a fool, expecting my charm to win her over when all she really wanted was a glimpse of my sincerity.' He rescued the rose that lay at his feet, twirling the stem in his fingers. 'Helping Marianne escape Rawdon hasn't improved matters.'

'It made no difference. Flora had made up her mind to marry Edward before she knew you'd gone.'

'No matter how it might seem, I only ever meant to do right by everyone. You believe that, don't you?'

Knowing him the way she did, Madeline had no doubt about Hugh's honourable intentions. He'd assumed the role of her protector after the death of their father without question or complaint, despite the damaging effect on his own life and his social standing. Now he'd done a similar thing for Marianne after her cry for help. If for no other reasons than these, he deserved to be happy.

Everything about Flora's manner convinced Madeline that she loved him, even if she felt too compromised to admit it. Somehow, Madeline had to find a way to put everything right. It was the only way to repay Hugh for his sacrifices.

Chapter 35

Madeline waited a few days before visiting Flora at Mountview. Hugh's unexpected reappearance over lunch had given both women much to digest. Now the reason behind Marianne and Hugh's disappearance had been revealed and there'd been time to consider it, Madeline wanted to know if Flora had had a change of heart. Surely, she couldn't favour Edward now Hugh had shown himself to be the hero of the story.

Flora was sitting in the corner of the drawing room, diligently working her way through a pile of mending. There was nothing in her manner to suggest she was soon to marry into the Booth family and become mistress of her own home, if not ultimately mistress of Mountview itself.

Mrs Booth was in her usual position on the chaise longue, the late summer breeze from the French doors gently blowing her curled fringe as she slept. Mimi, who appeared to have shifted her allegiance to the person who lavished the most loving care on her, gently snored at Flora's feet.

Mrs Norton, stationed in her usual hard-backed chair, scowled when the maid showed Madeline in.

'I'm surprised you have the nerve to show your face here after the trouble your brother has brought to this family. Have you any idea of the damage he's done? Dear Marianne can never hold her head up in good society again, and poor Rawdon is a broken man.'

'Forgive me for disturbing you,' said Madeline, responding to the coarse welcome with a smile. 'I've come to see Flora.'

Ruffled by Madeline's courteous reply, Mrs Norton sniffed. 'We'll forgive you for nothing.'

'We mustn't blame Miss Crosby for the behaviour of her brother,' said Flora. 'And from what I've been told, Mr Crosby's actions were entirely honourable.'

Madeline thanked her with a smile. It was a surprise to hear her speak so candidly and heartening to hear her defend Hugh.

After standing up to her aunt, Flora was emboldened enough to put aside her mending and invite Madeline to sit beside her. Despite everything, she still didn't appear to have the authority to ask the maid to bring tea and nobody else seemed inclined to propose it.

Mrs Norton continued to look dagger-eyed. The atmosphere was as icy as a New York pavement in winter, but it was nothing Madeline hadn't suffered before, and she refused to let it unsettle her. Madeline had to get Flora alone if there was to be any chance of having a heart-to-heart about Hugh.

'Shall we take a walk in the garden?'

Flora nodded, rising mutely from her chair until Mrs Norton intervened. 'You'll do no such thing. You'll both stay right here where I can see you.'

Anyone would have thought Flora was a disgraced child the way she was spoken to. Madeline clenched her jaw, fighting the temptation to say something as Flora returned to her mending. Madeline was only one wrong word away from being thrown out of the house and she wouldn't risk it until she knew what was going on in Flora's mind.

'It's time you remembered your place,' continued Mrs Norton, snarling through her words. 'If you have ideas of becoming

Edward's wife, you need to improve your ways and think twice about the company you keep.'

Mrs Norton's voice must have woken Mrs Booth from her afternoon slumber, because she suddenly shifted herself into a more upright position. 'Miss Crosby. I didn't know you were expected.' She blinked once or twice, her eyes adjusting to the afternoon light. 'We—'

'She wasn't expected,' interrupted Mrs Norton. 'Nor is she welcome.' She sniffed, her expression full of contempt. 'And she's yet to tell us what she's doing here.'

'No doubt she's come to congratulate Flora on her forthcoming marriage to Edward,' said Mrs Booth, hardly bothering to stifle a yawn.

So, the marriage was still going ahead, in spite of everything. Madeline smiled, disguising what she really felt about the news. 'I—'

'I'm surprised she has the nerve to show her face after what her wretched brother did to our beloved Marianne,' said Mrs Norton, trampling over Madeline's unfinished sentence and repeating what she'd already said for the benefit of Mrs Booth.

'I've explained what happened with Marianne,' said Flora, stabbing her needle into a fraying shirt collar. 'Rawdon was proving to be an impossible husband. Mr Crosby was good enough to rescue her before she came to any further harm.'

'Harm indeed,' snapped Mrs Norton. 'How about the harm that's been done to her reputation and to Jane's? How about the harm it's done to the family business now Rawdon's bank has withdrawn the promise of its investment? The hotel chain is in ruins; ruins I tell you. And it's all because of *her* brother.'

The financial problems faced by the hotel business weren't due to Rawdon's failure to invest, but because their customers had abandoned them since learning about the brothels. Madeline wasn't prepared to incriminate herself by correcting Mrs Norton's assumption. Edward knew she was behind the exposé in the newspapers and had been discreet enough not to reveal it to the rest of the family. It was more consideration than most people would think she deserved.

'I don't know how she has the nerve to set foot in this house,' she repeated for the third time, jabbing her finger at Madeline.

The facts Hugh had related in Flora's company were only part of the story. Hugh had refused to abandon the sisters while they were alone in New York and in need of his protection. The reason the three of them had stayed so long in the lodging house was because Marianne insisted on waiting for the bruises on her face to fade before she boarded the steamship. These were the secrets that were never shared, the horrors that were swept under the carpet when advantageous marriages were talked about.

'My brother considers what he did an act of mercy,' said Madeline. 'Marianne asked to be rescued. Her life wasn't her own while she remained living under Rawdon's roof.'

'Of course her life wasn't her own,' said Mrs Norton. 'She was Rawdon's wife. He was her lord and master. What did she expect? I engineered the match for the good of the family's social standing, and for the financial benefits it would bring to the business. Tobias had talked about expanding the hotel chain for years. This was a way of gaining the means to do it. Life isn't a fairy tale, Miss Crosby. It was a marriage of convenience. Marianne was wise enough to understand that until your brother interfered. She was given a grand house to live in and fine clothes to wear. She knew there was a price to pay for the wealth and privilege that had been handed to her on a plate. What else could the ungrateful girl have wanted?'

Not to be beaten by her husband, thought Madeline, *or to be kept apart from those she loved. Not to live in fear or be spied upon, or kept a prisoner in her own home.* There was no point in saying it. In Mrs Norton's world, these abuses were an acceptable price to pay for social status and monetary gain.

Mrs Booth yawned, stretching her arms above her head. 'It's all so terrible. I don't know how I can be expected to stand it. Even poor Mimi is out of sorts. Look how she tucks herself beneath Flora's skirt.'

All eyes shifted to the dog who had pushed her little body against Flora's ankles, claiming it as a sanctuary from Mrs Norton's ranting. Realising all the eyes in the room where on her, Flora leaned down and gave Mimi a reassuring rub behind the ear.

'At least our dear Edward has come to our rescue,' continued Mrs Booth, without much enthusiasm. 'He'll save the hotel business in the absence of Tobias and Theo.'

Madeline took advantage of the mention of Edward's name to bring the subject around to the reason for her visit. 'Is there any news on the wedding? Have you set a date?'

'Not yet,' said Flora. 'Edward's been so busy rescuing the hotel business, there's been no time to think of it. He left for New York almost the moment we returned from Wisconsin, and I haven't seen or heard from him since.'

Madeline observed Flora as she calmly sewed the fraying edge of a shirt collar. She didn't seem sorry about the delay to the wedding or Edward's absence.

'They shouldn't be too hasty when it comes to getting married,' said Mrs Booth. 'I can't do without Flora now. Losing both my beloved daughters, and Theo to Italy, has left a great hole in my life. I despair over what's to become of them without my wisdom to guide them. Flora's my only comfort.'

It was noticeable that Mrs Booth made no mention of missing her husband or her regret that he hadn't asked her to accompany him on his extended trip to Switzerland.

'There'll be plenty of time to think about the wedding later on,' said Flora, reassuring Mrs Booth with a weak smile.

'So, the two of you are in no hurry to marry?' asked Madeline. 'I thought your cousin might want to get it over and done with quickly.'

'It seems not,' said Flora, failing to meet Madeline's eye.

'Over and done with' was a clumsy way of describing it, but Flora didn't react to the implication. As always, she was putting duty before her own wishes, doing as the Booths told her to without question, even if it went against her heart's desire.

Madeline considered Flora's expression, trying to work out her thoughts. After almost a lifetime of hiding her true feelings, she was as skilled at dissembling as Madeline herself. Defeated in the purpose of her visit, it was time to leave. There was no hope of speaking to Flora alone today. Mrs Norton and Mrs Booth had closed ranks around her so closely she might as well have been protected by guard dogs.

Madeline's mother used to say, 'There's a Jack for every Jill.' She never lost her faith in love, even as she was passed around the paying customers. Since meeting Edward, Madeline had come to understand that faith. While there was still a chance of putting things right between the four of them, she wouldn't give up. She cast her eyes around the grand room before she said goodbye. For all the gilding and the finery, there was no trace of love, and nothing shone quite brightly enough to disguise the dark heart of the family who revelled in its shallow glory.

Chapter 36

It was the following week. Madeline still hadn't had an opportunity to speak to Flora alone, despite repeatedly inviting her to lunch and to go horse riding. If she couldn't be tempted by an outing on Brodie, then nothing would tempt her to visit. Flora's confidence as a horsewoman had grown during the times she'd spent riding with Madeline and Hugh. As far as they were concerned, the gentle mare was hers in all but name.

A polite refusal had been sent in reply to every invitation, each time with a different excuse. In a moment of weakness, Hugh suggested tying a bow around Brodie's neck and delivering her to Mountview as a gift.

'Riding does Flora a world of good, Maddie. Even if she doesn't want me, it's only right she has the horse.'

It had taken an hour of discussion to persuade Hugh out of his extravagant gesture. Madeline couldn't make him see how his generosity and his impetuous behaviour could work against him.

'I don't doubt the goodness in your heart, Hugh, but others don't always see the genuine motivations beneath your actions.'

'I only want to do good where Flora's concerned, Maddie. I want to make her happy, and for her to know how much I care about her. Brodie will do that for me, won't she?'

In an attempt to pacify him, Madeline sent a further invitation, imploring Flora to join her for an afternoon ride. A polite refusal was delivered within the hour, this time without an accompanying excuse or expression of regret. Madeline sensed Mrs Norton's controlling hand at work. If Madeline was to reconnect with Flora, she had to bide her time and be clever about it. Madeline had faced down far worse dragons than Mrs Norton and the slight was nothing to her.

With the Booths keeping their distance, it was a surprise when Finch knocked on the drawing-room door just after breakfast one morning and announced Edward had come to see Madeline. Hugh had gone to play tennis at the Casino, and Madeline was alone.

Unprepared for the unexpected visitor, Madeline gave Finch a troubled look. 'Do you think I should agree to see him?'

Finch blinked two or three times while she thought about it. 'It couldn't do any harm.'

Edward strode into the room as if he'd rehearsed his entrance a hundred times. 'Forgive the interruption, Miss Crosby. This isn't a social call.'

'Are you going to tell me that every time you visit, Mr Booth?'

Her comment was enough to make him stumble. She pointed to the chair directly opposite her. 'Please take a seat before you fall over yourself.'

She was being cruel and she knew it. His sudden presence had caught her off guard, and her wit was her only weapon.

Finch was still hovering by the door, waiting to see if she was needed. Madeline caught her eye, reading her warning to go easy on him. Surrendering to the housekeeper's wisdom, she replied with an almost indiscernible nod. Satisfied by the assurance, Finch quietly left them alone.

'I hope Flora's well.'

Edward cleared his throat. 'Yes.'

'I've invited her to visit no end of times, but she always seems to be busy with one thing or another.'

'Yes.'

Madeline felt her irritation growing. If she was only to receive one-word answers from him, they'd never get anywhere. If this wasn't a social call, then there had to be another purpose to his visit. She sat up straight, folding her hands in her lap and softening her tone. For all her outward hostility, she was delighted to see him.

'What can I do for you, Mr Booth?'

His eyes had always been the warmest shade of brown, like pools of liquid chocolate. Now, as he looked at her, they were nothing but dried husks, as if all the life had been removed from them. The joy had gone from him, and in its place she saw nothing but grief and exhaustion.

'Are you all right? You don't look so well.'

She knew what had happened to cause the change. She had happened. Madeline. Her rejection had broken him. Now, his hasty engagement to Flora, which was a result of his misplaced love, was set to destroy him. He hadn't so much given up as given in to the impossible situation the two of them had created, and by doing so, made everything so much worse.

'I'm perfectly well, thank you for asking, Miss Crosby. Striving to restore the fortunes of the family business has taken its toll on me, but it's nothing a good rest won't cure.'

'Then you should make sure you get it.'

Madeline's words came out more as an admonishment than the message of reassurance she'd meant to offer. She cursed herself for her lack of judgement. After a lifetime of building her defences, whenever she tried to say anything heartfelt, it always came out wrong.

He looked as if he expected her to beat him with a stick. 'The hotel chain has been through a challenging time, but my efforts to put the business on a more ethical footing are beginning to have a positive effect. Since I released a statement, explaining the evolution of our values and outlining the work we're doing to help the women who were previously exploited by the business, our customers are slowly returning to us. There's still a way to go, but I believe our new approach has even gone as far as to bring new people to our doors.'

'It proves there are benefits to be gained from doing the right thing,' said Madeline. 'It's a shame your father and his father before him didn't understand that.'

There was a long pause before Edward responded, as if he were working out the best way of expressing what was on his mind.

'I've come here today with a proposal.'

'A proposal?'

It was as if the clouds had lifted and the sun had suddenly burst through. Had he finally confessed his mistake to Flora and withdrawn his offer of marriage? Had she released him from his obligation to her? Were they both now free to follow their hearts? Was this the start of a happy ending for all of them? Madeline steadied her voice as she asked the next question.

'What kind of proposal?'

'It's regarding your charitable work.'

Her heart dipped. His interest in her charitable work wasn't unwelcome, but a part of her had hoped he was still interested in her, that he had a different proposal altogether. She tried not to betray her disappointment in her voice.

'Go on.'

'I'm only too aware of what you've done, and what you continue to do, to help the women who assisted you to expose the brothels associated with the hotels. I'd like to build on the work you've already started. There are, I've discovered, many more women who would benefit from support of this kind.'

'What is it you're proposing?'

'I'm asking for your assistance in setting up a charity with a broader remit, one that would aim to help any woman needing refuge from exploitation of whatever kind. A place of safety to run to, where she could be given protection from an aggressor and help finding decent employment and a new life. A place for all women, no matter what their social background.'

His description of the kind of women he planned to help extended to Marianne, trapped in an abusive marriage with no escape, as much as it applied to women at the less privileged end of the social scale. Vulnerability came in all guises. Family wealth and social standing didn't always guarantee personal safety or happiness.

She wondered if he'd come to this idea after learning of Marianne's escape from Rawdon, after hearing of Hugh's intervention to rescue her. As her brother, Edward hadn't been there for her. He'd let her down, and as a man of principle, he must have felt this failing keenly.

'It's a commendable plan, Mr Booth. What part do you expect me to play in it?'

'I expect nothing from you, Miss Crosby. You owe me nothing. But I'd be grateful if you'd share your experience to help me understand exactly what it is these women need and what would most benefit them. I know my limitations, my social awkwardness. I'd like you to teach me how to win people over, how to convince them of the necessity of rescuing these women.'

'You mustn't think of it as rescuing them, Mr Booth, but more of helping them to rescue themselves. Any work you do must be done in collaboration with the women and not simply for them. This is about their lives after all, and they must have a say in how they're changed. Each woman has her own desires, her own ambitions, and that should be respected.'

'You see, Miss Crosby, this is exactly why I need your help. It would never have crossed my mind to think in that way, and I could never put it into such words. Please say you'll help me in whatever capacity you choose.'

How could she say no when he looked at her so eagerly, now a spark of hope had finally returned to his eyes?

'I'd be happy to act as your adviser and offer financial support.'

'Thank you, Miss Crosby, thank you.'

She tempered her reaction to his obvious delight. As things stood, their charitable work was the only thing that would connect them, but at least it was something, and something was better than nothing.

'I'll send you a list of suggestions and we can discuss them another time.'

She got to her feet, indicating it was time for him to leave. They'd spent too long together already and she couldn't risk them becoming too familiar.

He nodded, grateful for every morsel she threw him. 'I look forward to working with you. I'm only sorry that . . .'

'Sorry for what?'

It was cruel of her to press him when she knew what he was sorry for, and how impossible it was for him to speak of it without being disloyal to Flora. He sighed, his despair expressing more than a spoken apology could ever hope to.

Madeline couldn't forget the note he'd sent after Flora's coming-out ball. It had only amounted to a few words, but they'd gone straight to her heart and buried themselves deep. His sentiments held strong. Hardly any time had passed since he'd expressed them, not only in the note, but also during the walk they'd taken along the beach. Still, they'd moved into a different world and there was no going back.

It was impossible to pinpoint the exact moment she fell in love with him. It had been a slow, gentle shift from admiration for his work to something more. When she'd finally admitted it to herself, it had felt like coming home, like placing her head on a soft pillow after a tiring day. And yet it had been impossible for her to forgive him for the crimes of his father, and his father before him, even though he'd played no part in them and now strived to atone for them. She lowered her eyes from his gaze and turned her back, leading him to the door.

'I'll see you out. Finch will have left your hat and gloves on the hallway table.'

'Thank you, Miss Crosby. Thank you for giving me your time.'

And with those few polite words, they parted, until the next time when similar stilted words would pass between them. And so it would continue, until the coolness they pretended to feel became real and there was nothing else. When all was said and done, after the way she'd been so quick to judge and condemn him, it was the best prospect Madeline could hope for. Still, as she watched Edward leave, her heart ached with an overwhelming sense of loss, and with the regret of what might have been.

Chapter 37

Hugh had suddenly become mad for tennis. He said the activity helped shake off the despondency he felt at failing to win Flora, at least for the time he was running around the court.

'When you strive to keep your eye on the ball, it forces you to shut out everything else and live in the moment. While you're rooted in the present there's no room in your head for past regrets.'

Madeline couldn't imagine where this new way of thinking had come from, but he was looking leaner and fitter for all the extra exercise, and his determination to spend two hours a day practising gave him a reason to get up in the morning.

'You should try it, Maddie. You've been spending too much time alone lately. It'll do you good to get out.'

Her heart sank at the thought of having to partake in any sport that didn't involve a horse. She only gave in after Hugh presented her with a tennis racquet, her initials engraved on the handle.

'I'm only agreeing to play to prove how much I appreciate your gift,' she said, trying to hide her unease. 'You know I never take anything you give me for granted.'

The prospect of running around after any kind of ball always brought back the horrors of school. Alongside her rigorous academic education, she'd been obliged to take part in team sports, which for an outsider like Madeline was always agony. However well-bred the girls were, they knew she wasn't one of them. It was beyond their limited sensibilities not to show it, not to consider how it felt to be snubbed, to be seen as not quite up to the mark, to be the last to be chosen for the team.

Now, as Madeline entered the Casino in a white muslin dress with her new tennis racquet tucked under her arm, she wondered how long it would be before her presence was noted, before eyebrows were raised among the observers around the courts and whispers exchanged behind lace gloves.

She grabbed Hugh's arm, holding him back as he headed straight for the nearest available court. 'I'd like to watch the other players first to see how it's done.'

They settled on a bench on the edge of the courts, observing the young men in tight, white breeches, soft shoes and flat caps throw themselves around the space, skidding on the grass and hallooing each time they scored a point, each time the ball was called out. For all it was meant to be a competitive game, it seemed to Madeline that it was just an excuse for running about and showing off.

They'd hardly watched a complete set when Madeline heard the sharp ring of a familiar voice behind them.

'I don't see why we had to drag ourselves all the way here when you have a perfectly good lawn at home on which to chase a ball around.'

It was unmistakably Mrs Norton. Madeline's teeth clenched in response to her presence. The only saving grace was that she was unlikely to acknowledge them in a public place.

'Miss Crosby. I thought it was you.'

It was another familiar voice. One she only heard these days in her dreams. Edward. Suddenly, he was coming towards her, his tennis racquet tipped at a tidy angle across his shoulder. 'I didn't know you played tennis.'

Madeline took refuge behind her most combative smile. 'I

don't. Hugh gave me a racquet, and I only agreed to come to show him how grateful I am for his gift.'

'And are you grateful enough to actually play a match?' he asked.

'Now I'm here, I'm not sure even Hugh can tempt me onto the court. I've never been one for running around and waving my arms above my head.'

'Let me guess. You've never played and you're worried you'll fail to score any points and the result will be a love match.' Edward blushed as he realised what he'd said. 'What I meant was—'

'Miss Crosby. I'm so glad to see you,' said Flora, her unexpected appearance rescuing Madeline from the awkwardness. Until that moment, Madeline hadn't realised she was there. If she'd shifted her attention from Edward's face for just a second, she'd no doubt have spotted her.

Madeline gave Hugh's arm a reassuring squeeze as he dropped his head to one side and gazed at Flora, who was doing her best to pretend she hadn't noticed him. All the while, Mrs Norton stood apart from the group, but still within hearing, thereby confirming her position as chaperone.

'Are you here to play tennis?' asked Madeline, admiring Flora's plain cotton dress, which was so finely stitched she must have made it herself. Lovely as it was, the simplicity of it wouldn't have looked out of place on a housemaid.

Flora shook her head. She looked as anxious at the prospect of playing tennis as Madeline felt. 'I asked Edward if it would be all right to come along and watch him play. I've never seen a match before.'

Mrs Norton scowled at the back of Flora's head. 'Some people are too selfish to consider how their insistence on gadding about inconveniences the rest of us. We're not all lucky enough to have time for fun and games.'

It seemed an odd comment from someone whose life was devoted to ease and pleasure, to living at no cost to herself in the house of her sister and her wealthy brother-in-law, but Madeline prevented herself from remarking on it.

The colour rose in Flora's cheeks. 'There was no need for you to come. Edward and I could have managed quite well without a chaperone.' She lifted her eyes to him. 'Isn't that right?'

Edward nodded. 'Of course. We are cousins, after all.'

Cousins. The word hung in the air, causing all interested parties to look away from one another. The awkward silence was broken by Hugh, who clapped his hands as if he'd suddenly had a good idea.

'As my sister is reluctant to play, will you allow me to give you a tennis lesson, Miss Pierce? I promise not to make you run around the court or wave your arms above your head, especially as Maddie thinks it's an unbecoming thing to do.'

Flora blushed. 'I don't know, I . . .' Confounded, she looked to Edward for an answer.

'A hundred times no,' interrupted Mrs Norton. 'Have you learned nothing from what happened to Marianne and Jane? Their lives are ruined thanks to this brute.'

'Of course you must play,' said Madeline, made furious by the slur. She handed Flora her racquet. 'Take this. You'll be in good hands with my brother, I promise.'

Once again, Flora glanced at Edward, appearing to plead for his permission to follow Hugh onto the tennis court. Edward was too busy staring at the ground to notice Flora's entreaty until Madeline spoke up for her.

'You don't mind if my brother teaches Flora to play tennis, do you, Mr Booth?'

Dragged from his thoughts, Edward gave Madeline a distracted smile. 'What? Of course not.'

With her authority overruled, Mrs Norton followed them to the far side of the court, determined not to let Flora or that 'terrible man' out of her sight, muttering that the family couldn't risk another fall from grace at the hands of such a charmer.

After they'd gone, Edward sat beside Madeline on the bench. He looked straight ahead as he spoke. 'I'm glad to see you. There's so much I'd like to talk to you about.'

Madeline kept her eyes fixed on the court, watching Hugh as he gently coaxed Flora onto the grass and showed her how to hold the racquet. It was easier to concentrate on how the two of them were getting on than to think about Edward sitting next to her.

'Thank you for your letters of instruction, Miss Crosby, and for the generous donation you made to the Trident Charitable Foundation.'

Since their last meeting, Madeline had been as good as her word in advising Edward on his new charity. Knowing it would be too awkward to meet face to face, she'd sent her suggestions in a series of letters, leaving him free to be guided by her experience should he wish to do so.

'They weren't instructions, Mr Booth. I was simply airing a few ideas. You're free to take them or leave them.'

'I would never dismiss anything you suggest. You know how I hang on your every word.'

She gave him a cold look. He'd overstepped the mark and they both knew it.

'Whenever I try to match your wit, Miss Crosby, it always seems to misfire.'

'Then I suggest you stick to plain speaking. That way, there can be no misunderstanding.'

The barb was enough to silence him. The truth couldn't be spoken without the whole world crashing down on them.

A few minutes passed before Edward tried again. 'Thank you for writing those articles for the newspapers, explaining the work we're doing to help the women exploited by the brothels. Judging by the letters I've received, they've helped to rehabilitate our reputation with the general public.'

The articles had been written anonymously, but Edward must

have recognised Madeline's voice in the words. There was no other way for him to know she was behind them.

'It was never my intention to put the Trident hotel chain out of business. I would never have forgiven myself if your employees had found themselves out of work as a result of my actions. I simply wanted an end to the exploitation of the women in your brothels.'

'Not my brothels, Miss Crosby.'

She gave him a sideways glance. It was the only admission she was prepared to make to his point, which she couldn't deny was well made and accurate.

'I shall continue to work for their cause and for any other women who require help,' he added.

'I don't want revenge for what happened to my mother. I only want to make sure such things don't happen again.'

He nodded, not looking at her. 'I only wish I could travel back in time to ensure it never happened at all.'

A sudden burst of laughter from the tennis court saved Madeline from having to reply. Flora was pointing at Hugh and laughing for all she was worth. 'You took your eye off the ball, Mr Crosby. It was the thing you told me never to do.'

Hugh was standing on the other side of the net, arms outstretched, his racquet abandoned at his feet. 'You've defeated me, Miss Pierce. What can I say?'

Glad of the distraction, Madeline got to her feet and applauded Flora's victory. 'What's the score?'

'One game to love,' replied Flora, glowing with the success. 'It's only beginner's luck, but I shall wallow in the triumph of it anyway.'

Madeline thought of the long evenings she'd spent with Hugh when she was younger, how he'd taught her to play chess and any number of card games by allowing her to win just often enough to bolster her confidence until she was proficient enough to win on her own terms. She'd never let on that she'd worked out his strategy but was grateful for the inherent kindness that lay behind it. Now, she could see him doing the same with Flora, bringing her out of herself, little by little. It proved he hadn't given up hope of winning her heart, even as Mrs Norton scowled at him from the sidelines.

'So, what happens now?' asked Flora. 'Do we play another game?'

'Only if you're willing,' said Hugh.

Flora batted the racquet against the side of her leg, demonstrating her readiness for another game. 'Remind me of the scoring again, Mr Crosby. Where do we start?'

Hugh picked up his racquet and tossed a ball gently over the net. 'We start with love, Miss Pierce. It's your serve, so please be gentle with me.'

'Such a strange way of scoring,' said Edward. 'I've never understood why it's called that.'

'If you want my opinion,' said Madeline, 'love shouldn't be brought into anything. Not until its power has been reduced to that of a fever, which can be cured with a few days of bed rest and a little sipped water.'

Seemingly unsettled by the sorrow of her words, Edward called to Flora to give up the game, insisting the afternoon had grown too hot to be chasing a ball. Madeline had flustered him again with her directness. Would she never learn to tread more gently?

Hugh led Flora off the court. For all his exertions, he'd hardly broken a sweat. 'Until next time, Miss Pierce, we'll allow the current score to stand. I'm determined to pick up where we left off.'

'With me having beaten you,' insisted Flora, triumph lighting up her face.

Hugh shook his head. 'No, Miss Pierce, it's the start of a new game. You know what that means.'

Flora paused before she said it, recalling the afternoon's lesson. 'Love all,' she murmured, casting her eyes briefly at Hugh. 'Love all.'

Chapter 38

Flora appeared at Beachlands a couple of days later. Madeline had offered her an open invitation before they parted at the Casino and Flora had sidestepped her aunt's pressure to refuse the hospitality.

She was red-faced when she arrived, as if she'd dashed all the way from Mountview, a bunch of dahlias from the garden already wilting in her hand.

'The roses have finished,' she announced, offering up the flowers. 'Hopefully, these will pick up once they're placed in water.'

Madeline took the flowers as if they were precious. 'There was no need to bring a gift.' She handed the flowers to Finch who muttered something about trimming the stems to revive them before putting them in a vase.

They'd hardly sat down when Hugh came dashing into the room, the timing of his presence suggesting Finch had rushed to inform him of their visitor.

'Miss Pierce, it's a pleasure to see you.'

It seemed that for now it was all he had to say. He threw himself down on a nearby sofa and sat on his hands, gazing at Flora's face, while her eyes roved every corner of the room to avoid looking at him.

'Flora brought us dahlias,' said Madeline, desperate to begin a conversation. The atmosphere in the room was so tense she expected the windows to shatter at any minute.

'Red ones,' added Flora.

'To match your eyes,' said Madeline without thinking. 'When the pollen irritates them, that is,' she added, trying to cover her awkwardness with a laugh.

Flora looked horrified. 'I had no idea the flowers would trouble you. I'll take them away again.'

'My sister likes to make fun at my expense,' said Hugh. 'Pay her no attention.'

The room fell silent as the three of them pictured Hugh sneezing over the wilted dahlias. Madeline couldn't believe the situation had come to such a pass.

'Don't you have something for Miss Pierce?' she asked, drawing Hugh's gaze from Flora's face, which appeared to be growing redder than the dahlias under his scrutiny.

Hugh jumped to his feet. 'Yes, I have a gift for you, Miss Pierce, yes. How could I have forgotten such a thing?'

Flora leaned back in her chair as if she were being attacked by a wasp. 'I couldn't possibly accept anything from you, Mr Crosby. You've already been so generous.'

'How, Miss Pierce? In what way have I been generous?'

To his credit, Hugh looked confounded by her assertion. Madeline assumed Flora was referring to the way he'd helped Will find a better job in New York, or the way he'd offered her the use of Brodie whenever she wanted to go horse riding. Perhaps she was referring to the gift of the amber dress for her coming-out ball, which had after all been Hugh's idea, even though he didn't want Flora to know it. But it turned out to be none of these things.

'The way you came to Marianne's rescue has put the whole family in your debt, Mr Crosby. No one had the courage to risk a scandal by rescuing her. I don't believe anyone else even had the presence of mind to see the situation for what it was. You were the only one not blinded by Rawdon's wealth. The only one not taken in by his blundering fool act, when underneath it all he was a controlling bully.'

It was the most either of them had ever heard Flora speak uninterrupted, and brother and sister remained silent while they took it all in.

Finally, Hugh blew out his cheeks, clearly taken aback by Flora's straight talking. 'I'm glad you see it that way, Miss Pierce. I did what I did to help Marianne. Causing a scandal was the last thing on my mind. My only regret is that I didn't think more carefully about the effect it would have on her reputation or that of her sister.'

'Experience has taught me that reputation is no substitute for happiness,' said Flora. 'I'd throw propriety to the wind just to live one day feeling truly loved.'

It was as if a canon had gone off in the room. Madeline glanced at Hugh, as if to question what she'd just heard. Was she reading too much into it or had Flora just admitted that she regretted agreeing to marry a man who didn't love her?

The following silence must have made Flora realise the implications of what she'd said. She clapped her hand over her mouth. 'I'm speaking in general terms, and in no way meant . . .' She stumbled, searching for the right word. 'Anything,' she added. 'I didn't mean . . . anything.'

It was a rare thing for Madeline not to have a witty retort to hand, but this time, she knew better than to risk saying the wrong word and scaring Flora away.

'Anyway,' said Hugh, changing the tone of the conversation. 'Your gift. I'll fetch it for you right now.'

He'd fled the room before Flora could further refuse the offer of the gift. She gave Madeline a weak smile. 'Your brother is too generous.'

Madeline returned the smile and changed the subject to the first thought that came to mind.

'How is Edward?'

'He talks of nothing but you.' Unsettled by her recent announcement, Flora seemed to blurt out the words without thinking. 'When I say he talks of nothing but you, I mean he talks of the charity work the two of you are doing together.'

This was more than Madeline had anticipated. For everyone's sake, she'd been clear about the boundaries of their working relationship.

'I wouldn't go as far as to say we're working together. I've offered him the benefit of my experience, that's all. Our connection amounts to nothing but the exchange of a handful of letters.'

Madeline had resisted the compulsion to write to Edward every day when the letters were the only thing they had between them. Just putting the words, 'Dear Mr Booth' onto paper brought him closer. Sometimes, she could almost imagine he was in the room with her, standing at her shoulder, nodding at her thoughts as they flowed from her pen.

But of course, it was all nonsense, which was why she restricted the number and the frequency of the letters she wrote, forcing herself to limit the time spent at her writing desk thinking of him. If she gave into it, she could always find an excuse to write to him, to spill words onto the page just to have his attention. Now she knew how her letters were received, it was all the more reason to resist the temptation.

'Here we are.' Hugh charged back into the room. 'Sorry I took so long, but I had the devil of a job making a fancy bow out of the ribbon. I had to ask Finch to tie it for me.'

Flora stared at the elaborately wrapped gift, which despite Finch's ingenuity with the ribbon was undoubtedly a tennis racquet.

'I had your initials engraved on the handle, just as I did with Maddie's,' said Hugh.

Flora unwrapped the gift and stared at it. 'It was very kind of you, Mr Crosby.'

'Perhaps we can continue our tennis lessons,' said Hugh, the hope in his voice enough to break anyone's heart.

'I'd love nothing more, Mr Crosby.'

'And we must go riding again. It sounds silly to say it, but Brodie misses you.'

'You must visit more regularly,' added Madeline. 'I'd love to continue our afternoon rides.'

Flora's attention remained on the ribbon as she smoothed it out and folded it into a neat bundle. 'I have so many family commitments these days. I can't promise anything.'

'Surely Mrs Booth could spare you for a few hours to get a little fresh air and exercise,' said Hugh.

'It's not only Mrs Booth. There's Edward to think of.'

Hugh appeared to visibly shrink at the mention of Edward's name. 'Of course. Forgive me. I assumed too much. It's a bad habit of mine. It comes of always being given my own way as a child. It wasn't good for me.'

'Not at all. You shouldn't think that of yourself, Mr Crosby.' Flora got to her feet. 'I must go. Mrs Booth will be wondering where I am.'

'You didn't tell them you were visiting?' asked Madeline.

Flora shook her head. 'It was a spur of the minute decision.' She glanced out of the window. The grey clouds that had been threatening all day had finally burst open and the rain was coming down in sheets.

Noticing the change in the weather, Hugh jumped to his feet. 'Allow me one minute while I arrange for our carriage to take you back to Mountview.'

'I'm fine to walk. I don't want to put you to any trouble.'

'It's no trouble,' said Hugh. 'I won't have you getting soaked.'

'You can borrow one of my cloaks,' said Madeline, noting Flora's thin cotton dress and pale gloves.

Flora held up her hands in protest. 'I couldn't possibly—'

'I insist.' The offer of a cloak gave Madeline the opportunity she'd been anticipating. 'I'll run upstairs and fetch one for you while Hugh has the carriage brought round to the front of the house.'

Wrapped in one of Madeline's cloaks, Flora was almost in tears as Hugh handed her into the carriage. 'Mrs Norton will scold me when she sees the trouble you've gone to on my behalf.'

'Then you must learn to take no notice,' said Madeline, who'd learned to deal with more than her fair share of scorn. 'Her cruelty isn't worthy of your attention and her jealousy is her own concern.'

Hugh nodded, the rain dripping from the ends of his hair. 'Maddie's right.' He closed the carriage door, checking it was secure. 'Say you'll come on Tuesday to ride with us.'

Flora nodded as the driver instructed the horses to pull away, her hand raised as she mouthed her silent goodbye.

Madeline observed her brother's crestfallen face as the carriage made its way through the tall iron gates and disappeared out of sight.

'Did I do wrong, Maddie? Did I overstep the mark?'

She took his arm, leading him inside out of the rain. 'I don't know, Hugh. We find ourselves at the centre of a conundrum, and we can only hope there's a way to solve it.'

It was no good leaving things to fate, and already she'd set her carefully worked-out plan in motion. It was only by taking matters into her own hands that Madeline could strive to give everyone the happy ending they deserved. There was no saying it would work, but the least she could do was try.

Chapter 39

Tuesday afternoon came and went with no sign of Flora and no word to explain why she wasn't able to join them for a horse ride. Madeline and Hugh waited for her well into the evening, the atmosphere growing gloomier between them with each passing hour.

'She must have forgotten,' said Madeline, trying to lift Hugh's spirits. 'She seemed distracted all the while she was here the other day. She'll be mortified when she finally remembers.'

'She left the tennis racquet behind,' said Hugh. 'It was a stupid gift and she probably didn't want it.'

'You're reading too much into it,' said Madeline. 'Her life isn't her own.'

'And it never will be while she's beholden to the Booths. It'll only get worse if she marries Edward. If only I could rescue her . . . if only . . .'

Madeline poured him a cup of coffee to distract him. 'You've done enough rescuing for now. All is not yet lost. Let matters rest for a while. Sit back and watch how things play out.'

Hugh tested the bitterness of the coffee before helping himself to sugar. 'You're up to something, Maddie. What is it?'

'Nothing,' she said, regretting she'd betrayed even the slightest hint of her plotting 'Nothing at all really.'

It was unfair to give him hope when there was no guarantee the plan would come to anything. Her actions had been risky and were as likely to backfire as much as they were to succeed, but desperate times called for desperate measures.

There was no word from Flora during the days that followed, no apology and no explanation for her absence, which was now not only an absence but a determined silence.

Every time Hugh raised the subject, Madeline repeated her insistence that she must simply have forgotten the invitation or was busy waiting on Mrs Booth, rather than risk taxing his mind with theories that something more significant had prevented her from visiting.

The following few days soon became ten days, and then two weeks. Madeline was beginning to think her plan had failed when a letter finally arrived. Flora's tiny writing on the poor-quality paper giving her away as the sender even before Madeline had opened the envelope.

She wandered into a quiet corner of the garden to read it where no one would see her. Whatever news it contained, she'd have to prepare Hugh for it, whether it was good or bad.

Dear Miss Crosby,

Forgive my long silence, but the recent upheaval in my life has left no time for writing to you until today.

Firstly, I apologise for failing to honour your invitation to go horse riding the last time we met. All I can say in my defence is that events overtook me, and as a consequence, the idea of being in your company, of pretending ignorance on certain important matters, was unthinkable.

If you have already checked between these pages, you'll have seen that I've returned the letter I discovered in your cloak. Forgive me for the indiscretion. It wasn't my intention to invade your privacy, but as I pushed my hands deep into the pockets, I couldn't help but find it. I pulled it out to save it dropping to the floor, expecting it to be a dressmaker's bill or a receipt of some kind. You can imagine my surprise when I realised it was a note from Edward to you, written at the time of my coming-out ball and professing his undying love.

You can try brushing it off by saying hearts are fickle, that things are said in the heat of the moment that are later regretted and best forgotten. I can believe this to be true of many men, but not of Edward, whose character I know to be steadfast. He speaks so rarely of his feelings that no amount of protestations on his part or yours could persuade me that the love he expressed in his few simple words is not deeply felt.

I recently confessed to you that I knew Edward loved another woman, and that she would not have him. I had no idea at the time that you were the woman in question.

Before you insist that Edward loves me, I will concede that of course he loves me, but there is love, and there is love. I will always be dear to Edward, but only as a brother loves a sister, the way a cousin loves a cousin. Having read his letter to you, I understand the difference between this kind of love and the love a man feels for the woman he would rather marry.

I beg you not to split hairs with me, Miss Crosby, as I sense you will be itching to do, playing your wit against my dull logic. There is a directness and an intensity in the way Edward expresses his love for you that I have never experienced from him and I know I never shall. His passion for you comes alive on the page. The fact that you kept the letter close to you so long after it was written tells me that his feelings for you are reciprocated.

You no doubt have your reasons for refusing him. Knowing what you told me of your past, I can imagine what they might be and do not blame you for it.

As a woman of beauty and financial independence, you are able to make choices that those of us who are less fortunate are in no position to make. We are forced to compromise, to take what is offered and be grateful for it, even though such expediency is rarely a recipe for love or happiness.

I agreed to become Edward's wife out of a sense of duty to my family, and gratitude for the home the Booths have already given me. None of my reasoning has changed. Lacking in fortune or prospects, the marriage will give me financial security and a place of safety that would otherwise be unavailable to me.

You will protest at this and be quick to remind me of your brother's devotion. However, the immoral behaviour of his father with his long line of mistresses is common knowledge. For all your brother's protestations of constancy, he is his father's son. I cannot put myself at risk of becoming his mistress. It's too late to guard my heart against him, and to be used and discarded by him would destroy me in too many ways.

Given what I now know of Edward's love for you, I have begged leave to delay our wedding for a year. It is a test of Edward's resolve as much as mine. If we are to marry, our hearts and minds must be clear of impediments. If we are certain of our path, a year of separation should make no difference.

For this reason, I have left Mountview and the protection of the Booth family and have found a respectable position as a paid companion to a widow here in Newport. You might view this as a step down the social scale, but the tasks Mrs Taylor requires are no more arduous than those I performed for Mrs Booth.

Please do not pity me or scorn me. I am perfectly well placed in a respectable home, and the fact that I am earning my own living has gone some way to restoring my sense of dignity.

Miss Flora Pierce

P.S. I will, of course, return your cloak at the earliest opportunity.

Madeline read Flora's letter several times as she tried to take it all in. Planting Edward's note professing his love in the pocket of the cloak before lending it to Flora hadn't had the effect she'd hoped for. Any other woman would have broken off her engagement in the light of such evidence, but not Flora. It was a testament to her lack of self-worth that she was willing to sacrifice herself to a loveless marriage out of a sense of gratitude and family duty.

Madeline's plotting had backfired and she was mortified by the catastrophic change her meddling had caused to Flora's circumstances. Having set out to improve everyone's lives, her actions had only served to degrade Flora's situation further, obliging her to leave the protection of the Booths' family home and forcing her to find work as a paid companion.

After giving it some thought, Madeline came to the conclusion that Flora wouldn't have shared quite so much information if she hadn't wished it to be passed on to Hugh. After all, she could have returned the note without any explanation or simply put a match to it. And so, it was with the best of intentions that Madeline showed Flora's letter to Hugh.

Hugh walked around the garden while he read it, frowning against the sun as he turned the pages over, reading and rereading them until he was exhausted.

'What do you make of it, Maddie? Do you think she's trying to tell me in her own sweet way that she loves me?'

Given the circumstances, Madeline was careful not to give him too much hope. 'She's saying she's going to marry Edward even though she doesn't love him.'

'She doesn't trust me with her heart. That's what she's saying, isn't it? You can't blame her.' He stared into the distance where the sun had begun to set. 'Marrying Edward is such a selfless thing for her to do. Have you ever known a kinder person, besides you, Maddie?'

The last thing Madeline felt was kind. 'I don't know what to make of it, Hugh. I really don't.'

It didn't matter that Flora had rejected Hugh and was pledged to another. He was still completely devoted to her.

'Something has to be done; don't you think so, Maddie?'

'Don't do anything rash, Hugh. Remember how you scared her off last time.'

Still, Hugh was right. Something definitely had to be done. Things couldn't be left as they were. It was Madeline's mission in life to help lift women from their vulnerable stations, not degrade them further with her matchmaking schemes. It had been badly done, very badly done indeed.

Chapter 40

Flora took advantage of her first afternoon off from her employer to return Madeline's cloak. She turned up at Beachlands unannounced and passed it to Finch on the doorstep, declining the offer to hand it to Madeline in person.

'Please thank Miss Crosby for her kindness in allowing me to borrow it.'

Madeline watched the scene from the drawing-room window, observing the way Finch encouraged Flora inside, insisting Madeline would be sorry to miss the opportunity to thank her for returning it, especially as she'd gone to so much trouble to freshly launder and press it. Flora refused so adamantly that Madeline thought she was going to have to intervene. Eventually she gave in, her shoulders sagging under the weight of Finch's kindly insistence.

Less than a minute later, the housekeeper appeared in the drawing room, announcing Flora's presence. Madeline crossed the room to greet her, pretending she hadn't witnessed the scene on the doorstep. 'Flora, I'm so happy to see you.'

'Forgive the intrusion, Miss Crosby. I only came to return your cloak. I didn't mean to interrupt your day.'

Madeline gestured to the empty room, bringing Flora's attention to a discarded novel on the armchair, the sheet music abandoned on the desk. Her mind was too unsettled for reading, and now Edward no longer visited, she'd lost interest in playing the harp. 'As you can see, I'm very glad to have my idleness interrupted.'

'You're all alone.' Flora's face fell at the realisation.

'Hugh's gone to play tennis at the Casino. He'll be back any minute.'

Flora blushed at the mention of Hugh's name. 'That wasn't what I meant. I wasn't wondering where he was . . . I was just . . .'

'That's a pity,' said Madeline, trying to rescue Flora from her embarrassment. 'He'd be delighted if he thought you were thinking of him.'

The horrified look on Flora's face told Madeline she'd gone too far. The last thing she wanted was to scare the poor creature away. Hugh would never forgive her. Madeline tried another approach.

'Thank you for your recent letter. I'm sorry I didn't reply, but you gave no address.'

'That was remiss of me. I hope you'll forgive me for it.'

Flora hadn't wanted to be found. Not then, anyway. Perhaps today she felt differently. She was here, after all. 'There's nothing to forgive. Have you settled into your new position? Is your employer kind?'

Flora gave nothing away in her expression and it was impossible to know how keenly she felt the lowering of her status, whether she actually looked forward to eventually becoming Edward's wife. And if she did, why had she chosen to take a job rather than marry him straight away? Did she really think a year of separation would make a difference to everyone's feelings?

'My employer, Mrs Taylor, doesn't have a dog, which makes the job easier, but neither does she have a garden.'

'Then you must come and enjoy ours any time you wish. The chrysanthemums have just come into flower. I'll cut some for you to take away with you before you leave.'

Madeline glanced out of the window whenever Flora looked

the other way. Hugh was expected any minute. If she was to engineer a meeting between the two of them, she had to keep Flora occupied until he arrived.

'You'll stay for tea,' she exclaimed, insisting Flora take a seat. 'We have so much to catch up on.'

They were on their second pot when Hugh finally returned, red-faced and with his hair uncombed after his game of tennis. He must have slipped in through the back door after taking a shortcut through the garden, which is why Madeline hadn't seen him enter the house.

'Miss Pierce. How wonderful it is to see you.'

His lack of surprise at Flora's presence suggested to Madeline that Finch had intercepted him on the way in and told him she was here. His urgency to greet her also explained his dishevelled look. He didn't usually appear downstairs without a wash and brush up.

Flora flushed at the sight of him. 'Mr Crosby. You do look well.'

'I'm hot and bothered from a game of tennis, I'm afraid.' He ran his fingers through his unruly hair, nervously trying to tidy it. 'I still have your racquet. You left without it last time. I kept it safe. I won't let anyone else touch it. It has your initials on it.'

Initials that would change the moment she married Edward. 'You look as if you need to cool down,' said Madeline to her brother. 'Shall we take a walk in the garden? I promised Miss Pierce some chrysanthemums to take away with her.'

Flora shot to her feet as if a gun had gone off and glanced at the clock. 'Is that the time? I really must go. It's later than I realised. Mrs Taylor will be wondering where I've got to.'

'You said it was your afternoon off,' said Madeline, frowning at Flora's sudden panic.

'It is . . . I mean . . .'

'But it's only three o clock. Surely Mrs Taylor can spare you a little longer?'

'Please come for a stroll in the garden, Miss Pierce,' said Hugh. 'I want to show you the new rose beds.'

Knowing how much she loved roses, Hugh had created a rose garden at the bottom of the long walk just beyond the herbaceous border, in what had previously been an uninspiring patch of lawn. Madeline had watched him plan the layout during the past weeks with an eye to what he knew of Flora's taste. Still, he hoped against all reasoning that one day she'd be there to enjoy the flowers alongside him. However much the odds were stacked against him, he refused to give up on the idea of Flora becoming his wife. It was this determination more than anything that had convinced Madeline, that for all his previous flirtations, he truly loved her.

Flora's eyes drifted to the open window, to the promise of the scent of late summer flowers carried on the warm breeze. 'I'm sorry, I can't. I have to go. I should never have come. It would be wrong of me to go into the garden with you. You must believe me.'

She fled the house before Hugh could beg her to stay. Madeline grabbed his arm as he threatened to go in pursuit of her. 'Don't,' she whispered, her heart almost breaking at the sight of his despair. 'Let her go, Hugh. Let her go.'

Chapter 41

With Flora settled in her new position, and Edward running the family business in New York, Madeline thought the enforced distance and the demands of their occupations would drive a wedge between the four of them, and they wouldn't see each other again, however much they wished it.

Madeline continued as an adviser to the Trident Charitable Foundation and remained an active fundraiser, while Edward, who found there weren't enough hours in the day to run the hotel chain as well as manage the charity, delegated the responsibility for overseeing the foundation to the redoubtable Miss Harper, who, out of either forced circumstances or choice, had devoted her life and considerable energy to good works rather than marrying and raising a family.

Before appointing her, Edward had written to Madeline, offering her the position, insisting there was no one else more fitted to the job and no one who could be more trusted with the responsibility of it. Madeline could have listed a dozen reasons for turning it down, but none of them would have shown her in a good light. In the end, she gave no reason for her refusal, choosing instead to focus on her continued support of the charity from a distance.

And so, it was out of the blue that Madeline received an invitation to the opening of a lodging house in Newport for women in need of a refuge, funded by the foundation.

She examined the note, written in the now familiar hand of Miss Harper. Edward hadn't taken the trouble to write to her himself. Despite her disappointment, she knew this was as it should be.

'You're invited as well.' She handed the note to Hugh, wondering what he'd make of it. 'Will you come?'

He frowned, as if the question were a curious one. 'Do you really think we should go?'

It hadn't crossed her mind that she should consider turning it down. She hadn't been invited to the opening of any of the New York refuges that were already up and running, but as this latest one was only across town, Miss Harper had probably felt it was only right to include her. She was, after all, one of the foundation's major benefactors.

It wasn't so much that Madeline wanted to attend the opening ceremony, but as they'd gone to the trouble of inviting her, she felt she should go. With the empty autumn days spreading before her, it wasn't as if she had much else to occupy her.

In the past, Hugh would never have considered refusing an invitation to a social event, but since learning of Flora's impending marriage to Edward, he'd shed much of his cheerful veneer and become increasingly withdrawn. These days, his afternoons were largely spent at the Casino playing tennis, where he was gaining a reputation as being the player to beat, his evenings spent quietly at home with Madeline. Everywhere he went, he seemed insensible to the coterie of women who had set out to gain his attention. Having been marked as eligible since his youngest days, their flattery and attempts at winning him, as if he were some kind of sporting trophy, were nothing but an irritant.

'I think we should go,' said Madeline, tapping the invitation against her fingers. 'We don't socialise enough these days.' There was no saying Edward would be there and even if he was, she couldn't allow it to matter.

She decided to wear one of the new dresses that had recently arrived in a trunk from the House of Worth in Paris. The twice-yearly order was borne out of habit rather than necessity, and she justified the extravagance with the thought that her regular order helped keep a legion of seamstresses, milliners and lace makers in work.

The dress, made of a deep rose-coloured silk, was a determined change from the lighter summer gowns she'd previously worn in Newport, and indicated a step away from the frivolity of those past months, of the mistakes she'd made. It was time to draw a line beneath what had happened and start again. There was, after all, no point in looking back and nothing to be gained from wanting what was lost.

Her resolve to focus on what was ahead of her foundered as soon as the buggy pulled up outside the newly renovated lodging house, where Madeline was expected to cut the ribbon on the door and declare the refuge open. It wasn't the crowd that had already gathered to celebrate the opening that affected her, but the sight of Edward, his eyes eagerly searching her out. Her heart swooped before dropping like a stone. He wasn't supposed to be here. By all accounts, he rarely left New York these days.

She allowed herself a glance in his direction, the most careless of nods as he stepped forward to welcome her.

'Our guest of honour has arrived,' he said to no one in particular.

'I had no idea you'd be here.' She hadn't meant to say it, but the words were out before she could stop them.

'I'm here to represent the foundation. This is the first refuge we've opened outside of New York. I wanted to mark the occasion.'

'Then perhaps I shouldn't have come.'

'Please don't say that, not after . . .' His words drifted off, as if he had no way of finishing what he wanted to say.

Madeline was as lost for words as he was. She sighed. 'Anyway, here we are. It's nice to see you. Are you pleased to see me?'

'*Pleased* doesn't begin to express how I feel at seeing you, but I thought we'd agreed never to discuss such things again.'

'From now on, we'll only talk about the weather. We can't go wrong with that.'

'And the foundation,' he added, grasping at straws. 'We'll always have that to bind us.'

She was rescued from having to respond by the appearance of Hugh, who came over to shake Edward's hand.

'Congratulations on the opening of another refuge, Mr Booth. Your reputation for good works goes from strength to strength.' As Hugh spoke, his eyes drifted to the figure who had just appeared quietly at Edward's side. Flora. He lifted his hat to greet her. 'Miss Pierce, if I can still call you that.'

It was his way of asking if she was married, or whether she was still determined to wait a year before becoming Edward's wife. Madeline was as eager to know the answer to his question as her brother.

'You can.' Flora avoided his eye, giving nothing away in her answer beyond the fact that she and Edward still weren't married.

'I'm delighted to hear it,' said Hugh, blundering in with more enthusiasm than Madeline had seen him display in weeks. Seeing Flora appeared to have brought him to life again, and if anyone else noticed how blatantly he expressed his pleasure at learning Flora and Edward weren't married, nobody commented on it.

Flora was wearing one of her homemade gowns, which had been simply fashioned in everyday cotton, her hair arranged in an easy style by her own hand beneath her plain bonnet. Working as a lady's companion seemed to have had no outward effect on her appearance, which only went to show that her situation hadn't really changed much after all. She'd simply swapped one mistress for another, and at least this one had the decency to pay her for her labour.

Before Madeline could engage Flora in conversation, a woman shouldered her way in between Flora and Edward, who in a rehearsal of their future life together were standing side by side with the cool distance of a long-married couple between them.

'There you are, Flora. Aren't you going to introduce me to your charming friends?'

Startled by the intrusion, it took Flora a moment to drag her attention from her shoes. 'Forgive my rudeness. Mr and Miss Crosby, please allow me to introduce my employer, Mrs Taylor.'

Mrs Taylor waved her fan in admonishment at Flora's words. 'There's no need to call me your employer, my dear. We're friends and companions.'

Flora blushed. 'Forgive me. I—'

'Of course, we don't really need an introduction,' continued Mrs Taylor, her eyes widening as they contemplated Hugh's face. 'You won't know me, young man, but I knew your father. It's quite startling to see how much you resemble him when he was your age.'

'You knew my father?'

Mrs Taylor grinned. 'Intimately. What a man he was.'

Beyond her fancy feather-tipped hat, her heavy eyelids, and the ruffles around the collar of her dress, designed to hide the damage the passage of time had inflicted on her once firm skin, lay the remnants of a beautiful woman. Madeline knew enough about her father to imagine how he'd have pursued her in her younger days. Hugh must have had the same thought because he changed the subject before she could reveal something they were all better off not knowing.

'This is my sister, Miss Madeline Crosby.'

A frown crossed Mrs Taylor's face, highlighting the lines her open smile had done so much work to banish. Instantly, Madeline felt the cold weight of her judgement and braced herself for a disparaging comment, or worse still, the mortification of being completely ignored. She'd faced down such responses many times with good grace and was determined to do so again if she had to.

'You're Crosby's daughter?' Mrs Taylor asked, her lips pursed to match her frown. 'I don't recall him ever mentioning he had a daughter.' She fluttered her eyes as if to summon her thoughts before quickly abandoning the effort. 'It's no surprise. Most men are only ever interested in talking about their sons.'

Her expression softened as she examined Madeline's face, all traces of judgement gone. 'You're such a sweet young thing. You probably weren't even born when I knew him.'

'Mrs Taylor has lived in France for the past twenty-five years,' said Flora, as if to justify the gap in her employer's knowledge.

'She's right. I'm at least a quarter of a century out of touch with any of the goings-on in society.'

'You haven't missed much,' said Hugh, deflecting Mrs Taylor's attention from Madeline before she could start asking questions that would be too awkward to answer. 'It's all nonsense.'

Edward must have sensed the negative tone creeping into the conversation because he rubbed his hands together, bringing the subject back to the reason they were gathered.

'Miss Crosby, perhaps now would be a good time for you to say a few words and cut the ribbon for us.'

He handed her a pair of scissors and pointed her towards the door of the lodging house, where a small number of local people had gathered, their eyes fixed on Madeline. She gave a short speech, made up on the spur of the moment because she hadn't realised something so formal would be expected of her, and tried not to feel too self-conscious.

The applause that followed, the bouquet thrust into her hand by Miss Harper, reminded Madeline that the people who'd gathered to hear her speak weren't there to look down on her, but to acknowledge the good she'd done. For once, she was being accepted for herself and for her actions rather than being judged for the circumstances of her birth or the mistakes of her parents.

She ignored Edward's steady gaze, glad of the distraction Mrs Taylor offered as she bustled up to her.

'How gracious you are, my dear. What a lovely speech you made. The way you talked about those poor women in need of refuge came straight from your heart. No one listening to you could fail to be moved or indeed, inspired to make a donation to such a worthy charity.'

Hugh gave her hand an encouraging squeeze. 'She does her mother's memory proud.'

It was the last thing Madeline needed to hear. The day had already been packed with unexpected emotion thanks to the sight of Edward, and Hugh's kind words were enough to tip her over into tears. She took a deep breath burying her face in the fresh flowers.

'We should leave.'

'Must you go already?' asked Edward. 'It's been so long since I've seen you. I mean . . . I was hoping to tell you about the foundation's future plans.'

Madeline glanced at Flora, wondering what she must think of Edward's keenness to see her, how he hadn't even bothered to hide his desire for her company, but as always, Flora was unreadable. Just like Madeline, she was too used to being judged to give anything away.

'Perhaps another time,' said Madeline. She forced a smile, trying to keep her tone casual. 'Finch will have our tea waiting for us.'

Edward followed her as she began to walk away. 'I'm returning to New York tonight. There might not be another time.'

It was unfair of him to pursue her company like this, whatever justification he thought he had for it. She had little defence against his determination to see her, on whatever terms that might be. Did he not know the power he had over her? Could he not see his own desperation?

'There's no need to rush off, Maddie,' said Hugh. 'Finch won't mind if we're late. The cake will keep.' He looked at Flora. 'You'll join us?'

His question had a lilting quality that was almost a plea.

Madeline could have cried for him, just as much as she could have cried for herself, and for Flora and Edward.

'I'm required to attend to Mrs Taylor. My half-day isn't for another two weeks.'

'Blast it, Flora,' said Hugh, unable to contain himself any longer. 'Has it really come to this? What is it you're playing at?'

'I'm asserting my independence, Mr Crosby. I can't tell you how good it feels.'

Despite her assertion, Flora's eyes told a different story. It was time to leave before they all ended up in tears.

'You must have tea with us tomorrow afternoon,' said Mrs Taylor, breaking the silence that was beginning to feel like stalemate. 'I'll be delighted to have your company.' She passed a roving eye over Hugh. 'And I'm sure Flora would love to see you.'

Edward gave a slight bow. 'Forgive me, but I'm expected in New York first thing tomorrow morning. The business won't run itself. You'll have to do without me.'

'We're all learning to do that, Mr Booth.'

Once again, the words were out of Madeline's mouth before she could stop them. How ill-judged it had been to let her guard down. She should have thought before speaking, before going in with another smart remark. It was her nervousness that did it. Whenever she felt anxious, she was guaranteed to say the wrong thing.

'I'm sorry for it,' said Edward, refusing to look at her as he replied. He raised his hat to Flora and Mrs Taylor, nodding at Hugh as he turned to leave, bidding them a polite goodbye before retreating to his waiting carriage.

Mrs Taylor sighed, as if she didn't know what to make of all the tension. 'You have my permission to go after him, Flora, to say goodbye properly. He is your fiancé, after all.'

'It's fine,' said Flora. 'He's gone now.'

Mrs Taylor shrugged. 'I suppose that's what comes of agreeing to marry a cousin. You don't mind seeing the back of one another.'

Having openly expressed what she probably only intended to think, Mrs Taylor beat her fan wildly in front of her face, even though the heat of the season had long passed.

'Enough of this talk.' She nodded to Flora. 'Please give Mr and Miss Crosby one of my calling cards.' She winked at Hugh. 'We'll see you at four o'clock tomorrow afternoon, and you'd better not be on your best behaviour.'

Flora handed over the card, giving them both a bleak look. 'I'm sorry,' she said, for no particular reason that Madeline could determine.

After saying goodbye to Flora and Mrs Taylor, Madeline and Hugh stood in the street, both carefully avoiding Miss Harper, who was desperately trying to catch their attention. There was to be a guided tour of the lodging house, followed by a reception with tea and cake, and she was desperate for them to attend.

Although Madeline had made it her life's mission to fund the refuges, she couldn't face being obliged to step inside one, knowing it would only revive memories of her mother's last days in the back room of a cheap hotel. If there'd been a place of safety for them to run to, things might not have turned out the way they did. She turned her back on the building, handing the bouquet to an old woman who happened to be passing on the street and looked at Hugh.

'Let's go home,' she said. 'I've seen far too much of the real world for one day.'

Chapter 42

It was Flora who opened the door to Madeline and Hugh when they arrived at Mrs Taylor's apartment the following afternoon.

'Is there no one else to answer the door?' asked Madeline, who was shocked to see Flora carrying out the duties of a maid. She'd assumed that as Mrs Taylor's companion, she occupied a higher position in the household.

'Of course, but it's her afternoon off. Mrs Taylor would have answered the door herself, but she's busy rearranging the chairs in the parlour ready for your arrival.'

'Is that our guests, Flora?' Mrs Taylor's voice rang through the apartment. 'Don't leave them standing in the hallway, show them in.'

The parlour, heavily scented with patchouli, was exactly how Madeline expected it to be. The dark green papered walls and patterned carpet giving it an atmosphere of an expensively appointed cave. The velvet drapes at the windows and the heavy lace curtains shadowed the natural daylight, the gilding on the mirrors and the picture frames serving as the only hint of brightness in the room.

The chairs, which wouldn't have looked out of place in the eighteenth-century French court, had been artfully arranged around an occasional table, as if they'd been set for a game of cards rather than afternoon tea. The plush sofa, pushed to the corner of the room and shaded by a large screen for privacy, suggested Mrs Taylor still lived in hope of being compromised by a romantic assignation.

Despite her years spent living abroad, Mrs Taylor didn't appear to have shaken off the tastes or the habits of the old New York society from which she hailed, and if pressed, would no doubt claim to be part of the self-appointed social aristocracy.

Knowing how the members of this closed world liked to gossip, Madeline was on her guard. It would only have taken one indiscreet conversation for Mrs Taylor to have discovered Madeline's true origins, and given her forthright manner, she would no doubt feel fully entitled to express her opinion on the subject.

'Do sit down, Miss Crosby.' Mrs Taylor narrowed her eyes on Madeline as she surveyed the room. 'The atmosphere's a little stuffy, I'm afraid.'

Madeline blanched at the thought that Mrs Taylor was able to read her mind. 'It's charming.'

'None of it is my choice. The place belongs to a friend of my late husband's. I'm only staying here temporarily.' She gestured to Flora who was standing beside the door, checking the room to make sure everything was in order. 'Would you mind bringing in the sandwiches and the cake now, my dear?'

Flora swiftly left the room, having failed to acknowledge Hugh, despite his desperate attempts to catch her eye. The following silence was quickly filled by Mrs Taylor.

'So, tell me, Miss Crosby. Do you have a husband in mind, or are you still breaking men's hearts by giving them hope, only to then dash them?'

Madeline glanced at Hugh, unsure how to answer such a direct question. 'Well, I—'

'Please tell me you're breaking hearts. You have to make the most of your allure while you still have it. The passage of time completely destroys a woman's power. The older you get, the less noticeable you become, until one day, you wake up alone and discover you're invisible.'

Madeline was saved from having to respond by Flora returning with the tea. Hugh leapt out of his chair to help her with the tray, frowning at the silver teapot, the plates of sandwiches, fruit tarts and scones.

'Did you prepare all this yourself?' he asked.

'Heavens, no,' said Mrs Taylor, appalled at the suggestion. 'We had the food sent in. I don't expect dear Flora to wait on me hand and foot.'

The sandwiches were dry, the edges of the bread where the crusts had been removed curling at the edges, the salad leaves wilting between the room-warmed slices of cured salmon, confirming that everything had been prepared hours ago and transported across town.

Madeline took a sip of tea to encourage the first bite down, suddenly missing Finch's careful management of the food that was presented to them at home, appreciative of the small attentions she now paid to her comfort, just as she always had to Hugh's. The days of over-brewed tea, of her sheet music being purposely knocked to the floor were long gone.

Mrs Taylor's eyes remained fixed on Hugh as he made sure Flora was comfortably settled in the chair beside him. Unbidden, he'd dropped a slice of lemon in her tea, proving he remembered how she liked it.

'You don't have to be on your best behaviour, Mr Crosby. I've been reliably informed that you're just as big a rogue as your father ever was. Why else do you think I invited you here today?'

'You've been misinformed,' said Flora, almost jumping out of her seat in her eagerness to come to Hugh's defence. 'He's not a rogue at all, no matter what anyone might say.'

Mrs Taylor raised her eyebrows. 'You have very strong opinions regarding this young man.'

'He showed my cousin, Marianne, a great deal of gallantry when she needed help.'

Mrs Taylor turned her attention back to Hugh. 'Indeed, I hear you rescued a damsel in distress. At least, that's one version of events.'

'It's the only version,' said Flora, before Hugh could speak up for himself. 'I also saw him put himself in great danger to save a little boy's life.'

'Is that so?' asked Mrs Taylor, smiling at Flora's sudden animation.

Flora nodded. 'Miss Crosby was also there.'

'It's true,' said Madeline. 'The little boy was stuck up a tree.'

'It wasn't just any tree,' said Flora. 'It was right on the edge of a cliff. One slip and Mr Crosby would have fallen to his death.'

'You're making much more of it than it was,' said Hugh, slurping his tea to hide his embarrassment.

'It goes to prove you're not a rogue,' said Flora. 'If it had happened in a novel, you'd be the hero.'

Mrs Taylor rolled her eyes. 'I don't know what kind of books you've been reading, my dear, but I think we need to find you something less sentimental.'

Taking the comment as a criticism, Flora sank back in her chair. 'Forgive me, I—'

Hugh let out an awkward laugh. 'There's nothing to forgive, Miss Pierce. I'm flattered to know you think so well of me, although I tend to consider myself the fool rather than the hero.'

'I've learned that a man can be many things, Mr Crosby,' said Flora. 'It would be too cruel and ill-considered to judge anyone on first impressions.'

'I'm delighted someone has something generous to say about me,' said Hugh. 'It's never usually the case.'

Mrs Taylor pursed her lips. 'From what I've been hearing, there are plenty of young women out there determined to flatter you.'

Hugh put down his teacup with a clatter. 'They only do so out of self-interest, I can assure you. None of them are as selfless as Miss Pierce. She sees the good in everyone.'

Madeline changed the subject before Hugh started to complain about how misunderstood he was. Even though she agreed with him, nobody wanted to hear it while they were struggling to swallow curled-up sandwiches.

'Do you intend staying here long?' Madeline asked, remembering how Mrs Taylor had mentioned her current living arrangements were temporary.

'Not so long,' said Mrs Taylor. She turned to Flora. 'I might as well tell you now. I've decided to return to Paris.' She gestured to the room, the plate of stale sandwiches. 'This place won't do for me at all. It's too gloomy, the food inferior. America is no match for Europe. Having lived on the continent for decades, I find the society here too prim, the values old fashioned, even in Rhode Island.'

'You're returning to Paris?' asked Flora. The news seemed to come as a shock. Whatever plan she had in mind, the sudden termination of her employment didn't fit into it.

'I am, my dear. You'll come with me, of course. I simply can't do without you. The travel will broaden your mind as well as your horizons.'

Hugh stared at Flora. 'You'll be in another country.'

'That's the whole point,' said Mrs Taylor. 'Flora should see more of the world before she decides whether she should settle for marrying her cousin.'

'But I've already agreed to marry him,' muttered Flora, as if she were thinking aloud, rather than announcing it to the room.

'You can't go just like that, Miss Pierce,' said Hugh. 'You simply can't. Think of us poor creatures you'll be leaving behind.'

Mrs Taylor raised her hand to silence his complaining. 'You're beginning to sound like Mr Booth, following your sister down the street like a lost puppy at the opening of the women's refuge yesterday. Don't think I didn't notice. What's wrong with you young men? You do nothing but pine and whimper? Where's your backbone?'

'But—'

'Flora has a paid occupation,' continued Mrs Taylor, interrupting Hugh's objection. 'She's perfectly entitled to make her own decision as to whether she should stay or go. I'm offering her the opportunity of a lifetime. Surely you wouldn't begrudge her that.'

'When are you planning to leave?' asked Madeline, discreetly putting aside her half-eaten sandwich.

'Within the month,' said Mrs Taylor. 'Now the decision has been made, I see no point in delaying.'

But had the decision been made? Madeline looked at Flora, whose expression betrayed a mixture of shock and indecision. 'How do you feel about a trip to Europe?'

'It won't be a trip,' said Mrs Taylor. 'I plan to stay for good. Flora will thrive there; I have no doubt. She needs removing from certain controlling influences.'

If nothing else, Mrs Taylor wasn't shy of speaking her mind.

'It's a lot to decide in a short time,' said Madeline.

'Moving to a foreign country is reversible, unlike an ill-considered marriage,' said Mrs Taylor. 'Don't you agree, Flora?'

Flora shuffled in the chair. 'There's a lot to consider. Paris is so far away. I might not see the people I'm most fond of ever again.'

'It's a great opportunity,' said Madeline, reaching across the table for Flora's hand, 'but forever is a long time to miss someone.'

'Paris is a wonderful city,' said Hugh. 'It's the most romantic place in the world. If you're to see it, Miss Pierce, you should see it with someone you love.'

'You can't rely on Mr Booth to take you once you're married,' said Mrs Taylor. 'He'll be too busy running his hotel business. The fact that he's not here right now, courting you, tells you how it's going to be with him. If you want to see Paris, you need to take matters into your own hands. I'm giving you that opportunity.'

'I've always wanted to go to Europe,' said Flora.

'But not in service to someone else,' said Hugh.

'You think her freedom would be any different, travelling as a wife rather than as a paid companion?' asked Mrs Taylor.

Madeline gave her brother a narrow look, warning him to think twice before he said something he might regret. It wasn't Hugh's place to beg another man's fiancée to stay close by him or to talk to her of love. The conversation was becoming far too heated and she didn't want to give their hostess any further material for gossip. Hugh was talked about enough in society as it was. And if Mrs Taylor was aware of Madeline's origins, she'd so far had the good grace not to mention them. It wouldn't do to make an enemy of her.

'I'm sure whatever you decide will be the right decision,' said Madeline, trying to cool the tension. She made a point of glancing at the clock. 'Is that the time? We really must go.' She thanked Mrs Taylor for her hospitality and stood up to leave before their hostess could insist they stay for another stale sandwich.

Flora followed them to the door. 'I'll show you out.'

The three of them stood in the hallway while Flora handed Madeline her parasol. 'Thank you for coming. It's been so nice to see you both.'

Her tone was flat, as if there was no meaning behind the words. She could have been talking to the fishmonger, or any stranger passing in the street. She'd shut herself down from all thought and feeling. Hugh was losing her before he'd even had a chance to win her back.

'You won't do anything rash, will you?' asked Madeline.

Flora gave her a puzzled look. 'Such as what?'

'Don't leave the country.'

The words burst from Hugh before Madeline could stop them. She nudged his shoulder, warning him to stay silent and forced him out of the door. 'Come and see us soon,' she said. 'Come any time you can. Don't wait to be invited. You're always welcome.'

It wasn't only Hugh who was upset at the prospect of losing Flora. She was the only true friend Madeline had ever had.

'I'll try.' Flora addressed the words to Hugh, although she probably didn't realise she was doing it.

'What happens now?' asked Hugh, as they stood in the street outside Mrs Taylor's apartment. Madeline shrugged. As hard as she tried, she couldn't coax him away.

'What if Edward insists on marrying Flora straight away to prevent her going to Paris?' he asked.

'I wouldn't worry about that yet,' said Madeline. 'She seems determined to delay the wedding.'

Madeline had been struck by the change in Flora's character. Working for Mrs Taylor was having a positive effect. She'd never seen her so confident, so willing to voice her opinion. The old Flora would never have spoken up for Hugh in such a way, and certainly not in front of the Booths.

'If she goes to Paris, I've lost her anyway.' Hugh threw up his hands as if the solution to his problem was waiting to be snatched from the air. 'What shall we do?'

'We wait,' said Madeline, 'and have a little faith.'

'Faith in what?'

'In love, of course.'

Hugh frowned. 'You're not plotting again are you, Maddie? Remember how badly it turned out last time. It was planting Edward's love letter in your cloak for Flora to find that got us where we are now. I don't blame you for it, even though it is partly of your doing.

'Flora striking out for independence is one thing,' he continued, 'but delaying her wedding to Edward instead of calling it off altogether is a disaster. She's too honourable for her own good, if you ask me.'

'I'm not plotting this time,' said Madeline. 'I've learned my lesson.'

She wished she could have given her brother a different answer, but this time there was no plan and she was afraid to admit that she had no idea how to fix the situation. It seemed Flora and Edward were lost to them once and for all.

Chapter 43

Flora took advantage of Madeline's open invitation to visit during her next afternoon off. Madeline rose to greet her as soon as Finch showed her in.

'I'm so glad you came.'

When Madeline made the invitation, she hadn't expected Flora to act on it, but here she was. Perhaps there was hope after all.

'You must say if I'm disturbing you.'

'Hugh is playing tennis at the Casino. You've rescued me from a very dull afternoon. Tell me all your news.'

'I'd like your advice, if you don't mind.'

Madeline's heart sank. Since planting Edward's letter in her cloak for Flora to find, she'd lost all confidence in her own wisdom. She also had too much at stake to risk influencing Flora. It wasn't as if she was a disinterested party, after all.

'I'm not sure I can help, but I'll be happy to listen.'

'I have to give Mrs Taylor an answer as to whether I'll go abroad with her or not.'

'What have you decided?'

'I've always wanted to travel, but if I go to Paris, I might never have the opportunity to come back. I won't be able to pay for my return passage on what I earn as a lady's companion.'

'What does Edward think?' It was almost as if Flora had forgotten she'd pledged to be his wife, as if she considered the wedding to be delayed forever.

'I wrote him a letter, explaining my situation. He replied, reminding me how much his mother is missing me since Uncle Tobias refuses to return from Switzerland and while Marianne, Jane and Theo remain in Italy. Also, Mimi is missing her daily walks.'

'Did he not ask you to stay on his account? You're supposed to be marrying him, after all.'

'He's too busy running the hotel business to think of himself. I've never known a man so driven to put right the mistakes of his father.'

Madeline nodded, thinking how like Hugh he was in that respect.

'I agreed to be Edward's wife and feel bound to honour my pledge and yet . . .'

'And yet?'

'The reason he gave for wanting to marry me is no longer valid. He has rebuilt the reputation of the business without needing to present himself as a respectable married man.'

'It doesn't mean he won't still marry you,' said Madeline.

'What if that wasn't the true reason for asking me to marry him? What if it was simply a reaction to being rejected by the woman he truly loves?'

Flora's words touched a nerve. 'Edward is a man of honour. He wouldn't go back on his word.'

'But what if he's already regretting it? I've hardly seen him since the proposal.'

'You said yourself he's busy rebuilding the business. It's probably no more than that.'

'The hotels are doing better than ever before,' said Flora. 'He credits you for the improvement in the fortunes of the business and for the success of the charitable foundation.'

'I offered him advice and money, that's all.'

There was a long silence before Flora spoke again, as if she were gathering the courage to make a confession.

'When I accepted Edward's proposal, I was a different person. I know it's only been a few weeks but working for Mrs Taylor has given me a new perspective on life. I've learned that I can take care of myself. I don't have to be grateful to anyone. My social status might be lowered, but I can be my own woman. I now know it's possible to live independently. I can even set aside some of my wages to help pay for Susan to go to college. I'm more capable than Mrs Norton ever allowed me to believe.'

It was a miracle to see how much Flora had grown in confidence. She even sat more upright in the chair. The old Flora would never have been able to command a room, whereas the new Flora had such an air of dignity, she probably wasn't even aware of it.

'What do you think, Miss Crosby? Should I marry Edward or go to France with Mrs Taylor?'

'Moving abroad would be a great change and would remove you from everyone you know and love, while marrying Edward would be an irreversible move.' Now Madeline sounded like Mrs Taylor. The old woman was more astute and more aware of the situation between the four of them than she'd given her credit for.

'I don't have to do either, of course,' said Flora. 'I could stay here and find a new position as a lady's companion.'

It was such a clever solution that Madeline wondered why none of them had thought of it before. 'There lies your third option. I'll help you find a new position if that's what you decide to do. I'll start making enquiries today.'

Flora's face brightened. 'Perhaps you could speak to Finch for me. She might know of someone who's looking for a companion.'

'I'll do that.'

'But would it be the right thing to do?' asked Flora, suddenly less certain. 'I owe the Booths so much. It's my duty to repay their generosity by marrying Edward and providing an heir to the family fortune.' She sighed, as if her reasoning were forever destined to run in circles. 'What do you think I should do, Miss Crosby?'

It would be easy to tell Flora not to go through with the wedding, but it would be wrong to do so. Flora had to come to her own decision, otherwise how would they know it was the right one?

'The best way to show your gratitude to the Booths is to let them see you living happily. Edward wouldn't want you to settle for a life that was anything less purely out of a sense of obligation. Nor would he want you to try to guess what you think might make him happy and for you to base your decision on that.'

'You make it sound so easy when you put it like that, Miss Crosby.'

'Follow your heart, Flora, for your own sake. It's all anyone is asking you to do.'

Flora was preparing to leave when Hugh arrived. Calling to Finch to bring him some lemonade, he charged into the drawing room, red-faced and sweating from his tennis match. He stopped when he realised Flora was there.

'Miss Pierce. You always seem to catch me when I'm hot and bothered.'

Her eyes lingered on his damp shirt, clinging to every contour of his chest. 'You've never looked so well, Mr Crosby. Now, if you'll excuse me, I was just leaving.'

He trailed behind her as she made her way to the door. 'Can I accompany you anywhere?'

'It's kind of you to offer, but no thank you. I can manage perfectly well by myself.'

Madeline laughed at his eagerness. 'You're in no state to accompany a lady anywhere until you've washed and changed your clothes.'

'Fair point, Maddie.' He turned to Flora. 'Then my carriage is at your disposal.'

'There's no need to trouble yourself, Mr Crosby. Mrs Taylor's apartment is only a short walk from here. The fresh air will do me good.'

'Then I hope to see you again soon.' There was a questioning lilt to the statement that turned it into a plea.

'Flora might be looking for a new position as a lady's companion,' said Madeline. 'I promised to help her find one, just in case she decides she needs it.'

Hugh raised his eyebrows, trying to appear casual. 'Is that so? Does this mean you're not going to France?'

'I haven't made up my mind yet,' said Flora, pinning him with a direct look. 'I'm starting to enjoy being in control of my own destiny.' She turned to Madeline. 'Don't worry about calling Finch to see me out. I'll find my own way.'

Hugh watched through the window as she left the house. 'There's a remarkable change in Flora. Is it anything to do with you, Maddie?'

Madeline looked at him in all innocence. 'I take no credit for it. Now she's away from the influence of the Booths, she's finally become the person she was always destined to be. If you ask me, it's no more complicated than that.'

Still, Madeline was delighted to see the change in Flora. It gave her hope that there might be a happy ending in store for the poor girl after all.

Chapter 44

It was the following week when the letter arrived from Flora. The notepaper was much better quality than the last time she wrote, leading Madeline to conclude that Mrs Taylor had offered Flora free use of her stationery.

My dear Miss Crosby,
 Please forgive the familiarity of my greeting, but I hope you'll allow me to refer to you as dear. You've been such a kind friend that it's how I shall always think of you. Yet again, you're the first person I reach out to when it comes to sharing my news. Who else would I turn to in such times? Who else could I trust?
 The wise words you offered when we last met stayed with me long after we parted. I couldn't shake off your idea that the only way to show gratitude to the Booths for everything they've done for me is to live a happy life. It's a different way of thinking about how I should honour my duty to them, but I've come to see that it makes perfect sense.
 Since leaving the protection of the Booth family and working as a companion to Mrs Taylor, the world has opened itself up to me, and for the first time, I find I have choices.

The challenge has been to decide which one would enable me to achieve the happiness I seek.

I could pretend it was a hard decision to make, but it would be untrue. After considering your advice, the answer quickly became clear. Now, I am writing to tell you my momentous decision. Take a deep breath, Miss Crosby, and prepare yourself for the news, for I have broken off my engagement to Edward. Although he was surprised by my decision, I don't believe he was disappointed. I will leave you, Miss Crosby, to consider the reason for this.

Despite the move to France with Mrs Taylor being the thing that prompted me to make this decision, I have decided not to go with her. Instead, I shall stay in Newport, where I hope to find a new position as a lady's companion. Mrs Taylor is recommending my services to many of the women in her social circle and talks of me in such glowing terms that I'm confident of finding a new situation before long.

I hope that by staying in Newport we'll be able to see much more of one another. Please remember me to your brother.

Ever yours,
Miss Flora Pierce

Madeline's hand gripped the paper as she read the letter. Flora had done it. She'd finally had the courage to release herself from the sense of duty that had been imposed on her by the Booths from an early age. And she'd done it for the right reason, to give herself the freedom to pursue her own happiness.

She would share the news with Hugh as soon as he returned from playing tennis. In the meantime, she composed a reply to Flora.

My dear Flora,
Never apologise for calling me dear, for that is what you are to me, and I hope always to be the same to you.

I congratulate you on your decision to call off your engagement to Mr Booth. It might not be an appropriate sentiment to express to mark something that has been broken, but the fact that you've chosen to take this step shows that in your heart, you knew the marriage would never have made you happy. What you said of your cousin's reaction tells me it wouldn't have made him happy either. By releasing yourself from your obligation you have released him too. If that isn't a display of love, then I don't know what is.

I'm delighted you have decided to remain in Newport and I know Hugh will feel the same when I tell him. I've been as good as my word in my quest to help you find a new position and I believe I've hit upon the ideal situation for you. Tell me when you're next able to visit and I'll arrange an interview.

Your dearest friend,
Madeline Crosby

Chapter 45

Hugh took a little convincing when Madeline told him of her plan. She was arranging a posy of purple pansies in a vase in his study when she explained it.

He looked up from his correspondence and scratched his head. 'I don't know, Maddie. Flora's very independent these days. It's one of the things I love about her. She might not appreciate your meddling.'

Madeline thought the same, but if she was going to put things right, she had to give it a try. If it failed, she'd convinced herself no harm would come of it.

'You'll support my plan, though? I won't go ahead with it unless you agree.' This wasn't strictly true because she'd already set things in motion.

'You know I can never deny you anything, Maddie.'

She leaned across the desk and kissed his cheek. 'Thank you.'

'It makes me nervous, though. What if it goes wrong?'

She thought of Edward's letter, planted in the pocket of her cloak for Flora to find, and the damage it had caused. It had been a lesson hard learned. 'This is different.'

Flora arrived promptly at four o'clock just as they'd arranged. As always, her dress was as neat as a pin, without a ruffle or a scrap of lace to adorn it, her hair neatly arranged beneath her plain grey bonnet.

'I hope I'm not late for the interview. I'd like to set a good first impression.'

Madeline wanted to cry for the frugality of Flora's dress, the anxious look in her eyes. She deserved so much better than this. 'You're right on time.'

Flora glanced around the drawing room, expecting to see her prospective employer. 'I'm too early, aren't I?'

'You're perfectly fine,' assured Madeline. 'There's nothing to be nervous about. You're among friends.'

It mattered that Flora found the right situation. Everything depended on it. Madeline couldn't bear the thought of her having to return to the Booths or become a burden to her family in Wisconsin. She'd come too far to take a backward step. Madeline saw it as her duty to see she was comfortably settled. If anyone had earned the right to be happy, it was Flora.

'Has the lady I'm here to see not arrived yet?'

'As it's not strictly a social occasion, I thought it would be best to have the meeting in Hugh's study.' Madeline held out her hand, encouraging Flora to follow her. 'You won't have seen the room before. It's too gloomy for my taste. You must tell me what you think of it and how we can improve it.' She walked into the study without knocking, the melody of her voice the only advance warning of their arrival.

'Here we are,' said Madeline, beckoning Flora to step inside. 'I'll ask Finch to bring some tea. There's bound to be fruit cake. I could smell it baking when I went down to the kitchen this morning.'

Hugh was sitting behind the desk, his arms folded across his chest as he stared out of the window. Whatever correspondence he was supposed be attending to seemed to have been forgotten.

Flora's step faltered as soon as she saw him. 'Mr Crosby, I didn't realise you were here. Aren't you supposed to be playing tennis?'

'I have a more pressing matter to attend to today.'

'Then I'm sorry for disturbing you.' She glanced at Madeline. 'We should find somewhere else to conduct the interview.'

Hugh rose from his seat, encouraging Flora to sit down. 'Won't you stay for a minute?'

'Another time, Mr Crosby. I have an important appointment to keep.' She turned to Madeline standing silently by the door. 'There must be some mistake.'

'There's no mistake,' said Madeline. 'Please stay and talk to Hugh while I fetch the tea.'

Madeline slipped out of the room before Flora had a chance to refuse, leaving the door open barely an inch. Instead of going to the kitchen, Madeline pinned her ear to the gap. The tea would have to wait. Hugh couldn't blame her for listening in after she'd gone to all this trouble for him.

'I'm a little confused, Mr Crosby. I thought I was here to discuss the position of lady's companion to one of Miss Crosby's acquaintances.'

'You are, Miss Pierce. You might remember I mentioned to you before, how very much I'd like you to be my companion.'

Madeline held her breath during the following silence. She imagined Flora sitting upright in her chair as she slowly came to understand why she'd been invited here today.

'I made a terrible hash of it when I proposed to you the first time, Miss Pierce. I allowed my enthusiasm to get the better of me and have no one to blame for it but myself. I'm sorry if I offended you.'

'You don't have to apologise, Mr Crosby.'

'What I'm trying to say in my clumsy way is that I'd like to make the offer again, if I have your permission to say it.'

'I'm not sure I understand. What is it you'd like my permission to say?'

'To ask you to marry me.'

Madeline heard the scrape of his chair as Hugh moved from behind the desk. Risking a peep through the tiny gap in the door, she saw him get down on one knee at Flora's feet and reach for her hand.

Having seen enough to know they no longer required her interference, Madeline closed the door quietly behind her and crept downstairs to the kitchen to update Finch on the developments, the certainty of success fluttering in her stomach. After that, she would go to the cellar to check the champagne was nicely chilled, just in case there happened to be a reason to celebrate.

Chapter 46

Flora and Hugh planned to marry the following spring. It was a steady, gentle courtship that could only have one inevitable ending. It was Flora who insisted they take things slowly, while continuing her work as a lady's companion to an acquaintance of Mrs Taylor's throughout the autumn and winter. Her experience of paid work was the first taste of independence she'd ever had and she was determined to relish it for a few months at least.

Not daring to risk losing her a second time, Hugh respected her wishes, resigning himself to enjoying the anticipation the intervening months generated before their wedding. He'd waited so long for the honour of being able to call Flora his wife and have her live with him at Beachlands that a few more months were nothing, considering they'd be spending the rest of their lives together.

During this time, Madeline took pleasure in getting to know Flora and embracing her as the sister she'd never had, witnessing her grow in confidence and self-assurance as she discovered a power and an agency she'd never before experienced. For Flora, the love story with its happy ending was as much a love story with herself as it was with Hugh.

Mrs Booth took the news of the engagement in her usual

languid stride, expressing her bewilderment as to how it had come about, wishing only to know if Mimi could play a part in the wedding ceremony as she'd missed out on a role in *A Midsummer Night's Dream*. She did so want to see her dressed in a smart little cape, or at the very least, wearing a ribbon in her collar to match the satin trim on the bride's dress.

No one knew Mrs Norton's opinion on the match, because after so many years of harsh judgements and interference, she wasn't there to give it. She'd complained so much about missing her dear Marianne that Edward had paid for a one-way passage to Italy, enabling her to join her beloved niece and leave the rest of them in peace.

There was no word on how Marianne or Jane felt about sharing their tiny apartment near the Spanish Steps with their overbearing aunt, but in one of his rare letters to his mother, Theo mentioned she was determinedly worming her way into the Italian nobility with the intention of marrying Jane off to a duke. Marianne, as a divorced woman living on a small allowance grudgingly provided by her father, had no romantic prospects beyond the penniless poets and exiled starving artists who haunted the Caffè Greco.

Tobias Booth remained in Switzerland, his stay at the sanatorium having become a permanent way of life. Edward was proving to be a great success at running the Trident hotel business, and with Mimi being the love of Mrs Booth's life, Tobias appeared to have come to the conclusion that there was no longer any place for him in America. With the laws against prostitution being more strictly enforced by the day, largely thanks to Edward's campaigning, the consequent threat of prosecution for his past crimes meant there was nothing to tempt him home.

Throughout all this time, Edward remained in New York, working to recover the reputation and the fortune of the hotel chain. Acting now as the head of the family, he arranged for Mountview to be shut up for the winter. Mrs Booth, along with Mimi, returned to their home in New York, where she rattled around the over decorated, un-peopled rooms, bemoaning the loss of Flora more than she ever mentioned missing her own daughters.

The charitable foundation Madeline had advised Edward on setting up was now firmly established. Refuges, designed to welcome any woman in need of an escape from their threatening domestic environment, or relief from any kind of want, were already beginning to appear in many of the major towns and cities in America.

There was no longer any personal correspondence between Madeline and Edward. Everything to do with the business of the charity, which was the only thing that bound them, was delegated to Miss Harper. If Edward wondered whether Madeline still kept the note he'd sent, the one Flora had discovered in the pocket of her cloak, he never created an opportunity to mention it.

If he'd have asked, Madeline would have told him that of course she'd kept it after Flora returned it. It was a precious item, having played its part in bringing Flora and Hugh together, but it was so much more than that. It was a reminder that once she'd been loved by an honourable man, a man who'd loved her for who she was, no matter where she came from, a man who had taken her at face value and found it to be enough.

Whenever Madeline felt the despair of loneliness overwhelming her, she would take the note out of her bedside drawer, and remind herself of the words, as if they weren't already carved on her heart.

My dearest Madeline,
  Forgive me the impertinence of calling you dearest, but it's what you are to me. However cruelly you try to dismiss me, I love you and I always will.
  Edward

When Hugh and Flora's wedding day finally arrived, Madeline knew to put aside all sad thoughts of what might have been for her and Edward. This was her brother's and Flora's day and nothing would spoil it. It was time to resume her habit of putting on a brave face, to show herself as the happy, witty Madeline who everyone knew and revered, even if she wasn't loved for it. After all, she wasn't completely unhappy. She had a life of privilege and the satisfaction of being able to use her wealth to do good in the world. Beyond this, the happiness she felt for Hugh and Flora had to be enough to gratify her, at least for the day of the celebrations.

She was pleased to act as Flora's maid of honour, while Will gave away the bride in the absence of their father, who was too indisposed by his drinking to attend the wedding. Edward sat in the front row of the church alongside his mother and Mimi, and the rest of Flora's family, watching the couple take their vows. The formality of the ceremony dictated there was no opportunity for Madeline and Edward to speak. It was Flora's day and all eyes remained on her, just as they should.

When the invitations were first sent out, Madeline had worried that no one would come to the wedding. Not for any reason to do with Hugh or Flora, but because of their association with her, the illegitimate daughter of a prostitute. Despite the reputation she'd gained for her charity work, Madeline was still viewed as an outsider by the society into which Hugh had been born. The last thing she'd wanted was to be the reason people stayed away from his wedding. She'd offered to go abroad and miss the day altogether to avoid any awkwardness, but Hugh wouldn't hear of it, and neither would Flora.

'There's no wedding without you, Maddie,' Hugh had said in a huff. 'Weddings are about family, and that's what you are. There's no one dearer to me than you and if people won't accept you, then they're not welcome at the wedding.'

When it came to it, few people refused the invitation. The prospect of fine food, wine and dancing was too tempting to turn down just for the sake of some young woman who didn't come up to the mark. After all, none of them were obliged to acknowledge her presence when they saw her in the church or as she circulated the room, making sure their glasses were regularly topped up with champagne.

The wedding breakfast was held on the lawn at Beachlands. It was the first time a party had taken place there since their father's death. Finch, who insisted on taking care of all the arrangements, went to great lengths to make sure the caterers were up to scratch, while overseeing every tiny detail, from the cut of the crystal glasses to the folding of the linen napkins. Dressed in a cornflower-blue silk dress, and brandishing a smile for everyone, she could easily have been mistaken for the mother of the groom. As she confessed to Madeline on the eve of the wedding, the tears spilling from her eyes, 'Hugh is the closest I have to a son and I want to do him proud.'

It was with this same sentiment that Madeline ensured Finch was seated at the top table and treated as one of the family, because in everything but name, that was what she was.

Custom dictated that Madeline danced with Will, so there was no need to worry about Edward asking her for the first dance. Given the way she'd refused him in the past, there was little prospect of him requesting any of the following dances either. She didn't interrogate her heart too much as to how she felt about this because it wouldn't do to be seen at her brother's wedding with swollen eyes or tear-stained cheeks.

Even though her duties as maid of honour kept her busy, there was ultimately no avoiding Edward. The bride and groom had cut the cake, and Madeline was handing out the slices when he finally approached her.

In spite of it being the happiest of days, his eyes were still husks. For a moment she wondered if he regretted not being the one Flora had chosen to marry after all. It was the nervous twitch of his mouth, the tired look of him that seemed to go bone deep that caused her to rethink her suspicion. He was working too hard, still trying to make amends for the past crimes of his family's business, punishing himself for the damage inflicted on Madeline's mother and so many others. Killing himself with overwork was no way to do it.

'You're still working too hard, Mr Booth,' she said, dropping a large slice of cake onto a plate and thrusting it into his hand.

He leaned back from the knife, clogged with jam, cream and crumbs, as she wielded it in front of his face to emphasise her point.

'You told me the same thing once before, Miss Crosby.'

'Then nothing's changed.'

Edward kept his eyes on the knife as Madeline plunged it back into the cake, peeling another slice from the main tier. 'It seems we've reached a stalemate.'

He moved to one side as she continued to serve oversized portions of cake to the guests who'd gathered around her in a huddle, forks poised. No amount of smoked salmon or champagne had dulled their appetite for cake, while Edward's plate remained untouched, his attention elsewhere.

'Once you've finished your duties as maid of honour, will you dance with me?' he asked.

Madeline looked forlornly at the splodge of cream that had dropped from the edge of the knife and landed on her dress. The silk was ruined. She looked up at him, irritated by the stain.

'My duties won't end until the celebrations are finished, Mr Booth, until the carriages have taken everyone home.'

'And so, I'll wait until then.'

Unnerved by his attention, she dropped the knife, silently cursing her clumsiness as it landed on the floor with a clatter. Before she could retrieve it, Edward reached to pick it up.

Finch must have seen Edward down on one knee in front of Madeline because she dashed across the room and touched her gently on the arm.

'Allow me to serve the rest of the cake. It's time you enjoyed the celebration.'

'I must go up to my room and change,' said Madeline, frowning at the stain on her dress.

Edward scrambled to his feet. 'Please don't change, Miss Crosby.'

The words burst from his mouth with such energy she suspected he'd only meant to think them rather than voice them. She gave him a curious look. 'Would you rather I appear ridiculous in front of the guests?'

'Not ridiculous, just . . . imperfect. It makes me feel a little more worthy of you.' He put aside his untouched cake. 'Now you've been released from your duties, you have no excuse not to dance with me.'

The sun was already beginning to set as he led her across the lawn, past the string quartet to a secluded bench. Now he had Madeline's attention, he didn't seem inclined to dance after all, just being in her presence seemed to be enough.

Madeline had wished for this moment for so long and yet now she was finally sitting beside him, she was lost for words.

'The dress is ruined,' she sighed, not knowing what else to say.

'Does it matter?'

She shook her head. 'Not in the least. I know a clever dressmaker who'll repurpose the fabric and turn it into a different dress, which will probably be even finer than this one and much more fit for everyday use.'

'Then you mustn't be ashamed of the stain when something good will come of it. We all have them, even if we try to deny them. Some go much deeper than yours. My family's go back three generations, at least.'

Madeline laughed. 'Now I don't think you're talking about my dress at all.'

'However much we try to change the past, it will always remain.'

'How many times have I told you, Mr Booth, that you work too hard?'

He cleared his throat, a sure sign that he was nervous. 'The secret of happiness is to not let the past define our present or our future. It requires a good deal of forgiveness, of ourselves, as well as of others.'

She felt her heart give at the sincerity of his words. 'Have you forgiven yourself yet, Mr Booth, or do you intend to continue to punish yourself with overwork?'

'I should have believed you when you first hinted to me about the brothels. I shouldn't even have needed you to tell me. I should have paid attention to what was going on behind closed doors. I should have stood up to my father sooner and involved myself more closely in the family business.'

'I take that to mean you haven't forgiven yourself.'

'I can't do that until others forgive me.' He turned to look at her, his eyes brimming with the question he lacked the courage to ask.

She stood up from the bench and held out her hand. 'You promised me a dance.'

When he failed to move, Madeline tried again, her palm upturned as she presented it to him. 'You once said, if you weren't bound to Flora, you would ask me to be your wife.'

He looked up at her, as if he could hardly believe what she was saying. 'Miss Crosby, I . . .'

'I'm offering you my hand now, Mr Booth, if only you'll accept it.'

The sun had gone down and the light was fading. Somewhere in the distance, the musicians played as Madeline and Edward danced into the night, living only for the moment, and for the future that lay ahead of them. Hour after hour they held each other, long after the music had stopped. Now they'd finally come together, nothing would ever part them.

A Letter from Theresa Howes

Mansfield Park has the reputation of being the least loved of Austen's novels. Even when it was first published it was less popular than her other works. The problem for many readers seems to be with Fanny Price, who appears too dull to be an Austen heroine, and a little too perfect.

We all like our heroines to make mistakes, just as we make them in our own lives. It's only by learning from these mistakes that our heroines earn their happy endings. 'Suffering virtue' isn't anywhere near as fun or interesting to observe.

There's also something unsatisfying about Fanny marrying her cousin, Edmund Bertram, when he's been in love with the beautiful, spirited Mary Crawford for most of the novel. To many readers, Mary is the true heroine of *Mansfield Park* with her wit and her human failings, which make her more entertaining and relatable than Fanny.

It was these controversial elements of *Mansfield Park* that inspired me to write a reimagining of the novel, with a more proactive heroine and an alternative ending. To achieve this, I chose to tell the story from the point of view of a heroine who is more like Mary than Fanny.

An American Scandal offers a respectful nod to certain plot elements of *Mansfield Park* but my intention to create a different ending, written from a different point of view, inevitably led me to change the story considerably.

As with my previous Jane Austen reimagining, *A Matter of Persuasion*, I have set the novel in America's Gilded Age, when the position of women in society and the strict codes of behaviour between men and women were close to those of Jane Austen's world. Similarly, the distinction between old and new money meant people were brought up to know their place in society and not to step outside its boundaries.

The Gilded Age was a time of rapid economic growth in America. During this period, the gap between rich and poor continued to increase, along with the exploitation of workers. It is this backdrop that I was interested to explore in the situations and origins of my characters. I also wanted to show the challenges people had to face, no matter what their station in life.

I've loved Jane Austen's novels since I first read *Pride and Prejudice* at the age of twelve. To my mind, no other writer has ever come close to Austen's subtlety, her wit or her social observations. *An American Scandal* is a result of my admiration and respect for her genius.

If you enjoyed *An American Scandal*, I'd be grateful if you would consider leaving a review. I love to hear what readers thought, and it helps new readers discover my books.

Many thanks,
Theresa Howes

X: https://twitter.com/HQStories

Goodreads Author – Theresa Howes

Website: www.theresahowes.co.uk

A Matter of Persuasion

New York, 1882.

Amy Eaton is a bestselling authoress, much to the embarrassment of her family. Proudly 'old money', they see her professionalism as an impropriety. Despite their undisguised disdain for her, Amy is bound by a promise she made to her dying mother to look after her two sisters and father.

Eight years have passed since Amy gave up the love of her life, after her mother's best friend persuaded her not to marry him. But now Wareham is back: a rich, self-made man in search of a wife.

Doing her best to forget the life she might have had with Wareham, Amy must learn how to navigate her small social circle without letting her true feelings show. As new and unexpected situations arise, will Amy defy expectations and choose her own path?

The French Affair

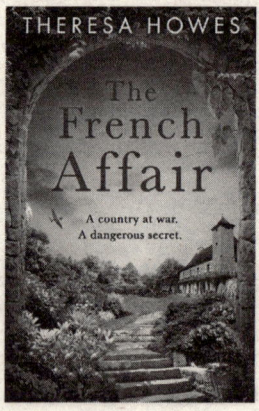

A country at war. A dangerous secret.

After a failed honey-trap mission for British Intelligence leads to the breakdown of her marriage, French journalist Iris escapes to Dijon, seeking refuge in the cottage of her beloved aunt, Eva. But Eva is gone, the streets are full of distrust, and Iris is soon followed by the very last man she wants to see – the British civil servant and traitor she was tasked with catching, now keen to rekindle their affair.

Eva's home used to be a comforting place, where the locals sought out Eva's homemade tinctures and cures and gifted jars of fresh honey from the garden. Now it is a place of danger, where threats loom in every corner. And as Iris spends more time there, she discovers a secret that will change the way she sees her aunt forever – and the course of her own life too . . .

The Secrets We Keep

1944, the Cote d'Azur.

Artist Marguerite Segal is recruited by British Intelligence into befriending Etienne Valade, a local priest. Her mission is to persuade him to pass on information from the high-ranking German officers who attend his church: evidence of their war crimes.

Connected by a passion for art, Marguerite and Etienne soon fall in love, but their association increasingly puts her at danger of violent reprisals. With his church frequented by Nazis, Etienne is a suspected collaborator, and distrust is high.

And Marguerite is keeping her own secret too. Like the Jews whose identity cards she forges to hide them from the Third Reich, she is hiding behind a false name, her true identity and past known only to her closest friend.

Marguerite must get hold of the documents that will condemn the German officers, but, in a world where everything is at stake, can she truly trust anyone – even the man she loves?

Acknowledgements

So many people worked tirelessly behind the scenes to help create this book and I'm grateful to everyone. The first thanks go to my agent, Juliet Mushens. I wouldn't be writing this without your kindness and support. Thanks also to the rest of the team at Mushens Entertainment, Rachel, Emma, Alba, Catriona and Den. It's an honour to work with you.

Thanks to everyone at HQ who have nurtured the book from the first idea to publication. In the editorial team, I'd like to thank, Georgina Green, Sophia Allistone and Audrey Linton. Also, Rebecca Jamieson, Teresa Palmiero and Michelle Bullock. In marketing, I'd like to thank Lou Nyuar, Jo Rose and Emily Gerbner. In publicity, Georgia Hester and Caitlin McCoy. Thank you to Anna Sikorska for the cover design. In sales, I'd like to thank Emily Scorer, Hannah Lismore and Lauren Trabucchi. In Finance, thank you to Aziz Siddiqui and Kelly Spells. In Operations, thank you to Sarah Renwick and Laoise Culloo, and to Francesca Tuzzeo in Production.

Thank you to all the readers who continue to pick up my books when there are so many others in the world to choose from. Thank you to all the book bloggers, reviewers, librarians and booksellers who work so hard to spread the word about the joys of reading and encourage the right books to land in the right readers' hands.

Thank you to Jane Austen for inspiring this novel in the first place. I'm in awe of your genius. Thanks to fellow authors for your friendship and support, Annabelle Thorpe, Aliya Ali-Afzal, Tessa Harris and Kate Hamer. Thank you to Jean Hudson for being such a proud aunt. Thanks to Mum and Dad, Janet and Brian Wood. I'm so lucky to have you. Thank you to Claude, the cat, and finally thank you to Bill. None of this would have happened without your love and support.

Dear Reader,

We hope you enjoyed reading this book. If you did, we'd be so appreciative if you left a review. It really helps us and the author to bring more books like this to you.

Here at HQ Digital we are dedicated to publishing fiction that will keep you turning the pages into the early hours. Don't want to miss a thing? To find out more about our books, promotions, discover exclusive content and enter competitions you can keep in touch in the following ways:

JOIN OUR COMMUNITY:

Sign up to our new email newsletter: http://smarturl.it/SignUpHQ

Read our new blog www.hqstories.co.uk

X: https://twitter.com/HQStories

f: www.facebook.com/HQStories

BUDDING WRITER?

We're also looking for authors to join the HQ Digital family! Find out more here:

https://www.hqstories.co.uk/want-to-write-for-us/

Thanks for reading, from the HQ Digital team